THE TOUCH OF AN OUTLAW

He buried his head in her chest and let out a long sigh, then kissed her wildly as if a hunger for her had almost killed him.

She laughed as he stood, holding her in his arms, and walked over to his bed. He tossed her atop the covers and stared down at her for a long moment before joining her. "It's cold in here. You should be under the covers, dear."

As the first light shone through the open windows, he tugged the front of her gown open. "If you just want to be touched and nothing more, then touch you I will."

His fingers shoved the cotton aside a moment before his warm hands covered her breasts. "But I plan to do so all over."

When she gasped, he kissed her deep as his hands made his promise true.

After a while, he rose his head to look into her eyes. The pain she'd seen was gone, and passion had taken its place. She whispered between gulps for air. "Again, Michael. Touch me again."

He pushed the gown off and lowered his mouth to her peak.

Crying out from the pleasure, she rocked back and forth. He moved back to her mouth, holding her face in his hands as he kissed her.

"Is this what you want, my love?" His words whispered against her mouth.

"Yes," she answered.

D1624542

Collections by Jodi Thomas, Linda Broday,
Phyliss Miranda, and DeWanna Pace

GIVE ME A TEXAN

GIVE ME A COWBOY

GIVE ME A TEXAS RANGER

GIVE ME A TEXAS OUTLAW

Give Me A Texas Outlaw

Jodi Thomas
Linda Broday
Phyliss Miranda
DeWanna Pace

ZEBRA BOOKS
KENSINGTON PUBLISHING CORP.

ZEBRA BOOKS are published by

Kensington Publishing Corp.
119 West 40th Street
New York, NY 10018

Copyright © 2011 by Kensington Publishing Corporation
The Outlaw copyright © 2011 by Jodi Thomas
Trouble in Petticoats copyright © 2011 by Linda Broday
Texas Flame copyright © 2011 by Phyliss Miranda
Most Wanted copyright © 2011 by DeWanna Pace

All rights reserved. No part of this book may be reproduced in any form or by any means without the prior written consent of the Publisher, excepting brief quotes used in reviews.

Zebra and the Z logo Reg. U.S. Pat. & TM Off.

ISBN-13: 978-1-61129-749-2

Printed in the United States of America

Contents

THE OUTLAW

JODI THOMAS

Chapter 1

January 15, 1852
Big Bend Country, Texas

Cozette Camanez straightened the pearl-white lace of her wedding gown, hating the dress almost as much as she hated herself. Everything about her life was a lie and it was all about to come crashing down around her.

Two months ago she'd made a mistake. She'd trusted a man she thought she loved and found out one stormy night that he wasn't worth loving, or trusting.

The next morning, she'd thought she could walk away, as he had, but when it was far too late to admit what had happened between them, she'd discovered he'd left her with a reminder of what he'd done to her. A reminder that would cause her father to disown her.

Desperate, she did the only thing she could think to do. She lied. First to herself, then to others, building a world around her as she had as a child. The lies grew so thick, they now walled her in, making escape impossible.

Leaning back on the old wooden church pew of the ranch mission, Cozette wished she could close her eyes to everything and just drift away into nothingness. She took a deep breath, inhaling the musty smell of dust and cobwebs and candle wax.

She'd rushed home with her broken heart to find her father dying. She couldn't tell him the truth then. He was in enough pain already. If he knew she might be pregnant, he'd probably use his last breath to yell at her.

But, as the days passed and he grew weaker, she thought her secret might be safe. She sat beside his bed telling stories of an imaginary love who planned to come for her. She even lied and told her father that they'd already been married by a judge in Austin. As she guessed he would, her father complained that as soon as her love arrived, they'd be married by the priest. Until then, her father had claimed it wasn't a real marriage.

The rafters rattled as the wind blew through the holes in the old mission roof. Cozette looked up into the shadows of the loft thinking how hard it would be for an imaginary groom to appear tonight.

She'd thought she would slip away once her father recovered a little, or passed. Maybe she'd be gone for a few months, or even a year, and return home, an imaginary widow with a real baby. Only she'd gone too far with details, saying her husband planned to meet her at the Grand Hotel in Odessa.

When her father took a turn for the worse, her Uncle Raymond told her she had to stay. He took the liberty, without telling Cozette, to send word for the man waiting for her in Odessa to come to the ranch.

From then on, her ball of lies began to unravel amid wedding plans. The house staff took over. They all knew the road to Odessa. A week's journey in a wagon, half that on horseback. As they helped Cozette care for her father, they prepared for the proper wedding. It would have to be as soon as the groom arrived, for her father's days were numbered.

Whispers circled in the hallways. The groom would be

there in a few days, the housekeeper announced to everyone, and the maids began to clean while the cooks cooked. A week at the most, the housekeeper reasoned. Later, everyone except Cozette decided it would be three days if the weather held.

Two days.

Tomorrow.

And finally, last night they all agreed that he'd come before dawn.

Cozette thought she'd go mad worrying about when her imaginary groom would show up. She'd even let them dress her in her mother's dress to wait though she knew she was waiting for no one.

Then, her father, who'd never forgiven his wife for delivering him with a girl as their only child, did something Cozette never expected. At her uncle's insistence, her father changed his will, leaving the huge ranch not to Cozette, but to her legal husband.

Cozette jumped off the bench and began to pace. Lying on the pew trying not to think wasn't working. She had no one to blame but herself for this mess. She'd piled one lie on top of another and the chaos that was about to start at dawn, when no husband showed up, would be her funeral pyre.

She'd promised her father a hundred times when she was growing up that she'd never lie again. Without her mother to buffer his rage, he'd die hating her, disowning her, demanding she leave and never return. Her father and her uncle weren't men who tempered rage. They didn't just get mad, they got deadly, and at dawn they'd both be furious with her.

Without a husband showing up to claim her and the baby growing inside, her uncle would inherit the only home she'd ever known and kick her out with his dying brother's blessing.

Since she had no hope of an imaginary husband showing up, she had only one path left. She planned to pray herself dead before morning and save everyone else the trouble of murdering her.

There was no other way out.

Better to die now with the priest waiting outside the door. He could perform the funeral. Cooks were baking all night for the wedding breakfast. It would serve as the meal for the wake. More gifts and guests would arrive tomorrow. Everyone would attend her funeral instead of a celebration. After all, they were much the same. All the women cried and everyone would say how nice she looked.

A rustling sounded in the loft. For a second Cozette thought she might be rescued, maybe by a tornado, or a hailstorm, either of which would take everyone's mind off the wedding. Then reality weighed against her heart. A storm wouldn't make the ranch hers. Nothing would. Until a few hours ago her father had wanted the priest to perform the marriage at his bedside when the groom arrived, but he'd finally demanded she marry in the tiny chapel. She'd seen the blood in his handkerchief each time he coughed and guessed the reason.

The rattling above came again. Cozette refused to turn around, thinking the rat in the church must be huge . . . almost big enough to be an uncle. Her father loved the ranch, but Uncle Raymond saw only a fast way to make money. Her beloved San Louise would be sliced up and cannibalized within months, because with no groom, her uncle could chop it into small farms. One of the oldest Mexican land-grant ranches in Texas would vanish.

Shouting came from beyond the chapel walls. Cozette pressed her cheek to the window. She could die in a few minutes when all was quiet, she decided. She saw shadows of men run from one building to another, but she couldn't tell what was happening. Shouts echoed through the foggy night air and she thought she heard gunfire near the barn.

As she pushed away from the window, she became aware

of someone behind her. Before she could turn, the barrel of a gun pushed sharply against her back.

"Turn around pretty lady and you're dead," came a voice low and rich.

"Who are you?" she demanded, thinking of the old stories she'd heard of outlaws raiding the ranch years ago.

The laughter only inches behind her chilled her blood.

"I'm a bandit come to relieve you of the burden of your wealth. I'll start with that necklace."

She tugged off the heavy gold necklace and handed it to him. "Take it and be gone."

"And the ring." He was so close to her she could feel his warm breath on her bare shoulders.

She jerked off the gold band she'd bought for herself before she left Austin.

"A willing victim?" the robber said. "A change from what I expected." His voice was more educated than she thought a bandit's might be, but the steel of his weapon seemed no less deadly.

"Is that all you want?" she asked as she stared out into the night wishing the gun in his hand would go off and end her misery.

"Oh, we're taking plenty. I checked out the chapel, and my band is loading all your wedding gifts in a wagon."

"Good," she said.

"You don't seem upset that we're taking everything of value."

"I could care less," she answered.

"Don't play games with me, miss. I may not kill you, but my gang wouldn't hesitate."

Cozette placed her hands on the windowsill, fighting to see beyond the thick glass. "Your gang? They wouldn't be three short fat men dressed in black."

"What makes you say that?"

"They're being led away by several of the ranch hands.

I don't know how mean they are but one looks like he might be sobbing."

The outlaw pushed her against the window as he looked out. His strong fingers rested on the back of her neck, holding her, but not hurting her. His touch was as warm as the glass was cold.

"That's them." He mumbled an oath. "Great, I leave them for five minutes and look what happens."

"My men will come after you next." She tried to wiggle away. "They're probably already checking every building on the ranch."

For one second his hand slipped against her hair and she twisted to face him. She drew in a quick breath to scream, but his stormy eyes stopped her. He was tall, and darkened by the sun, but his eyes were unlike any she'd ever seen. He was young, maybe only a year or two older than she, yet the sadness in his stare held a hundred years of sorrow.

"Great!" He pulled her from the window. "You've seen my face. Now I have to kill you."

"Good!" she shouted back. "Shoot me!" Heaven had answered her prayer.

She straightened against the wall, bracing herself for the blow. "Shoot me right in the heart." Cozette closed her eyes and waited.

After holding her breath for as long as she could, she let out the air and glared at him. The outlaw was just standing there staring at her.

"What's wrong? All you have to do is pull the trigger."

"I can't just shoot you in cold blood. Not with you ordering me to. In that dress you look like a doll on top of a wedding cake."

"Well, I'm not taking it off, so shoot me."

She took another breath, closed her eyes, and waited. No blow came.

This time when she opened her eyes, he'd lowered his gun to his side. "What's wrong now?"

"I can't, lady. I know it's the outlaw code to shoot anyone who can identify you, but I can't."

All the tension of the day exploded inside Cozette and he was the only one around to take her bottled-up rage. "You are absolutely the worst outlaw I've ever seen. You must have the dumbest gang in creation if they follow you. All you have to do is aim at my heart and shoot me. Then I won't be around to testify and you can go bungle some other job."

"Look, lady, if you want to die so badly, why don't you just take my gun and kill yourself."

"Suicide is a mortal sin. I was schooled by nuns in Austin until a month ago. I know the rules and I always follow them," she corrected him with a bold lie, but then lying seemed to be her main profession of late. "I don't expect a low-down, worthless outlaw to know anything about right or wrong. I'm surprised you aren't lying out somewhere, your dead body feeding the buzzards, or swinging from a tree by rope." She pointed her finger at him. "Now stop wasting time and shoot me!"

He shoved his gun in the holster and stared into her face. "No. Maybe I should tie you up and gag you. I'd enjoy the silence and that should give me time to go spring my three uncles and get out of this place by dawn. I knew this was a bad idea from the start."

"Just shoot me, please." She couldn't believe the answer to her prayers was standing right in front of her refusing to cooperate.

"I can't. Someone will hear the shot." He tried to reason with her.

"Then choke me." She pulled the collar of her gown open, popping several buttons.

He closed the fingers on one hand around her slender neck, but he didn't tighten his grip.

He was so close to her she could feel his heart pounding. "Please, do it," she whispered. "If you don't I'll be forced to watch my father die knowing his only child lied to him. I'll be disgraced and kicked off the ranch by an uncle who hates me."

He studied her with those fascinating, stormy blue eyes that seemed to see all the way to her soul. "Why don't you just tell your father the truth?"

"If I'm not married by the time he wakes up tomorrow, I'll break his heart. He never had much to do with me, thought my mother was a fool for listening to my stories. As soon as she died, he sent me to the nuns and, as far as I know, he's never even read the letters I wrote. He's giving his brother the ranch rather than let me have it unless I marry." Cozette knew she was babbling, but she didn't care. She needed to confess, and an outlaw wasn't likely to judge her.

"Don't you have friends, relatives, the law who will help you?" To her surprise the outlaw actually sounded concerned.

"No one who would stand against my uncle once my father is gone. I'm sure the will is legal." She paused, then tried another angle. "My uncle will kill your gang. He's done it to others who tried to steal from the ranch. They say he beat a cook almost to death for stealing three chickens. My father's a hard man, but his brother twisted one more step into cruelty."

The bandit let go of her neck and backed away. "You've got a mountainload of problems, lady." He handed her back the ring and necklace. "I wish I could help you, but right now I've got my own worries. Those three fat little outlaws in black are all the family I've got, and I'll do anything it takes to save them. I thought if I came along with them tonight, I'd keep them out of trouble, but that plan obviously didn't work."

Cozette stared at the jewelry in her hand. She cared nothing about it or all the wedding gifts. All she wanted was her land, someplace to live, somewhere to raise the child she carried. "Are you sure you won't kill me?"

He smiled, a sad smile as if he was sorry he'd disappointed her. "I can't, lady."

"Then marry me." Cozette covered her mouth, not believing what she'd said, but the logic of it slammed against her. "The priest won't help me. I've lied to him as I did to everyone else. They all believe my husband is coming tonight. But, if I told him you were that man, he'd marry us and my uncle would have to watch the land pass to my husband."

"But I'm not your husband. How's he going to feel when he shows up and finds his wife married to me?"

"He won't show up. I made him up and the land won't really be yours—you'll just hold on to it for a while, then pass it back to me."

The stranger looked confused. "Why?" he asked as if he really didn't want to know the answer.

She glared at him. "Because I may be pregnant." It was the first honest thing she'd said in so long, and it felt good.

"How did that happen? Imaginary men don't get women pregnant." He met her stare, and she swore she saw a bit of a blush flash across the outlaw's face in the candlelight. "Never mind," he corrected. "I don't want to know."

She rushed on, not wanting to remember, much less explain. "I have to marry or lose everything. If you won't kill me, marry me."

"Great plan. What would keep your uncle from just shooting me a minute after the ceremony?"

"The minute we're married, as my husband, you own the land. If you die, it's mine. The ranch hands will stand with whoever is the rightful owner. Some of them don't agree with the way my uncle has been taking over since my father's been sick, but they're afraid to cross him, knowing he could be their boss soon. If they know the ranch will pass to you, they'd stand with you."

A grin lifted one side of his mouth and she thought he looked almost handsome. "What's to keep you from killing me?"

"I'll make you a deal. Marry me and stay with me until my uncle goes back to his place at that gambling hole he calls his town, and then I'll let you take that wagonload of wedding loot out of here." She hesitated, then added, "But if you don't leave when I tell you to, I *will* shoot you, myself."

"How long do I have to stay?"

"Not long. A few days. A week at the most. Just until the guests leave," she lied. "My uncle will suspect a trick. I'll need time to make sure I'm protected. But, while you are here, acting like my husband, you'll have to play the role."

"What about my uncles?"

"If I save them from the rope, will you consider my proposal?"

"Why trust me, lady?"

"You're a thief, I'm a liar. Seems a good match." She thought she saw a bit of hurt flash in his eyes as if she'd insulted him.

When he looked back at her, his blue eyes had turned hard as gray, cold steel. "You've got yourself a deal," he said as if she'd just chosen an impossible task. "Get my uncles freed and I'll play your game. I'll marry you and stay here until the ranch passes to me, and then I'll leave it to you."

"Stay here," she whispered as if afraid to hope. "I'll be right back."

Before he could say a word, she rushed to the tiny side door of the chapel with her wedding dress flowing like a huge white cloud behind her. She tapped twice and a priest opened the door. Then she vanished.

Chapter 2

Michael Hughes walked to the window and stared out into the chilly winter night. She was the most beautiful thing he'd ever seen, and the craziest. The woman made snakes look predictable. He had no hope of her managing to free his three dumb uncles. After all, she was a prisoner herself from all he could tell.

If he had any sense, he'd run. Michael laughed. If he'd had any sense he never would have come back to the Big Ben country. He'd been twelve when his uncles talked him into playing lookout for one of their schemes. They'd failed at robbing a bank and he'd been the only one who got caught. Without parents, Michael had had no one to stand with him before the judge. He'd been sentenced to six years of hard labor.

The first few months had been hell. Then the warden's wife, Mrs. Peters, noticed him and demanded he be assigned to help her. She was six feet tall and as hard as nails, but she was a Quaker on a mission. She ran a school that forced education on every child she managed to catch and draw into her one-room school.

Michael cleaned the schoolroom, built the fires, and stayed with her all day doing whatever chore she yelled for him to do. At night he helped the cook wash up after supper before a guard came to put his chains back on and take him to the huge bay where prisoners slept. When it got warm enough that first spring, he took off his ragged coat to chop wood. Mrs. Peters noticed bruises on his arms and knew he'd been mistreated at night in the cell block. She demanded he be allowed to sleep in the school, and she wasn't a woman even the warden would cross.

With regular meals and a place where he could sleep without fear, Michael began to grow. The animal he'd almost become calmed. In three years he'd read all the books she had and practiced math until he was faster than her with figures. Mrs. Peters never told him so, but he guessed she was proud of what she'd done. Every month she managed to find more books for him to read and she always insisted on calling him Michael, never Mickey or Mike, like his uncles had.

When he was released at eighteen, she gave him the only clothes he'd ever had that weren't hand-me-downs and said she saw great things in his future.

Mrs. Peters told him many times that he was a child never to be loved, but he could manage to be useful if he worked hard. Only, in the two years since he'd seen her, he hadn't managed to be that to anyone. If this crazy bride needed him, he'd do what he could, if for no other reason than to prove Mrs. Peters right.

The Quaker had been wrong about the great things in his future. With men drifting into Texas looking for work by the hundreds, there were no jobs, and even if there had been, no one wanted to hire an ex-con. Michael's years in prison left him unskilled for most manual jobs and the few he got drove him insane with boredom. Finally, he drifted back to the only family he'd ever known. His three uncles.

The three hadn't changed much, but Michael had. He

saw them for what they were, bumbling idiots who loved him simply because he was kin to them.

Uncle Abe couldn't count past seven but liked to cook any meat the others shot or stole.

Uncle Moses followed what he called his laws and believed everything bad that happened in his life was somehow caused by him not adhering to his rules. Of course, the laws included reversing his socks every morning so they'd never wear out and eating all his meals with the same spoon.

Uncle Joseph was the true thief in the family. He stole everything he found not tied down. He even stole from his brothers. They'd long ago given up on trying to talk him out of his habit and now just looked for whatever was missing among his things.

Michael thought he could keep them out of trouble. In the months he'd been back he'd made them clean their shack and clear the plot behind the house for a garden. Then, they convinced him to come along on this one robbery. The people were so rich, they wouldn't notice a few things missing.

Michael's plan was to ride along in case they got in over their heads. He'd thought to hide away in the church for an hour while they wandered around the sleeping ranch collecting all they could carry. Once they made it off the ranch, the uncles would fall asleep and he'd take back their loot.

Even his robbery of the bride had been only a trick. He knew he wouldn't leave with the jewelry. He'd thought she heard him enter and was about to scream when she leaned against the window.

Great job he'd done, Michael thought. Unless he could think of something before the crazy bride got back, he'd be swinging with them from the nearest tree come dawn. She was probably running for help now and laughing that he'd agreed to wait.

The bride, he thought. She was the most beautiful little

thing he'd ever seen, and when he'd touched her neck, he knew he'd never touch anything that soft again. But she had to be nuts if she thought her imaginary husband could have gotten her pregnant.

"Psst," a sound brought him back from his worrying. "Psst, Mr. Outlaw."

She was back. The nutty princess in white.

"The priest has gone to get your uncles. I told him how we were in love and of course in a family way. I said you wanted to marry me but you had to have your family present. Father Timothy also agreed not to wake my father."

Michael stared at her, wondering if he'd ever be able to tell if she was lying or telling the truth.

"The priest agreed to tell whoever is guarding your uncles that they were here for a secret wedding. Once he's got them in his chambers, he'll marry us."

"What about your uncle? He might want to stand in for your father."

She moved out of the shadows and he saw her shy smile. "I told Father Timothy I was embarrassed because of the pregnancy and our hurried wedding without the blessing of the church. I said I preferred to marry now before as few people as possible. He went along with the idea, assuring me that my uncle only wanted me to do what was right and marrying the man I've already bedded would be wise."

Michael watched her closely. "The truth never crosses your shadow, does it?"

"Not often. My mother used to say life is far more interesting when looked at from a different angle."

"Well if we do this I'd like your word that you'll play no games with me. No lies between us from here on out. We'll be honest with each other for the few days the marriage lasts."

"Outlaw honor?"

Michael guessed she'd already figured out he wasn't much of an outlaw. "Outlaw honor."

"Fair enough. We have a deal then?"

"We have a deal."

The priest opened the door and whispered, "Miss Cozette, are you ready? I have the three witnesses."

Michael reached and took her hand. He didn't miss her slight jerk of panic, before she calmed and let him pull her toward the door. "Come along, dear," he said, realizing he'd never used the endearment before. "It's time we married."

"Yes . . ." she whispered.

"Michael," he filled in the blank, guessing, like Mrs. Peters, his short-time wife would call him by his real name.

"Yes, Michael," she confirmed.

They followed the priest into a small room already full of his chubby uncles. The three looked a little the worse for wear and frightened. Uncle Abe wiped his bloody nose with his sleeve. Uncle Moses was shaking his head as if he could wish himself back home. Uncle Joseph ran his fingers over a brass cross as if judging its size before he tried pocketing it.

Michael felt sorry for them. "It's all right," he whispered. "There's not going to be a hanging. I'm getting married and everything will be fine."

Uncle Joseph wrinkled up his face. "You stealing a bride? That ain't right, Mickey boy. It just ain't right."

Michael laughed. He'd finally found something Joseph wouldn't steal.

Chapter 3

"Do you wish to marry this woman of your own free will?" the priest asked.

Michael hesitated, knowing that if they went through with this ceremony, at least one man, her uncle, would want him dead.

The priest huffed with impatience. "Sir, you have already touched this woman?"

"Yes." Michael couldn't lie there. He could still feel the softness of her skin on his fingers. He had touched her, if not in the way the priest was hinting.

"Then in the eyes of the church you are already married."

Michael felt like he was whirling in a storm. Cozette stood close, holding his arm as if she needed support. His Uncle Moses started crying and mumbling something about never seeing a wedding up close. The priest glared at him as if he were dirt-rolled evil, which only made Moses cry harder.

All in all, the wedding was worse than first light after a three-day drunk.

They both said what the priest told them to say and did everything he told them to do. When he finished, he looked at Michael and said simply, "You may kiss your bride."

Michael stared down at her and realized she looked as miserable as he felt. Somehow he found that one fact calming. Touching her chin lightly with his fingertips, he tilted her head and brushed her lips with his own.

She tasted newborn and fresh, nothing like the few saloon girls he'd kissed.

Her lip quivered slightly and he knew this lady might have known a man, but she'd never been loved. She'd never been kissed with tenderness. Deep down, he understood something she might never tell him.

"It's going to be all right, Cozette," he whispered to her. It was the first time he'd said her name and he wished he could believe his own words. "We'll get through this and you will be safe. I swear it."

Her eyes rounded and part of the fear he'd seen there vanished. To his surprise, she believed him.

This time she took his hand and asked, "Will you go with me to my father's bedside? I'd like him to meet you when he wakes."

Michael nodded once and opened the mission door for her. They stepped out into a crowd of men, all with guns raised at him.

The priest hurried out. "Do not worry!" he shouted. "All is well. They are married. This is the man our Cozette picked as her mate."

For a moment, Michael feared those would be the last words he'd hear on earth. None of the cowhands looked like they'd be bothered if his new bride ordered him shot.

Then, surprisingly, the cowboys lowered their weapons and stepped forward to shake his hand.

Cozette's laughter came too loud to sound real. "I know everyone expected us to wait until morning, but I wanted my father to meet Michael as my husband." She waved her hand across the crowd. "I know my uncle plans a wedding breakfast and I'd like you all to wash up and join us at first light."

The wranglers gave a hoot and started toward the bunkhouse.

Michael noticed his three uncles slowly backing into the shadows. "That means you three also." His words froze them in midflight. You'll be joining us for breakfast and you'll behave yourselves."

"There's a well behind the house where you can clean up if you like," Cozette added without venturing any closer to the three outlaws. "I'll have towels and soap set out."

"W-what's going on here?" Uncle Joseph stuttered out his demand. "This don't seem right. W-we ain't never been invited to w-wash or eat nowhere in our lives."

"It's right." Michael knew he couldn't trust them with the details of the marriage. A few drinks and all three would be telling everything they knew about how their nephew found a bride in the middle of a robbery.

While they watched, he kissed Cozette's cheek and motioned for her to go ahead into the front door of the big house. "I'll be with you in a moment, dear."

She glanced at the uncles and broke into a run. Michael had no idea if she feared them or simply got downwind of them.

Once she was out of sight, he turned to his kin. "I need you all. I can only trust family in this matter of life and death."

"W-what can w-we do, get horses, find guns?" Joseph asked. "I'll steal a few. It was just pure luck they caught us the first time. W-we can grab a few bags and be long gone before they notice."

"No." Michael shook his head. Flight seemed always their first thought. "I need the three of you to stay close and keep your eyes open. There are men here who didn't want us to marry. They might mean my new bride harm. I don't want them getting close to Cozette."

"Who's Cozette?" Abe asked.

Michael fought the urge to thump him hard. "My new wife, remember, the woman I just married. The one who told you to wash."

"Oh," he said. "The one in white. I remember now. You called her dear. I never knew you had a dear one, Mickey boy."

"Yes, and we've got to protect her"—Michael stared at them—"with your lives if necessary."

They looked at one another as if he were speaking a language they didn't quite understand. "We're bodyguards?" Moses whispered.

"Yeah, you've been promoted from outlaws." Michael hated to admit it but he did need them. He had no idea what he was stepping into, but it had to be bad if she was willing to die to get away. It offered him no comfort that he was her second choice tonight.

"Now there are three rules you've got to remember. Listen close. One, no drinking. Two, no stealing. You can eat all you want, but rule number three is that one of you is to be armed and standing near my dear wife at all times. I don't want anyone, and I mean anyone, laying a hand on her. She's in danger."

Abe scratched his bald head. "Mind my asking where you got this pretty little wife? You never mentioned her."

Michael said the first thing that came to mind. "We met in church. I didn't know she cared about me, but when she mentioned marriage, I thought it was a good idea."

They all nodded as if he'd explained. Michael had the feeling if any woman had ever mentioned marriage to any one of them she would have been forced to take all three. They came as a set.

"Now, clean up and wait for me inside." He smiled as they hurried around the house, heads down. The food might sound good, but washing had always been treated like a disease.

Michael didn't know what he expected to see when he walked into the main house on the ranch, but a mansion wasn't it. The place shone grander than the hotels he'd seen in Fort Worth and Austin. It had a long staircase and candles everywhere on tall gold candlesticks.

He straightened, feeling out of place. No way did he belong here. How could he hope to pull this off? He knew nothing about ranching and even less about women.

Cozette waited at the bottom of the stairs talking to an old woman who looked like she might be the housekeeper. He just stood watching Cozette and wondering how he could even be allowed on the same planet with such a creature.

When she noticed him, she moved away from the old woman and walked toward him, her hand out.

"We need to see my father, but the doctor is with him now." Her fingers closed around his. "Maybe we can talk while we wait."

He let her lead him to a long bench outside two massive doors. All his life everywhere he'd been had been small: his uncles' small cabin, the jail cells, the one-room school. For the first time ever, indoors he felt like he could stand tall and breathe without using up too much air.

She sat next to him, almost touching. "We need to get things clear between us. I'm aware that I may have tricked you into this but I want to be fair now. You've done no less than save my life."

He nodded, aware that she was leaning into him. "It seemed the only way out for us both." He didn't bother to add that she hadn't given him much choice in the matter.

She nodded her agreement, then whispered, "My father has consumption. His lungs are filling with blood, so we can't stay long. Only a minute. Last year he moved into his study because the stairs got too much for him." She looked down at Michael's fingers, still laced in hers. "I'm not close to him. When I was little, he was never around. I thought he hated me. I wasn't much of a consideration in his world."

Michael found it hard to believe she wouldn't be loved.

She was rich. She had a grand home. Hell, she even had him for the asking.

She continued, "My mother was French and never really fit in here in Texas. I guess he thought I never would either, because most of the time I was home from school he managed to be somewhere else. When my mother died, it was like he wished I'd disappear. I remember one Christmas at the school he sent me to, he forgot to send someone after me. I ate Christmas dinner with the sisters and, of course, there were no presents allowed."

He closed his hand around hers. He'd never received one gift for birthday or Christmas, but he found himself feeling sorry for her. Little angels in white should have presents to open.

She met his gaze. "Promise me, for the time we're pretending, you'll never be cruel to me."

"I promise," he said, "only we're not pretending. We are married. I'll try to be a good husband, and when I leave, you'll have this place for you and your baby if one grows inside you."

One tear drifted down her cheek. "Thank you," she whispered. "I'll owe you a great debt. Is there nothing you ask?"

He closed his eyes and leaned the back of his head against the wall. Finally, he formed the words. "If you wouldn't mind, I'd like to touch you now and then." He lifted his hand as if showing her an example. "I mean you no harm, but I've never been near anyone so fine."

She frowned. "Are you making fun of me?"

"No," he said, surprised.

She pouted, then shrugged. "I'm a fallen woman about to trick my father, who is on his deathbed. I've been used and tossed away by one man, which makes me worthless, and I never plan to have another. If all you want to do is hold my hand or brush my cheek, I'd say that's a fair enough price for risking your life."

To his surprise, she frowned. "I must tell you, though, I don't like to be touched. It's not something I'm used to. My father never touched me. The nuns never touched me, and the one man who did touch me hurt me. You'd probably be doing me a favor, making me a little less jumpy around men. So touch all you like."

"I'll not hurt you," he added, trying to figure out if she truly meant what she said. "And I've already touched you, when I started to remove your necklace and again when I put my hand around your neck."

She smiled. "For a murder attempt, it was rather gentle."

They both laughed and for the first time he thought this scheme of hers might work. She'd have her land, his uncles would have their loot without fear of jail, and he'd have a memory of a time when he'd been allowed close to perfection.

A few minutes passed before the huge wooden door opened and an old doctor limped out. "You can see him." He shook his head. "I had to ask twice before he'd agree to see you. He doesn't seem to want to use up what little energy he has left."

She stepped past the doctor. Michael followed.

The room was huge and built to impress. Against long windows, a massive desk stood on a platform one step up so that whoever sat behind would be eye level with anyone standing. Books lined the walls into a seating area big enough to hold a full-sized bed. There, a man rested, his dark weathered skin contrasting against the white sheets.

Michael stared at Duke Camanez. Somehow, Michael thought he would have been bigger, but he looked small beneath the covers.

"Father," Cozette whispered as she stepped closer. "Father. I've brought my husband to meet you."

The dying man's eyes opened slowly. He looked at his only child with a cold, uncaring gaze. "You look more like your mother every day, child, and are just as worthless, I'm sure."

Then, without expecting her to respond, he looked at Michael. "So, you married her. She's no more than a bit of a girl, not strong enough to bear many children, I fear." Camanez coughed and blood trailed out of the corner of his mouth. "My condolences. She's made of lies and lace, you know."

"I know." Michael smiled as if he thought Duke Camanez was telling a joke. He'd heard of the rancher—everyone within five hundred miles had heard of the man who ruled his ranch like his own private kingdom.

Michael offered his hand and was surprised when the frail man took it.

"You're a fool who fell for her beauty," Camanez said in a whisper. "I can't blame you, son, I once fell myself." He took time to breathe, then continued, "Keep her pregnant if you can and don't give in to her tricks. Maybe she'll give birth to sons who will run this ranch one day. I pray they get your build and not hers." He coughed, then added as he fought to breathe, "Try not to run the place into the ground before you pass it on to my grandsons."

Michael had no idea what to say. Camanez's hand slipped from his as the old man's body shook from a round of coughing.

A nurse moved from the shadows and put her arm around him as she wiped away blood dripping from his chin.

The doctor mumbled as he pushed them toward the door. "Don't come back until tonight. I'm giving him enough laudanum to let him rest the day away. I fear you've excited him, doing him more harm than good."

As soon as they were outside the door, Cozette straightened as if she'd been slapped hard and was refusing to cower. "I'll be right back," she said and disappeared down a hallway. A moment later he heard her feet tapping up a wooden staircase just out of sight.

He didn't know if he should follow. Was she upset, hurt,

or embarrassed at what her father had said? Or, he reasoned, could it be morning sickness?

Michael returned to the entrance hall, noticing the sunrise shining bright across twenty-foot windows. It crossed his mind that it would take a dozen suns to lighten the sorrow in this house. He'd never considered himself as knowing much about women, but compared to Duke Camanez, he was a knight. If he hadn't heard the words he never would have believed a father could be so cruel to his only child. Apparently, he saw her as only a means to grandsons. His only chance that his blood would continue to own the ranch he called San Louise.

His uncles stood a foot inside the door looking as out of place as pigs in a parade. To their credit, they had tried to clean up. Their faces and hands were washed and they'd slicked back their dirty hair. He thought of Mrs. Peters back at the school near the prison. She probably would have taken one look at these three and had them planted in the dirt in hopes that whatever sprouted might be cleaner.

He joined them as they surveyed the place.

"We could take a dozen of these candleholders and they'd never miss them," Joseph whispered.

Michael glared at all three. "Rule two. Don't take anything," he said softly and all three nodded.

He watched them move around the room, staring at every piece of furniture or painting as if they were appraising its value. Strangers began to come down the stairs and from the hallway where his part-time wife had disappeared. They hung in small groups like travelers at a train station showing little interest in people around them.

Michael guessed some were employees, some might be relatives, but he had no idea if they were holding a death watch or waiting for a wedding. If he had to define their look, it would be curiosity more than sadness or joy.

Five minutes later, they all turned and watched Cozette

slowly come down the steps. The feeling that she was too beautiful to be real crossed his mind and he considered the possibility that this was all one long dream. When he'd first begun to read, he'd dreamed that the places and people in books were real, but he'd seen no evidence of it until now.

She played a role before him she must have been born to play. She greeted the sleepy guests who were down the stairs and the cowboys stepping inside, their hats in hand, with the same graceful smiles and comments.

Only one, an older man in black, looked like he hadn't been asleep. He stormed down the stairs glaring at Cozette, then searched the room until his gaze settled on Michael.

Michael knew if looks could kill he'd be dead.

Before being introduced, he had no doubt this was her uncle, Raymond Camanez. The man who would have inherited everything if she hadn't married.

Raymond said something sharp to her as she made the introduction, then glared at Michael as if he knew something was wrong but couldn't quite see the flaw. Then, like a storm breaking, his features cleared. Cozette's uncle Raymond took a step toward Michael, offering his hand.

When Michael took the man's hand, Raymond pulled him close and whispered, "You're a walking dead man for tricking me out of this ranch."

Michael stared as the older man pulled away smiling as if he'd just wished them well.

Cozette had moved away, probably to stay out of reach of her uncle. Michael could find no words to answer the threat, but he planned to keep watch. He might not know much about women, but he'd seen enough evil men to know one on sight.

The priest arrived and offered a blessing to the house. Then women came from the kitchen with huge trays of food. The ranch hands began to take their seats along a dining table long enough to hold two dozen people.

Cozette moved toward Michael. "You'll sit at the head of the table," she whispered. "I'll sit at the other end."

"No." Michael shook his head. "This is our wedding breakfast. You should stay at my side." He moved to the head of the table and pulled a chair from the wall.

She gave him a puzzled look, then smiled as if proud he was willing to play his part.

As they ate, Cozette introduced him to a few of the hands and they made more introductions. By the time breakfast was over, he could call most of the men by name and, surprisingly, they treated him with respect.

Cozette explained that he'd ridden for four days to get to her and made a joke about how he'd look far better when he got cleaned up.

Michael didn't miss how the men seemed to ignore Raymond Camanez when he stood. He was no longer their boss and every man on the ranch knew it.

The trouble was, Michael wasn't sure he would be up for the job. He could ride and shoot fairly well, but he knew nothing about running a ranch.

He glanced at Cozette and saw a brush of fear shadow her eyes as well. If they didn't pull this off, he didn't want to think about what might happen.

Her hand was icy when he closed his fingers around hers and stood, pulling her up with him. "If you will excuse us, gentlemen, I'd like to take a few minutes to get reacquainted with my wife."

They all laughed and mumbled low comments, but Michael didn't care. "Let's make this believable," he said only for her to hear a moment before he swept her up.

"Good day, gentlemen!" He laughed as they shouted while he started toward the stairs.

She wrapped her arms around his neck and buried her face against his shoulder.

Lowering a kiss on her cheek, he whispered, "Which way?"

"Up," she answered, her lips touching his. "All the way to the back of the hallway."

A cheer went up from the men behind them and Michael paused on the steps long enough to finish the kiss she'd started. The rest of this job he'd signed on for might be frightening, but her lips tasted like heaven.

When he finally let her breathe, her cheeks were rose colored with embarrassment, but she smiled up at him. Without a word he carried her up and set her gently on her feet once they were out of sight of those below.

She moved to the waiting maid and gave instructions in a low tone. The maid nodded and hurried away without looking up at Michael.

When they were alone, Cozette opened the last door on the left of the hallway. "My uncle took the first room when he came here after my father had moved downstairs. It's the biggest bedroom. He didn't know that my parents' rooms were always the last rooms."

She walked into a warm room done in colors of the earth and bathed in sunshine. Michael didn't want to act the fool, but he had a hard time keeping his mouth from dropping. He'd never seen such a room. Books lined two walls, and the view beyond the window panes seemed endless.

He glanced back at his uncles thundering up the stairs, Uncle Abe still eating. Before he could say anything, Cozette stepped in front of him and pointed. "Gentlemen, you'll find your rooms being readied in the guesthouses off the garden."

"We get a room?" Abe mumbled. "We'd be fine in the barn."

"No," she insisted. "You're family now. I've asked for baths and fresh clothes to be sent to your rooms."

"But . . ."

Michael didn't know if they were thinking of the rule to never leave her, or dreading the bath, but he said, "I'll watch over my wife, you three do as she says. We all could use a few hours of sleep."

They weren't about to argue with the woman who saved their lives. They all nodded and hurried back down the stairs.

Michael turned to her. "When I'm not close, I want one of them with you at all times. If for any reason I have to be gone, one will be sleeping in this hallway outside your door."

She walked back into what had been her father's room. "That's not necessary."

"I saw the way your uncle looked at us. I insist."

"Already being bossy. I don't like rules."

Michael hesitated, feeling like he might step a foot too far in any direction and be in quicksand. "I'll go along with however you want to play this except where your safety is concerned. Fair enough?"

"Fair enough." She moved to the windows, her black hair shining in the sunlight.

For the first time he thought he saw her relax a bit. She trusted him. It made no sense, but somehow he had the feeling that the only person for miles she believed in was him, the outlaw who tried to frighten her last night.

"This is not your room," he guessed, for there was nothing feminine about the space.

"No," she answered, opening a panel he thought might open into the hall. Only it led to a bathing room larger than most hotel rooms he'd seen. She crossed the tile and opened another door. "This is my room." The end of the hallway had been closed in to connect the rooms.

Michael smiled. It looked exactly like what he would imagine her room would look like. She didn't have the tall windows or the walls of books, but she had a fireplace and comfortable chairs in an alcove, where she could spend quiet mornings. Her colors were in the earthtones of spring.

"I keep both my doors locked whenever I'm in my room

and I'll tap on the bathroom door before entering in case you're bathing."

"Fair enough." He tried to act like he understood. The room she'd called the "bathing room" was almost the size of his uncles' entire house.

Three maids banged their way into the bathing room, causing Michael to take one step into her quarters. "What's going on?"

"They're getting your bath ready. I asked them to lay out extra shaving equipment. By the time you've finished, we'll have a few trouser lengths let out and jackets aired. There should be something waiting on your bed that will fit you."

"I have my own clothes." He looked down. His trousers and shirt might have been bought off the shelf at the mercantile, but they were the best he'd ever owned and not more than a week dirty.

"You're my husband. By marrying me you now own one of the biggest ranches in Texas. I can help run the ranch, but you'll need to look the part."

"We need to talk." He began unbuttoning his shirt. "As soon as I've followed your orders and had my bath, I need to know more about this ranch if I'm going to be of any use."

She smiled, her hands on her hips, her eyes watching his hands as they worked the buttons. "I'll be waiting in my room with a hot cup of tea and maps of the ranch when you're ready." She blushed when she noticed he was watching her watch him.

She closed her door and he wasn't surprised to hear the lock click. He kicked the other door closed with his boot and stripped off his clothes. She might think he understood her, but he felt like they were barely speaking the same language.

An hour later, he looked in the mirror and almost didn't recognize himself. His hair was clean and combed back, his clothes probably cost more than he'd ever made in his life all put together, and his boots, though too tight, were fine leather with tooling along the sides. It seemed unbelievable that people kept such clothes around for guests who might need them.

He tapped on her door. After a moment, he heard the lock give and she stood before him in a white blouse and midnight blue riding skirt. If possible, with her hair down and her boots disappearing into her skirt, she looked even more beautiful.

"Come in, sir." She grinned. "You sure do clean up nice. If I didn't know better I'd think you were born to wear those clothes."

He had no idea what to say. He couldn't think of a compliment for her that wouldn't make him sound like a fool.

"How does everything fit?" she asked as she moved to the seating area.

"The boots are too small, but someone came in the bathing room and stole my clothes and boots while I was dressing."

"The maids. They'll bring them back in a few hours, all cleaned and polished. I'll order you new boots by mail tomorrow."

"So, dressing me is part of the bargain." He didn't like the idea, but he did like the clothes.

She shrugged. "I guess so. It seems only fair. After all, I'm the one asking you to play a role."

He almost said, "Any chance undressing you is part of my bargain?" but he feared any boldness might frighten her. Showing affection downstairs was one thing; being bold here in the silence of her room would be quite another.

She took her seat on one side of a small table set with tea and smiled up at him as if they were old friends.

He gambled and brushed the top of her head with his hand.

As before, she stiffened at his touch, but made no comment. He had a feeling they were both thinking of the bargain they'd made. He'd play the part and she'd let him touch her from time to time.

He took his seat, swearing to himself that before he left her she'd at least not jump when he touched her.

She poured him tea, which he didn't drink as she filled him in on the workings of the ranch. She showed him maps and explained her family history.

He was quiet and polite until she pulled out the monthly expense records. The figures, so carefully kept, interested him. "Mind if I study these?" he finally asked. "If I can follow the income and output, I'll understand the runnings of the ranch better."

"I would say you could talk to our bookkeeper. I don't know his first name. Everyone always calls him Mr. Fiddler." She frowned. "I haven't seen him since I came back. In fact, I haven't even thought to ask about him. He's probably around somewhere."

Michael raised an eyebrow, but said nothing as she continued.

"The past three years' records are on my father's desk downstairs. I saw my uncle looking at them the morning I found out my father's terms for the will. While you're here take as active a part in the running of the ranch as you like." She hesitated a long moment and added, "But never forget our bargain. As soon as the ranch is safely mine, you and your uncles will leave and for your trouble I promise your wagon will be packed."

"I'll hold to my bargain, Cozette, and I'd like to look over the accounts," he said, almost angry that she felt the need to remind him of their pact. He didn't add that since she'd probably be by her father's side the records would give him a reason to stay close.

She opened her mouth as if to question, then reconsidered and nodded in compromise. Last night he'd watched her change from a frightened child to a woman taking control of her life. She'd never be easy to manipulate again and he knew he'd never even try.

He smiled as she fiddled with her tea. He knew he was the only one she had to trust. An outlaw who had threatened to kill her was all that stood beside her now. Michael had seen the look in her uncle's eyes. He wanted the ranch and might just be willing to do anything, including killing them both to get it.

Michael planned to stay by her side until he knew she was safe. He would do so even without the promise of a wagonload of goods.

Chapter 4

The newlyweds came down for lunch late. Cozette didn't miss all the smiles and winks at Michael. He remained the gentleman, never letting on that he knew she'd thrown up her breakfast. He hadn't even raised his head from the book he'd been reading when she forgot to close his connecting door. When she'd visited her father by way of the back stairs, he'd followed and quietly remained at the desk by the window until she'd told him it was time for lunch.

He'd covered his hand over hers a few times during the meal, and when he knew someone was watching, he'd made an effort to brush her cheek with a kiss or lightly circle his arm over her shoulders. Because of her father's illness and the newlyweds' need to be alone, the few guests who'd come quickly made excuses to leave. By afternoon, all the ranch hands had returned to work and the house was quiet.

When she'd excused herself to sit with her father, Michael followed without a word. He'd walked her all the way to the chair by her father's bed, then kissed her hand and said he'd be at the desk across the room.

She'd expected to find her uncle in her father's room and was relieved to see only the nurse.

Shadows were long when Michael excused himself and

left the room. Cozette stood and stretched, then walked around the big desk, noticing that Michael had been studying the records all afternoon. She stopped at the tall windows and stared out at her ranch, loving it so much her heart ached to realize how close she came to losing it.

She brushed her fingers over the slight bulge just above her knee where she'd strapped a gun to her leg. A few months ago she believed everyone to be good and fair. She thought her uncle loved her and only wanted her to be happy when he'd sent a letter introducing the son of a friend.

Fredrick Bates had shown up at her school with flowers and his aunt as chaperone. The nuns had let her go riding with him and to dinner in town as long as the aunt went along. After all, he had the proper family introduction and Cozette was a year older than most girls who left the school. They'd let her stay on another year only because her father had insisted.

Cozette thought she was in love with Fredrick by the fourth outing. He spoke French to her and swore she had angel eyes. When his aunt retired early on the fifth evening, she'd been excited to spend the time alone with a man who pampered her so.

Fredrick had teased her and told her he planned to seduce her as they entered his private quarters. She'd been fool enough to laugh and play along when he kissed her and flirted with her. When the hour grew late, she'd told him she had to go, but he changed. Seduction turned forceful and demanding.

For a moment she thought he was still teasing, and when talk turned to action, she'd been too shocked, too young, too naive to even fight.

It had all been over in a few minutes, and when he pulled away, he'd seemed furious at her. The man who'd spoken his love for her in French stood, straightened his clothes, and said he'd done what he'd been paid to do. He'd left her there, her dress torn, her heart broken as if she were no more than the scraps after a meal.

She'd cried for a while, then walked back to the school and pretended nothing had happened. If she'd said a word she would have been expelled. Her father would have disowned her. Proper young ladies didn't get themselves into compromising positions.

So, she'd held her tongue and come home as soon as she could find a reason to slip away.

Once on the ranch, she'd realized the truth. The letter introducing Fredrick was in Uncle Raymond's handwriting. He had paid a man to dishonor her.

When she said nothing, he must have thought the plan hadn't worked. Then, he'd talked her father into changing his will. He probably figured she'd be too afraid to even talk to another man after her encounter with Fredrick. Uncle Raymond must have thought he'd planned it all out where he would win the ranch without a fight. Half the family wealth had never been enough—he wanted it all.

Her grandfather had fought the Apache for this land, her father had fought outlaws and raiders more than once, and now she knew she'd have to fight her uncle. No one was ever going to stand in her way. The land was hers, paid for with blood and sweat. She would have made a bargain with the devil himself to keep it.

Looking at the chair where Michael had been sitting, she wondered if that hadn't been exactly what she'd done. After all, he was an outlaw. His only three relatives didn't look like they'd completely evolved from animals. Moses snorted like a bull and Joseph smacked when he ate. She couldn't even see Abe clearly for all the dirty hair hanging in his face.

But Michael Hughes looked like he was born to play the role of a rancher. All dressed up, he looked like a perfect gentleman, but he seemed to be holding his cards close to the vest and waiting for her to give him just enough power to take over or run. When the time came, how hard would it be for him to walk away from a ranch this size with only a wagonload of trinkets? By law all her property now belonged to him. Would he give it back when the time came?

She stood and moved to the gun chest. Lifting the false bottom to the shelf, she retrieved two more small Colts. One for beneath her pillow, the other to hide in this room. She'd not be caught unprepared again. The nuns might not have taught her to fight, but they had taught her to reason. She wanted to believe in Michael, but she'd learned the hard way to be prepared.

From the window, she watched her new husband cross through the garden. He didn't turn to the cabins where his relatives stayed but opened a side gate. Taking long strides he walked into the untamed pasture beyond the trimmed and groomed walls of the compound.

He was almost to the trees running along a creek behind the house when he stopped. She watched as he leaned his head back and stared up at the cloudy sky like a man trying to find his bearings.

For the first time, she wondered if he felt as trapped by their bargain as she did. If he hadn't agreed to her crazy scheme he might have been killed last night. Yet, even knowing all she had to do was yell and he'd be trapped, he'd bargained for his uncles' lives. He'd also handled her setting all the rules with more class than she might have in his place. She'd made it plain that he'd play the part of master over all he saw, but she'd make the final decisions on anything pertaining to the ranch. She'd hold all the power. As her father slipped farther and farther from the world, she'd take her place.

One of the ranch hands fell into step with Michael as he walked back to the house. She saw them talking and wished she could hear what they were saying. The ranch hand tipped his hat in salute when he veered off at the garden gate.

Cozette put one of the guns in the pillows by the alcove and noticed he hadn't touched his tea again. Next time they talked, she'd have coffee for him even though he hadn't complained or asked. The least she could do was make him comfortable in his cage.

Chapter 5

Michael walked slowly back onto the house grounds. He was supposed to join her at dinner, but he had no idea when dinner would be. At the prison there were only two meals. One served at dawn, the other an hour before dark. That way men could use daylight to work and everyone would be shackled in by dark and no extra light was needed.

He'd hated those nights. A boy sleeping in among men who yelled and swore and cried. The silence of the classroom was a welcome change. He hadn't minded that he slept on the floor with a single blanket at night. The warden's wife gave him clean clothes every Monday and made him bathe once a week. When he'd finished and dressed, she'd always inspect for dirt under his nails or ears that weren't scrubbed.

If she found nothing, she'd say, "You'll do" and walk away without another word.

He ate his meals on the back porch of the warden's house. Their cook gave him scraps at first. No matter what or how little was on the plate, Michael thanked her every morning and night. Eventually, the meals got better. After a few months, she even gave him a tin with leftover biscuits in it. "You ain't much older than the kids in that school. It ain't fair you don't have no lunch."

Michael thanked her and that night he tasted his first dessert. One scoop of apple cobbler.

When he was growing up with his uncles nothing had an order. Supper or any meal, for that matter, came when the food was done. If nothing was caught and cooked, they ate like chickens scratching around for bits of food.

He passed through the pasture gate and into the courtyard wondering if the San Louise Ranch ever had cobbler.

He saw Abe and Joseph walking out of their small rooms along the row of cabins Cozette had called guesthouses. His uncles were dressed in wool trousers without a single patch and well-made broadcloth shirts.

"Hold up, Mickey!" Abe yelled. "You get a look at our quarters? Real sheets and two blankets each. One of the maids came by to tell us she'd pick up our laundry and sheets every Monday to wash. Imagine that."

Joseph shook his head and stuttered, "They'll w-wear them out w-washing them that often."

Abe took his time chewing his words before he spoke, as he always did when he wasn't sure of something. "How long do you figure we're staying?"

Michael wished he could tell them the bargain, but he'd given his word. "Behave yourselves and you can stay as long as I do."

Abe tried again. "When your pa married our sister, he took her away. The marriage didn't take, I guess, 'cause she was back before all the seasons changed with you in her belly. When she left us she kept saying it was forever. Mickey, you ain't never used that word once."

Michael had heard the story of how his mother left them a hundred times. They did all they could when she went into labor, but she died giving birth to him. Then his uncles stole a goat and somehow kept him alive. He was about seven when he realized his uncles barely had a brain among them.

He tried to make one detail clear to them. "I'll stay a while but we'll have to leave eventually. This is Cozette's ranch, her land, not mine. Never forget that."

They both nodded and turned toward the bunkhouse.

"Aren't you coming in to dinner?" Michael asked.

"Nope." Abe smiled. "We've been invited to the bunkhouse kitchen for chili."

Joseph grinned. "W-wish we could invite you, boy, but it w-wouldn't be right. You're going to have to eat in the big house w-with all those people w-watching to snatch your plate before you get a chance to lick it clean and more forks than anybody ought to have to put up w-with."

Abe frowned. "One of them fell in my pocket this morning. I guess you'd better take it back before they miss it."

Michael took the fork. "No stealing while you're here, remember?"

Abe's head bobbled, but Michael doubted the message would log.

He walked back to the house. Inside the kitchen, he dropped the fork on a work table and moved on. The place had more rooms than he could count. There were sitting rooms and proper parlors. Cozette's father's office was bigger than most banks, with closets and doors going off in almost every direction. While they'd looked over the map she'd mentioned her father hadn't smoked in weeks, the area near the desk still smelled of cigars. Michael decided to ask if the bookkeeper smoked. If he did, he couldn't have been away long even though Cozette hadn't seen him.

When Michael finally wandered into the main entry hall, he found Cozette waiting on the third step, her elbows on her knees and her chin in her palms. She still wore her white blouse and riding skirt.

"Am I late?"

"No, you've plenty of time to change for dinner. I laid your clothes out myself."

He frowned. "Why would I change?"

She smiled. "I've wondered that same thing most of my life. All I know is my uncle invited guests again. He's not talking to me directly, but apparently he's not ready to leave and needed a reason to stay. The charade of a wedding dinner with neighbors is as good a reason as any to delay his departure."

"How's your father?"

"The same." She looked up at him, her eyes filled with sadness. "He doesn't squeeze my fingers anymore and he won't open his eyes when I talk to him. I get the feeling he wishes I'd stay away."

Michael took her hand firmly in his grip. He had no idea what to say. The old man was having a hard time dying just as he'd had a hard time living. Cozette had been as starved for love growing up as Michael had been.

He tugged on her hand and pulled her into his arms as she stood. For a moment all he did was hold her against him guessing that the feel of another standing heart to heart was as foreign to her as to him.

She held on tightly for a moment, then smiled her thanks up at him.

"If I dress for dinner," he tried to make light of what had just passed between them, "I'm guessing you will have to also."

She groaned. "Of course, and wear my hair up. After all, I'm not a child any longer. I'm a proper married lady." They moved up the stairs, holding hands.

"I like your hair down." He winked at her. "It brushes your bottom when you walk."

She slapped at his ribs and laughed. "A gentleman never refers to a woman's bottom."

He liked her teasing. This was a side of her he hadn't seen. "I'm sorry, but you know, dear, I'm not a gentleman and I like looking at your bottom as well as your hair." He slowed slightly to take in the view before she pulled him along.

They reached her room, where Moses slept outside her door.

"I slipped past him," she confessed.

"Don't do it again." He hadn't meant his words to roll so hard.

She looked up as if she might argue, then turned and disappeared into her room.

He woke his uncle and told him to go eat chili, that he'd guard his own wife tonight. She didn't like being ordered— he needed to remember that. She expected him to be a gentleman and he wasn't sure how. The one compliment he'd given her apparently wasn't proper. If their marriage lasted beyond dinner tonight, he'd be surprised.

Chapter 6

Cozette jumped at the tap on their connecting door half an hour later.

"Ready?" he said when she shoved the lock free.

She didn't miss his smile, but he looked nervous and somehow that one fact calmed her. With only a slight hesitance, she motioned him into her room.

She couldn't help but stare at him from head to toe. He looked striking in his tailored evening jacket and white shirt hugging his tan throat. "Almost," she whispered. "I can't get the latch of my necklace to hold. Would you do it for me?"

Handing him the jewelry, she turned her back. Her hair was already swept atop her head, so he should have no trouble. Standing very still, she waited.

"Got it," he said.

She felt for the necklace even knowing it wasn't there. "No, you haven't."

He laughed. "No, I meant I figured out how this thing works. Now hold still and I'll rope it around you."

She felt his warm fingers work the lock at the back of her neck. Then his hands drifted down, smoothing the chain along her throat. She didn't move as his long fingers fanned out over her bare shoulders and gently held her still. She could feel his breath against her cheek, but he didn't move.

"Are you finished?" she asked, waiting for him to let go of her shoulders.

"Yes." His voice was oddly low. "I'm just enjoying the view from here. I think I like it better than I do the one of you walking away. You seem very nicely rounded in several places."

She turned preparing to snap at him, but he was even closer than she thought. They were almost touching. The warmth in his eyes shocked her, as did the honesty. He wasn't flattering or playing with her, he was simply telling her how he felt. He had no reason to play games with her. They both knew the bargain between them was already set.

She raised her chin slightly. "It's time to go downstairs."

He took her hand and put it in the bend of his elbow, then led her down the steps to a dozen people waiting to see the newlyweds.

Cozette smiled when she saw them. Most of the women had been friends of her mother's from years ago. She remembered them coming to visit when she was little, but they'd stopped dropping by after her mother died. Uncle Raymond would have to be on his best behavior. Even if he was furious about the marriage, he couldn't afford to let on in front of them or the powerful husbands who stood at their wives' sides.

Michael remained near, smiling but saying little. He asked where each guest's land was and if it bordered San Louise, then talked of the weather, but little else.

Her mother's friends seemed to tolerate Raymond more than like him. By the time dinner was served it was plain they came to see her and the man she'd picked to marry. Judging by their smiles, the neighbors liked her new husband just fine.

The only thing Michael did out of order was pull up her

chair beside his when they walked in to dinner. The guests laughed and kidded him about being a new husband. One lady even commented that it was the dearest thing she'd ever seen.

About the time the main course was served the talk turned to books. Cozette tried to shield questions meant for Michael. She wasn't sure he was well read and she didn't want these people to hurt his feelings. But, after a few moments, she realized they were united in their mission to get to know him.

When she glanced at her uncle she knew that somehow he was behind their curiosity. He must have planted a seed that her new husband was not good enough for the princess of San Louise.

Finally, a man on their left asked Michael, point-blank, what he thought of *Moby Dick*.

Michael set down his fork and said simply, "I think it's a wonderful study on social status and it makes you speculate on your own personal beliefs as well as your individual place in the universe." He fought down a smile, probably proud of himself for remembering most of a review he'd read. "I also think, at over eight hundred pages, it's a bit longer than it needed to be."

The room was silent for a moment, and then everyone talked at once. He'd somehow passed the test and been accepted. For the rest of the meal, no one bothered even to look at Uncle Raymond.

"You read," she whispered near Michael's ear when she got a chance.

"Yes, dear." His hand moved over her skirt and brushed her leg. Then, without hesitation, he kissed her lightly.

Cozette blushed and pushed his hand off her skirts. He might read, but as far as his manners, he would barely be considered housebroken. No man, not even a husband, would touch his wife's leg in public. Thank goodness they were at the end of the table, where no one could see.

The table roared with approval over the kiss as she slipped her hand beneath the table and pushed his hand away a second time.

"Do it again! We missed the wedding!" someone yelled. "At least we should be allowed to see a real kiss."

Michael waited until she turned in his direction. This time his hand gripped her leg with determination and she felt the heat of his fingers through the layers of her gown. With his free hand, he lifted her chin and lowered his mouth over hers.

The kiss was sweet, tender, but his hand moved purposefully up her leg with shocking familiarity. After a few moments she pulled away. Anger flashed before she realized they were on the same side. His bold actions made everyone believe they were in love, and her shocked hesitance only led them to believe that the girl was becoming a woman.

Michael smiled down at her as his hand beneath the table moved back to her knee, straightening the silk gown as he went, as though he could somehow erase the feel of his hand.

The crowd clapped and yelled. "Look," someone shouted, "she blushes with just a mere kiss!"

Cozette wanted to jab him hard in the ribs but he was playing the game they'd agreed to play. No one in the room would suspect they'd married for anything but love or maybe passion.

All evening he kept her close. He played with her hand while someone read poetry, and when the evening progressed and the wine flowed, and they no longer became the center of attention, he remained close, always touching her hand or arm, or brushing his leg lightly against hers.

She considered the fact that he might be trying to drive her mad. After all, he'd have everything if she went crazy.

Each touch seemed a fraction bolder than the last. She found herself warming to each, waiting for the next.

People grouped together to sing around her mother's piano. Two old men were sound asleep near the door, their brandy still in their hands. To her surprise, Michael moved even closer to her after her uncle retired.

Cozette felt the length of the day. With no sleep the night before, she couldn't remember when she'd last had any rest. She'd tried for an hour in the afternoon, but there was far too much to do. Now, with the warmth of him beside her, she melted against him, no longer worrying about what was proper.

He seemed to understand, putting his arm around her and pulling her close, then brushing her cheek as he encouraged her to rest her head on his chest.

She didn't protest, surprised at how good it felt to have someone watching over her. The guests fell away, their goodnights little more than buzzing around her. Even the doctor's report that her father was resting comfortably hardly registered.

When they were alone, Michael pulled her onto his lap and cradled her against the soft arm of the settee. "Sleep, my dear. I'm right here to watch over you."

She felt his hands brush along her side and his lips kiss her temple, and then she drifted deep into sleep.

When she awoke, he was carrying her up the stairs. Embarrassed at being carried to bed like a child, she didn't move or open her eyes.

He went to his room and crossed the space between to hers. Without a word, he gently laid her down on the bed. She didn't move as he unlatched her heavy necklace. His fingers drifted down and brushed lightly over the rise of her breast, and then he moved to her feet and removed her shoes. His hand glided up her leg to just above her knee where a strap held her gun in place. He didn't seem surprised by the weapon but simply removed it and pulled her skirt back down.

The thought crossed her mind that if he went any farther she'd scream, but she knew no one would come to stand between a husband and a wife on their first night together.

His hands slid along her sides from knee to shoulder, and then he tugged the covers to her chin and moved off the bed.

She expected him to cross back into his room, but he didn't. He locked her door, pulled the curtain across the alcove, stoked the fire, and removed his boots and jacket.

Then, very carefully, he lay down atop the covers at her side.

With her eyes closed, she tried to breathe slowly as if asleep as his hand moved across her waist. He stretched, then was still and his breathing calmed.

She risked a glance as she turned to face him.

He was sound asleep.

Chapter 7

When Cozette woke the next morning, Michael was gone but his new boots and coat remained in her room, looking very much like he'd tossed them there before taking his bride to bed.

She stood, removed her wrinkled dress, and hurried into her morning clothes. She wanted to check on her father before the rest of the house came awake.

The doors between her room and Michael's were open. His room was empty and for a moment she thought her part-time husband might be gone. She stared out the window until she spotted him in a corral near the main barn. He was on horseback, circling the corral as if testing one of her father's horses. He wore the tailored trousers and starched shirt she'd left for him along with the leather vest. He looked the part of a rancher.

Two of her three uncles-in-law were hanging on the fence watching Michael. She had no doubt the third little round man was outside her door on guard.

The two on the fence both had on the clothes she'd sent down for them to wear. She'd picked the largest clothes from their stock of work trousers and flannel shirts and asked one of the girls to hem all the pants up at least six inches.

How could Michael be so tall and lean and have three relatives who looked like tree stumps?

As she watched, one of the uncles opened the gate and Michael bolted out across open land at full gallop. He could ride. Not like a gentleman from the East might ride, but like a cowhand used to living in the saddle.

After a few minutes, he turned the horse and raised his hand. Several riders joined him. Within minutes they were galloping at full speed toward the open range. Just before they crossed the ridge, he turned his head toward the house . . . toward her.

Cozette stepped back as if she'd been caught spying. She darted out the bedroom door and headed down the back stairs to the kitchen. The sound of her chubby bodyguard rattled along behind her.

In the kitchen she sat Uncle Moses down at one of the work tables and promised not to try to slip away. "Stay here and have your breakfast. I'm going to check on my father. You can watch the door to his office while you eat."

Moses nodded, liking the idea of being able to stand his guard while sitting at a table eating.

Cozette hurried down the hall wishing she'd checked on her father before she'd gone to bed. She knew there was nothing she could do for him, but still she needed to know when anything changed.

The doctor was sitting beside the bed when she entered the office. A stack of bloody towels nearby was almost as high as the mattress.

The doctor shook his head slowly. "No change and I don't think we could wake him this morning if we tried."

She moved to the other side of the bed and took her father's hand. His fingers were colder than they had been the first day she'd returned home. He no longer opened his eyes, or spoke to anyone. He might not be in pain, but he was less with the living than he'd been yesterday.

"I've made him as comfortable as I can," the doctor whispered. "His heart grows so weak I'm not sure I hear the beat sometimes."

She looked up at the doctor and he added in a voice so low he almost mouthed the words, "I'll be surprised if he's here much longer."

Cozette nodded and took her place beside the bed. A few hours later she was aware of the doctor leaving and of Michael coming in. He walked to her side and kissed her cheek without saying a word. She watched as he moved to the massive desk and began looking over the accounts. His trousers were stained, his shirt was sweaty, and his old boots were dusty. Her husband was looking more and more like the rancher she'd asked him to become.

When the housekeeper brought lunch, he stopped long enough to sit across from Cozette by the window. She ate only a few bites. When she smiled her thank-you to him for not trying to talk to her, he seemed to understand.

As they finished and stood, he pulled her to him for a tight hug, and then she tugged away and went back to her watch. He followed as if she'd need him to hold her chair. When she was seated once more, Michael brushed his hand over one lock of her hair.

"When there is time," he said as he rested his hand gently on her shoulder, "I'd like to talk to you about the books."

She nodded, thinking more about how she liked this man's gentle touch . . . almost comforting, almost loving. "I don't know much. Mr. Fiddler can answer your questions."

"I've asked about him," Michael said as he brushed her shoulder. "No one has seen him in days."

"I'll worry about it later," she said as she stared down at the man who liked being called Duke but never took to the name Father.

He had never been there for her, or her mother if the stories were true, but she had to sit beside him now in his last hours. Maybe she just wanted to show that she was a better person, or maybe she didn't want even him to be alone. All his life he'd considered his only daughter worthless, yet she was the only one to stand near in his final hours.

She listened to the shallow intake of breath after breath . . . until there was none. The late sun shone golden across the windows as she realized he'd passed.

"Michael," she whispered, knowing that he'd come to her side.

When she felt his arm circle around her, she collapsed into his embrace wanting nothing more than to step away from the world for a moment.

She was barely aware of him taking her upstairs. When he laid her beneath the covers, she curled into a ball and cried softly. For a while she was alone, but then she felt his weight move the bed and he was at her side again. He pulled her into his arms and held her without saying a word. As always, his hands moved over her, only tonight she found comfort in his touch.

The next morning Cozette moved as if in a dream through the funeral of her father and the reading of his will. She ignored the angry looks from her uncle, knowing he wouldn't dare say a word with people filling the house and spilling out onto the yard. To no one's surprise, her father's will was short, leaving everything, not to family or kin, but to his only daughter's husband with the request that he always treat her fairly.

She slipped up the back stairs as Michael saw the lawyer out. Cozette needed a few moments alone. She'd lived in the eye of a tornado for weeks and, finally, the storm was settling.

After refusing to let a single tear fall in front of others, she washed her face in cold water and went to greet those who came to pay their last respects to a hardworking but never-loving man.

She noticed Joseph watching her from his chair near the back stairs as she stepped into the hallway. Reluctantly, he abandoned his breakfast and downed the last of his coffee before following.

From the other direction, Uncle Raymond appeared suddenly in her path and stopped her progress with an iron grip around her arm. He twisted cruelly, slamming her against the wall. "We need to talk." Anger flowed like hot lava around her. "You think you got away with something here, but . . ."

Uncle Joseph bumped into Raymond like a blind bull, knocking her uncle a few feet down the passage and away from her.

"Oh, s-sorry," Joseph said. "I was so busy eating I didn't even notice you blocking the w-way." He smeared sticky fingers covered in warm cinnamon and sugar along Raymond's buckskin vest. "You really should go get you one of those rolls w-while they're hot."

Raymond hissed, "You'll be as sorry as your nephew."

"Oh, I am," Joseph whined. "There w-was still some g-good finger licking on that hand when I touched you. I'll miss those few b-bites."

Raymond swore.

Joseph straightened. "I don't think it's right to talk that w-way in front of Mickey's dear one."

For once Raymond was too upset to form words. He decided to storm off.

Cozette smiled at Uncle Joseph, seeing for the first time how her husband could love such a man.

"Thanks," she said, realizing that Michael might have been right to enlist three bodyguards for her.

"I d-do my best," Joseph said simply. "You're Michael's

pretty little bride. I can't let anything happen to you on my w-watch."

He followed her into the huge dining room and stood in the corner looking about as invisible as a two hundred–pound frog, but she didn't care. This morning he was her knight in shining armor.

She greeted her guests, offered them food and coffee. The room was almost full when Michael walked in. He didn't seem to see anyone in the room but her. He walked right up to her, circled her waist, and kissed her forehead with tenderness.

Two wranglers she recognized as having worked for her father for years followed a step behind Michael like war lieutenants storming into battle.

"It will all be over soon," he whispered to her. "Until we have time to talk, these men will be on watch."

She looked into his blue-gray eyes and saw worry. Something had changed, but her father's funeral was no time to talk.

"It'll be all right," he said, brushing his hand over her arm.

She had no idea what he was talking about, but she believed he'd keep her safe. She'd picked an outlaw to trust, and somehow, he'd proved worth the loving.

She remembered the way he'd readied her for bed last night. He'd carried her to her room, tugged off her shoes, and pulled the pins from her hair. He'd even slid his hand beneath her skirts and removed the small Colt strapped to her leg just as he had the night before. Only last night she thought she remembered his fingers lingering longer along the soft flesh above her knee. When he'd unbuttoned a few buttons of her blouse, his knuckles had traveled down the valley between her breasts.

She'd moaned softly meaning to pull away, but his gentle touch calmed her. The next time his hand moved between her breasts, he'd caught her moan in his kiss.

He'd done everything almost exactly like he'd done the night before, only last night he hadn't slept on top of the covers. They both might have been fully clothed, but they'd slept with their bodies pressed together.

As before, when she'd awoke, he was gone. She'd found him downstairs making all the plans for the funeral.

Now, as people passed by to tell her of their sadness over the death of her father, Michael did exactly what he'd signed on to do. He acted the part of the perfect husband.

He even walked her to her room when all had left. She was surprised he'd ordered tea and sandwiches for her. With one kiss, he ordered her to rest. When he left, she had no doubt one of his uncles was just outside the door.

Chapter 8

As the day passed, Michael checked on his sleeping wife several times before he finally settled in the study to work. A few of the ranch hands he'd become friends with dropped by to offer suggestions on what needed to be done on the ranch. With the Duke's illness and Raymond only doing what had to be done, much had been neglected.

Michael took the men's advice but knew he'd have to check the books himself. No one could find the bookkeeper named Fiddler or remember exactly when he'd left. Michael noticed there were slight changes in the printing of numbers starting about four weeks ago. The handwriting was close, but whoever had started keeping the books had a heavier hand.

The nurse passed in front of the desk at dusk and lit the lamps. Michael barely noticed. What he was discovering in the accounts of the ranch was shocking. For the last six months, since Uncle Raymond had been helping run the place, small amounts of money had gone missing. Sometimes bills were double paid while others went weeks on the books without any payment. Each month the amount disappearing off the books grew.

Then, the last month, the month before Duke Camanez

died, nothing went missing. Apparently, Raymond was so sure he would inherit, he'd stopped stealing.

Michael frowned, wondering if the answer more likely might be that whoever was stealing feared being caught.

"Sir?" the nurse said softly as she lifted her bag.

Michael glanced up unsure whom she was talking to, but she was looking straight at him. "Yes?" he managed.

"If you don't mind I'll leave now. I've packed up all the doctor's things."

"Thank you," Michael said. "Thank you for being so kind."

She hesitated, then added, "If you and the missus need me when the baby births, I'll be happy to come."

"You know about the baby?" He couldn't believe Cozette would tell anyone.

"I've seen the signs, but don't you worry about me saying anything. The first one sometimes comes early. Nobody will count the months. You just send word if you need me."

He managed a nod without raising his head as she closed the door behind her.

He tried to go back to the books, but he couldn't focus. He'd seen the signs too. His bride hadn't been lying when she'd said she might be pregnant. She was pregnant.

Forcing himself to concentrate, he decided to work on one problem at a time, knowing deep down that if she was truly with child, he wouldn't be able to keep his word and leave her.

He wasn't aware of anything but the books for a while, then, out of the corner of his eye, he saw Cozette slipping through the door.

With her puffy eyes and red nose, he had no doubt she had been crying. She smiled as she neared. "Thanks for handling everything today," she said as she moved closer. "I don't know what is the matter with me. I thought to only nap and ended up sleeping the day away."

"You're welcome," he answered, wishing he could read her mind as she walked closer. "There was no need to wake you. You needed the rest."

When her hand brushed over his head, he jerked in surprise. He hadn't expected her to touch him. That hadn't been part of the bargain. A few times she'd taken his hand or put her fingers on his arm, but nothing like this—almost a caress.

"You look like you belong in that chair, Michael. The housekeeper told me you've had the men do more work today than they've done in a month."

He pushed his chair back. "Come closer," he ordered gently, loving the easy way she came to him as if they were lovers.

She slowly moved against his side and he handed her his handkerchief. As she blew her nose, he pulled her onto his lap. As always, she hesitated like she might refuse his closeness, then relaxed against his arm.

"Are you all right?" he asked, playing with a curl of her hair.

"Everyone has been so nice," she said, then laughed that little giggle she had that wasn't really a laugh at all. "Well, everyone except Uncle Raymond, who is, at present, eating his dinner surrounded by your uncles because he keeps trying to get close to me."

Michael brushed his hand over her shoulder and along her arm. The need to touch her grew stronger every hour. He'd learned that once he was close to her, she quickly grew accustomed to his touch and no longer tightened her muscles as if expecting a blow. Either she was learning to trust him, or she saw him as no more than a bothersome gnat to be ignored.

As Cozette talked about the guests and all they'd said, he

slowly moved her hair away from her neck and leaned close enough to brush his mouth along her throat.

When she didn't react to his light kisses, he opened his mouth and tasted her skin. He could feel her pulse beneath his lips. Curling his fingers into the collar of her dress, he tugged to reveal more of her neck. The material gave to his demand, showing the rise of her breasts against the black of her dress.

"Are you listening?" she said, tugging away so that she could look him in the eyes.

"Yes, dear," he lied. So she wouldn't consider standing, he circled her waist as he pushed the chair closer to the desk. He wanted her close enough to feel her breathing. "But before you continue I need to show you something I've found." His hand rested just below her breast and he almost forgot what he was saying. She was perfection in his arms.

She leaned over the books unaware that he now cupped the bottom of one breast in his hand.

He pulled her back and whispered against her ear. "I love touching you." His fingers closed gently over her breasts. "Am I hurting you?"

She shook her head. "I think I like the feel of you touching me." She took a breath, letting the front of her dress press lightly against his hand. "It seemed a strange request but I've found it comforting."

He moved his fingers over her, needing to feel all of her. "And pleasurable," he whispered.

She stopped breathing for a moment, then took a deep breath and sat perfectly still while his fingers tightened once more. "And pleasurable," she admitted.

He watched her face for any sign that she wanted him to stop. He saw none.

He kissed her ear. "I love being near you. The best part of the bargain we made was you agreeing to let me hold you."

She giggled. "I had a feeling you'd say that. You're an

easy man to get used to." She gently pushed his hand away. "Now, tell me about the books."

He smiled in agreement to her suggestion, knowing he'd never be able to concentrate if he didn't. As his hand brushed over her one last time, he promised, "Later."

She managed a shy smile. "Later."

They pored over the books for half an hour with her questioning and recalculating every step and him fighting the urge to touch her as he answered her questions.

When she took extra time refiguring what he'd already checked, he didn't mind at all. As she studied the books one last time, he lightly began to brush his fingers over her gown. He'd gone long enough without the feel of her in his hand.

She'd grown used to him and except for now and then absently pushing his hand away she didn't seem to mind his attentions. He kept his touch light, a promise between them.

Finally, when he thought he might go mad, she turned to him and smiled. "You're brilliant. Now I have a reason to demand my uncle leave. It's obvious he's been robbing my father for months."

To his shock, she leaned close and kissed him quickly on the mouth.

When she started to pull away, he whispered against her ear, "Do that again."

And she did. Soft, light kisses that turned to fire as they lengthened. When she'd pull away her eyes were huge with wonder and her mouth pouty. Then, she'd smile and he'd ask for more.

They played the game until the housekeeper tapped on the door to remind them that it was well past dinnertime.

When they sat down to a late meal, neither seemed to want to talk. They both knew the bargain they'd set. As soon as Raymond left, there would be no reason for Michael to stay. Their time together was coming to an end and neither wanted to waste a minute of what they had left.

Finally, when they moved to the parlor with their cobbler, Cozette smiled. "You played your part of loving husband well. I'm growing very used to your kisses, sir."

"You're an easy woman to kiss, to cherish. That first man you knew, who hurt you and left you, was a fool."

"How do you know he was the first man? Maybe I've had many lovers before."

Michael shook his head. "In the study you were learning to kiss. If you'd had a lover, you would already have known." He winked at her. "By the way, you're learning very well."

She blushed as she winked back. "I think I need a little more practice if you don't mind."

"I don't mind at all. A woman with child should already have learned such things."

He watched her carefully, guessing she was about to lie. "The truth, remember. Always the truth between us."

She looked down at her bowl. "It's worse than you think. He didn't just hurt me and leave me with a child, he was paid to do so. Paid to dishonor me." She gulped down a sob. "And somehow it is all my fault. I should have fought harder or killed him. I should have . . ."

"It's not your fault."

She shook her head. "My father said I have my mother's blood. Several times I heard him tell my uncle that it was just a matter of time before I disgraced the family."

He cupped her face in his hands. "I didn't know your mother, but if you are like her, she must have been a wonder." He moved his thumbs across her cheek. "Tell me about her."

In the shadows of a dying fire she told him all she remembered of a loving mother. When she could think of nothing more, they sat side by side.

Finally, she patted his leg. "Thank you. I needed to remember. No one mourned my father's passing but I remember how it was when she died. I think I cried today because I'm alone, not because I'll miss my father."

"You're welcome." He covered his hand over hers for a moment. "And you are not alone. I'm right here beside you."

Standing, he pulled her gently up and kissed her cheek. "It's time we called it a night. Do you think you can undress yourself tonight? I've work still to do on the books." He didn't add that he wanted to hide the records while Raymond was still in the house. If the books were lost, it would only be his word against Raymond's.

She looked up at him. "Of course. You're right. It is late. Will you be sleeping in my bed?" It was such an innocent question, but there could be only honesty in the answer.

"Do you mind? I enjoy holding you while you sleep. I know you're safe."

"I don't mind," she whispered. "Just don't wake me when you finally come to bed."

He knew they were both adults, but there was something almost childlike in the way they trusted without reason. He wasn't sure what she thought. Maybe she believed nothing would happen. Maybe she was simply living up to the bargain he'd requested.

But there was nothing childlike in the way he felt about her. Each brush of her arm or taste of her lips only left him wanting more. Two days ago he thought he'd be happy just to be able to be near her, but now he wanted more, much more.

In the eyes of God and by law they were man and wife, but in her eyes, he was no more than an outlaw she'd made a bargain with to hold on to her ranch. He had a feeling she would have found another way if he hadn't been near.

If he took advantage of her, he'd never forgive himself, but if he walked away without loving her, he'd regret it until he died.

He walked her to the stairs. After she took the first step she turned and said good night.

He didn't turn her hand loose. "Kiss me good night," he whispered with more need than demand.

Slowly, she leaned forward. "Yes, dear," she answered as she pressed her lips to his.

He closed the distance between them as if he were starving for what she offered.

When she finally ended the kiss, she was breathless.

"That was . . ." She couldn't find the words.

"Perfection," he helped. "Good night, dear. When I come to bed I'll not wake you, but I make no promises not to touch you."

Her eyebrows lifted and she whispered, "Oh."

He smiled. "Would you like another kiss, my wife, or can you wait until I'm beside you?"

"No." She stumbled up the next step. "Though I've no complaints about the one."

He fought the urge to follow her up the steps. "You might think of wearing a gown tonight. I'm sure you're tired of my wrinkling your clothes. I'll kiss you again when I come to bed."

"I'll be asleep," she said, her eyes wide awake.

He grinned. "I won't mind."

She turned before he could say more and disappeared up the stairs.

It took every ounce of his willpower to make himself walk to the office. His time was limited but he wanted to give Cozette something and the proof of her uncle's embezzlement might keep her and her child safe. She might like flirting with him but that didn't mean she wanted to give him half the ranch. He'd learned a long time ago to expect nothing.

Michael worked late into the night, forcing all his energy into his work so he wouldn't think of the woman upstairs waiting for him to share her bed, but not her life.

Finally, when the numbers started to blur on the page, he

hid the books beneath the sickbed, blew out the lamp, and climbed the stairs. He walked through his room, removed his shirt and old boots, and tossed them on the floor. A new pair of boots stood at the end of his bed along with a clean set of clothes he knew would fit him perfectly. She might not want him around long, but while he was there she treated him with more kindness than anyone ever had. He would miss the coffee served to him every morning and the cobbler every night.

When he lowered onto her bed, she was asleep, as she'd promised she would be. For a while, he just watched her, wondering what life would be like if she really belonged to him.

His hand moved beneath the covers. Only one layer of soft cotton separated his touch from her body. He moved near her soft breath and touched her lips with his as his hand began to explore.

The feel of her washed away all the exhaustion. He traced the outline of her breasts and slid his hand over her slightly rounded tummy, wishing it were his child growing inside her. When he moved her head onto his shoulder she made a little sound in her sleep, but she came to him willingly.

He began at her ear with his light kisses. When he reached her mouth, slightly open and waiting, he couldn't resist.

He felt her come awake slowly, one sense at a time. She shyly kissed him back. He ran his hands into her loose hair and pulled her head off the pillow as he rolled and brought her on top of him.

In the shadows he watched her look down at him with sleepy eyes. "Kiss me again," he whispered.

She smiled and did as he requested.

Before her lips pulled away, he whispered, "Again."

She giggled and wrapped her arms around his neck.

The kiss exploded with passion. She was fully awake now and wanting his nearness as much as he wanted her.

When they finally had to stop to breathe, he rolled her on her back. "Now again, if you don't mind."

"You don't have to keep asking. I've no plan to stop until you beg me to."

"I'll take that challenge."

This time, as their lips touched, he cupped her breast and brushed his thumb across the peak. She reacted as he hoped she would, by pulling him close.

"I want you so much," he whispered between hurried kisses.

He told himself they were married. He had every right, but he knew he'd make love to her only when she said she wanted him. He knew if he ever took her as his real wife, he'd never leave. Not her, or the ranch, or the child she carried. There were some things a part-time husband could never do as part of a bargain.

He broke the kiss and looked down at her. In the pale light of the fire her lips were swollen, her hair was spilled across the pillows, and her eyes shone bright with unshed tears.

He rolled away, onto his back. Her silence had told him all he needed to know. He might want her, but she didn't want him . . . not in the way he needed her. If she had she would have said something.

Mrs. Peters's words came back to him. *You'll never be loved, but maybe you'll make yourself useful.* That was all he was to her. Useful.

He'd fallen for a woman who didn't or wouldn't love him. He'd fallen into hell.

Chapter 9

Cozette pretended to sleep the rest of the night. Until he'd told her he wanted her she'd thought they were simply playing a game. He was touching her, she was enjoying it. When he'd said he wanted her, she knew he was no longer playing. He hadn't said he loved her or wanted to stay forever. He simply wanted her, and she'd already had one man in her life who'd simply wanted her.

She felt him slip from her bed long before dawn. He hadn't touched her since he'd rolled away from her, so she had no warmth to miss.

Maybe she should have said she wanted him, but she wasn't sure she'd ever want a man in that way again. It hadn't been a pleasant experience. In fact, the mating had hurt when she'd been forced down without warning.

Michael might be gentle and kind, but she wasn't sure the act wouldn't still hurt.

She had loved his kisses, though, and the way his hands touched her as if they were worshiping her. She'd even thought of asking him to touch her again, but she didn't know how. That kind of honesty had never circled so near before.

She slipped from the bed and crossed the bathing room to his bedroom. He'd pulled on clean trousers and was sitting by the open windows tugging on his old boots. The cold air blew her gown as if pushing her back, but she tiptoed toward him.

He didn't look up but she had a feeling he knew she was there.

"Your new boots should fit far better," she said calmly.

When he didn't look up, she took one step more. "Are you mad at me?"

"No," he answered too quickly.

"Good," she played along as she moved closer. "Then, you'd have no objection to a good-morning kiss."

"It's a long time until morning," he mumbled before looking up at her, and a moment later she was running into his arms. He was her only friend. The only one she could trust. She couldn't stand to see hurt in his wonderful blue eyes and know that she'd caused it.

"You promised you'd never be cruel to me," she whispered. "Don't turn away from me now."

He buried his head in her chest and let out a long sigh, then kissed her wildly as if a hunger for her had almost killed him.

She laughed as he stood, holding her in his arms, and walked over to his bed. He tossed her atop the covers and stared down at her for a long moment before joining her. "It's cold in here. You should be under the covers, dear."

As the first light shone through the open windows, he tugged the front of her gown open. "If you just want to be touched and nothing more, then touch you I will."

His fingers shoved the cotton aside a moment before his warm hands covered her breasts. "But I plan to do so all over."

When she gasped, he kissed her deep as his hands made his promise true.

After a while, he rose his head to look into her eyes. The pain she'd seen was gone, and passion had taken its place.

She whispered between gulps for air. "Again, Michael. Touch me again."

He pushed the gown off and lowered his mouth to her peak.

Crying out from the pleasure, she rocked back and forth. He moved back to her mouth, holding her face in his hands as he kissed her.

"Is this what you want, my love?" His words whispered against her mouth.

"Yes," she answered.

Slowly, he gentled as he removed her gown and lightly brushed over her body with his fingertips. When she shivered, he rolled her onto her stomach and stroked her back, dipping lower until his hand covered her bottom.

He didn't say anything as he explored her body with bold strokes that warmed her skin.

Part of her couldn't believe she was letting him. Knowing he wanted her wasn't the same as loving her, but it was close. Reason told her she never wanted another man, but emotions warring in her wouldn't allow her to stop him. Just seeing the pleasure in his face made her happy. He was a good man who'd had very little pleasure in his life, and it pleased her greatly to know that she could offer him something in return for all he'd given her.

She finally curled next to him and he pulled a blanket over them both. They fell asleep with her head on his shoulder and his hand spread across her stomach.

When the household began to wake, Cozette stirred, loving the warmth of him near.

He opened one eye and looked at her.

"Can I have my good-morning kiss, please?" she pouted.

"Of course," he said, "but only one."

He kissed her soundly and pulled away. "Tonight I think maybe you should forget the gown. It will only get ripped. I plan to repeat our early morning activity."

"I'll keep that in mind," she smiled.

"Don't worry. If you forget, we might have to do it twice."

She blushed. "Oh, I see. I should probably warn you my memory's never been good."

"Don't worry. I'm here to help."

They both laughed, but she didn't miss the warm fire in his stormy blue-gray eyes.

She tugged the covers around her as she watched him dress. She wanted to ask him if he'd be happy just touching her and nothing more, but she wasn't sure she wanted to hear the answer. When he left she'd keep the memories of their nights together close to her heart. She might not have a real husband, but she'd know that once, for a few short nights, she'd been touched completely and lovingly.

After he strapped on his gun belt and lifted his hat, he crossed to the bed and kissed her on the head. "All day, I'll think of you here like this and long for the night."

He was gone before she could answer. Without giving any thought of what was proper, she curled back under the covers and went to sleep in his bed.

Her day could wait a little longer to begin.

Chapter 10

By the time Michael reached the barn, he'd calmed some. Another night of touching his wife without making love to her would surely kill him, but he'd gladly die. He'd known she wasn't sleeping after he'd pulled away in the night. He'd lain awake angry at how she'd reacted when he'd told her he wanted her. Surely she wasn't so young to believe that all they were playing was a game.

When he'd left her bed and gone back into his room, he'd still been angry and hurt. She was spoiled and he appeared to be no more than a puppet husband. She'd hardly noticed how he'd been organizing the ranch and getting it running back on track.

Then, she'd come to his room, tiptoeing like a child and looking every ounce a woman in her thin gown that hid little from view. For a moment he'd thought of telling her how impossible her request was. To touch her and not love her was ridiculous. But then, she'd ran to his arms and he'd known he'd have to try.

He knew he hadn't been as gentle as he should have been when he'd tossed her onto his bed, but she hadn't complained, hadn't protested or pulled away. And, once he'd gentled his touch, she'd let him handle her body, exploring, caressing, tasting wherever he liked. She'd given herself to him in every way but one. The one way only a woman can give herself completely.

He knew without thought that no other woman would ever satisfy him. If he didn't have her, he'd be unfulfilled for the rest of his life.

He walked to the corral, tossed a lead rope around his horse, and entered through the back of the barn, his mind still filled with thoughts of Cozette.

Two hands were at the front of the barn looking out toward the house as he neared. Neither noticed him.

The tallest one complained, "Raymond promised us all a bonus after he got rid of the brat of a girl. But she married, so who knows how long a bonus will be coming, if ever."

The other added, "We won't have to wait more than a few days, I'm guessing. I heard one of the men say Raymond plans to get rid of them both."

"Run them off or kill them?" the tall man questioned.

"Probably make it look like an accident, or better yet make it look like those three bumbling uncles of his killed them. The sheriff will take one look at those three and start looping a rope."

"Well, I'm not waiting around to be thought of as part of a killing. I hear there's work up north. I think I'll head out before something happens."

"You'd better stop complaining or the same thing will happen to you that happened to Fiddler."

Michael released the strap on his Colt and moved forward. "What happened to Fiddler?" he asked slowly.

Both men jumped and reached for their guns, but Michael cleared leather first.

"We don't know, boss," the tall one said as he lifted his hands. "We was just talking."

"There will be no bonus from Raymond. He got his

inheritance forty years ago and squandered it if rumors are true. His brother built this ranch without any help."

Michael lowered his gun as he continued, "Raymond has no right to the ranch, gentlemen. My wife is not leaving and there will be no accident."

He thought of firing them but reconsidered. He couldn't afford to make enemies too quickly. "I'd like you men to decide if you want to work for me for a fair wage or pack your gear. But, understand, if you stay, you stand with me, not Raymond Camanez."

The two men glared at each other. They were hard men, but not fools. Jobs with good wages and regular food were hard to come by. "We stay," one said and the other nodded agreement. "None of us believed Raymond anyway when he talked of bonuses when he took over. He's all talk."

Michael holstered his Colt. "All right. I've an assignment for you both. See if you can find out what happened to Fiddler and do it without Raymond, or anyone you think might be with him, aware that you're looking. We need to find the bookkeeper if he's still alive."

Both men nodded.

Michael eyed the shorter of the two. "Smith, right?"

"Yes, sir. Ace Smith." The man seemed surprised Michael remembered his name.

"I'll expect that report tonight. I'll meet you in the chapel after supper."

Both men tipped their hats. "We'll do our best," Smith said.

Michael moved away to saddle his horse. It crossed his mind that he could have passed the job along to someone else, but he believed a man should always take care of his own mount. Besides, if accidents were predicted, he wanted to make sure no one got close.

He saw Smith and his friend saddling up. The tall man walked over to Michael while his friend waited in the morning sun. After a few moments of just standing, the man said,

"Mind my asking why you didn't fire us on the spot, Mr. Hughes?"

"No, I don't mind." Michael climbed on his horse. "I knew a lot of men once who no one gave a second chance to. Some were worthless, but others might have made better men if anyone had let them try."

"Fair enough. We want you to know, we don't hold nothing against your little wife. Thanks for giving us a shot." The man turned to move away.

"You're welcome, Phil." Michael finally thought of the second man's name.

He rode out knowing Cozette would be safe with his uncles watching over her. He needed to make sure the ranch hands were with him and the only way was to spend the day in the saddle. When he reached the cattle he was glad to see two dozen hands already hard at work.

Michael took the time to talk to each man. He mostly asked questions, unafraid to let them see how little he knew. By the end of the day he knew every man and that they were his men.

When he rode home he was tired but satisfied. Part of him couldn't believe that Cozette's uncle would think of killing her, but he might not feel the same about Michael.

He wanted time to look over the accounts one last time. They'd agreed they'd confront Raymond tomorrow. It seemed cruel to kick him off the land the day after they buried his brother.

Michael had told his uncles to guard his wife and that at least one of them should always keep Raymond in sight. He smiled as he walked into the office guessing that Cozette's uncle probably had had a horrible day with one of them tailing him.

An hour later, he looked up from the books to find rain splattering softly against the huge windows of what he thought of as his study.

"My study?" Michael whispered, knowing that this wasn't and would never be his study, or his ranch. He'd been playing a game of make-believe.

The woman upstairs would never be his wife. It was all pretend. Somehow he'd gotten caught up in her fantasies. The pretty little liar had taken down the outlaw without one shot. When he left this place he knew his heart would be staying behind.

Thunder rattled the night and lightning flashed. Michael closed the books, no longer able to stay away from Cozette.

He was at a run when he reached the stairs and almost collided with the housekeeper.

"Sorry," he managed, trying to look respectable and not like the wild kid he was.

She smiled. "The missus said you'd be home late. She asked that I bring supper up to her room tonight."

He nodded as if he wasn't surprised. "What about her uncle?" Michael didn't want to sleep without knowing where Raymond was.

"He left a few hours ago."

"For good?" Michael hoped.

"No." The housekeeper frowned. "For a ride, I think. He said he wouldn't be back for dinner this evening and I heard him say he'd shoot anyone who tried to follow him."

"My uncles?" Michael asked, worried that one of them might have tried.

"They're all three in the hallway. Said they wouldn't leave your dear one until you got home." The housekeeper smiled. "I had a meal sent up to them and the cook is baking cookies for them now. Dear little men, all three."

Michael wasn't sure she didn't have them mixed up with some other three short fat men. He'd never heard anyone pay them a compliment.

When he reached the top of the stairs, there they were, all on guard. "You watch over my wife today?" he said sharply bringing them all to attention, or as much to attention as they could get.

"We did," Abe said. "Had to quit watching Raymond, though. None of us can ride well enough to trail him, so we decided to all guard her."

"Plus, here w-we don't miss meals. That's something to c-consider." Joseph pulled two forks from his pocket and placed them on the hallway table. "I w-wasn't going to take them, Mickey, I w-was just keeping them in case more food w-wandered by. Food comes along here as regular as a train. I ain't never s-seen the like of it."

Michael said good night to them and reminded them that hot cookies were waiting. He realized that for the first time in his life he was proud of them and, more important, they were proud of themselves.

He opened the door to his room and walked across to the bathing room separating him from Cozette.

The door was closed, but not locked. When he pushed it slowly open, he swore his heart stopped. She must have just stepped from the tub, her body still dripping as she reached for the towel.

He saw her completely. Her beautiful face, her long damp hair, her rounded breasts and pleasing bottom. She took his breath away along with the power to speak or think.

When she turned and smiled at him, he couldn't move.

"Good evening, Michael," she said shyly. She lifted the towel and put it around her back, leaving her front still open to his view. "I thought we'd have a quiet dinner and talk."

She began to wrap the towel around her, but his hand shot out to stop her. "Later," he said, staring into her eyes. "First, I have to hold you."

She tugged away from him and crossed the towel over her. "No, first you have to take a bath. Like all ranchers, you smell like a horse."

He would have argued, but she began unbuttoning his

shirt. He just stood as if stone while she removed his shirt and gun belt. When she began unbuttoning his trousers, he stopped her. "I'll bathe," he said. "Alone."

The pouty lip he'd spent hours thinking about came out, but she turned and headed to the door.

He had stripped and slid into the tub and was already thinking of what he wanted to do with her when the door to her room opened. She was still wrapped in her towel, but she was dragging a stool behind her.

"What do you think you are doing?" he asked with a smile.

"Watching," she answered.

"I should have locked the door." He blew out all but one of the candles beside the bath.

"There's no lock on your side, only on mine." She sat down as if waiting for the play to start.

He gave up. He scrubbed off a layer of dirt as fast as he could and then asked for a towel.

She pointed to one three feet away and didn't make a sound when he stood and grabbed it. Looking at her was one thing, but having her stare at him was quite another. He planned to tell her so over breakfast.

"What's all this about?" he asked as he dried.

"I've decided to change the rules a little. You seem to be having so much fun touching me, I thought I'd touch you tonight, if you don't mind."

He studied her trying to figure out what she was up to. They both knew that tonight might be their last night together. Tomorrow they'd confront Raymond and run him off the ranch. Michael knew several men working for her who would be great bodyguards just in case Raymond decided to come back.

When he left her, he'd leave her well protected.

It occurred to him that she must want tonight to be a memory they'd both take with them.

He crossed the room and stood above her, his towel now draped low around his hips.

She looked up at him without fear. She might never learn to love him, but she'd learned to trust him.

His fingers slid along her slender throat as they had when they'd first met. For a moment, he tightened his grip as he had in the chapel, holding her firmly, but not hurting her. Then he lowered his mouth and kissed her.

It wasn't a hungry kiss, but a slow, loving kiss that warmed them both. His fingers moved down her throat and over her shoulders, then shoved her towel away. "I love the way your skin feels," he whispered into her mouth as he pulled her up and kissed her again. "I don't think I could ever get enough of you."

Every moment, every move, he expected her to tell him to stop, but she didn't and he couldn't shake the feeling that tonight he was a part of her fantasy.

She didn't say a word. She opened her mouth, welcoming him as his hands branded across her body. Timidly she brushed her finger over his chest and along his arms. Her touch was so tender it was almost painful. He knew he was lean with a few too many scars across his body, but she didn't seem to notice as she touched him.

He turned her toward a long mirror, pressing his body against hers as he watched his hands move over her. She leaned her head back and kissed his throat as her hair tickled across his chest.

He had to try one more time. "Love me, tonight," he whispered in her hair. "Be mine for one night."

She turned in his arms and kissed him as she pressed against him silently, giving him the answer he'd waited for.

When he rubbed his chin against her cheek, he felt her tears and pulled away enough to meet her gaze. "What's wrong?"

"Nothing. I just didn't think it could be like this. I didn't expect it . . ."

He understood and pulled her close. Both their towels were forgotten as they moved to her bed and he pulled the covers back. She lay down and waited, looking unsure.

"I promise I won't hurt you, but if you'll let me, I want to make love to you."

She didn't answer. This time he didn't pull away. He saw all he needed to see in her warm eyes as her soft hands trailed along his body and she tugged him closer.

He kissed his way down her until he came to the slight rise at her middle. "I love you," he whispered, "and I'd love this baby growing inside you if you'd let me. I want it to be my baby. After tonight. After we've made love. There will be no other past but me and tonight."

He hadn't planned the words. He wasn't sure if he'd said them aloud or not, but when he kissed her where the baby grew, her hands moved into his hair and held him to her.

The storm rattled outside as they made love slow and easy. She was shy and he was uncertain, but passion washed over them smoothing everything into mindless perfection. They floated in the warmth of each other unaware that time existed. For two young lovers there was no past or future, only this moment.

When he held her to him afterward, he kissed away her tears. She hadn't said a word and he wasn't experienced enough with women to know whether her tears were tears of joy.

He just held her close and whispered his love for her, wondering if there was any chance she'd believe him . . . wishing he had a lifetime ahead to tell her how he felt. But tonight, this time, this place, would have to be his lifetime. All before, all after, didn't matter.

When Cozette was sound asleep, Michael slipped from her bed and dressed, already missing her before he left her room. He had a meeting in the chapel tonight, and then he'd be back to wake her.

Tonight, he'd know the truth about Raymond. He'd know how to keep her safe.

He walked from her room and put his boots on in the hallway. They were a perfect fit. Within a few minutes he let himself into the chapel.

Smith and the tall man named Phil were waiting for him. They both looked tired and wore dusters soaked in rain.

"What news do you have?" he asked, in a hurry to be done with the meeting and get back to Cozette.

"A farmer north of here found Fiddler's body two days ago. The farmer didn't recognize him, being most of his face was shot off, so he took the body into town."

Phil stopped talking and his partner continued, "Sheriff said he knew at once who it was. Said he'd noticed the ink stains on Fiddler's hands once. The sheriff also noticed once that the bookkeeper had the longest fingers—piano hands he called them—with ink spotting heavy across his knuckles."

"Any idea who killed him?" Michael asked.

"No. He'd been dead for a while. Folks claimed they could smell him an acre away. Sheriff had him buried."

Michael thanked the men. They talked as they walked back to the house. Both were convinced Raymond had something to do with the killing, but with a body already in the ground and any clues washed away by the rain, they weren't likely to prove it.

Michael noticed the study's lamps were lit, burning low, when he walked into the house. He remembered blowing them both out just before he hid the ranch records under the bed. Caution set his nerves on edge as he walked into the study.

Cozette sat very still in the chair behind the desk. Her

hair was down and wild around the heavy robe she wore. When she looked up at him, he saw terror in her eyes.

He took two steps toward her before he realized someone was standing behind the door waiting. He'd stepped into a trap.

"Come on in," Raymond said from behind him. "Your bride and I have been waiting for you to come back."

Michael faced the gun as he backed toward the windows and away from his wife.

"I know you two thought you could get away with this trick you played on my brother, but I've finally decided to put a stop to it." He moved to the center of the room so he could keep an eye on both of them. "So, the only question is, which one should I kill first? With this storm no one will even notice the shots."

"Kill me!" Michael shouted with enough anger to rattle the windows. "Because if you don't, I swear I'll kill you if you harm her."

Raymond must have found his power over them amusing. "Oh, so you've fallen in love with the family tramp. Did she tell you she's already been with a man and she's barely out of school?"

Cozette let out a yelp and Raymond turned his gun on her.

He smiled. "I've even heard the house rumor that you're with child. What would your father say? He'd shoot you himself rather than let you disgrace this family."

"It's my child!" Michael shouted. "And she's my wife. She's had no other lover but me."

Raymond pointed the gun at him. "Then you are a bigger fool than I, for she's tricked you. I've had enough of you both. It's time to—"

Something short and round barreled into Raymond like a freight train, knocking him off his feet.

The gun fired, clipping Michael in the shoulder as three men jumped on Raymond like hungry dogs on a fat rabbit.

Pain shot through Michael's body as he watched his wife scream and rush toward him. He could hear his uncles pounding away on Raymond but nothing seemed real. All seemed part of a dream, even Cozette.

Then, all went quiet in his world. All went black and he circled in midnight water until he could see or hear nothing, not even his own heartbeat.

When he awoke, he was spread out on one of the couches along the wall and the doctor was smiling down at him.

"'Bout time you decided to wake up and join us. You're a lucky man, son. The bullet hit only muscle and I dug it out without much trouble."

Michael sat up slowly and looked around. "Where's my wife?"

"She'll be back in a minute. I made her go get dressed if she was going to insist on sitting with you. She told me she was in a family way and planned to stay close to you."

"Raymond?" Michael asked.

"He's on his way to town. Sheriff said he'll have charges filed in the morning for attempted murder of you and the murder of a man named Fiddler. Seems Fiddler told my nurse one afternoon while she was with the old man and Fiddler was doing the records that if he ever showed up dead they should look in the books for the murderer. Your wife showed us where her uncle had been stealing for months. We may never know if Fiddler was part of the theft and just got scared or if he found out the truth and confronted Raymond. Don't guess it matters much, he's dead either way."

Michael's head pounded. It was over. Cozette was safe. She'd never be bothered again. He leaned back and rested until he heard her come in with his three uncles right behind her.

"How is he?" she asked the doctor as if Michael weren't staring right at her.

"He's fine. A good night's rest and he can be back in the saddle tomorrow." The doctor began packing up his bag.

"I'll be heading out tomorrow," Michael said. He'd keep his promise to her.

To his surprise anger flashed in her eyes and she stood. "You're not walking out on me and the baby."

All three uncles said, "*Baby?*" at the same time.

She nodded toward them. "That's right. The doctor just confirmed I'm pregnant. Right?"

"Right," the doctor mumbled, obviously trying to stay out of the argument.

Cozette stared down at Michael. "Am I or am I not your wife?"

"I'm not deaf, dear. Of course you're my wife."

"And is this your baby growing inside me?"

He stared at her remembering his wish. Remembering how he told her there was no time, no one before him. "It's my baby."

"Then, Michael, you are not going anywhere." She whirled to the doctor. "You might not want to leave yet. I may have to shoot him in the leg to convince him to stay."

To his surprise the uncles looked like they were on her side. They all stood behind her, their knuckles white and ready to beat him to a pulp.

"It ain't right," Uncle Moses said. "Getting her pregnant and talking of leaving. It ain't right, Mickey."

Cozette pulled a pistol from behind one of the pillows. "I may be a widow, but I don't plan on being left."

She pointed the gun at him and all three uncles folded their arms and waited.

"Don't shoot." He smiled. "I'll stay, dear."

"How long?" she asked without lowering the gun.

"Forever if you'll say you love me."

She grinned. "Then I won't shoot you, because I do love you."

All three uncles nodded as if they understood what was going on. The doctor shook his head, totally lost.

Michael raised an eyebrow, wondering if he'd ever be able to tell if she was telling the truth. He guessed he'd just have to stay about forty or fifty years and find out.

He might not be much of an outlaw but somehow he'd managed to steal the lady's love.

Holding his side, he stood. "I think it's time we said good night, dear."

She smiled and moved beneath his arm as if they were now an old, settled married couple.

He pulled her close, knowing that in the future he'd be whatever she wanted him to be, but he'd be beside her.

Once the couple was halfway up the stairs, Uncle Abe shouted, "Mickey! How long you figure we're staying?"

He glanced down at the three men who'd done their best to raise him.

"Forever," he said.

"Forever," she whispered beside him.

TROUBLE IN PETTICOATS

LINDA BRODAY

Chapter 1

South Texas, 1878

From the back, the man standing in her father's study was extraordinary, with a broad back that tapered to a narrow waist and muscular thighs that drew his black trousers taut across a well-shaped behind.

Her pulse quickened in response.

Suddenly, as if sensing her presence, he whirled.

Larissa Patrick sucked in a quick gasp.

From the front, he was a mixture of undeniable danger and charm. In that instant she realized why a moth flew into a flame even though the fire would kill it. It was captivated by the light and nothing else mattered. Looking at the stranger, she knew such an attraction.

His forceful stance combined with the dangerous aura about him set her heart racing. Hair the color of darkest midnight brushed his collar. Deep lines that seemed carved into the tanned rugged features with some kind of sculpting tool spoke of a life lived outdoors.

So did the worn dusty boots on his feet.

Following the man's long lean lines, her gaze moved to the lethal Colt he wore on his hip. The leather of the holster appeared as supple as melted butter. Only something that received a lot of use could look so worn and pliable. Her gaze slid to the thin leather strap that secured the holster to his leg.

No lawyer she'd ever seen wore a tied-down, low-slung Colt.

All the lawyers she'd known had been doddering men well past their prime.

Doddering definitely didn't describe the man before her; not by a long shot.

Despite her father's explanation for the visitor, she didn't believe for one second that he was there to impart legal advice.

Everything about this stranger shouted that he lived on the wrong side of the law.

And that he preferred it that way.

She was as positive as anything that he'd never seen the inside of a law office . . . except maybe to employ a solicitor. Furthermore, the mocking smile and amusement in his startling blue gaze said he knew she knew it and dared her to comment.

The flutters in her stomach intensified under that crystal blue gaze as cool and deep and mysterious as a fathomless pool.

Her father had insisted she make the man known as Johnny Diamond welcome on the Four Spades Ranch.

The instructions had been explicit. She was to make sure the supposed lawyer had full access to every part of the house, barns, and grounds and not question any request.

Why? Her brain scrambled for answers.

Able to finally break free from the handsome visitor's stare, she turned her attention to her father, who was seated behind his desk with his hands steepled in front of him. Dunston Patrick was hiding something. And she meant to find out what he kept from her. As soon as she could get a word with him she'd demand to know where Beth had gone. She'd looked the ranch over and could find no trace of her younger sister anywhere.

"There you are, Larissa," her father said. "I'd like you to meet Mr. Johnny Diamond. Mr. Diamond, my eldest daughter."

"My pleasure, ma'am." Their guest covered the space between them and instantly dwarfed Larissa, all five feet two inches of her. He shifted the worn felt hat he held and offered his hand. "They sure grow 'em mighty pretty here in Texas."

The quiet, deep timbre of his voice scraped along her nerve endings. Larissa accepted his handshake, admiring the firm grip. One other thing was wrong—the calluses on his palms. Men who made their living reading books and interpreting the law had smoother skin. At least the few she knew did.

Last but not least, there was the matter of his name. It seemed one a man two steps in front of the law might own. Unless she missed her guess, it was as made up as his occupation.

What did he really do? And what business did he truly have with her father?

The whole day had been one puzzle after another.

"Thank you for the compliment, Mr. Diamond." She tucked her hand in the folds of her dress when he released it. "Welcome to the Four Spades. Will you be staying long?"

"Afraid not." His glance shifted to her father. "I'll ride out after our . . . business . . . is done."

"Could I offer you some coffee or tea, perhaps?"

"No, thank you."

Dunston Patrick swiveled in the chair behind his desk and waved her away. "Now run along. We have work to do."

That she'd been so brusquely dismissed chafed something raw inside her. Though she'd long known that her father viewed her and her sisters with cold disregard, it stung that he'd do so in front of a stranger. Even an outlaw one.

Larissa turned toward the door and hesitated.

"What do you want now?" Dunston had picked up the four of spades from a deck of cards and flipped it over and over on his desk. Larissa had long grown accustomed to seeing that particular card. It was never far from her father's reach.

Though she'd fully intended to wait until they had a private moment, she found she really couldn't. This was too urgent and her father might not be free for hours.

Her teeth captured her bottom lip. "I've looked everywhere and Beth seems to have vanished. I can't shake this feeling that something horrible has happened."

Her father's ruddy cheeks paled. He ran his fingers through a thick shock of white hair before he blustered, "Your sister is perfectly fine. She pestered until I gave in and let her go spend some time with your sister Charlotte. You know how impatient she's been to see Charlotte's new baby again."

On the surface that made sense. But it didn't convince her. Larissa had checked Beth's room and all of her clothes and belongings were there. Besides, a ten-year-old wouldn't go anywhere by herself. Charlotte lived a day's ride from them. That meant Beth would stay overnight at the very least. And even if she had forgotten to take a nightgown and some dresses, Beth most definitely wouldn't have left behind the baby quilt she'd stitched for little Matthew. Beth had been so proud of her handiwork and couldn't wait to give it to the new babe.

Larissa's stomach lurched painfully. What was her father keeping from her? She straightened her spine and raised her chin. "How did she get there and why wasn't I told?"

"As usual, when there's a decision to be made you were off riding Arabella before breakfast. I had Jonas take her."

That explained why she'd not seen Jonas Flynn, their ranch foreman, today.

But it was odd that her father hadn't said anything last evening. Surely he'd known then. She might've wanted to accompany Beth. Larissa hadn't seen Charlotte since Matthew's birth two months ago when Larissa and Beth had both gone to help their sister out during her lying-in. This pregnancy had been extremely difficult for Charlotte.

"Wasn't this decision rather sudden, Papa? Neither you nor Beth breathed a word of these plans to me." Besides she'd raised Beth almost single-handedly after their mother died giving birth to the girl. Dunston Patrick had shown Beth little affection or interest, whereas Larissa knew her baby sister inside and out.

All these facts frightened her more than she'd been since the night her mother died.

"I do as I think best." Her father's sharp tone let her know he didn't have to explain his actions to her. "Leave us be now and close the door behind you."

Her eyes met Johnny Diamond's before she exited the room. She caught the slight nod of his head. She detected a mea-sure of sympathy, which seemed odd coming from a total stranger who wore a Colt that advertised his disregard for the law.

Larissa made up her mind that it was time she got some answers by whatever method she had to do it. She hurried from the house and around to the open window of her father's study. Bending low, she crept forward.

"I don't come cheap, Mr. Patrick." She recognized Johnny Diamond's deep voice.

"Don't mind paying for results," Dunston shot back.

"Why me, if you don't mind me asking? I'm curious why you didn't send for the U.S. Marshal."

The hair at the nape of Larissa's neck rose at mention of

the lawman. That confirmed Diamond's appearance didn't have anything to do with law work. She leaned closer.

"Let me explain something, Diamond. I didn't become the cattle baron I am today without making scores of enemies, one of whom regrettably is Marshal Dallas Banks. I knew I had to hire someone who doesn't have an ax to grind with me if I stood a chance in hell of getting Beth back."

Suddenly the world around Larissa spun. Blood pounded inside her head while a cold, deadly stillness invaded her body.

Beth has been stolen from us.

Larissa strangled a sob before it could escape.

Dunston continued, "And I also know it's going to take someone with your reputation to do the job. A renegade like you can go places where a lawman can't."

"Do you think the kidnappers are men you might've had sour business dealings with?" Diamond asked.

Her father snorted. "Without a doubt."

"Care to elaborate?"

"I wouldn't know where to start. The list is . . . rather long." Dunston's voice held bitterness and anger.

"I have to ask. Why not just pay the ransom, Mr. Patrick?"

"Even had I been so inclined, which I'm not, I can't immediately lay my hands on the huge sum they're asking for my daughter's return. Not without selling off part of my herd or land. My holdings as well as my daughter are mine and I intend to keep 'em. I'm trusting you to rescue Beth in a timely fashion. If you don't think you can do the job tell me now so I can get someone else."

Suddenly Larissa prayed Johnny Diamond would accept what was asked of him. She only wanted to get Beth back.

The sooner the better.

Didn't matter the cost.

Or if they had to place their trust in an outlaw's hands.

The familiar creak of her father's desk chair reached her

ears and she knew he'd stood up. When Dunston Patrick spoke again his voice came from right above her. He was probably staring out the window at Patrick land, which stretched as far as the eye could see and then some. The scratch of a match, the smell of sulphur, and she knew her father had lit a cigar.

If he looked down he'd see her. She pressed herself closer to the side of the house, making herself as small as she could.

"Are you wasting my time here, Diamond?"

"I will get your daughter back. There's no question of that." Dangerous confidence colored Johnny Diamond's terse tone. He wasn't bragging; he stated fact. "I just don't know if you'll like how I do it."

"As long as you make the sorry thieving yahoos pay. I need to send a message that no one steals from Dunston Patrick. You do that and you and I won't have a problem. Whatever you have to do to accomplish that is your business. But if I had my druthers, I'd prefer you end their miserable lives and silence them once and for all."

Larissa quickly put her hand over her mouth to squelch her startled protest. Her father was more interested in seeing the culprits pay than in Beth's welfare. Beth could've been nothing more than a horse or a prized piece of land. They were all possessions to the great Dunston Patrick. Larissa didn't know who he was anymore. And maybe she'd never really known.

"If they've harmed a hair on Beth's head I'll take exception. Hell will seem mild in comparison to what I'll unleash on them," Johnny Diamond vowed.

"Diamond, just make sure they won't come back and try the same thing again a month or a year from now. Understand me, I want them stopped and stopped for good. Any questions?"

"What about your daughter Larissa?"

Larissa jolted at hearing her name on the stranger's

lips. Johnny Diamond had said it so easy like he'd known her forever.

"What about her?" her father snapped.

"Begging your pardon, but don't you think she has a right to know about her sister? She clearly suspects."

"Larissa is my concern. You just worry about upholding your end of the bargain."

So he didn't even plan on telling her. Anger rose. If a subject didn't pertain to the smooth running of the house, he wouldn't discuss it with her.

"I suppose this concludes our business." Diamond's deep voice carried through the open window. "I've got to collect some provisions before I take to the trail. Unless I miss my guess they'll cross the border into Mexico. That's where I'd go if I were running from the law."

Larissa wondered how many times he'd dodged into Mexico until the heat died down. Sounded like it'd been pretty often.

"You could be right," Dunston agreed. "Don't worry about your supplies. I have everything you need right here at the ranch."

"Including a packhorse?" the younger man asked.

"Yes, including that. It'll save time we don't have."

"Appreciate it, Mr. Patrick. Then I reckon I'll be on my way if you'll give me half of the money we agreed on. I'll scout around and with luck can pick up a trail before nightfall."

"Good. I like a man who takes a bone and runs with it."

Larissa heard the dial on her father's safe clicking and the door swinging open. Her mind was made up. She backed away from the window and ran.

She needed to hurry.

Chapter 2

Johnny Diamond looked for Larissa Patrick as he strolled for the front door. There was no sign of her. Disappointment wore like a woolen winter shirt. He'd have liked to have seen her again. Maybe he would when he asked for the promised provisions.

Intelligence had shown in her velvety brown gaze. She was much too smart to buy the bill of goods her father had tried to sell her.

Dunston Patrick had done her a disservice.

Larissa was nobody's fool. He'd seen that much.

The wild tale of Beth going to visit their oldest sister wasn't the only lie Larissa had caught. The brown-haired beauty had clearly seen through the flimsy lawyer story as well. He'd seen it in her fluid gaze.

But as Patrick had gruffly reminded him, Larissa wasn't his worry. He'd best focus on the job at hand and leave well enough alone.

He let himself out and adjusted his hat at an angle that blocked the harsh sunlight from his eyes. He'd do some checking around and see if he could scare up some tracks.

That the ransom note told Dunston Patrick to leave the money at a line shack on the most remote section of the ranch in five days told him the kidnappers didn't stay together. Most likely at least one of them was still in the area.

Maybe the accomplice was one of the ranch hands.

Regardless, his gut told him they'd taken the young Patrick girl to a border town to wait. Then, if Patrick didn't come through on the ransom, they could easily sell the girl to willing buyers.

Five days to complete the job. That wasn't long.

A squint at the sun told him he had about three hours before dusk.

Blue Boy, his Appaloosa gelding, nickered and shook his head when he spied Johnny. The animal didn't appear none too happy to be tied to the brass ring in front of the sprawling two-story ranch house.

"Quit your bellyaching, Blue. I won't be much longer."

Giving him a baleful stare, the horse dropped his head to nibble on a sparse patch of buffalo grass.

An hour later, leading a laden packhorse, Johnny mounted Blue Boy and headed south. Near as he could tell, four men had tied their mounts in a stand of juniper not far from the ranch house in a little arroyo. They must've lain in wait there, biding their time. Evidently, after the house had grown dark and everyone was asleep, they'd stolen into Beth Patrick's room through an open window and grabbed her.

An easy plan. And it'd gone off without a hitch.

No one had learned the girl was missing until morning.

Johnny followed their tracks until one set veered off from the others. One man had indeed stayed behind to collect the ransom while the other three hid the girl.

The group of men acted like they'd done this before. The plan appeared well thought out and implemented.

He made a mental note of the three sets he'd be tracking. One horseshoe was missing a nail and the deep impression of one of the other horses said the man who rode the animal carried a heavier load.

Johnny had just happened to be staying in the nearby town of Sonora for a few days, considering his options. At first light, Patrick had sent a rider from the ranch with a message for Johnny and the offer of a job. He'd wasted no time in satisfying his curiosity. Plus, his funds had gotten very low. The work meant he could replenish his coffer and set more money aside for that horse ranch he'd dreamed of owning.

It was past time for him to make a change and become respectable.

If it wasn't too late.

A short while later, still on Four Spades land and a good distance from the ranch house, he turned sideways in the saddle. Dust rose in the direction he'd just come. He took a spyglass from his saddlebag and held it to his eye.

One horse and rider was coming fast. He was too far away to see many details other than that the rider was a slight figure. Could be a boy.

Johnny got the horses out of sight behind a clump of scrub oak. He didn't have long to wait. When the mysterious mount came even to his hiding place, he leaped out and hauled the rider to the ground.

The figure fought like a wildcat but couldn't break free.

She was soft with curves in all the right places.

And she wore a riding skirt.

Her hair spilled from the confines of a dark floppy hat. "Let me go!"

No one had eyes the color of rich fertile earth except Larissa Patrick. She stared up at him, her eyes snapping with fury.

He slowly eased his weight off her, got to his feet, and offered her a hand. She hesitated before taking it.

"Dare I ask why you're following me?"

Larissa beat the dust off her skirt with her hat. "You can lead me to my sister."

Johnny's head jerked. "How did you know Beth has been taken?"

The beautiful woman chewed her lip and had the grace to blush. "I sort of overheard you and my father talking."

"You were snooping, you mean."

"That's pretty blunt, Mr. Diamond."

"I never mince my words. I believe in calling a spade a spade. Saves time. And a whole lot of energy."

"That's admirable, I guess. At least for a made-up shyster. I think we've both done our share of swapping ends with the truth today. What happens now that you've caught me?"

"I'm going to turn you around and send you home. Either you'll get your sister killed or the kidnappers will capture you too and you'll be no good to Beth. You're much better off waiting at the ranch and letting me do my job. Do I make myself clear?"

"Is that an order, Mr. Diamond?" she asked stiffly.

"Take it any way you like, but you're going back."

"I can help you. I know it."

"No."

"Won't you even discuss it?"

"No."

"She's my sister. I have a right to help rescue her."

"No, and that's final." He reached for her horse's reins.

Tears welled in her eyes and her lip trembled. "I feel so helpless. Won't you even consider it for a second?"

The lady had spunk, Johnny gave her that.

"Good-bye, Miss Patrick. I have a job to do and I'm burning precious daylight standing here arguing. Let me help you onto your horse so I can go about my business."

Larissa straightened her spine. "You don't have to get snippy."

A long-suffering sigh escaped his lips. "Just go home. Your father will wonder where you are."

"My father could care less about Beth or me."

Johnny wanted to pull her into his arms and soothe her hurt. He'd witnessed Dunston Patrick's ill treatment of her, seen her embarrassment. He didn't hold with a father being rude to his own flesh and blood.

"You're just upset. If Dunston doesn't care for Beth, why did he hire me to find her?" he asked, trying to ease her anguish.

She shrugged her shoulders. "He's concerned with appearances, for one thing. He knows this makes him look weak. If his enemies smell blood in the water, they'll attack. All I know is that Beth and I mean little to nothing to him. We're not his precious cattle. And we're not the son he always wanted and dreamed of someday taking over the ranch. And maybe it's nothing more than besting the men who took something from him. You don't know my father."

"Grant you that. But please don't make my job more difficult than it is. I wouldn't be able to focus on your sister if I was worried about protecting you."

"I can look after myself. And I've been taking care of Beth since she was born. I'm the only mother she's known."

Johnny blew out an exasperated breath. "Okay, ma'am, here's the deal. I'm tired of this nonsense. You are not going with me. If you continue to follow, I'll have no choice but to take your horse and let you walk back to the house."

Larissa gasped. "You wouldn't do that."

"Try me."

"Of all the nerve!" She planted her hands on her hips. "You're impossible. Oh, all right. Just promise me one thing."

"What's that?"

"That you'll tell Beth I love her and bring her home to me."

Johnny relaxed and allowed a fleeting smile. He thought she'd ask for something a bit harder. "I'll do that anyway, but if it makes you feel better, I promise to treat her as if she's my own family."

She turned away but not before he caught the quick flash of tears brimming in her eyes. He cupped his hands, making a step for her. She placed a booted foot in them and threw a leg over the saddle horn. "Thank you, Diamond."

"No problem." It was all he could do to touch the brim of his hat with a forefinger in farewell and pretend he hadn't seen her heart breaking.

His life might've turned out differently if he'd had someone like Larissa at home waiting for him to return.

Or a mother and father to provide love and support.

But all he had, all he knew, was the outlaw trade.

And Sam Whiskey.

If it hadn't been for Sam, those Comancheros would've killed him too, right along with his parents and sisters.

This was a hard, unforgiving land, just as Sam Whiskey had preached. To get by, a man had to be as tough as a piece of boot leather and twice as mean as a water moccasin.

Johnny shook himself and climbed into the saddle. It was time he got to the task of following the trail that would lead to Beth Patrick.

The kidnappers were smart. They'd taken time to erase their tracks on several occasions and doubled back on the trail more than once to try to throw him off. He'd had to use all his tracking abilities to stay with them.

His enemy was nightfall. He couldn't see the trail in the dark. His only choice was bedding down for the night. Besides, Blue Boy and the packhorse would need some rest.

He only prayed the ones he trailed did the same.

The moon had risen by the time Johnny decided to stop. With no trees around and precious little vegetation, he led Blue Boy down an embankment to a narrow draw that held a trickle of water. He could at least have coffee in the morning without using the water from the canteens he'd brought along.

After unsaddling Blue and unloading the packhorse, he hobbled them within easy reach of the stream. After spreading his bedroll, he rooted around in his saddlebag for some jerky. It'd have to do for supper. A fire would likely be seen. He didn't need a target on his back.

He'd just stretched out and was dozing off when he caught the sound of boots crunching on the rocks.

Instantly awake, he reached for his .45 and crept stealthily up the side of the embankment. The full moon cast a silvery sheen over the south Texas desert landscape. He flattened himself against the hard ground that still carried the heat of the summer sun even though it had long since set.

A dark horse stood silent a short distance away.

And beside the mount was a figure that was slowly coming his way.

Johnny eased himself back down the embankment just enough until he was out of sight. He quietly worked his way down the side until he figured he could come up behind and get the drop on the culprit.

The strange horse hadn't moved but the rider had made a bed on the ground on a bedroll.

So much for thinking it might be one of the kidnappers. They wouldn't be that careless.

Guided by the moon's rays, he snuck up to the sleeping form. Placing his Colt to the side of the figure's head, he ordered, "Stand up nice and easy and you won't get hurt."

A feminine scream rent the air and Johnny's conscience pricked. This was no threat, it was a frustrating setback.

Larissa Patrick leaped to her feet with her fists balled. "Diamond, what on earth are you trying to do, give me a heart attack? I thought you were one of the kidnappers."

"It'd serve you right. You aren't supposed to be here." He

holstered his Colt. "I told you to go home. But here you are, continuing to dog my trail every last step of the way. What do you have to say for yourself?"

"She's my sister and I'm going." Larissa's chin jutted defiantly.

"So you flat out lied."

"I told you what you wanted to hear. It's a free country, isn't it?"

"Oh, lady, you have no idea how much trouble waits for you."

Chapter 3

The dangerous softness in Johnny Diamond's voice made goose bumps dance up and down Larissa's spine. She wasn't exactly sure what he meant, but it appeared she may have bitten off a mouthful of something she'd have trouble chewing.

She tilted her head back to look up at him. Dern! He towered over her like a sturdy oak tree that had been battered by storms but still stood tall and proud. She felt so small beside him, but safer than she ever recalled being.

Light from the moon washed his face in silvery shadow. She searched the lines of his face for signs of anger or that she'd provoked him past the point of all reason.

But she found nothing except boiling frustration. Although, the fact she nettled him was a true and accurate statement.

Larissa wet her dry lips. "You may as well let me go with you, because I'm not going to stop following you. And like I told you earlier, I have talents that you might need before this is all said and done."

He mumbled something under his breath. In one swift motion, he jerked the bridle from the ground and slipped it over Arabella's head. Then he slung the saddle that had taken every bit of strength she'd had to remove back onto the horse's back.

"Please don't make me ride out at this time of night," she begged, stifling pure panic that threatened to be her undoing. "Arabella might step in a hole and break a leg."

"Grab your bedroll," he growled.

"You can't ask this of me. Just wait until daylight."

Diamond paused to stare. "I'm not heartless, ma'am. I'm going to take you down this draw where I'm camped. You'll be safer. Besides, no reason to have two separate campsites."

"You're saying I can stay?" she pressed in a breathless voice, daring to hope.

"For now. I'll decide what to do with you after some shut-eye." He turned to lead Arabella down the incline.

Larissa scrambled after him, unable to keep back the smile that persisted. At least she'd have time to think of valid arguments to make when dawn arrived, the main one being that she had no sense of direction. There was no way she could find her way back to the ranch. She didn't even know where they were or in what direction the Four Spades lay. The most sensible thing would be to go with him. If only she could think of a way to inform him of the decision she'd already made and try her best to persuade him to her way of thinking.

His camp seemed orderly enough, but she quickly saw he hadn't made a fire. He probably had his reasons for that.

Johnny Diamond pulled the saddle and bridle off Arabella and hobbled the mare alongside his Appaloosa and the packhorse. Larissa liked that he took good care of the animals. That said something about a man, especially one who was an outlaw.

He turned to her. "Do you want something to eat? I didn't build a fire because I didn't want to advertise my presence, but I can rustle up some grub if you're hungry. Some jerky maybe?"

Larissa spread her bedroll a short distance from his. "No, thanks. I brought some cold biscuits and ham left over from breakfast. I ate it back down the trail. I'll be fine until morning."

Whatever she did, she didn't want to be a bother and have him kick her out on those grounds.

"Then I reckon I'll turn in. It's been a long day."

She watched the way his shirt drew tight across the hard planes of his chest when he yawned and stretched and dropped onto his bedroll. She quickly ducked her head before he noticed her ogling him. The man clearly didn't sit behind a desk all day. Even if she hadn't glimpsed his rippling muscles, she could've told that much by his sun-bronzed features.

No, Johnny Diamond was at home in the outdoors.

When she settled down and felt it safe to do so, she glanced his way again. The cagey outlaw removed his holster and laid it beside him within reach. Somehow that simple act made her feel warm and protected. Earlier he hadn't wanted her to stay where she was above the embankment. Said she'd be safer here with him. She certainly wouldn't dispute that.

Shifting her weight, trying to get comfortable, she wondered where her sister was and what she doing.

Please, God, watch over Beth and protect her from the evil intentions of her captors. Her eyes filled with tears as she stared up at the star-filled sky.

"Diamond?"

"Yeah," he answered.

"How much time did the kidnappers give my father to pay the ransom?"

"Why?"

She propped herself on an elbow to look at him. "I just want to get a clear picture of what we're up against."

"What *I'm* up against you mean. I have five days."

A quick intake of air almost choked her. It would be near impossible to find Beth in that short a space. "Do you think you can find her by then?"

"Don't know why everyone keeps asking me that. I'll get your sister back."

Larissa suspected the steely confidence he projected into his voice was for her benefit alone, but she appreciated the effort nonetheless. A lump formed in her throat.

"What'll happen to her if you should fail?"

"I won't." Again his voice brimmed with quiet resoluteness. "You'd best get some sleep and quit worrying your pretty little head. Daylight will come before you know it. And I have a far piece to ride."

They did indeed, but Larissa wasn't finished. "Where do you suppose those men have taken Beth?"

A deep sigh troubled the night air. "Most likely to a border town. That's where their trail seems to be leading."

"I hope they're not being mean to Beth." She'd heard tales about outlaws and criminals and what such men were capable of. She didn't know how she could bear it if they were mistreating her sweet, loving baby sister.

"If they want to continue drawing breath, they'd best treat her gently."

The sudden venom spewing from Diamond's voice startled her. She knew he meant every word of the threat and that gave her comfort. And somehow she knew the money her father paid him played perhaps only a tiny role. She suspected he'd do the job if he received no compensation at all.

Her outlaw did what he did out of a deep sense of justice.

Larissa lapsed into silence. For a while she listened to the sounds of the night. The howl of a lonesome coyote. The whisper of the gentle breeze rustling the tall grasses.

The gentle babble of the small stream, thankful for the deluge several days ago that briefly gave the creek life.

And Johnny Diamond's quiet breathing just feet away.

Though he slept, she had the feeling that the slightest sound out of the ordinary would awaken him instantly. He'd spring up with his Colt in hand, ready to battle any threat, real or perceived.

A big smile stretched across her face as she flipped over and got comfortable.

She'd never felt so protected by anyone. Not even her father. Especially not her father. He kept her from harm because it was his duty—and the fact he'd fight tooth and nail to keep someone from taking what was his, not because he valued his own flesh and blood.

Dunston Patrick had shown her no love or softness. Every chance he got he voiced regret that she hadn't been born a son. Daughters were of little consequence to the great cattle baron except for what they could do for him.

But her father's worst sin of all was rejecting Beth, blaming the girl for his beloved wife's death in childbirth. Were he half the man of Johnny Diamond, he'd go after Beth himself, instead of hiring it done. If he truly cared.

Her thoughts turned to how she could sway the outlaw to take her with him.

Johnny Diamond's eyes popped open at the sound of someone rifling through the provisions he'd taken from the packhorse's back.

Lying still, he glanced around the campsite. Light from the pink dawn revealed Larissa Patrick. Curiosity kept him from moving. He'd lie there and see what she was up to. He didn't have to wait long. She drew out the battered coffeepot and a tin of coffee.

Johnny propped himself on an elbow. "Morning."

Larissa jumped and whirled. "You scared me."

He sat up and pushed to his feet. "Serves you right for sneaking around and making yourself at home with my belongings."

A flush crept up her face and settled in both cheeks. "I was just going to make some coffee for you. I'll put everything back where I found it. I thought you might like some stout brew before we ride out."

He reached for his holster and strapped it around his hips. "Time to get up anyway. I'll scare up some firewood. A pot of coffee sounds real nice and I think a fire will be safe enough."

Some spindly shin oak grew near a limestone outcropping several hundred yards away so he headed in that direction, keeping an eye out for dead branches. With luck he found enough to build a passable fire. It wasn't long before Larissa handed him a cup of the hot brew where he was seated on a big rock.

"Have you given any thought to letting me ride with you?" she asked with hope lacing her words as she sat on another rock opposite him.

A glance at her and his heart caught in his throat. Her large expressive eyes seemed to see past the ugliness that so often had scarred his life. That the thick fringe of her lashes gave her eyes a dark sooty appearance didn't help to slow the blood rushing through his veins.

He took a swallow of the coffee and scalded his tongue. He willed his heartbeat to a slower gait before he trusted his voice. "You have me over a barrel and I think you know that, ma'am."

"I don't know what you mean."

"I believe you know exactly what I'm talking about. I can't spare the time to take you home and it's too far and too dangerous for you to go back by yourself." Johnny pushed back his hat with a forefinger. "The only solution is to take you with me and pray to God that I can get you and your sister back home safe and sound."

"Thank you, Mr. Diamond."

"Another thing—don't call me mister. Johnny will do, or just Diamond."

"I can do that."

Hell, if he told her to eat a horse dumpling she'd probably be agreeable as long as she got her way.

"We're going to ride hard and travel fast. I'll leave you behind if you can't keep up. Your sister's life hangs in the balance. Remember that when you get so bone weary you don't think you can ride another mile."

"I understand."

"And no complaining. I don't want to know when your stomach rumbles, your body aches, or you need to visit the necessary. And another thing—I like the quiet. I can't abide someone who prattles on and on."

"You won't regret this, Diamond."

"I already do." He could see the handwriting on the wall and they hadn't ridden out of camp yet. Just trying to keep his thoughts from constantly wandering to her would be nigh impossible. Keeping from kissing her would tax him to the limit.

"I won't be any trouble. I promise."

She didn't know that trouble seemed to be her middle name.

Chapter 4

Larissa stooped at the water's edge to wash the few cooking utensils they'd used. Johnny found his gaze drawn to her trim figure as he broke camp.

The woman enticed him. And he didn't like the feelings she'd awakened in him. He mentally listed all the reasons why he couldn't—wouldn't—give in to the needs she made him acutely aware of.

Number one, she was far too persistent, in fact to a fault. Any other woman would've turned back and gone home.

But then, that could be reason to admire her, he reckoned.

Number two, he couldn't concentrate on the job Dunston Patrick had hired him to do with her around. And if he couldn't keep his focus on the task at hand it'd get someone killed, either Beth, Larissa, or him. Maybe all three of them.

Number three, it was downright uncomfortable the way his body hummed when she came near him, as was the current that arced between them when they touched.

And number four . . . He stopped. The biggest reason of all was the way his body betrayed him. A certain part of his anatomy refused to listen to any scolding. It was constantly trying to leap to attention. He'd run out of ways to hide the evidence. She'd notice before long and then what?

No, he didn't have good sense in letting her ride along.

He rolled up his bedroll and laid it beside his saddle. That Larissa had taken it upon herself to help with the chores without being asked hadn't escaped him.

Clearly, the woman made herself useful to repay him for not running her back to the Four Spades. He turned his head to hide the grin that spread across his face.

He prayed that the decision to let her come wouldn't rear up and bite him in the butt. She could be of some help, he grudgingly admitted. Larissa knew what her sister looked like whereas he had only a vague description. Sometimes a man had only a split second to react in a situation and needed to have confidence in his choices. She could possibly give him that.

He gave her another sidelong glance as he doused the campfire, using sand rather than water so it wouldn't smoke and give away their location should anyone happen to be in the area.

With the hot embers buried with sand, he threw Blue's saddle over his shoulder and headed toward the mount, still aware of where Larissa was and what she was doing every second.

Indeed, how could he not?

It seemed she'd aroused every last fiber of his being.

Keeping Blue Boy between them, he boldly admired the handsome woman who was no bigger than a sack of feed. He bet he could practically put his hands around her waist and touch his fingers on the other side. And though the top of her head barely reached the middle of his chest, she had bountiful curves in all the right places.

Definitely all woman.

A red-blooded, warm woman who put herself in danger to save her little sister.

Blue Boy snorted and tossed his head. Johnny gave himself a mental shake. Nothing could be gained from dreaming for something that was out of his reach. He was an outlaw, plain and simple. He couldn't change that fact. And until today he'd been perfectly content with his life. But now, he found no pleasure in doing as he wished and the devil take anyone who spoke a word against him.

Living by the gun had become a way of life for him.

There was no denying that he'd oftentimes enjoyed the rush of adrenaline when he'd squared off against an opponent.

Now, he suddenly saw that what he'd mistaken as satisfaction had been reckless and irresponsible behavior. His life was nothing but remnants of blood and destruction.

Johnny made a vow to change things . . . just as soon as he got Beth Patrick back and safe.

They rode out just as the sun poked its sleepy head over the eastern horizon. He picked up the kidnappers' trail and tracked it due south.

The brilliant orange sun had climbed midway in the sky when the wind shifted and really began to blow. He noticed a red-hazed wall bearing down on them. His stomach clenched as he tasted the grit in the air, which smelled earthy and dank.

They were riding straight into a deadly sandstorm.

It was coming fast and hard, too fast to seek shelter.

He pulled up. Snatching off the bandana from around his neck, he gave it to Larissa. "This'll protect you somewhat from the sand. Tie it over your nose and mouth. Looks like we're in for it."

From experience he knew the damage biting sand would do to her exposed skin and wished he could spare her.

"What about you?" she asked, quickly doing as he requested.

"Don't worry about me." He dismounted and rummaged in his saddlebag. He pulled out one of his extra shirts and ripped off a big piece. After removing his hat, he tied the uneven square around his head where it would shield his face. It wasn't the best in the world, but it'd keep him from swallowing half of the grit in Texas. He wedged his hat back on his head so it wouldn't easily blow off. Larissa's hat was also anchored well, he noticed, the rawhide strips tied under her chin.

"Maybe we can find a cave in those limestone cliffs just ahead," she suggested, pointing toward them.

"That's my thinking," he agreed.

They'd ridden less than a mile when the storm overtook them, blotting out the sun and erasing their tracks. Johnny grabbed the reins of Larissa's mare and added the strips of rawhide to the packhorse's halter in his hand. He got a death grip on them in order to keep them all together in the zero-visibility sand blast.

To make matters worse, the limestone cliffs they'd headed for had disappeared. A man could get lost and wander in circles in these situations.

Sand whipped his clothing and cut into the soft tissue of his eyes. He could barely breathe without getting a lung-ful of the grit. To make matters worse, tumbleweeds slammed into the horses' legs. It took every bit of strength to control the animals. They kept rearing up, and if he hadn't had a firm grip on the reins, they'd have bolted.

It seemed an eternity before Johnny and Larissa reached the rock wall of the cliffs. He helped her dismount. They found refuge of sorts by pressing close to the rock face.

"Gotta rest the horses a bit!" Johnny yelled, leaning close to Larissa's ear.

If she replied, the fierce wind swallowed up her words. He just gave her a nod. As they huddled there, he scanned the area as far as he could see in the brown murkiness for signs of one of the hundreds of caves known to litter the limestone rock. They'd need somewhere to hole up for the night and rest.

He saw nothing.

After an hour or so had passed with no sign of the storm letting up, he helped Larissa onto her horse. He walked alongside the cliff, leading all three animals, keeping an eye out for a cave.

Just when he was ready to give up and suggest they hunker down as best they could under an overhang, he spied the yawning mouth of a cave up ahead. Wasting no time in escaping the brutal wind, he hurried them inside. He lifted his hat and removed the makeshift bandana. Looking around, he could see that, while it wasn't a large cave, there was enough room for Larissa and him and the three horses.

Johnny hung his dusty hat on the saddle horn. He then put his hands around Larissa's small waist and helped her down. She lost her footing and grabbed his arm to keep from falling. The contact jolted through him.

"Are you okay, ma'am?" He relished her warm body pressing against him and was loathe to let her go.

"I'm sorry. I'm just exhausted."

He fingered the strings to her floppy hat that were tied under her chin. Untying them, he removed her hat and the bandana from her face.

His knuckle grazed her cheek in a gentle caress. He couldn't have said what came over him to do so, but it seemed as natural as breathing. The pulse in the hollow of her throat beat wildly. Her lips parted ever so slightly.

But before he could kiss her, Larissa suddenly stepped away, brushing back her hair. "That wind stole every bit of my energy. I haven't seen a sandstorm this bad in ages."

"It's something else, all right." He stepped to his and Larissa's mounts and unsaddled them.

Conscious of the woman's every move, he knew instantly when she stumbled to the packhorse and began working the knots loose in the rope that secured their provisions to the animal's back.

He hurried to her side. "Let me get that. You sit down and rest."

Evidently too tired to object, she did as he asked, picking a spot against the wall of the cave.

He got the packhorse unloaded and stacked the supplies next to the wall before he noticed Larissa slumped in a heap on the rocky floor.

Grabbing one of three canteens, he went to her. "Here, drink up."

Noticing he had yet to put the canteen to his lips, she shook her head. "Only when you do. If you don't drink, I don't either."

"Lady, you're in no position to haggle."

"Give my portion to Arabella. The animals are two steps from a shallow grave now." She could do her part to ration if he could.

"So are you. Think of your sister," he persisted.

"One small drink then." Larissa reached for the water and took a sip. "Now, are you happy? It's your turn."

"If there's any left after I take care of the horses."

Larissa knew he'd hornswoggled her. He had no intention of wetting his throat. She watched him pour their precious water into his hat and let each horse drink.

"I don't think we're too far from Devils River. It should have water in it this time of year," he offered over his shoulder. "By my estimation we're probably half a day's ride out. I can wait. With luck, this sandstorm will die down and we'll make better time."

With the animals cared for, he came and sat down next to her. The companionable way his shoulder touched hers brought sudden warmth. She felt totally alive and well cared for.

Waning light revealed the layer of dirt caked on every portion of his face that had been exposed to the elements. She guessed she probably looked the same and for a minute yearned for her room at the ranch, where she had all the water she needed. A cool bath would do wonders for her sagging spirits.

She ran her tongue over her cracked lips to moisten them.

Surely her father had read the note she'd left. Although separated by thirty miles of wasteland she could feel his anger.

But she chose to look forward rather than backward. She still believed she'd done the right thing.

She reached for the bandana that lay beside her, then tried to wipe some of the sand from her face. The dry cloth didn't do too good a job, but at least it probably got some of it.

Twisting toward her, he held out his hand. "Give me the bandana."

Johnny Diamond, the man who seemed to guard his thoughts as if they were locked in a bank vault, folded the square piece of fabric and ordered, "Hold still."

With the softest touch, he gently brushed her cheek. "Missed a spot."

The crooked grin he flashed stole her breath. That glorious smile revealed a row of white teeth. And she knew at that moment that he had more than a little devilment in him. He'd break her heart if she wasn't careful.

"Diamond, how close do you think we are to the kidnappers?"

"I can't hazard a guess." He returned the bandana to her. "It depends on whether they got caught in the storm too."

"But if not?" She struggled to keep fear from her voice. Losing control now would benefit no one. She'd not give Johnny Diamond reason to leave her behind. Beth needed her.

Still, the man on whom they'd pinned their hopes didn't have to tell her valuable time was wasting away.

Their five days was down to four and the clock ticked.

"I've never been any good at playing the 'if' game." His

quiet answer calmed her rising panic. "Don't throw the baby out with the bathwater just because of a little thing like nasty weather. The pure and simple fact is we have right on our side. We'll win this fight, mark my words."

"But the wind will have destroyed their tracks. How will you know where they've gone?"

"We'll just keep heading south toward Del Rio. It's the most logical place. We'll look there first and if we can't find your sister, we'll try up and down the border. I won't give up. My gut tells me we're looking in the right direction."

"You don't deal in iffy speculation but you rely on something so vague as your gut?"

"It's rarely wrong. I'm alive today because of my well-honed instincts. And before this is all said and done you might be thanking God for them, if you don't mind me saying, ma'am."

Larissa bristled at the set-down. "Diamond, you're more prickly than a horned toad on a hot rock."

He rubbed his eyes. "Sorry. I wasn't always like this."

"Did you just wake up one day and decide to live on the wrong side of the law?" She'd blurted the question before she'd had time to consider that it probably wasn't the wisest thing to ask an outlaw. Only now that she'd spent some time with him he didn't exhibit the sort of characteristics she associated with someone who spurned the law at every turn.

No matter what he'd done or the crimes he'd committed, Johnny Diamond had principles. She had a feeling when he believed strongly in a cause he put everything he had into it.

A startled look swept Johnny's ice-blue gaze. It was like staring into the cool depths of an iridescent pool. "My life didn't take this turn of its own accord. You might say circumstances led me to follow this path."

Now she was intrigued. "Circumstances?"

"Yep. I was born in the mountains of Kentucky. When I

was fourteen, my family sold everything they had and came west. We traveled with a wagon train until we reached Texas. My father decided to split away. He'd heard of cheap land for the taking as far as the eye could see on the Llano Estacado."

Larissa had a feeling this story wouldn't have a good ending, but she itched to know that he'd once had a normal life. "I've heard of the Llano Estacado in west Texas where the grasses appear as endless rolling waves across the prairie. It must be quite mesmerizing."

"It is. The only thing was, no one warned my father of the danger." Johnny wearily rubbed his eyes.

She waited for him to continue and when it seemed he'd said all he intended to she prodded, "You can't leave me hanging in suspense. What danger?"

"Comancheros, for one."

An icy chill invaded her. Mention of Comancheros struck fear in the hearts of God-fearing folk. They were a murderous band of men who preyed on the weak and on ill-prepared travelers. She'd heard tales of them killing, raping, and sometimes selling hostages. They traded guns and whiskey to the fierce Apache in exchange for captives and stolen horses.

"I'm sorry I pried. I can see this is too painful for you." Her words barely rose above the shrieking wind.

Johnny didn't act like he heard her. He seemed to be reliving the nightmare. "They killed my father right off. He was the lucky one. I watched them rape my mother and sisters and I prayed they'd just kill them and end their suffering. But when they finally shot them, the world went so still. The birds quit singing, the breeze stopped blowing, the mules ceased their complaining. That silence was the sound of death."

Larissa ached for him. She had no idea how a person would cope after tragically losing his entire family. "What happened to you? How did you get away?"

"After the deadly quiet, the Comancheros argued about

what to do with me. Just as they decided to trade me to the Apache, a stranger suddenly swooped in on a horse with pistols blazing. I never saw anything like it. He grabbed me up and we hightailed it for the cover of a nearby arroyo. He single-handedly held off eight Comancheros. When night fell, we slipped away and rode for our lives.

"The man's name was Sam Whiskey. He was an outlaw and I owe my life to him. He took me under his wing. Taught me to shoot, track, and stay alive. When I'd learned enough, I went looking for my family's killers." Johnny's features were as though carved from granite, his tight voice as unyielding as tempered steel.

They sat for a long time shoulder to shoulder, immersed in their own thoughts.

Larissa didn't have any doubt that he'd found the men. She also knew that he'd exacted his form of retribution.

And he'd paid for it with his soul.

Johnny rose and stood at the mouth of the cave, staring out at the red-tinged sky. His square jaw seemed braced as though daring the world to take its best shot.

Unshed tears filled her eyes. She stared at his broad shoulders that had borne so much weight. Johnny's family had wanted nothing other than owning some land and living their lives. Instead what they found in Texas was a killing ground. Shame swept through her. At least she still had a father who walked, talked, and breathed. But she'd wanted far more.

She vowed that when this was all over she would try harder to have a better relationship with Dunston Patrick . . . if at all possible.

Chapter 5

Johnny Diamond dreamed of pools of sparkling blue water. It was there simply for the taking. The water was so real he could taste it, feel it trickling through his hand, sluicing over his head.

He awoke to find the inside of his mouth as dry as a sunbaked piece of boot leather. It was still dark, must be very early morning if he were to hazard a guess.

The winds no longer shrieked like a demented banshee.

He couldn't see Larissa, but gentle breathing came from her bedroll, which she'd lain out next to his. He wished he had some water for her. It didn't matter so much that he went without, he just didn't want her to be miserable. He wished he had enough for drinking . . . washing up . . . making coffee.

And if wishes were horses he'd have a ranch bursting at the seams with the beautiful animals. He let out a long breath. Taking care not to wake her, he stole over to look out of the cave.

Blue heard him and nickered softly.

Johnny looked up at the millions of stars. "I'm a fool," he angrily whispered. "I shouldn't have told Larissa about my past. I should've kept quiet."

Thanks to his loose tongue she knew exactly what kind of man he was—the killing sort. He'd wanted her to look kindly on him. For once in his life he wanted someone to see the kind of man he wished he could've been before evil touched his life and moved in to stay.

But now she'd seen the unvarnished truth and probably rued the day she'd followed him from the ranch.

Not that he didn't rue it either. His conscience balked at suddenly finding himself responsible for Larissa Patrick. He didn't want anyone's life being dependent on him. He wasn't any good at looking out for others.

Hell, he hadn't even been able to save his mother and three sisters!

What would Larissa think if she knew he'd hidden like a scared jackrabbit as bullets shattered their skulls?

He stood there cursing himself until the inky sky lightened with pink and golden hues. It was a new day.

"Larissa, time to wake up. We need to be going." He moved to the dark shape on the bedroll and lightly shook her shoulder.

She came awake instantly, her eyes finding his in the soft light. Her hair was a tousled mess, dirt streaked her face, and her clothes were wrinkled. He didn't think he'd seen a more beautiful, stubborn woman.

"Good morning." Her brilliant smile turned the brown of her eyes a rich chocolate. She had little to be overjoyed about, but neither the lack of water nor a fierce sandstorm that could strip the hide from bone seemed to dampen her spirit. She never wasted breath complaining.

"Let's ride while it's still cool. Maybe we can make it to the river before the day heats up too much."

Half an hour later they took to the trail again.

Just as the sun heated in earnest, Johnny saw a cloud of vultures circling the sky ahead. His gut clenched. Such scavengers feasted on something dead.

He knew the minute Larissa saw it too. Although she didn't speak, she straightened as alarm swept her features.

He wished he could assure her it couldn't possibly be her sister, but the words wouldn't come, for he knew all too well the price this land sometimes exacted on its travelers.

And of all people, he knew the depth of viciousness that lurked in the hearts of men.

Urging the horses to a faster pace, he pushed them onward. They'd find out soon who or what baked in the scorching heat. He wasn't a praying man, but he found himself uttering a prayer that the vultures' meal wasn't Beth Patrick.

They rode down into a dry wash, up the bank on the other side, and rounded a stand of mesquite. The vultures' big wings flapped noisily as they took to the sky. It was then Johnny got a look at what they were feasting on.

The bloated body of a dead horse brought relief.

Judging from the amount of sand that had blown up around one side, it had been there since early yesterday.

Johnny dismounted and handed the reins to Larissa. Covering his nose, he went for a close look. The poor animal had been shot through the head. At least someone had put the horse out of its misery. He guessed it had probably died of thirst and from being ridden too hard. A good look at the horseshoes told him this animal made one of the three sets of prints he'd been following since leaving the Four Spades Ranch. That meant two of the kidnappers rode double.

They might meet the same fate as this horse if they didn't reach water soon.

He returned to the horses and looked up at Larissa. Seeing her dry, cracked lips made his chest tighten. "How are you holding up?" he asked quietly.

"I'm all right. How much farther to the river?"

"We should be there soon." He took Blue's and the packhorse's reins from her and swung back into the saddle. "Maybe a couple more miles. Don't worry, we'll make it."

"I'm not worried. You'll get us there."

Larissa's quiet confidence brought a lump to his throat. Until he'd met her, only Sam Whiskey had put much stock in his abilities.

Sweat drenched their clothing by the time Devils River came into view. The horses smelled the water and took off at a gallop. The river was narrow but the glistening water was a sight to behold. The horses didn't stop until they stood in the middle of it.

Johnny helped Larissa from her mare. He hung his hat and holster on the saddle horn and moved upstream before he cupped his hands and scooped the water into his mouth. He drank his fill and then some. Only after he'd wet his parched throat did he submerge his head, then his whole body.

"We made it! We really made it." Larissa, who'd followed him upstream, stretched out her arms and fell backward into the water.

When she came up, Johnny's heart stopped. Her clothes were plastered to her body. Every curve, every peak and valley stood out with crystal clarity. And she didn't know the effect it had on him. If she'd had any inkling she'd have gotten on her horse and hightailed it out of there so fast he wouldn't have known what hit him.

He swung away to hide a grin and doused his head with water. As if that would cool the rising heat. He doubted a bath in frigid ice water would return his body to a state that wouldn't betray his thoughts.

Larissa Patrick could tie him in knots without half trying.

After some time he waded out of the water, and retrieved his holster from his saddle horn and the Winchester from the scabbard. Plopping down on the bank, he emptied the water from his boots.

"Can we camp here for the night?"

He didn't miss the hopeful note in Larissa's question. "As much as I hate it, we'll have to ride on. We need to get to Del Rio. But we'll have to rest the horses for a bit. I'm going to build a fire and make some coffee. Might see what game I can scare up for a quick meal. Hungry?"

"I could stand to eat something," she answered. "If you can."

Before she emerged from the water and he embarrassed himself, he shoved his feet back into his boots and headed for the nearby brush to find some wood for a fire. He took his time, giving her ample opportunity to set her clothes to rights. When he made it back a short while later, she already had the coffeepot out, filled with water and coffee.

And not too much later, they roasted some quail over an open fire and sipped on cups of coffee.

Larissa wished they didn't have to ride on, but she understood. Their five days was now down to three and they had yet to reach Del Rio, if that was where they'd find Beth. They had no assurances of that. Like Johnny had stated, the gang of kidnappers could be anywhere up and down the border.

Every time she thought of her innocent sister in those mens' clutches an icy chill ran through her blood. Finding Beth seemed a daunting task.

She turned the stick over the fire with a quail skewered on the end. Johnny had skinned and cleaned the birds in no time, a skill acquired only from lots of practice. She gave him a sidelong glance, her cheeks heating at the memory of how her blouse and riding skirt had clung to her when she'd gotten out of the river. She'd been so overjoyed to have reached water that she'd given no thought of her modesty. No wonder he'd suddenly disappeared. In his own thoughtful way he'd given her time to make herself presentable.

Her heart swelled.

Johnny Diamond was no ordinary outlaw. He could

easily fit into the most discerning social circles had he a mind to do so.

And yet he chose a life that could get him killed.

Or rather, as he'd explained, this life had chosen him. He hadn't had much choice in the matter, given the way the Comancheros had erased his whole family from the face of the earth and made him an orphan in the bargain.

It was small wonder he had an ancient look in his eyes as though he'd already lived several lifetimes, although he couldn't be but a few years older than she.

Taking advantage of his preoccupation with his own roasting quail, she boldly assessed the man who sent a wave of heat careening through her belly each time he touched her.

His broad shoulders bore the weight of the world with such ease, the holster around his lean hips lent undeniable strength, and the iridescent blue of his gaze could pierce right into her soul and see all her shortcomings.

Her attention was drawn to his dark hair that brushed the top of his collar. No matter how many times he kept pushing back the stubborn lock that fell onto his forehead, it insisted on doing what it would. There didn't appear to be any taming it. Larissa wondered what his hair would feel like on her fingers.

"Like anything you see, ma'am?" he growled.

She jumped as a hot blush crept into her cheeks. "I was just . . . I didn't mean . . . I truly have better manners," she finally got out. "I apologize."

Lord, he must think her terribly rude!

"And that's another thing . . . can we please dispense with the ma'ams?" she added in a rush. "Makes me feel so . . . old."

"If that's what you want, Larissa." He pulled the quail off his skewer, dropped it on a tin plate, and blew on his fingers. "I think these are done. Hand me yours and I'll take it off for you."

"Thank you," she murmured, passing over her skewer.

"Diamond, how do you suppose the kidnappers will know if my father doesn't pay the ransom?"

"They left one man behind for that purpose. I'm sure it's arranged for him to send a telegram to his compadres. Your father is going to keep a watch on that line shack and nab the man when he shows up to collect the ransom money."

"So he'll never get a chance to send the telegram." Larissa chewed her lip. "When the men who have Beth don't get word, they'll . . ." *Kill her,* she added silently.

He laid a tanned hand on hers and spoke as though he'd read her mind. Maybe he had. "They won't get a chance. I'll already have Beth far away by then."

All of a sudden the enormity of the task hit her.

It all depended on a man who hated himself for caring about what happened to people. He seemed to consider that part of him a weakness.

He didn't know it made him stronger.

Chapter 6

The town of Del Rio came into view in the afternoon of the following day.

Their five days had dwindled to two.

Johnny Diamond knew it would take a miracle to find Beth before the deadline, but he didn't share that with Larissa. She was a bundle of nerves without adding more worries. He wouldn't smash her hopes for a positive outcome.

He scanned both sides of Main Street as they slowly rode from one end to the other. The border town was typical of others up and down the Rio Grande. It was dirty and drab and many buildings leaned precariously.

Except for tinny piano music blaring from one of several saloons, the town appeared quiet and docile. But he knew that was misleading. Once darkness descended it would become a wild and wooly place. He'd have to do his best to keep Larissa out of sight.

That would be a chore, given her stubborn streak.

Drawing up in front of The Texas Spur, the only hotel in town, he threw his leg over Blue's neck and slid from the saddle. "I'll get you a room before I scout around. You can bathe and put on some fresh clothing."

He put his hands around her waist and lifted her to the

ground. His hands lingered on her a tad longer than needed, but if she noticed, she kept quiet.

"I'm not the only one in need of a bath." Though she was weary to the bone, sparks flashed in her eyes. "If you can put it off so can I. Will you stay here at the hotel?"

"Figure I'll bed down at the livery, where I can get a good look at the horses without raising a lot of questions. If it works out where I get a chance to visit the bathhouse, I will. If not, it'll have to wait. It's not my first priority right now."

"Diamond, don't think you're going to get rid of me this easy. I came to find Beth and that's what I aim to do," she said stiffly.

Johnny pushed back his hat with a forefinger. "Would you stop with that? I'm not trying to get rid of you. I'm going to have to hang out for a bit in the saloon to see what information I can ferret out. It's not exactly the place for a lady of your caliber." He gave her a wry grin. "Now, are we going to haggle out here in the street the rest of the day or are you going to go into the hotel like I suggested?"

"Like you ordered, you mean. You're giving me no choice."

Johnny ground his teeth but kept his voice calm and low. "I didn't mean that like it sounded. It's just that I have a few million things on my mind. Time is short and so is my patience, it seems."

Larissa finally withdrew her claws. "I'll do as you ask simply because you have me over a barrel. But don't forget about me. I want to know what you find out no matter how large or small."

"I promise to tell you the minute I learn something. Okay?" She gave a curt nod.

Breathing a deep sigh of relief, he got her a room and gave her some money for a new change of clothes. Then he took the horses to the livery. He briefly scanned the other horses that were boarded. He didn't have a chance to inspect their hooves without raising suspicion, though. He'd have to do that after the livery owner went to bed.

Leaving the stables, he strolled toward the nearest saloon.

The sign on the false front proclaimed it to be The Red Eye. Johnny stepped inside the swinging doors and took note of the place. The sawdust floor said the owner was either frugal or lazy. His gaze shifted to the patrons.

Four men at the back played cards. Three customers stood at the bar swilling whiskey and talking. It was early yet for most men. The two working girls seemed bored. The one who was the most heavily made up yawned big and ambled his way with her hips swinging suggestively.

"Hi, stranger," she said when she reached his side. "Care to buy a woman a drink?"

He gave her the once-over she probably expected and took her arm. Leading her to a nearby table, he pulled out a chair for her. "What'll be your pleasure, ma'am?"

"I'm partial to whiskey, but not the rotgut stuff." She patted her cloud of auburn hair. "I have my principles."

"I can certainly see that you do, ma'am."

"Oh, honey, I could listen to you call me that all night long," she crooned close to his ear before she sat down.

Johnny strolled to the bar and bought a bottle of good whiskey though he doubted she'd be able to tell it since she'd clearly had more than a few already. He just hoped all his effort paid off. He took the bottle and two glasses to the table, then pulled out a chair and dropped into it.

"Do you have a name, ma'am?"

"Sally. And what do I call you, honey?"

He saw no reason to give a false name since the kidnappers wouldn't know him, except maybe by reputation.

Besides, being an outlaw let him mix and mingle without drawing suspicion.

"Diamond. Johnny Diamond."

Her plucked eyebrows raised. "Sounds like the name of a wanted man."

"Would it make a difference?"

"Only to the law." She chuckled. "Thank goodness we're not bothered with any of that in Del Rio. Mind if I ask what you're wanted for?"

"You're a mite nosey for my taste, Sally." He scooted back his chair and started to rise. "Think I'll mosey on."

Sally quickly grabbed his arm. "Hold on, cowboy. Don't make a hill of beans to me who you are or what you've done. I'm just making a little harmless conversation."

Johnny relaxed into the chair and poured her a drink. He poured himself one too but left it untouched on the table. "You lived here long, Sally?"

"For a while." He wasn't the only one being evasive. She was definitely running from something.

"I reckon you know everyone around here then." He leaned close and stuck two dollars into the low-cut dress she wore. "I'm looking for a group of men. Heard they might be here. Was thinking I might join up with them. Seen any strangers in town?"

"Well, a couple of newcomers blew in here yesterday like a sandstorm sweeping across the plain. Looked like they were fresh off the trail."

Johnny caught Sally glancing off and poured his drink on the sawdust floor. "Happen to know where they're staying?"

"One of them, he was real mean looking, remarked to his partner that they'd wet their whistles before returning to camp. Got the impression they're staying outside of town."

That would fit. It'd be easier to keep Beth a secret out there all by themselves.

"Have they been in here today?"

Sally downed her whiskey in one big gulp. "Nope. Ain't seen hide nor hair of 'em."

He pushed back his chair and stood. "Reckon I'll see if I can find them. Appreciate the help, Sally."

"Sure thing, cowboy. Come back anytime. I'm always around. Maybe next time I can lure you upstairs." She winked.

He seriously doubted that although he didn't tell her. Larissa's luminous amber eyes framed by long, thick lashes crossed his mind. If he had a hankering for female companionship he knew where he'd go.

And he wouldn't have to be afraid of catching something.

By the time Johnny left the saloon, dusk had settled over the town. Things were beginning to pick up in the street. He headed for the livery. He'd saddle Blue Boy and take a ride.

Sitting on Blue at the edge of town, he pondered which direction to take. He ruled out north, the direction they'd come. The gang would need to be close to the water if they were camping out. The Rio Grande divided Texas from Mexico and was the only river in the area. His gut told him to look there.

He rode about a mile east and saw nothing. Disappointed, he returned to where he started and headed west. A few minutes later he saw the light from a campfire shining through some mesquite trees. After getting off Blue, he tied the horse to a branch and stole silently toward the camp.

Suddenly a female scream fractured the air followed by several men's coarse laughter.

The hair on his neck rose. His hand stole to the Colt on his hip. It slid with ease from the buttery softness of the holster and filled his hand. He crouched low and listened.

"You'll do as we say or else, missy," sneered a man.

Then came the sound of a hand connecting with a face and another warning. "If you know what's good for you you'll stop the blubbering and take off your clothes and be quick about it. I guarantee you won't like the lesson we teach you."

Dunston Patrick's words echoed in Johnny's head. *If I had my druthers, I'd prefer you end their miserable lives and silence them once and for all.*

A familiar resolve filled his chest. He didn't know how he'd go about it, but he would set whoever the captive girl was free or die trying. And if it was Beth, he would make the kidnappers pay dearly.

Lord knew they deserved whatever they got. It was what Patrick paid him to do. And like Sally over at the saloon had said, there wasn't any lawman in town. Johnny was Beth's only hope.

Inch by inch Johnny drew closer.

At last he could see. Three men were passing a small female back and forth between them as they would a whiskey bottle.

True, he couldn't clearly see the girl's features, but he guessed she could be Beth Patrick. He'd find out soon enough.

One thing for sure, the girl was there against her will.

Images of his mother and sisters flooded back. They'd fought the Comancheros with every bit of strength they had. And yet they'd lost their lives.

His jaw clenched. He'd been young then and unarmed. That was far from the case now. He'd not see another girl or woman perish as long as he could help it. Not this time. Not ever again. This time evil wouldn't win.

The girl screamed again in rising panic.

Johnny seized the element of surprise and leaped into their midst with his pistol cocked and ready. "Turn her loose."

The man who twisted the girl's arm in a punishing grip whirled. A jagged scar ran from one eye across his nose, then ended by his ear. "I don't know who you are, mister, but this is a private party. We don't cotton to anyone meddling in our business."

"If you need some convincing, I can oblige." Johnny's threat bore velvet softness that deceived. "Let the girl go."

The youngest of the trio licked his lips nervously. "We was only funning with her."

"She's not laughing. Neither am I." He spoke to the girl. "Come over here and get behind me."

But the brute holding her wouldn't release her. "The only way you're getting her is through me," the man roared.

Johnny was through trying to reason with men like them. He'd let his Colt do the talking. He quickly aimed and pulled the trigger.

Chapter 7

The bullet struck Scar Face in the leg. He dropped like a sack of feed, releasing his captive on his way to the hard ground. The sobbing girl ran to Johnny.

"Are you okay?" he asked her.

Her reply to the affirmative was low, the girl probably scared within an inch of her life. He could feel her trembling. He quickly tucked her behind him, keeping his Colt trained on the trio in case they drew their weapons.

Up close he realized she was quite a bit older than Beth. No ten-year-old had curves like this one, who must be in her teens. Disappointment swept through him. He'd hoped this would all be over now. But it seemed he'd only begun the chore of locating the kidnappers.

"Toss your pistols over here," he ordered Scar Face and his accomplices. Scar Face seemed to dawdle, maybe thinking to challenge Johnny. Or else catch him with his guard down.

Finally, the man evidently saw he had no choice because he obliged, albeit grudgingly.

Johnny instructed the girl to get on his horse, and then he collected the pistols and backed cautiously away from the campsite.

A mile down the road, he threw the firearms into a clump

of bushes. He doubted the trio would ever find them, which would make his job a tad easier. He'd still have to look over his shoulder, though. He sighed. He had trouble remembering a time when he hadn't.

Back in town, he returned the girl, who gave her name as Meg Frost, into the care of her father after explaining the circumstances.

"Thank you for looking after my daughter." Mr. Frost stuck out his hand and shook Johnny's. "I've been searching high and low for her and feared I'd never see her again."

"This is a dangerous town. Keep her close to you." Johnny took his leave, then left Blue Boy at the stables. The breeze suddenly died and he got a whiff of himself. Smelled like the south end of a northbound mule. A bath was definitely in order before he had supper with Larissa.

He stopped by the mercantile for some new clothes first. The owner was just flipping the sign to the "Closed" side. Johnny begged the man to let him in and was grateful when he did. He quickly picked out a shirt, trousers, and drawers.

Business was slow at the bathhouse. There were only him and two other bathers. It didn't take him long to get undressed and sink into the clean water he'd paid extra for. He kept his Colt within easy reach. A man could never tell when he needed a weapon, especially in a wild border town that had no lawman to ride herd over it.

Relaxing in the water, Johnny overheard a conversation on the other side of the cubicle. The words "Four Spades Ranch" made the hair on his neck rise. He sat quietly, straining to hear more of the exchange.

"Tomorrow's the deadline. We'll know what we gotta do."

"Think Patrick'll pay up?"

"He will if he wants to see his daughter again."

"Can you kill the little brat if it comes to that?"

"Never doubt my word. I'll do exactly what I say." The

voice was hard and mean. There'd be no yielding from that man.

"Well, I think y'all should've listened to me and snatched the older sister. Then we could've sold her in Mexico."

"What makes you think we can't sell this girl? I know a man in Mexico who likes 'em real young. In fact, I think we'll keep the ransom and sell her too. That'll serve Patrick right for swindling us out of our land."

"Hush, you fool. Someone might overhear us. These walls look a mite on the thin side. Never know who's listening."

After that, all Johnny heard was the splash of water.

He hurriedly dried and pulled on his clothes. He'd wait across the street. When the two came out, he'd follow them.

Luckily, night had fallen when Johnny emerged from the bathhouse. He took up a position in the inky shadows.

Two men stepped gingerly from the bathhouse a good half hour later. The burly one more resembled a wild demon animal than he did a man, with his mass of hair that stuck out in all directions and a full beard. In contrast, his bony partner stood but a little over five feet and wore a Mexican serape. Johnny fell in a safe distance behind and kept them in his sights.

The pair stopped by The Red Eye saloon. Johnny waited outside. He was mulling over whether to go in when they came out, carrying a bottle of rotgut. They took the alley beside the saloon and went into an adobe dwelling in the back that had the windows covered with some sort of black material.

Johnny carefully circled the dwelling, hoping to get a glimpse inside. But it turned out the only windows were the two shrouded ones in front. Disappointed, he settled down behind some barrels by the saloon's back door. He'd bet they'd come out when they'd drained the whiskey bottle and needed another.

As he pondered his choices of trying to wait them out or thinking of a possible ruse to get inside, a woman appeared.

The mystery woman walked right up to the door as bold as you please. There was something familiar in the gentle sway of her hips.

Light from the full moon struck her face. He jerked in surprise.

Larissa!

His heart stilled. What on God's green earth was she doing there? When she raised her hand to knock, the spit dried in his mouth. He had to stop her. She could ruin everything on top of getting herself killed.

He sprang from his hiding place, sprinted across the space between them, and grabbed her hand a second before it struck the weather-beaten door. A smothered scream left her throat as he quickly covered her mouth with his.

It was all he could think of to do.

Not that he hadn't wanted to kiss her. Tasting her had been on his mind from the second he'd met her in her daddy's study.

Larissa was warm and pliable in his arms. He could feel her heart beating wildly through the layers of clothing. Her lavender scent ignited his senses, driving all sane thought from his brain.

What was meant only as a way to effectively silence her became something deeper, some fiery passion that threatened to burn him alive. Johnny settled his lips firmly on hers and poured his heart and soul into the kiss.

His tongue swept through her parted lips exploring the wild honey sweetness of her.

He now knew how a wild steer on locoweed felt.

He knew that one taste of her would never be enough.

And he knew how deeply this woman was in his blood.

With eyes closed, Johnny prayed the moment would never end.

Once the initial shock passed, Larissa recovered her senses and fought the sudden assault for all she was worth. She'd known the danger when she'd ventured from the hotel. But she'd been anxious to find the house behind the saloon that the woman who'd brought up her bath had told her about. If only she'd been content to wait for Johnny.

"Wait just a cotton pickin' minute," the stranger urged.

Marshaling every last bit of energy, she finally broke the man's hold. "Let me go, you brute."

"Larissa, it's me." The husky voice came as a shock.

"Diamond?" She gazed up at the rugged moonlit features of the outlaw. "What are you doing?"

"Trying to keep you from—"

Just then the door to the adobe dwelling burst open.

Larissa found herself again yanked into Johnny's arms as he swung her around. She realized he'd positioned himself between her and danger. His protectiveness touched her.

Then his full lips again swept over hers and a mass of tingles cavorted up her spine and spread out to each nerve ending. A golden glow enveloped her.

Her knees buckled and all logical thought fled.

Lifting her arms, she slipped them around Johnny's neck and leaned into the hard wall of muscle of his chest. The softness of his hair brushed the backs of her hands. He smelled of wild Texas sage and saddle leather. And his dark whisker growth only enhanced the dangerous attractiveness that stole her breath.

"What's going on here?" came a surly voice from the doorway of the adobe house.

Johnny glanced up. She felt the rumbling growl low in his throat. "Do you mind? This is a private party. I have no intentions of sharing my woman with you. Get your own."

"If you don't want a bullet between your eyes, gringo, take

your little party somewhere away from here. *Comprende?*"
A Mexican in a serape closed the door halfway and light
from behind showed him glaring through the space.

Larissa jumped when Johnny swatted her bottom.

Her face heated.

"Come on, darlin', appears we're not wanted here." He
put an arm around her waist and drew her close, leading her
toward the front of The Texas Spur.

Out of earshot of the house, she jerked away from him.
"Honestly! You got a little carried away back there. I've
never been so manhandled in my life."

They now stood in light streaming from the hotel. The tic
in his jaw revealed his vexation. "I suppose you'd rather I
let you be shot? What was the meaning of you traipsing
about dark alleyways? Don't you have better sense?"

"I came here to find my sister, not sit in a hotel room."
She jerked her head, lifted her heavy skirts, and stomped up
the steps. The nerve of him! All she was trying to do was
help and this was the thanks she got. As she swept through
the hotel door, he grabbed her arm.

"Not so fast. I want answers. Why were you of all things
about to knock on the door of that adobe house?"

Aware they were drawing stares, she turned to Johnny
and purred, "Darlin', this simply isn't the place to air our
dirty laundry. Can't you wait until we're in private?"

"Of course, sweetheart." He put an arm around her waist
and directed her back out into the street, then hustled her
into the little eating establishment next door. "We might as
well eat. I'm starving. How about you?"

Eating was the furthest thing from her mind after the
searing kiss that had curled her toes, but she needed to find
out what Johnny had discovered.

Once they were seated, he demanded in a low voice,
"What were you thinking when you sashayed that cute little
behind of yours up to that door?"

Larissa gasped at his suggestive language that betrayed the fact he'd been looking at her attributes.

"The woman who brought me bathwater this afternoon told me that two gringos and a Mexican were staying at that place and that she'd heard the sound of female cries coming from it." She glanced at her reflection in the window where they sat. Her cheeks glowed with high color. Nettling anger, coupled with strange heady feelings, swarmed inside her head like a bunch of bees. And with small wonder, seeing all that had just taken place. "I couldn't very well wait for you to come back. Who knows when you might've remembered that I was sitting in the hotel twiddling my thumbs."

A waiter approached their table and took their order. Fried chicken and coffee for Johnny and roast beef for her.

At least Johnny waited until the man was out of earshot before he spewed, "And pray tell what were you going to say when they came to the door?"

"I was going to pretend I'd gotten the wrong house. Or ask for directions to the nearest stage lines . . . or . . . I don't know." She threw up her hands. "I was hoping a plan would come to me. Where have you been?"

Larissa glanced at him, seated across from her. She couldn't stay mad at someone whose touch, whose clear gaze, turned her bones to jelly. She'd been kissed before out behind the barn on the ranch but this was different. Much different. This was the first time she'd been kissed by a man who knew what he wanted and wasn't afraid to take it.

The depths in his blue stare did things to her no other man had done. And right now they were promising to take her to heaven and beyond.

A crooked grin curled one side of his mouth. "I like your dress. Looks real nice." His husky voice unleashed warm shivers. How could she hope to get her relationship with him back on even footing with him doing that?

Everything tilted at a crazy angle. She felt as though she stood on a floor that was higher on one side than the other.

Nervous, she smoothed the full skirt of the sprigged cotton dress she'd bought at the mercantile. They hadn't had much of a selection but she rather liked this pretty shade of daffodil. The only thing wrong was the neckline. It was a tad low for her comfort.

But that was probably what appealed to Diamond, being all male. Her face flamed. She clutched the neckline and gave it a yank. What she wouldn't give for a wrap of some sort, although in this stifling heat it would've smothered her.

Laughter erupted, crinkling the corners of his eyes.

Larissa was mortified. The best thing to do was get the attention off her. And fast. "I see you bought some new clothes, too. But you didn't answer my question. Where have you been since you left me at the hotel?"

Larissa tried to keep her thoughts on what Johnny was saying and away from the sound of that deep voice of his, which aroused every nerve ending. She sternly gave herself a talking to. She needed to focus.

But all she could think about was the way she'd thrown herself into his arms and the feel of his generous mouth on hers.

The reality that he'd kissed her only to keep those men from finding out who they were and why they were there lodged in her mind like a patch of thorny thistle.

It hadn't meant anything.

Yet she couldn't help wonder what it would be like if Johnny Diamond kissed her simply because he wanted to.

Chapter 8

"I got a glimpse of your sister back there." The second Johnny blurted it out he wished he could take it back. That wasn't the way to tell her. What an inconsiderate fool.

"That's wonderful!" Excitement flashed in her rich, earthy gaze. "Let's go get her."

Now she'd want to know how Beth looked and he wasn't prepared to share that the girl had a rope around her neck that was looped over a beam in the ceiling. He couldn't tell her that the kidnappers had shortened that rope so that Beth's tiptoes barely touched the floor. He'd seen that method of torture. When the victim got tired and let her feet lower, the rope would tighten and strangle her. Beth was also wearing a blindfold and was gagged.

No, he couldn't share any of that with Larissa.

But having her in his arms, her body against his had muddied his clear head. It was going to be a sleepless night in more ways than one.

"Just because I know where your sister is doesn't mean I can waltz in there, get her, and waltz right back out. I have to think of a solid plan." Planning was half of getting a job done. He didn't want any of them to end up on a cold slab. Unless it was the monsters who held Beth. Those he wouldn't mind.

Bands of fear encircled his throat. He had the lives of two people in his hands and he didn't know what the outcome would be for any of them.

"What did Beth look like? Have they hurt her?"

Her quiet questions slammed into him like a thick fist. He had no choice but to lie. Otherwise Larissa would probably take matters into her own hands, as headstrong as she was. He could see her marching up to that house, beating the door down, and demanding they release her sister.

And getting killed.

Johnny's mouth went dry. "I only had a split second. I didn't see a whole lot."

"Well, we'll know soon enough, I suppose. I know you'll come up with a solution. You have to."

"I appreciate your vote of confidence. Right now I'm fresh out of ideas. I know the house has only a door and windows in the front. It's the only way inside."

"What if we drive them outside some way?" she asked.

An idea niggled in his brain. Setting fire to the roof could do the trick. And he could be waiting. But was that best for Beth's safety? If he chose to do that, he'd have to use the cover of darkness. That meant tonight.

"That has possibilities, but just so we're clear, it'll be me, not you, who handles this." The waiter brought Johnny's coffee. He blew on it and took a sip. "I have some crow to eat, though. You were right. You've been a huge help. If I'd left you behind, I wouldn't have seen inside that adobe shack and wouldn't have known for sure where your sister is."

Larissa's wide smile lit up her face. "I told you so."

"Then you forgive me for being so . . . forward back there?"

A flash of tears glittered in her eyes. How swiftly her mood had changed. In a matter of moments she had gone from beaming to downright gloomy. "There's nothing to forgive. You were simply doing what you had to. Just forget it ever happened." She raised her chin a notch. "I already have."

Johnny could see he'd hurt her feelings. She'd taken his apology as a rejection. The kisses had clearly meant something to her. And they sure did to him too. *Sam Hill!* To try to explain that he was still sorting out his feelings would only muddle things worse. Better to drop the subject.

The waiter brought their food. Johnny breathed easier when she abandoned the conversation.

A little before midnight, Johnny awakened Larissa. While she gathered her things from the hotel room, he got the horses from the livery and tied them not far from the adobe structure behind The Texas Spur. He'd stuffed what supplies he could in the saddlebags, tied canteens that were full of water onto the horses, and traded the rest of their provisions for a saddle. Couldn't be helped. Beth Patrick needed a horse.

It didn't take Larissa long to meet him.

Careful to make no sound, he rolled a barrel to the side of the dwelling and climbed up to the thatched roof. Taking handfuls of dry tinder from a bag he carried, he arranged it in a pile and struck a match to it. It caught instantly.

Saying a prayer that the desperadoes wouldn't leave Beth inside to die, he sprang to the ground. He returned the barrel to its shadowy place beside the back hotel door and took up a position behind it.

Larissa crouched beside him, shaking like a scared rabbit. He'd have admitted to a case of nerves too if she'd have asked him. So many things could go wrong. He took her hand and squeezed it.

"It'll be all right. We'll get your sister," he whispered in her ear. "You just have the horses ready. I'll do the rest."

About that time there was a whooshing sound and the whole roof went up in flames. He slid his Colt from the holster and readied himself.

Men's yells filled the air. Within seconds, the front door opened and three figures ran out.

Johnny froze.

Beth wasn't with them.

Just before he dashed into the burning dwelling he saw her through the thick smoke that billowed from the door. The man with bushy hair had slung Beth over his shoulder.

In all the commotion, Bushy Hair didn't see Johnny until he stuck his Colt into the man's side. "Give me the girl," he ordered.

Both the short man who wore the Mexican serape and his sidekick raised their hands above their heads.

Bushy Hair lowered Beth until her feet touched the ground. Keeping his Colt trained on Bushy's heart, Johnny swept the girl to his side. Beth clung desperately to him, sobbing.

"Now, give me your weapon," Johnny barked.

"Ain't got one. It's in there." Bushy pointed to the inferno.

"You'd better hope so. How about the rest of you?"

The two men sullenly shook their heads.

I want them stopped and stopped for good. That was Dunston Patrick's last words.

But considering they were unarmed and Johnny had a real problem with shooting someone in cold blood, he warned, "Follow us and you'll die. I promise that."

"You better kill us while you have the chance, mister," said Bushy.

"I don't shoot unarmed men. You come and I'll have a bullet waiting with your name on it." Johnny backed toward the horses that Larissa had already untied and headed in the right direction. She made a great partner in crime.

"Beth, I'm so glad to see you." Larissa gave her sister a big hug.

"We'll have time for a proper reunion later," Johnny promised, putting Beth on the packhorse. "Right now, we can't waste time."

Larissa didn't argue. She pulled herself into the saddle and readied to ride.

When daylight broke over the desert landscape, they'd put a fair distance between them and Del Rio. And now that they could see where they were going, they'd be able to ride faster. He was glad Larissa and Beth were accomplished horsewomen. No matter how fast he rode, they easily kept up the pace.

At Devils River they stopped to rest the horses.

Larissa jumped from her horse almost before it halted and ran to her sister. Her heart stopped when she saw the dark bruises and the dried blood around one corner of Beth's mouth. Also visible was an angry red welt around her sister's neck. Larissa wrapped her arms around her younger sibling. She couldn't stop the sudden tears. How would they ever repay Johnny for bringing them back together?

"I was so worried about you. Are you okay?" Larissa asked.

Beth rubbed her forehead. "I'm okay now. I didn't think anyone would ever come for me. It seemed a long time."

"Let me introduce you to the man who set you free." Taking Beth's arm, Larissa led her to where Johnny stood by his horse watching them. "Beth, this is Johnny Diamond. He never gave up on finding you."

"Thank you for saving me," the girl said shyly.

A muscle twitched in Johnny's jaw and his eyes narrowed

when he saw the bruises in the bright sunlight. He offered a smile and stuck out his hand. "It was my pleasure. Nice to finally meet you, Beth."

Larissa gently massaged Beth's thin shoulders. "Come, let me wash your face. Would you like that? This is the only water for a while, so we have to take advantage of it."

Beth nodded.

Larissa tore a piece of cloth from the blouse she'd worn with the split skirt. Then taking Beth's hand, they walked to the riverbank. A lump formed in Larissa's throat, hindering her ability to swallow, as she tenderly washed away some of the traces of cruelty.

"Beth, did those men make you remove your clothes?" She hated asking, but she needed to know for her own sanity.

"No. They only beat me when I was too slow to follow their orders. And they tied a rope around my neck like I was an animal. Why? What did I do?" Beth's voice cracked.

Larissa's heart broke. "I don't know why, sweetheart. But you didn't do anything. Put that out of your mind."

She drew Beth close and held her. One way or another she meant to have justice for her sister. Johnny could make them pay, but if he refused, she'd find someone else to help her.

From the corner of her eye, Larissa noticed that Johnny was gathering material to make a fire. Her outlaw needed some coffee or she'd miss her guess. After leaving Beth at the water's edge, she located the beat-up pot and the ground coffee and got it ready for him.

After getting the fire started, Johnny stared intently into the distance.

She caught him scanning the trail behind them. He didn't have to tell her that trouble was coming. She felt it in her bones. The kidnappers wouldn't give up without a fight. They'd be out for blood this time.

Only this time they'd not take hostages.

Those men would kill them all.

And one had only to look at Beth to know they were capable.

Despite the scorching heat from the sun, shivers ran the length of her.

Larissa's glance found her sister. Beth had never harmed another being. She'd been so innocent before all this happened. Now she was covered in bruises and wore a haunted look. Who knew the full scope of all she'd endured that she locked inside her head.

Johnny touched Larissa's arm, startling her. "You and Beth need to stay close. Don't wander off."

"They're coming, aren't they?"

"I'm just being cautious, I reckon." Whether it was a grimace or a smile that quirked the corner of his mouth, it was gone as quickly as it had formed.

"I'll sacrifice myself before I'll let them have Beth again," she said in a brittle voice. "She's gone through things no little girl should have to." Larissa bit her trembling lip.

Johnny caressed her cheek with the knuckle of his forefinger. "I'll not let them have either of you."

"Why won't they leave us alone?"

"It has a lot to do with money. There's no explaining evil in a man's heart."

Johnny's parents' only crime had been in being at the wrong place at the wrong time. Beth had been safe in her own home yet the bad men had taken her. Her sister had been but a pawn that those men had used against their father.

Larissa's breath caught in her throat as she put it all together. "My father set these wheels in motion, either on purpose or accidentally. Either way, he's to blame. Beth paid for his bad decisions."

He sighed. "Appears that way."

"I always knew he was ruthless and craved power but I didn't know the full measure of it. I guess I didn't want to see the truth. When a person comes face-to-face with the facts, they have to make a choice. They can continue on and try to wear blinders or they can make changes." She gave him a weak smile. "I guess I was afraid to see too much, afraid of what I'd have to do about it."

"Change is hard, especially for a woman."

"I'm starting as of this minute. I want to hire your services."

"I still work for your father. What do you want me to do?"

"Hunt down those men and make them pay."

"I plan on doing that . . . free of charge."

"Another thing." She jutted her chin. "Just so you know, I'm not sorry you kissed me."

"I'm not sorry either." He pushed back his black Stetson, his crystal blues staring into her eyes.

Larissa's heart fluttered with his nearness. The air shifted in a strange way whenever he was close. She didn't have to close her eyes to remember the way his mouth had settled on hers as though she was a piece a land he was laying claim to.

She couldn't remember ever feeling so fully a woman.

His head lowered and she held her breath. It seemed he might kiss her again.

Instead, his breath ruffled the tendrils of hair beside her ear. "My dear Larissa," he drawled, velvet softness wrapping each word. "One of these days I'll accept what you're willing to give and I won't be shy about taking it."

Chapter 9

The setting sun splashed a myriad of orange and purple hues across the expansive desert floor that was littered with scrub brush. A day of hard riding had brought them to the limestone outcroppings in which Johnny and Larissa had ridden out the sandstorm.

Johnny pulled up near a cave and dismounted. "We have to stop. The horses are exhausted and we're not far behind them."

Larissa nodded and slid from her horse while he helped Beth off the packhorse. He wished Larissa had waited. He loved any excuse to put his hands on her, to feel the warmth of her body, the satiny texture of her skin.

Leading the horses into the rock shelter, he turned to watch her. Her hips gently swayed, her skirts swirling around booted ankles, as she moved to help Beth. He pictured Larissa in his bed wearing nothing but a come-hither smile on her face. He stumbled over an uneven place in the cave floor, so busy was he watching her.

He shouldn't be thinking about her.

Or bedrooms.

Or the way her hips moved when she walked.

Or kissing.

He had to keep his mind sharp so he could get them home alive. He turned his gaze away.

Although he hadn't said anything, he'd noticed a dust cloud behind them. At first he'd thought it was simply a dust devil, a swirling wind that formed a miniature cyclone. But since the dust hadn't died down as it should have after a while, he knew it was riders. Three or four of them if he had to guess.

And they were coming hard and fast.

A good way to kill a horse.

But if by miracle the horses somehow lasted, if they only rested them a short time and kept riding, they could catch up to them in a matter of hours.

He didn't like the sour feeling in his gut.

Nothing he could do about the situation except to get ready for a fight.

Had he been by himself, he'd have turned and ridden straight for them. Sometimes it paid to go on the offensive, instead of maintaining defense.

But he wasn't alone. He had responsibilities.

Johnny glanced at Larissa and her sister, who were sitting on the cave floor. Beth was sobbing quietly while Larissa held her, crooning softly. The girl had been through the backside of hell and he had no choice but to put her through more.

Turning, he unsaddled the horses. Then he grabbed his rifle and knelt in front of Larissa. "I'm going to see what I can scrounge for supper. Stay inside the cave."

"Be careful." She reached out to lightly touch his hand.

"I'm leaving my Colt. Just in case." Johnny laid it beside her.

In the waning twilight, he killed a couple of rabbits. He was walking back to the cave when he heard a gunshot. His blood froze and he sprang forward like a rock from a slingshot.

Near the cave entrance, he dropped the rabbits. Flattening himself against the limestone, he gripped the rifle and listened for voices.

Everything was quiet. He crept forward, his finger on the trigger of the rifle, every nerve taut.

Then he saw Larissa. She was pointing the Colt at the floor. He stole toward her and took the gun from her trembling hands. In the low light, he made out a deadly rattlesnake at her feet. He let out the breath he'd been holding.

Larissa thrust the Colt at him and threw her arms around his neck. "I was afraid I'd miss and the thing would strike."

"But it didn't. You did real good." He reveled in the feel of her in his arms, the rapid beat of her heart, the fragrance of her swimming up his nose.

Perhaps conscious of Beth's eyes on them, Larissa pulled away and took a tremulous breath. "I did, didn't I?"

"I couldn't have done better myself."

"Did you find some game for supper?"

"Rabbits. I dropped them outside the cave. Wasn't sure what I'd find in here." He picked up the snake and threw it out of the cave.

Larissa patted her hair, smoothing it back. "I'll hunt for some firewood while you skin the rabbits."

"No, stay in here with your sister. I'll fetch some wood. The evening's filled with predators." *Both the four-legged and two-legged variety,* he added to himself.

At least the cave would hide the campfire and not reveal their position. That was a plus. A hot meal would go a long way toward replenishing stamina for them all.

"I can't sit idle while you do all the work."

"You can get out the coffeepot and get it ready. A cup would sure be mighty nice."

A little while later, they had their stomachs full. Beth yawned big and stretched. Johnny spread out his bedroll beside Larissa's and offered it to Beth. He'd have no need for it. He'd stand guard while they slept.

It wasn't long before the two women bedded down. He took up watch near the cave entrance. The men would have to go through him to get to Larissa and Beth.

Their quiet breathing kept his thoughts focused on the job at hand. His life wasn't worth a plug nickel, him being an outlaw and all, but their lives were worth fighting for. His jaw hardened. Come hell or high water, he would ensure them a future to be and do whatever they desired.

In the quiet solitude of the night, he thought about his life. He'd give anything to go back and undo some of the things he'd done.

While he'd never shot anyone who hadn't fired at him first, he could've had more patience and looked for a non-violent solution.

He could've tried harder to be a better man.

None of that had mattered until now.

He'd never figured on meeting a woman like Larissa. She made him examine the choices he'd made.

What he wouldn't give to wake up beside her every day.

Suddenly Beth let out a bloodcurdling scream and sat up. *"No!"*

Johnny jumped to his feet and started toward her, but Larissa beat him, taking her sister into her arms and softly assuring the girl she was safe. He watched Larissa's devotion to Beth. Deep abiding love for her sister showed in everything Larissa did. As he thought of his own sisters, who perished on the Llano Estacado, his eyes misted. He'd give anything to be able to tell them how much he loved them.

He sat back down and watched Larissa calm the girl. It didn't take too long for Beth to go back to sleep. Then, instead of lying back down on her bedroll, Larissa came and dropped down beside him.

"A nightmare?" He moved until their shoulders touched.

"Afraid so. Frankly, I'm not surprised, seeing what she's gone through. Have you seen anything?"

Nothing but a wasted life.

"It's quiet out there so far," he answered.

"Johnny, you can be honest with me. I know you wouldn't stand guard if you didn't see the need for it. Any idea when those men will attack?"

"No. Just my gut telling me it'll be soon."

"You should've killed them back there in Del Rio." Her voice was as hard as a piece of flint. It startled him.

"Shooting unarmed men in cold blood isn't my style."

"They deserve it. It's going to take Beth a long time to get over this. Her little heart was pounding and her clothes were drenched. She's so terrified it doesn't matter if she's awake or asleep."

"We'll let her rest another hour or so and then we'll need to ride out. Want to get a jump on daylight. Maybe you should lie back down while you can."

Larissa shook her head. "I'm wide awake. I'll just sit here with you if you don't mind."

The company was nice. He sure wasn't about to turn down spending these quiet moments with her. He'd take as much as he could get and try to store it up for the long dry spells ahead.

The inky blackness had lightened to a heavy gray by the time they'd ridden a few miles. Larissa kept a close eye on Beth without trying to smother the girl. Johnny kept glancing behind and knowing what he was looking for brought Larissa chills.

A cloak of doom seemed to envelop them.

Larissa followed Johnny down a steep ravine. As Arabella was climbing up the other side her foreleg turned wrong and the mare went down.

Larissa screamed, more afraid for the animal than herself.

Johnny turned around and leaped from the saddle. He grabbed Larissa and pulled her free.

It was a struggle but the mare got to her feet, shuddering and shaking her head. Larissa rubbed her beloved friend's neck, speaking softly, while Johnny examined its foreleg. She prayed it wasn't serious. She'd had Arabella for eight years and wasn't ready to lose her.

"It's not broken, just a bad sprain," Johnny announced.

"Thank God!" Larissa wiped tears from her eyes.

Johnny's gaze met hers. "You and Beth will have to ride double now. This will slow us down, but we'll make it."

"And Arabella?"

"She'll make it too if we don't push her."

He cupped his hands to form a step and helped her up behind Beth. He grabbed Arabella's reins and mounted his Appaloosa. Mindful that they were sitting ducks, he urged the horses to a fast walk.

Trouble caught up to them when they stopped to rest the horses in the shade of a rocky outcropping.

Johnny shouted a hoarse warning and shoved her and Beth behind a group of boulders while he hurried back for their mounts. Breathing hard, he led the animals to safety as the first shots rang out.

Larissa put her arm around Beth as they crouched low. Bullets zinged into the rocks and over their heads. Johnny returned fire.

"Got you cornered now, don't we?" yelled a voice during a lull. "Whoo-ee! How you like them apples?"

"What do you want?" Johnny's curt question could've sliced through steel. It left little room to think he'd be open to compromise.

"Well, let's see. There's the little matter of money. You beat us out of the ransom. And we'll take the Patrick women."

"Not gonna happen," shouted Johnny as he reloaded his Colt.

"Oh no? Care to make a wager on that? There's three of us against you and two helpless females."

Helpless? Larissa would show them she wouldn't wring her hands and cower. Spying Johnny's Winchester in the scabbard, she sprinted for the Appaloosa. Keeping low, she returned. Ratcheting the lever of the Winchester, she took aim at the trio's hiding place. The men were lying on their bellies in the dry creek bed of a draw.

Johnny's gaze reflected admiration when he glanced her way. His regard filled her with warmth. It felt good to be of use.

The sun beat down on their heads. Sweat ran into her eyes, making them sting. Each time she grew weary, she had only to remember what they'd done to Beth.

"Larissa, trade with me." Johnny handed her his Colt and took the rifle. "I'm going to try to circle around and come up behind them. You keep shooting. Do you know how to reload?"

"I think so." The Colt was heavy so she gripped it in both hands.

He gave her a quick demonstration and laid a box of bullets beside her. "In case I don't make it back, I want you to save two bullets—one for you and one for Beth. Don't let them take you alive."

Hot tears threatened, but she held them at bay. "Okay. Promise you'll be careful."

"I plan on it." He leaned and brushed her mouth with his in a quick kiss.

Then he disappeared into the low brush.

Fear dried the moisture in her mouth. Could she look Beth in the eye and pull the trigger, ending her life? She swallowed hard.

Dear God she prayed she wouldn't have to.

Time dragged painfully slow. She kept her eyes on the creek bed. Nothing moved. Not a bird, a blade of grass, or a man who wanted them dead.

What was happening? Where was Johnny?

Beside her, Beth whispered, "I'm scared, Larissa."

"I know, honey. I am too. It'll all be over with soon. Johnny will get us out of this."

"You have feelings for him, don't you?"

Larissa recalled his muscled chest and how safe she felt wrapped in his arms. The gentle way he brushed her cheek with his finger. And his full lips on hers, taking and giving in equal measure.

"Yes, I guess I do. I didn't mean for it to be so obvious, though." Before she could say more, movement caught her attention. Three men strode from the creek bed.

Her heart gave a painful lurch.

Johnny Diamond led the way with a gun jammed into his side.

Chapter 10

"Pitch that hog leg down here, girly. You and your sister come out." The snarl made the hair rise on Larissa's arms.

"Don't do it!" Johnny yelled. "Remember what I told you."

Larissa met Beth's frightened stare. She could no more put a bullet in her sister's head than she could fly over the moon. The hand holding the Colt shook.

"You do as I say or I'll shoot him, here and now, right in front of you. What's it to be? Does he live or die? No skin off my nose either way." The man doing the speaking had the appearance of a shaggy grizzly. He had enough hair on his head and face for a dozen men.

Glancing at Beth's bruises, she knew the man didn't bluff. She weighed her choices. There were three kidnappers. Even if she managed to shoot one, there'd be two others to deal with.

And she might miss them and hit Johnny.

She couldn't take that risk.

"Larissa, they aim to kill us no matter what we do." As the words left Johnny's mouth, the hairy man hit him with the pistol. Larissa winced. Blood oozed from a gash on Johnny's cheek.

"You got three seconds to make up your mind. Then he dies." The warning carried in the stifling air.

She wet her dry lips and took Beth's hand.

"One. Two."

"Stop. We're coming." Larissa hurled the Colt toward them and she and Beth stood. Her legs trembled as she helped her sister down the rocky incline.

"That's more like it." The man's grin showed yellow rotten teeth. "You're a lot more reasonable than your papa."

Standing in front of the man, Larissa tried not to breathe his stench. If they were to die, she wanted some answers first. "Why are you doing this? What have we done to you?"

"The children must pay for the sins of the father."

She ignored Johnny's silent plea to keep her tongue. "What did Dunston Patrick do to you?"

"You're awfully curious, girly."

"I know my father wronged you somehow. He did a lot of people."

"You want to know?" The man wiped his mouth with his dirty sleeve. "The great Dunston Patrick gave me an ultimatum. I leave the land I'd bought and paid for or he'd make me sorry. But I refused to be run off. One night he sent some riders. They set fire to the house. I escaped the flames but my wife and son didn't. They were burned alive. He did the same to Pedro and McGee here."

Larissa gasped. Still, she wondered if the man truly spoke the truth. "How do you know those men worked for my father?"

"They told me. Besides, the riders pitched Patrick's calling card at my feet before they rode off."

Her stomach lurched. "What kind of card?"

"The four of spades from a deck of cards."

That confirmed it. The man's account was true. Her father had a lot to answer for, and if they got out of this mess, she'd make sure he would.

"I'm sorry for what they did, Mister . . . ?"

"Never you mind what my name is. And I don't want your pity. I want justice."

"Then seek it with Patrick," Johnny spat. "Leave his daughters out of it."

"Cain't do that." The man put his mouth by Johnny's ear and said softly, "Patrick set the rules. I'm only following them."

The man wearing the serape, Pedro, spoke up. "An eye for an eye."

"You never intended to give Beth back, did you?" she demanded, her stomach twisting with the knowledge.

"After we got rid of her, we were coming back for you. But that's enough talk." The man shoved Larissa and Beth toward his partners.

"Let's put a bullet in them right here," said the third man, McGee, who'd grabbed a sobbing Beth.

"Johnny Diamond has no part in this. He doesn't deserve to die." Larissa fought Pedro's crushing grip. "He's innocent."

"He shouldn't have decided to work for Patrick," came the answer from the hairy man. "We let him go and he'll dog us to the end of the earth. No, he dies right along with you and your sister."

Suddenly, Johnny swung. Six feet three inches of enraged outlaw filled her sights. He wrenched the gun from the hairy man's surprised grasp. And in the next instant Johnny fired a shot, hitting the man between the eyes. The force of the bullet sent the man flying backward to the ground.

"Let the Patrick women go," Johnny ordered, turning the weapon on Pedro and McGee.

Larissa watched the drama praying they'd listen.

But they didn't heed. Both men raised their pistols. Larissa screamed and shut her eyes. There were two gun blasts. When she opened her eyes, Pedro and McGee lay sprawled in the desert dirt and smoke still curled from Johnny's firearm.

She ran to Beth. "Are you all right?"

"I'm okay," Beth answered numbly, staring at droplets of blood on her hands. Larissa gently wiped McGee's blood from Beth's bruised cheek, then cleaned the girl's hands with the hem of her dress.

It was over.

Johnny Diamond had kept his word. He got Beth back and none of them got killed except the ones who'd tracked them down.

"Reckon we need some grub for supper. I'll see what I can find." Johnny slid his rifle from the scabbard at the end of a very long, draining day.

After burying the three kidnappers, they'd ridden back to the small stream where he and Larissa had spent the first night on their way to Del Rio. A quick glance found her tenderly checking Arabella's sprained leg.

Beth was washing her face and arms in the stream. The girl seemed obsessive about the act. Larissa had told him Beth was trying to scrub away all traces of the kidnappers' touch from her skin. The child didn't know the main problem was that their filth had imbedded itself in her head. It'd take a while to get that out. He knew a thing or two about that subject.

Larissa's eyes met his and she gave him a weary smile. "I'll find some wood for a fire and get coffee made."

Johnny moved closer. What he had to say was meant for her ears alone. "You do know the way to a man's heart. I'd just about strap a saddle to a mangy coyote for a cup of brew."

He lifted a finger and ran it gently across her lips. "I'd

give anything to kiss you right now. But once I start I won't want to stop. Guess it'll have to wait for a better time."

The pulse in the hollow of her throat throbbed.

"Yes. It might be best." Her throaty voice lowered. "We need to talk about some . . . things. Destiny smiled on us when you came to the ranch. I don't know what I . . . we'd have done without you, Johnny."

It was a two-way street. Larissa had changed him. She'd taught him that there was more to life than simply existing, going from town to town, not caring where he wound up. A man found joy in sharing the good with the bad. Nothing meant anything unless it was shared. It was time he thought about changing his life permanently.

He wanted Larissa with every fiber of his being.

"You give me too much credit. I only did what anyone with an ounce of decency would've done. The real heroes are you and your sister." He tucked a strand of hair behind her ear.

Maybe, just maybe she could find room in her heart for an unshaven, worn-out old outlaw. He could hope.

Johnny might've asked her about the possibility if Beth hadn't chosen that moment to interrupt them to announce she was hungry. His glance promised Larissa they'd talk later.

And he meant to say what was on his mind.

Two hours passed before he found his chance. Beth had crawled onto his bedroll and was sound asleep.

Larissa stared into the flames of the fire, deep in thought.

Sensitive to her low spirits, he moved to sit beside her on the rock next to hers. "Penny for your thoughts."

She turned. Tears in her eyes punched into his chest like a closed fist. "I doubt they'd be worth a plug nickel."

"Let me be the judge of that. What's on your mind?"

"My life. We'll be back at the ranch tomorrow. I refuse to live with my father another day after what he's done." Her heavy sigh drifted in the night breeze. "Nor will I subject

Beth to his care any longer. But where will we go? What will I do? I don't have the answers."

Johnny pulled her against his chest and wrapped his arms around her. "What about your other sister? Can you stay with her until you get your bearings?"

"Charlotte's small house is bulging at the seams. I won't add to their problems."

"Is there anyone in Sonora that you can stay with until you find something of your own? Are there other relatives?"

"None that I know about. Papa kept us isolated. Wouldn't allow us to have any friends. But maybe I can find a job in town. Don't exactly know what I'd do, though."

He kissed the top of her head, relishing the warmth of her body. "I've always found that a good night's sleep helps make things more clear."

"Your magic solution?"

Larissa leaned back to look up at him. The silvery moonlight bathed her in glorious rays. Johnny hadn't the will to resist temptation. He took her face in his hands and kissed her eyelids, the impudent tip of her nose, and the alluring curve of her jaw before moving to her mouth.

But he took his time. This was something he wanted to savor. He slowly outlined her rosy lips with tiny feathery kisses before capturing them in earnest.

Drawn to the soft curves now within his grasp, he cupped the gentle swell of her breast and knew he'd found heaven.

It was at that moment that he knew he couldn't live the rest of his life without her. She'd shown him just how empty and alone he'd been. He couldn't go back to his old ways as if nothing had happened. He'd changed.

Larissa Patrick gave his life meaning. He was nothing without her.

She returned his kiss with a passion and fire that made him grow weak.

Lifting his mouth from hers, he stared at her with wonder.

"I love you, Larissa Patrick. I never believed it possible, but I love you with all my heart and soul. Marry me."

"Marry you?" She'd barely breathed the words.

"I warned you that the time would come when I'd take what you were willing to give and I wouldn't be shy about it. The time is here. I'm not shy. I want you. I need you bad. So, what do you say? Do you think you can grow to love a set-in-his-ways outlaw?"

"Yes. I already do. I knew when you kissed me outside that adobe house in Del Rio. I was afraid that I read too much into it, though, and you didn't feel that way about me."

Johnny drowned in the depths of her liquid brown eyes that were rimmed with thick, lush lashes. "To set the record straight and get rid of any doubts you may have, you are my here and now. You are my always and forever. My future is tied with yours, pretty lady."

Chapter 11

Johnny's hoarse declaration seemed to squeeze through a narrowed windpipe that left the words bruised. Waves of heat flooded Larissa's blood. She reached up to caress the stubborn square jaw that was covered with dark stubble.

She loved this man, utterly and wholly.

A deep breath failed to calm the trembles that had left a quickening in her stomach. "That was very poetic, Johnny Diamond. My words are far simpler—I love you back. I'll be proud to be your wife."

Johnny kissed the hand that cupped his jaw, setting off another round of delicious tingles. "Now that we have that settled, I think it's time I came clean about something."

Larissa steeled herself. Was this where he'd tell her he was a wanted man? Maybe wanted for robbery or even murder? Maybe running from a rope? Well, it didn't matter. She'd fallen head over heels in love with this man, no matter what he'd done.

The night air didn't help her nerves. "I know everything I need to know about you. Let's let sleeping dogs lie. Okay?"

"I don't want anything to ever come between us. You ought to know the facts."

She sat back, putting some space between them. "If I

can't talk you out of it, then I guess you'd best say what's on your mind."

Johnny grinned. "Johnny Diamond is a made-up name. I was born Marion Applebaum. Sam Whiskey gave me the Diamond name, said it was more fitting for an outlaw."

Marion Applebaum? She worked hard to swallow the giggle. "Are you wanting to go back to your real name? Is that why you're telling me this?"

"It's your call. I want you to decide which name you want attached to yours."

"You've spent the better portion of your life being Johnny Diamond. Let's just stick with it if you don't mind."

"Glad you agree, because that was my thinking on the subject."

"Then you're not a wanted man?"

"Only by you. If you do, that is."

Larissa scooted close enough to hear the wild beating of his heart. She pressed her lips to his. "I want you more than you can possibly know. Any other things you want to get off your chest?"

"One other thing before we turn in." He gave her a leisurely kiss. "From now on, you'll be the keeper of my heart. I know you'll guard it well."

They crossed back onto Four Spades land midmorning the next day. Breakfast sat like a rock on Larissa's stomach. It would take all her gumption to confront her father. His stern, unyielding demeanor had always intimidated her.

But with Johnny on her side she could face anything.

She glanced at him, admiring the way he sat in the saddle, his broad shoulders straight, his eyes constantly scanning the landscape. From the hawk circling high overhead to the scurry of a jackrabbit through the brush, nothing got by him. He cast a long shadow over the land and the people who walked it.

To be the keeper of his heart was a scary thing. Even as

excitement spread with thoughts of spending her life with him, she didn't know if she was up for the huge responsibility.

He'd given her a great treasure.

Beth rode in front of her on the packhorse. The girl was fidgety and on edge.

Larissa put an arm around her. "Are you all right, honey?"

"Papa's going to be real mad."

"Don't worry your head about that. The only reason we're going to the ranch is to gather our things." Larissa and Johnny had already told Beth their plans to marry and that she'd live with them. Beth had seemed happy with the arrangement.

"But still . . ."

"You're not changing your mind about coming with Johnny and me are you?"

"No. I just hate having Papa mad at us."

"Some things can't be helped, I'm afraid."

An hour later, they rode up to the house. Dunston Patrick strode from the front door. His face was heavy and thick with anger. "It's about time you got back."

Johnny helped Beth down and reached up for Larissa. She slid into his embrace. Keeping his arm around her, he turned to face her father. "I got the job done. Didn't know you'd set a time limit on returning."

"You ought've left Larissa with the kidnappers," Dunston told Johnny. "She's no longer welcome here. She knew better than to defy me."

Johnny's arm tightened around Larissa. "Reckon we won't have a problem then, because she's coming with me."

Larissa's pounding heart was loud in her ears. "We're getting married. We only came to get Beth's and my things. We'll soon be on our way."

"Beth isn't going anywhere," Patrick barked.

"Just try to stop her. She knows the truth about you. We both know how you sent your men to burn down the houses that happened to sit on the land you wanted and would have by any means. You're a murderer. You have blood on your hands. We know how your men burned a man's wife and son alive." Larissa shook with burning fury.

Her father's eyes darkened in his mottled face. "They refused to leave. I had every right to do what I did."

"That's all you have to say? Nothing is ever the great Dunston Patrick's fault. It's always someone else in the wrong. Who knows how many others have died at your hands."

"That's none of your concern. I always provided for you and your sisters. You didn't complain about having plenty to eat and pretty clothes to wear."

"There's more to being a father than focusing on material things. We needed love, but you were unable or unwilling to give it. We needed to know that we mattered." She pulled Beth close. "We might as well have been one of your animals."

Dunston threw up his hands and whirled to go back inside.

"I'll have the rest of the money I earned." Johnny's voice sliced the air. "I completed my end of the bargain."

"By stealing my daughters? You'd best think again."

Larissa watched Johnny's jaw twitch. Foolish man, her father. He didn't know Johnny could simply take whatever he wanted, if that was what he had a mind to do.

Johnny's voice hardened. "I'll exchange the money for a wagon then, to haul Larissa's and Beth's belongings and we'll call it even."

Patrick shot them an angry glare. "I'll pile everything they own out here in front of the house and set fire to it before I let them take even a stitch of clothes. Everything they have I gave them. It all belongs to me."

Larissa was grateful for Johnny's strength around her or she would have collapsed.

She'd known her father would be angry. But refusing to let them have even their clothes was beyond understanding.

"Come on, darlin'." Johnny turned her toward the horses. "I'll buy you whatever you need. We won't beg him for a blessed thing."

Once they were all mounted on their horses, Johnny turned for one last word before they rode out. "Just know that we'll be stopping in Sonora for a word with the marshal. He'll be watching you, Patrick. Anything at all that goes wrong in this county he'll be coming after you."

Larissa didn't look back as they rode away. And she didn't take a deep breath until they were off Patrick land. It saddened her to leave the ranch where she had been born and raised, but excitement bubbled inside. Her place now was by Johnny's side.

Two weeks later, Johnny flicked the reins of the draft horses that were pulling their wagon. He draped one arm around his new wife and smiled. Larissa and he had said their vows in front of the preacher in Sonora. Right now he was more contented than a man had a right to be.

Larissa nestled against him. "How much farther?"

"Just around the bend, my darling Mrs. Diamond."

"Can't you give us a hint where you're taking us?" pestered Beth, who was perched on top of a trunk in the wagon bed.

Johnny grinned. "You'll see soon enough."

"Just one question, dear husband. This house and land is not from ill-gotten gain, is it?"

"I'm wounded." He placed a hand over his heart mockingly. "The place belongs to me lock, stock, and barrel. And I came by it honest. It belonged to Sam Whiskey, given to him by his parents. Sam passed it on to me when he died, seeing as how he didn't have any family left. I just never had a reason to live out here until now. Truth to tell, I found it really lonely. I figure you'll change all that."

He watched Larissa take in the lush rolling hills and quiet woods of the Texas Hill Country.

"It's breathtaking," she murmured.

"Thought you'd like it."

He urged the team around a crook in the road, turned into a narrow lane, and stopped in front of a two-story frame house. "We're here."

Beth barely waited for the wagon to stop before she hopped out and ran for a closer look.

"Oh my goodness!" Larissa exclaimed. "It's beautiful. I can't believe it's ours."

He jumped down from the wagon box and turned. Placing his hands around her waist, he swung her easily to the ground. Instead of letting her go, he tucked her next to him. He'd never tire of feeling her soft curves or listening to her heartbeat, steady and true.

He lowered his head and captured her mouth. She raised a hand to caress his hair. His breath became ragged with desire.

Finally she pulled away. "We have a lot to do before bedtime, Mr. Diamond."

"Yes, ma'am. Nighttime can't come soon enough for me, though," he drawled.

Her skirts swirled around his pants legs as they strolled toward their future.

He opened the screen door, then scooped her into his arms and carried her across the threshold. "This is a fine place to raise a passel of kids and enough food so we won't starve."

"And exactly how many kids is a passel?"

"I reckon ten or so oughta be enough."

"Good heavens! I'll have to unpack my rolling pin first thing. I'll need something to fend you off with," she replied with a twinkle in her fluid brown eyes.

Johnny chuckled. He couldn't wait to get started on their family.

For a man who'd once lost everyone and everything he owned, life was looking particularly rosy.

And all it had taken was finding trouble in petticoats.

Texas Flame

Phyliss Miranda

*To Elaine Standish, Kim Campbell,
Molly McKnight, and Ginger Porter,
fellow writers, friends, and critique partners
who have always known when I needed a hug
and when I deserved a kick in
the behind to keep me motivated.
Thank you, ladies.*

*In appreciation also to my coauthors,
Jodi Thomas, Linda Broday, and DeWanna Pace,
who helped me through the tough times
and celebrated the good ones.*

Chapter 1

Texas Panhandle, 1889

"Don't come a step closer!" Savannah Parker leveled her Winchester shotgun directly at Ethan Kimble's chest.

"Damn it, Anna, put that dern gun down," Ethan said harshly, trying not to allow his frustration with the fiery red-head to show. "I haven't given up four months of my life to chase you from Galveston to this blasted dugout to let you shoot me."

A small stone and timber shelter nested into the side of the canyon. Thunderclouds bellowing in an otherwise true blue Texas sky provided a backdrop for the red and gray layered canyon walls. No doubt the lawman would have to duck to get through the door of the dwelling if he were invited in, which he doubted was gonna happen if she had anything to do with it.

A mangy dog covered with splotches of red and gray mud stood guard at the woman's side, seemingly not too disturbed that a stranger had approached but certainly not willing to leave his master's side. Ethan figured if Anna hadn't been holding the gun with both hands that she'd be pettin' the dang wild-eyed critter.

Ethan took stock of the shooting end of the firearm, which quivered slightly. Although he'd known Savannah Parker ever since she was too short to pump water, he'd never known of her handling a firearm, and by the visible shaking of her hands, she hadn't had much practice since the last time he'd seen her. He'd certainly prefer to face a steady gun any day than a nervous shooter . . . woman or not.

"What do you want with me, *Dimples*?" She put extra emphasis on the nickname only she could get by with using.

"Don't you dare call me that, Savannah!" He deliberately used her given name in retaliation. "I guess it slipped your mind that you robbed your father's bank and snubbed the whole blasted town when you tipped your bonnet and said, 'Good morning,' before you ran off with the rest of *your* gang—"

"Ethan Kimble, I can't believe you're accusing me of such atrocities!" she blurted out. "What would your mama think?"

"I'm sure she was relieved that she didn't have any money in that bank, and since she didn't give a squat for your father, she might have even been happy." He swallowed hard but didn't let his guard down, making sure his shooting arm didn't move an iota.

A low growl came from deep inside the dog. His intensity was certainly a pause for caution. No doubt the tone in Ethan's voice was more threatening than even he would have liked. The hound bared teeth, to reinforce the earlier warning.

"It's okay, Bones," Anna almost whispered, but the dog stood his territory between his master and her visitor. Ethan sure wasn't all that confident that the son-of-a-biscuit-eater wouldn't lunge at him if he so much as sneezed.

"Get that confounded flea-bitten mutt under control or I'll—"

"You'll what? Shoot him?" She lifted the gun higher, but

from the look on the face of the fiery redhead she'd already made up her mind what Ethan would do.

"You know I've never killed an animal in my life unless it was for food. I don't figure on startin' now, so don't plan on eatin' a tough cut of mutt tonight," he retorted in chilly sarcasm, clenching his mouth tight.

"No, Ethan, I don't know what you've been doing since you left Galveston in your quest for fortune and fame." Savannah kept the Winchester pointed at the man, finger resting heavily on the trigger. "I presume you've been gallivanting across Texas hunting down outlaws. And, for all I know, you may have killed one or two along the way. You never liked to follow the rules anyhow." She let out a brief, shrill whistle.

Bones heeled at her feet while keeping a leery eye on the stranger.

Furor coursed up and down Ethan's spine. "I've been doing what I hired on for, something you know little about. Making a commitment and following through."

"You know nothing about commitments. As I remember, you hightailed it away from Galveston as soon as you found your calling and live a much more exciting life than you would have ever had working at Father's bank."

"I think it'd been a little crowded there. Don't you?"

She ignored the barb. "You could have been a lawyer, too, but you're more of a man who'd chase after the bad guys and give them some ol'-fashioned six-gun justice instead." She lifted her brows significantly.

"You don't have the slightest idea what I've been doing, Anna." He had to work hard to keep the memories of what had been going on for the last six years out of his mind. He'd become pretty dern good at keeping them at bay, but as it'd been since their school days, simply laying eyes on Anna uprooted him. It wasn't just her beauty—flaming curls hanging down her back and ivory skin that made him want to touch her—but something about her free spirit and spontaneity, and even her stubbornness, that seemed to draw him to her. But he wouldn't let that happen this time. Not again. There'd been too many warm beers and hot nights for him to go back now. He wasn't the bashful, deep-dimpled kid of yesteryear. He was a lawman. A fearless, up-standing Texas Ranger. A man who had experienced a heapin' dose of life since he'd rode away from Galveston.

"Let's put the guns down. One of us is fixin' to get hurt and you're much too smart to let that happen," he said.

"And, you're much too arrogant!" Her words were as cool as the water beneath the footbridge off to his right. "I see being a lawman hasn't changed you. You went to bed mean and woke up even meaner."

"How would you know? Remember, you never slept with me."

Anna leveled a stare at him equal to the Winchester pointed in his direction. "How could I forget?" She lowered the weapon aiming more at open space between the stream and him.

Ethan had chased the bodacious, emerald-eyed darlin' from the Galveston Merchant's Bank and Trust in Galveston to the Texas Panhandle and by dern he wasn't about to let the feisty gal, with or without a shotgun, keep him from taking her back home. And what a shame too. She looked like an angel with a devil's glare—almost a smile but defi-nitely etched with defiance. Nothing like the sweet, soft-spoken Southern belle who had robbed her father's bank and escaped, daring her family and friends to wish what they might about her involvement. Certainly not the girl he'd grown up with.

As if it were only moments ago, the same sadness cur-tained her face that existed when she walked out of the bank, flanked by the two robbers. Even today the look still haunted him.

For weeks afterward, he found himself drawn back to that moment when she looked him straight in the eye, as he stood outside the bank unable to step in and take a chance of getting her or a bystander killed. When only a fraction of a second could make a difference, he had no choice but to watch her prance away obviously pleased with herself. Although it should have been an emotional, disappointing moment to witness the robbery, it wasn't for Ethan, who only felt helpless and confused by Anna's expression that had reeked with a challenge: "Catch me if you can."

Considering the turn of events that wintry day, Ethan realized there had to have been a reason he'd decided it was time to come home and see his mama, particularly since it'd been a while since he'd made it back home.

Memories of that day still felt serene and bewildering to him. Savannah had left a life of comfort behind to commit a crime when all she had to do was ask for money. She'd never been denied anything in her life.

From miles away steady breezes wafted the air, carrying the smell of fresh rain, bringing Ethan back to the matter at hand.

He searched the face of the woman standing only a few feet in front of him. What had happened to change her? What circumstances had led to a life on the run? There was one thing certain: this lawman had no intention of getting involved with this woman ever again. The problem was he'd convinced her father that instead of hiring the Pinkerton Agency to chase her down, he should allow Ethan the opportunity to find her first. The sheriff had initially gone along with the plan, as had Ethan's captain, but at the time no one imagined that Anna and her gang would go on a rampage of bank heists up and down the Brazos River.

As Ethan had done all of his life, he took on his responsibilities seriously and planned to protect and return her before a less sympathetic lawman caught up with her.

But seeing Anna in the flesh brought back memories. Memories he'd been successful in keeping at bay until now. Memories of a prior life. A prior dream. A prior commitment.

Now, searching her face, he knew what his heart had told him years before: in her presence he seemed to lose control of all reasoning and could make a mistake that might cost him his—or worse yet, her—life.

Ethan watched as Anna shifted her gaze, focusing once again over his shoulder, toward a mesquite wood footbridge that joined the hill and the dugout nestled in with the other side of the narrow, zigzagging stream. A few straggly bunches of purple horsemint and Indian paintbrush dotted the path, hugging the posts.

Was Anna waiting for someone? If so, whom? As far as he knew the two men who had been her partners in the bank heists were in jail down south in Menardville. Ethan had personally seen a picture of the lookout man, Arlis Buckley, laid out to rest, as evidence of his demise. He was heavy bearded and thought to be in his twenties, although his hat had blurred his facial features somewhat. The picture had stuck in Ethan's mind because it was the first time he'd known of a sheriff requiring proof of death in order to pay the reward. As far as Ethan knew the reward still had not been collected.

But until Ethan knew what or whom Anna was watching behind him, he'd not let his guard down . . . nor his pistol.

Chapter 2

Ethan heard the crunch of boots on the clay dirt and scrunch grass being broken down long before he caught a glimpse of movement over his shoulder. He shifted his gaze back to Anna, who didn't take her sight off the footbridge. She raised her gun a bit, not totally pointing it at him, obviously distracted by the approaching sounds. The ruffling of grass indicated whatever neared wasn't of the four-footed kind, so that pretty much left only a human. Too heavy-footed for a woman yet not the footfall of a man. More of a meandering in their direction, not definite steps or anyone trying to hide his approach.

The shadow became longer and soft humming could be heard in the distance, a short concerto of the same notes over and over, very close together, a metronome of sounds.

Ethan turned quickly toward the figure ambling closer, settling his Colt directly on the ambusher's heart. He locked his finger on the trigger, knowing he had only a split second to get the draw on the intruder before he opened fire on Anna or Ethan himself. Most likely there were one or two gunmen hiding in the brush waiting to strike out when the firing began. Training taught Ethan to fire first and ask questions later, but a warning deep inside told him something wasn't right; neither he nor Anna was in danger. He prayed his instincts were on target.

Suddenly, Anna's scream penetrated his thoughts.

"Noooo! Ethan, don't shoot!" She stood petrified.

Unaware of Anna and Ethan's presence, a clean-shaven young man with dark hair touching his collar continued to count stones he held in his hand and hummed the same short tune repetitively. A leather pouch hung around his neck.

Seemingly forgetting Ethan had drawn his Colt, Anna propped the Winchester up against the hitchin' rail and with complete disregard for her own safety ran to the boy.

"Where did he come from? Who is he?" In rapid-fire succession, Ethan bombarded her with questions. "What is going on?"

Tenderly, with her hands Anna drew his attention up to her eyes but never touched him.

"Thirteen, thirteen," chanted the boy. "Thirteen rocks." He began to count the pebbles out one at a time, gingerly placing them in the palm of Anna's open hand.

"Dakota," she said softly. "Look at me."

The boy continued to count.

"Dakota, please look at me."

Gradually, he raised his head. With a blank stare, he said, "Thirteen, thirteen. Thirteen, just like you told me to find."

Ethan holstered his weapon almost in slow motion, giving his heart time to return to its normal rhythm. Realizing just how close he came to shooting an innocent child, the lawman wasn't sure if his legs could continue carrying his weight. He couldn't help but stare at the kid, whom Ethan surmised was not much older than Anna's little brother, Charlie. Scrawny and barely old enough to shave.

"Thank you." Anna grasped the rocks as if they were precious gems and lifted her head. "Dakota, I'd like for you to meet . . ."

Ethan caught Anna's eye and studied her. Neither spoke.

How in the world was she gonna explain to a kid that Ethan was a lawman coming to arrest her for bank robbery? Just like the day at the bank, her expression pled for understanding.

"He's . . . he's your . . ." Anna hesitated.

Ethan stared in disbelief. He didn't even know the dark-headed kid, so Dakota being his anything was nothing but a bunch of malarkey.

"He's your . . ." She took a deep breath, then finished, "Your . . . uncle. Your Uncle Ethan."

Shock ran rampant through Ethan's body. Uncle? What in the blue blazes was she talking about?

Dakota simply looked up, and with no recognition in his face, he recited in the same monotone voice, "Thirteen. Thirteen. Thirteen rocks." Then he added, "Uncle Ethan."

"Please wash up, Dakota." Anna examined the stones before depositing them in her apron pocket. "It's suppertime."

The young man did not respond. As though he didn't realize Ethan was there, Dakota simply walked to the pan of water heating in the sun and looked intently into it.

"Why did you go and do that for?" Ethan had to pull himself away from watching the kid. He tried not to be angry, but he knew he was doing a lousy job.

"Because his hands are dirty," she said matter-of-factly.

"You know I didn't mean why he had to wash up." Ethan found himself growling at her much like the mutt, who had now moved to the shade of a scrawny mesquite tree. "Why did you tell him I was his uncle?"

"What was I supposed to do, tell him, 'Hey, kid, meet the nasty old man who is going to arrest the only friend you have in the world and take her off to jail? Maybe hang her? Hellfire and brimstone, even shoot her'?" Her voice mirrored her frustration.

Ethan wasn't sure exactly how to respond to her accusations, mainly because he'd already thought the same thing. Now wasn't the time to confront the problem head-on, although he still had the upper hand. She was the one wanted for bank robbery, not him. "Do you realize I could take you into custody for pulling a gun on a lawman?"

"And I could have shot you for trespassing?" She turned and flounced toward the dugout, which wasn't a spit's throw away.

"I guess you also forgot about the wanted posters in every sheriff's office between here and Galveston? Not to mention the bounty on your head?" He tried successfully not to add, "Dead or Alive." Particularly since she still had a shotgun within reach.

She grabbed the Winchester in one hand and opened the iron-grated screen to the dugout. As if he'd told her she had an overdue library book, she simply retorted, "Consider me arrested."

Turning back, Anna offered up a sweet smile. "If you want supper, wash up."

Thunder in the west didn't hold a light to the roar Ethan felt in his body. Clouds churned bitterly overhead, announcing a thunderstorm much like the turmoil boiling in his heart.

Ethan was up to his ears in yucca and couldn't remember why he'd thought it was important to wade through the dang stuff in the first place.

Pausing, he raised his eyes to the sky and sent up a tiny prayer that Anna wouldn't ask to see an arrest warrant.

Chapter 3

The smell of beans attacked Anna when she entered the dugout. Gingerly, she closed the screen door behind her and put the Winchester back in the gun rack above the fireplace. She made her way to the stand that held a dishpan. Holding on to both sides of the stand, she took a deep breath, trying not to cry. She swallowed the tears and closed her eyes in an attempt to clear her mind.

Her heart stung from the jolt of reality just heaped upon her. Ethan had every right to take her into custody, and deep inside she realized what hurt the most was that he not only had the right but the duty to arrest her. It wasn't his job to judge whether her reasons were justifiable; it was his obligation to get her back to those who would.

Ethan had hit the nail square on the head, as he seemed to always do. Until that horrid day at the bank, she'd never had to stand up and be responsible for her own actions. Her father, if not her mother, always made an excuse or explained things away. But she'd never done anything all that bad—not until she was trapped into it. She now had to face the world—worse yet, her family—and take full responsibility for her own actions, but why in the blue blazes did Ethan Kimble have to be her redeemer?

Why did seeing Ethan again create such conflicting emotions within her? She should be more scared of being brought to justice than dealing with Ethan. She had to put the past aside, because safeguarding the young man with childlike qualities was more important than saving her own hide. She'd face the consequences of her actions, but not until Dakota was safe. It was as though she'd come full circle, once again doing what was necessary to protect someone she cared about.

Anna added some mesquite to the belly of the stove, then covered the cooling skillet of cornbread with a tea towel. She tasted a couple of beans. *Ugh, needs more salt.* She added a smidgen, knowing that the tad left on the shelf had to last for a while. On second thought she threw in a pinch more since this would most likely be the last meal she cooked in the dugout.

Stepping outside to check on Dakota, she caught sight of Ethan standing near a thicket of brush while a golden palomino lapped up water. With the storm brewing and light raindrops already falling, it'd be next to impossible to get out of the canyon before dark. The steep, flinty, and treacherous trail was dangerous even during daylight. The storm would give her much needed time to figure out what to do. Not only would escape be impossible, it would be stupid to try it. She'd been on the run too long and had been a pawn too many times, so this was the end for her. But how in the world could she ever come up with a reason simple enough for Dakota to understand why they had to go back to Galveston? He felt safe where he was, probably for the first time in his life. Where would he go? He needed her, and she needed him. But before she could explain anything to Dakota she had to somehow talk to Ethan and make the big man understand.

A chill coursed through her body. How in the living hell was she going to explain the kid to Ethan?

Dakota headed her way.

She met him halfway. "Come inside. It's suppertime."

"Storms, storms," he said without looking up. "Big storms."

After entering the dugout, the young man moved directly to a quilt folded up on the foot of the lone bed in the room. He removed it, then meticulously laid out the bed covering in the corner, making sure that the fabric was totally flat. At least as flat as it could be on the hard clay floor. When he was satisfied, he settled down in the corner with his back to the wall. He removed a deck of cards from the leather pouch around his neck and carefully went through the pack and removed two of the jacks. Placing them to the side facedown, he said, "Bad jacks," as though reprimanding them, then shuffled the remaining cards thirteen times. Once he finished, he sorted the remainder of the deck one card at a time onto separate squares of the quilt sequentially by ranking suit.

Anna was accustomed to his solitary game. When he completed all of the stacks of cards, he'd announce, "Three hundred twenty," then gather them up one suit at a time and return the deck to the pouch. Within seconds, he'd begin the whole process over again.

Although Dakota was absorbed in his solitude, Anna spoke softly as she worked. She didn't know if her words penetrated his thoughts or not, but talking to him gave her comfort.

"I've already set a place for Uncle Ethan twice but ended up removing it each time." She laid down a blue tin plate, along with a fork and knife on the table in front of the spare chair. "Guess I'd best find out if he plans to eat with us before I set him a place." She again removed the items and stacked them on the small sideboard next to the sink.

Ethan probably had better food in his saddlebags than she had to offer. So far Anna hadn't gotten hungry enough to try to chase down a wild turkey or prairie chicken, so dried beans and cornbread was their daily fare. The dried and preserved food she found in the root cellar, along with what she had brought along, had been devoured a while ago.

"Dakota," Anna said. "Do you remember when I tried to get you to go to Amarillo with me, and you were too scared to go somewhere you'd never been before? Remember me puttin' on a big floppy hat and rubbin' mud on my face so nobody would recognize me when I ventured into town for supplies?" She didn't anticipate an answer so continued on, "With only one horse everything I bought had to fit in the saddlebags." She couldn't help but smile to herself. "I don't think Troubadour was all that happy having sacks of sugar, cornmeal, and flour strapped across his back, but we made it home safely." She took two cups off the shelf. "Remember me telling you how nice Mrs. Diggs at the mercantile was?"

Anna never forgot the friendliness of the woman, particularly since she was so helpful and didn't ask too many questions Anna didn't want to answer. But when Mrs. Diggs asked if she'd been around long because she looked familiar, Anna gathered up her purchases and hightailed it out of Amarillo. She'd never risked returning to town again, with or without a disguise.

Whether Mrs. Diggs thought she really knew her or had seen a wanted poster, Anna didn't know. By now she had little doubt there'd be wanted posters of her from every county between the Gulf Coast and the Texas Panhandle tacked on the wall in the sheriff's office. Why had they been renamed the Texas Flame Gang anyway? The band of misfits, minus her, already had a seedy reputation as the Graves Gang under the leadership of the burley Cajun Gator Graves.

Anna walked over to where Dakota sat and squatted

down to his level. "Dakota, do you remember us talking about the ruts wagons make in the trails?"

He looked up at her, and to her it signaled an acknowledgment.

"If for some reason I'm not around and you get scared, go back up the trail, find the ruts, and it'll lead you to safety." She searched his face to make sure he was absorbing her orders, and it seemed he was. "Go find Mrs. Diggs, she'll keep you safe. Do you understand?"

"Ruts. Ruts. Ruts," he repeated before returning to his cards.

Satisfied he understood, Anna pulled to her feet.

Walking outside, she took a gander at the ominous clouds over the rim of the canyon. The temperature had dropped fifteen degrees in the short time she'd been inside. Behind the light showers, an ebony rain wall waited to attack. And if the previous few days' storms were any indication, it promised to be a gullywasher.

Since there was only one flinty trail in and out of the canyon, and the streams had already swollen miserably, they could be stranded for days if that happened. She wasn't sure if she ought to be happy or sad about the idea. It could work for her yet against her. Possibly, the longer she had to explain things to Ethan the better it could be. At the same time, just the thought of spending any more time than was absolutely necessary with the rugged, incredibly appealing lawman made her uncomfortable. He had made it crystal clear that his sole mission was to arrest her. On the other hand, technically she was already in his custody. She sure didn't hear him contradict her when she told him to consider her arrested. Surely there was some law on the books that said a wanted person couldn't arrest herself.

Anna stepped around the corner of the stone structure and movement near the corral caught her eye. She watched as Ethan removed a small, tan box from his saddlebags and took out the contents. Briefly the sun peeked between clouds. Sun rays danced off something very bright, more faceted than silver. He dropped the shiny object back in the container and took out what appeared to be a picture.

Although Anna felt more like a spy than someone announcing supper, she couldn't help but watch. He removed his hat, uncovering a full, thick head of blond hair. His hair color had always reminded her of the sand along the Gulf Coast. Today, coupled with his deeply tanned skin, it seemed even lighter.

Just as she was about to holler for him to come eat, Ethan dropped to one knee for only a fleeting moment. Holding the photo tight to his chest, he pointed to the heavens with his index finger, then effortlessly rose to his feet.

A sense of strength came to Anna. She remembered the gesture from years gone by and knew its significance. That left only one question. Whose picture did he cherish enough that just looking at it would move him so?

Ethan stuck the picture back into the box and secured it in his saddlebags, which he threw over his shoulder. He gave the gelding a pat on his rump, heaved his saddle over his other shoulder, then headed toward the dugout.

The sky opened and buckets of rain pelted the ground and everything standing in between. Ethan ducked his head and increased his gait from a fast canter to a full-out run.

The rain, combined with him bringing his belongings with him, answered one of her questions. He'd be spending the night.

Not wanting Ethan to catch her watching him, she stepped back inside.

Dakota had moved to the table and sat in his customary chair. He stopped straightening his silverware when she walked in.

"You're hungry, too." Not expecting an answer, she

continued on to the stove, removed the tea towel from the cornbread, and placed the pan on the table. Hurriedly, she set another place for Ethan and finished only seconds before the screen opened and the lawman walked in.

After dropping his gear on the floor in the corner, Ethan removed his dove gray Stetson and let the rain slide off it. He hung the hat on a peg next to the door. "Some rain you all have here," he said, then shot her his familiar schoolboy smile. That dern smile, with deep dimples on each cheek, always caught her off guard. And then there was the tiny indention in his chin. So enduring, but then he'd always used his dimples to get what he wanted. That's why she loved to fan the flames by calling him Dimples, especially whenever she had the upper hand on him.

Her mind whirled with mixed feelings, unnerving her somewhat.

Ethan pulled off his jacket and hung it beside his hat. Although his shirt wasn't soaked, it clung to every inch of his upper body, and she could imagine his wide shoulders tanned just as much as his face and neck. She still had memories of sneaking up on him when he was fixing fences at his pa's place when they were only in their teens. Of course, she had to make sure it was him, not his brother. From a distance they looked alike. It didn't take her long to be able to tell them apart when they worked outdoors because, unlike Robert, Ethan rarely wore a shirt and his pants hung tight and low against narrow hips. Some things never change, and that was certainly one of Ethan's enduring qualities that had only matured handsomely with age.

Over the last few months, during times when she wasn't sure she'd survive to see daylight, those memories gave her hope and sometimes warmth, but his dimples always made her smile.

Savannah Kathleen Parker, don't forget he's your enemy, not your sweetie, her heart chastised her.

Thinking only about the good times and nothing of the bad was beginning to make her unfocused on what truly mattered.

Nothing could stand in the way of making sure no one found out the truth . . . not even Dimples.

Chapter 4

The dugout was roomier than Ethan had imagined, with sturdy lodge poles holding the rafters high. As he expected the air was several degrees cooler inside than outside. Although the quarters were clean and tidy, it had the personality of a way station without the comforts. Even the pitcher and bowl on the stand near the lone bed was devoid of color.

The three ate dinner in total silence. If it hadn't been for the claps of thunder and pounding rain on the sod roof, there would have been no sound in the least. The mutt snoozed by the fireplace after gobbling up his share of beans and cornbread.

Ethan took his time eating, enjoying supper more than he had in a very long time. Tired of eating dried beef and hardtack on the trail was an understatement. Sharing a meager meal with Anna and Dakota, who made him feel right at home, was nice—except he sure could have passed on the one-woman Winchester welcoming committee. Certainly better than chowin' down a steak and all the fixin's in some fancy, faceless hotel dining room surrounded by people who didn't give a rip about him.

Sleeping arrangements in the dugout would be tight at best, so he'd do what he generally did: sleep under the stars.

Even rain wouldn't hold him back. He wished he had two bits for every night he bunked with Yellow Jacket in the livery or threw a camp near a creek. Every few days when he'd come across a town with a hotel, he'd rent a room so he could get a hot bath and a close shave. A shot of whiskey and an occasional warm bed was fine with him, but he'd probably choke to death if he had to make it a steady diet. He had to admit how inviting a comfy bed might be tonight.

Just the thought of cool sheets and a feather pillow sent old feelings rushing back even stronger than before. A riot of emotions ran harem scarem through his belly, reminding him that it'd be physically impossible to share such cramped quarters with the pretty, petite bandit.

The room continued to reek with deafening silence except for an occasional clang of metal against metal when someone rested a knife on a tin plate.

Ethan had avoided bringing up the subject of Anna's return to Galveston in front of the kid, but time was nearing. Preparations had to be made tonight, as they needed to leave at first light. It didn't look like Anna would have much packing to do. It'd take a good bit of the day, absent of rain, to ride out of the canyon and travel to Amarillo.

As much as Ethan wanted to get a message to her father, Alexander Parker, that he'd found his daughter safe and would be accompanying her to Galveston, he couldn't take the chance of Anna being identified by local lawmen. He'd memorized the railroad schedule, so he pretty much knew when to expect the train to Fort Worth, which would eventually take them to Galveston.

For a brief moment, several reasons to wash his hands of Anna and her problems galloped across Ethan's mind. He shook his head to dislodge the thoughts. How stupid could he be? Just because he didn't want to risk spending any more time with her than necessary, he'd never put her or the kid in danger. There was still a reward over her head. He'd told her father that he'd do everything humanly possible to keep her safe. They'd shook hands on the deal, and in Texas, a handshake was as good as his word any day.

He couldn't even get a good bath and shave before they left for Fort Worth, mainly because there'd be no place to safely leave Anna. Usually he'd deposit a prisoner in the local jail for a few hours, but not in this particular situation. It wasn't just taking a chance on her being recognized; for whatever reason he was unable to grasp, he just couldn't bring himself to do that to her . . . or the kid.

In the corral, Ethan had taken stock of the dapple-gray-rumped Appaloosa that looked strong enough to get them about anywhere they wanted to go. He had looked around but found no second saddle or any sign of another horse or pack animal. He surmised that Anna and the boy had rode double. Ethan wasn't sure what he'd do with the gray gelding but dern sure wasn't gonna leave his palomino behind. Yellow Jacket would probably be happy to have company in the train's livestock car.

Ethan didn't know exactly how to go about questioning Anna about the kid, and so far, she hadn't offered up any explanation.

How had he latched on to her? Ethan had already witnessed how protective she was of him. But before final arrangements were made to leave, Ethan had to know more.

Was he related? If so, why didn't she just say so? Had she picked him up along the way? Or did he come with the dugout? That being the possibility, he might be happy for the return of his privacy. That concerned Ethan since the kid was somewhere between grass and hay; physically more man than child, but just how experienced was he in taking care of all of his needs on his own?

One thing Ethan would not compromise on was making sure the kid got into the hands of people who would care for him, but he could not and would not be responsible for him all the way to the Gulf of Mexico.

Silence continued to suck life out of the room, while the winds howled flanked by booms of thunder that sounded like cannon fire.

Ethan took a gulp of lukewarm coffee.

Dakota downed his cornbread and after finishing his first plate of beans, dished himself another helping. Ethan watched as he carefully divided the beans into equal parts on the plate before he began eating three at a time.

Anna shuffled her food around on her plate before awkwardly asking, "What is your horse's name?"

"Yellow Jacket," Ethan answered, realizing she was obviously trying to make small talk.

"Nice name." Time crawled by before she up and said what was really on her mind. "How did you find me?"

Ethan was pretty sure this was another attempt to avoid the question they both had on their mind: what came next?

"I knew you'd head north, so when I didn't find you in Ransom Canyon, I knew exactly where you were headed."

"You knew or you were told?" Her normal soft, composed tone had turned sarcastic.

"I don't go off half-cocked based on what I've heard. I find out the truth for myself and make my own conclusions. You should know that." He ripped the words out impatiently, even for him.

Anna smiled benevolently as if dealing with a temperamental child.

Ethan struggled to retain self-control. Why did she frustrate him so? He knew the reason his mama offered up, and for a while he thought she was right, but that was a long time ago. It was best that those reasons stay undisturbed deep within his heart. But for the record, he only thought he was in love with Savannah Parker.

"Savannah, I remember your dad tellin' you that if he

ever needed a place to hide it'd be in the Palo Duro. He said that if anybody got all the way down to the bottom they could get lost with all the caves and streams. I figured you weren't a cave dweller since you don't particularly like confinement and might head for the colonel's abandoned dugout. Heard he built himself a big ranch house up on the caprock."

A thoughtful expression veiled her face, and she lifted an eyebrow as if to question his comment. He realized that something he said had given her pause for thought. Surely she wasn't hatching a plan to escape.

Her silence made him reconsider whether to tell her of any of his plans to get her back home, but common sense prevailed. It was in both of their best interests to know exactly what to expect from one another.

"Anna," he began but made the mistake of stalling a moment to get his thoughts together. He started again, "Anna . . ."

For the longest few seconds she didn't respond but finally said, "Yes, he has a ranch house northeast of Amarillo."

Anna returned to whatever was going through her mind, and he figured it wasn't necessarily being taken into custody that she was so concerned about. She'd know in her heart that her father wouldn't have prosecuted her, but she still had to worry about the bank robberies after she left Galveston. For some reason Ethan could not pinpoint, something a whole lot more serious lay heavy on her mind.

Suddenly, she seemed to deliberately veer off course. "Did you get your horse settled in? There's a lean-to, I'm sure you noticed. It's not all that big, but the horses can get out of the weather."

"Thanks. I found it and stored my gear," Ethan said.

"Good." She offered up a small arresting smile. "He's a beautiful palomino, so glad you got him settled in."

"Yellow Jacket likes to sleep outdoors, so I hobbled him—"

"Hobbled!" Dakota almost knocked his chair over getting to his feet. "Hobbled! Hobbled!" He rushed out the door.

Tight on his heels, Bones barely escaped through the heavy metal screen before it slammed shut.

Taken by surprise, both Ethan and Anna rose from their chairs. Ethan glanced from the door to Anna, who was visually distraught. She grabbed her waist and began to shake as though she'd suddenly caught a chill. Her face paled and she looked like her feet wouldn't hold her up.

Although Ethan wanted to go after Dakota, he grasped her by the shoulders to keep her from keeling over. Drawn between comforting her and following after the kid, Ethan took care of the most immediate need and gathered her into his arms and held her tightly against him.

"Are you all right?" he asked, knowing she was taken aback terribly by Dakota's outburst, but the fact that she felt so good in his arms didn't escape notice.

With her hand clutched against her chest, she whispered not so convincingly, "I'm okay."

"I'm going after the kid." He decided that although she was shaken Anna was being honest about being all right, but he wasn't so sure about Dakota. "It's raining, and he might get hurt. What did I say to upset him so much?"

She didn't speak, but he felt her stiffen beneath his touch. He pulled back and looked in her eyes.

"We've got to talk, Ethan." She barely lifted her voice above a whisper. "There're things that happened—things that took place while we were on the run that you should know about."

Ethan searched her face for answers but found none. "We'll talk later, but right now I'm concerned about you and the kid. Are you sure he's safe out there alone?"

She nodded her head. "He knows every nook and cranny

of this canyon. Please don't let his strange behavior make you think he's light in the head, because he isn't. He's extremely smart, but sometimes his mind can't control both his thoughts and his actions." She bit her quivering lip. "He's a survivor, and most times prefers to hide his feelings than to share them with others. He's been mistreated and doesn't trust anyone. He's just recently come around to me." She looked up at Ethan, melting his heart. "He's a good person and knows how to take care of himself."

Relief came to Ethan, but she'd brought up more questions than answers.

"What did you mean by things I should know, Savannah?"

Tears welled up in her eyes, and she simply said, "I'm not sure you'll understand."

"Whatever it is, I can help you get through it—"

"No, Ethan. This is one time I have to do this alone."

"You don't trust me?"

Anna turned away and began clearing dishes from the table. After a moment, she looked up and said, "I don't know who to trust, Ethan."

A tear rolled down her cheek.

Chapter 5

Anna wanted more than anything to trust Ethan, but his lawman's oath trumped anything and everything on the wrong side of the law. Right now, she certainly was on the wrong side. She couldn't afford to let him know the whole truth until she had Dakota safely out of harm's way. Ethan would be furious with her for what she'd done, but she didn't want Dakota dragged into it . . . if that was possible.

Ethan grabbed his hat, jammed it onto his head, and hurried out the door.

Anna removed her apron, hung it over a chair, and followed.

Sheets of rain blinded her. By the time she stepped from beneath the jutting rock overhang that protected the door, she could barely make out the lawman, who headed toward the lean-to.

Cold sopping dirt whipped around her ankles, making it harder for her to walk. Mud and water clutched the hem of her calico skirt and weighed it down to where she had to struggle with each step. She caught up with him by the time he reached the corrals.

"Son of a bitch!" he bellowed.

Angry flashes of lightning arched from cloud to cloud before zigzagging from cloud to ground.

Even with the thunder and wind gusts, she knew by the tone of his voice he was gnashing at the bit. He removed his Stetson, ran his fingers through his hair, and put the hat back on.

"What's wrong, Ethan?" She grabbed him by the arm, not so much to keep him from walking away, but to steady her so she didn't fall in the sludge.

He stared ahead. A muscle quivered in his jaw, betraying his deep frustrations. He set his chin in a stubborn line before hauling off and kicking the hell out of one of the corral posts, shaking the railing.

"What's the matter?" Anna asked again.

"I should've gone with my gut." Rain dripped from his hat. "But I never took the kid for a horse thief."

The accusation flying around caught Anna off guard.

"He's not a thief. Ethan, think about it," she spouted, trying to ignore the stinging rain slapping her on the face. "He couldn't have gone far in the rain. There's only one way out of the canyon and it's flooded, and he didn't take your saddle."

"Only because it wasn't here for him to steal." His jaw quivered. "I had Yellow Jacket hobbled right here, and now he's gone. What in the hell do you want me to think?"

"I know where he is, Ethan. He's taken the horses to higher ground, where they'll be safer."

"You know or you think you know? They were plenty safe here."

His words stung almost as much as the raindrops lashing out at her.

"He didn't think they were. Let's go back inside and I'll fix a pot of coffee. I can explain. Please trust me. He won't hurt Troubadour nor would he harm your horse. He's not trying to run away; he's just doing what comes natural for him. He might not be able to communicate with humans like we think he should, but he has a special gift when it comes to animals. He'll take care of them."

"He knows horses?"

"Better than anyone I know. So let's go."

The trip back to the dugout, although it was probably less than a hundred yards away, was even worse. Bucketfuls of cold rain came down harder, faster without giving them any reason to believe Mother Nature had any plans to make it stop.

The stream coming down from the headwaters of the Red River ran bank to bank with water hungrily lapping at the path. A quagmire of clay sucked her feet into the mud, hampering her every step. Torrential sheets of rain made it impossible to see the dugout clearly. When she lost her footing and almost fell, Ethan took her hand to keep her upright.

Thoughts of hobbling slid around Anna's mind like her boots on the red, soggy dirt, making her stomach churn and her throat tighten.

If only she'd paid attention and noticed that Ethan had hobbled his horse . . . if only.

There were no decisions left to be made. She would have to tell Ethan everything . . . or at least what she could without taking a chance on getting Dakota arrested.

By the time they reached the doorway, their boots and the hems of their clothes caked with mud, a prairie dog trapped in his hole during a flood couldn't possibly have been any more soaked. The only difference was Ethan and Anna weren't likely to drown.

Ethan held the screen for her but didn't come in. Instead he called out, "If you'll toss me my saddlebags, I'll change into something dryer."

"And with a lot less mud on them, too." Anna smiled, wondering if there was anyplace in the canyon that hadn't turned terracotta except for the dugout's floor. Well constructed, the structure was totally dry inside except for a tiny bit of moisture that had collected in the corner right above a nail used to hold up her clothesline.

Don't forget to repair the leak, one side of her mind warned, while the other remembered, *You won't be living here come tomorrow.*

A sad feeling overcame her. Like her mind, her heart had a difference of opinion. One part was sad about leaving the free-spirited and simple life of the new frontier to return to the fast-paced, hectic lifestyle of Galveston. And though anxious to see her family again, she dreaded facing her parents and having to come clean with them. It would hurt not just in her heart; it would hurt others she trusted.

Considering how much conflict she already had within her heart about telling Ethan the truth, she knew it would be virtually impossible for her parents to understand.

A clap of thunder caused Anna to jump and it certainly cleared her mind. How could she have forgotten the man standing outside her door soaked to the gills? Except for propriety's sake, there was no reason he had to change clothes outside in the pouring rain when the dugout was perfectly dry.

She had to raise her voice a little so he could hear her over the storm. "You don't need to change out there. I've got a curtain that separates the room in half, so we can both have our privacy."

Anna heard him stomping muck from his boots. By the time he entered, he'd already taken off his hat and unbuttoned his shirt, revealing a muscular chest covered with crisp brown hair. She had to pry her gaze away. Yes, ma'am, he'd physically grown into the man she always imagined he would. A powerful, well-muscled body moved with easy grace as he removed his shirt, exposing a big dose of his beautifully proportioned body. A more devilishly handsome figure she'd never seen. He shot her a smile that sent her pulse racing.

"Sorry about that." He reached for the curtain and pulled it far enough along to hide him from view. "Didn't mean to embarrass you."

"You didn't embarrass me. It's not like I've never seen a man naked before." She turned her back and began loosening the ties on her boots. "Plenty of them."

"Hmm, so if I didn't embarrass you, what caused that sweet little blush on your cheeks?" His boot hit the dirt floor with a thud. "And I wasn't naked. You wanna see naked, wait about ten seconds and pull the curtain back."

"Ethan Kimble, you're a scoundrel and have been ever since I've known you."

No denial from him. Honesty had always been his strongest attribute.

About as cold as Anna could ever recall being, she quickly undressed, dried her hair with a flimsy, thin towel, and slipped on dry clothes. He'd probably not be too keen on her wearing pants and a shirt, but with only one change of clothes, she had no choice.

By the time Ethan pulled the curtain open, dressed in a dry shirt and pants, the coffee brewed softly on the stove. She pulled two cups from the cabinet.

He seemed to make no attempt to cover his scrutiny as he looked her up and down as though he was appraising a mare. He drew in his lips approvingly, which only made his dimples entrench themselves deeper into his cheeks. So, if he disapproved of a woman wearing pants, he was doing a good job of covering it up.

The welcoming smell of strong, freshly brewed coffee seemed to soften the mood, reminding Anna of her parents when they'd sit and share after-dinner drinks in the parlor.

"We won't be gettin' out of this canyon until the water goes down, and from the looks of those clouds, that won't be for a while." He lowered his big frame into a kitchen chair. "So, you're stuck with me, Savannah, whether you like it or not."

Anna filled two cups of coffee and set one in front of Ethan. Before she could move her hand away, he caught it with his strong fingers. "We can't avoid this forever. It's time we talked."

The day had arrived that she'd had nightmares about for months . . . her day of reckoning.

Chapter 6

Ethan moved his hand away from Savannah's and accepted the coffee she offered but couldn't keep his eyes off her. As much as he'd like to ignore her, the soft glow of the low-burning lantern only highlighted her beauty. He wondered if she even realized how lovely she was, not just in looks but in actions. Although she was given every comfort of life growing up, she rarely took advantage of it. Unless one counted the times her parents would make unnecessary excuses for her behavior when they thought she acted inappropriately, reflecting poorly on them as parents. Like the pants and shirt she had on. No doubt Abigail Parker would make plenty of excuses for her daughter's lack of fashion sense. Frankly, he liked the way she was dressed, as it reflected her sense of independence, plus those pants looked pretty dang good stretched across her rump.

Anna was always at her mother's beck and call. Anna did things from the goodness of her heart, while her mama made sure everything she did looked good for her and her family.

Assisting her at the annual church bazaar to help needy children was one of his fond memories. His own mama used to say, "That girl would take in a grown wolf if she thought it needed help." He'd only known Anna to be considerate of others. Nothing like the spoiled brat she portrayed when she rode out of Galveston or the pistol-packin' mother grizzly who confronted him earlier.

But the problem still existed that he hadn't come more than six hundred miles to tout her attributes, but to take her into custody and protect her until he got her safely home.

Soft rain continued to pitter-patter on the roof.

"Who's going to start, Anna?"

She cupped the coffee mug in her hands. "I guess I should." She inhaled deeply. "The first thing you *need* to know is that I didn't know Gator Graves or Shorty Duncan before—"

"I'll be the judge as to what I *need* to know." Once the words were out he recognized how easily she could wind him up. The lawman in him took over, asking, "Then the witness who saw you in the dining room with Graves was lying?"

Just thinking back to his interview with Bradford Jackson III made his jaw tighten involuntarily. Ethan had never agreed on much with the man, but then he'd had plenty of good reasons, going back a lot of years. Most of the town folks, although sympathetic that he'd lost the sight in one eye as a child, still didn't trust the boot-lickin' flannel-mouthed bastard.

"Hear me out. Then you can grill me, Ethan." Her tone was velvet-edged steel. She shoved the coffee away from her and folded her hands together on the table. "Just listen, and it'll all make sense."

Useful investigating was always slow work, particularly since Ethan already had most of the facts. He found himself wanting to hurry her up and get to the information he didn't already know. He'd received updates on his hunt for Anna. He knew how and where all of the robberies took place and who was involved, so all he wanted to know was the why and what of them. Why did Anna, who had everything in the world a young woman could ever want, get involved in the first place? What was she forced to endure while on the run?

In order to draw the answers out of her, he'd have to be more patient and do the job he was trained for. Listen, evaluate, and sort out truth from fiction.

"Go ahead." Ethan folded his arms across his chest and leaned back in his chair. "I've always been a little impatient."

"A little?" She quirked a brow and shot him a wary smile that stung to the core. "I didn't know Gator Graves until he approached me at dinner one night. He presented himself as a jewelry salesman and had a Patek Phillipe pocket watch he knew I'd been looking for."

"For your mother's birthday?" he half asked, half stated. "What did it look like?"

"A beautiful piece of jewelry. Blue enamel with an inlay of red and pink roses, in a four-leaf clover design accented with diamonds." She rubbed her arm a little bit, as if trying to wipe away some of the ache in her heart. "It took me a while to save up for it."

Could be the truth. Ethan remembered seeing Anna's mother, Abigail, with a watch pretty much matching that description, and when he'd complimented her on her selection, she'd said it was a birthday gift but never said from whom.

"Go ahead," he coaxed her, wanting her to relax and give him every bit of information that might help.

"I agreed to meet him after my Theater and Art Guild meeting at the Fillmore Opera House. Before I knew it, he'd stuck a pistol in my side and forced me to the balcony . . ."

She buried her face in her hands and began to weep softly. Although he wanted to comfort Anna, Ethan refrained from touching her. She had to get her story told in her own way. Maybe something she said could help him save her from a life in prison.

Anna wasn't sure she could go on and tell Ethan all of the facts but knew she had to be honest with him. She loathed that she had lost her composure and let him see how fragile and vulnerable she was. The truth would be the only way he could help to save her, and she was on a slippery slope with it at the moment.

Anna crossed her arms on the table and rested her forehead on them. For the first time since she'd arrived in the Texas Panhandle with Dakota at her side, she allowed memories to flood the barriers she'd erected in her mind.

Praying for strength to coherently tell Ethan what had happened, Anna described how the cold steel felt pressed against her rib cage and how she tried to reason with the big Cajun and about staring straight ahead at the unlit stage of the Fillmore Opera House.

In slow motion the events of that day tore at her insides. As she told Ethan of the ordeal it shamed her that she hadn't fought back. Anna had always prided herself on being a bright woman and she couldn't believe how long it had taken her to realize she'd been lured to the theater by a madman. The Colt in her side had told her as much.

"Mon cher, *all ya have to do is follow orders,*" Gator Graves *said in a gruff voice, fringed with his heavy Cajun accent.* "I jest need ya to do a job and no harm will come to ya, *cher.*"

She challenged him by reminding him that she wasn't his dear anything, which made him even madder, so he threatened that if she didn't shut up and do what she was told, he'd shoot her right then and there.

The loathsome piece of hogwash demanded that she escort him to her father's bank. It soon became crystal clear to her that she was about to step right into the midst of a bank heist . . . of her family's bank!

And that being the case, it wasn't going to happen—not if she had anything to do with it. Her father, as did his father before him, worked endlessly to make certain the town's largest and most fiscally sound bank was successful. Through the war. Through reconstruction. Through a fire. They'd never been robbed or even, to her knowledge, threatened. She'd lay her life on the line to see that it didn't happen now. Not as long as she had a breath left in her.

Belligerently, she placed her hands on her hips, while her handbag precariously dangled in the crook of her elbow. "Give me one reason I should help you."

His hot, sour breath slid down her neck as he hissed, "So, ya wanna reason, girl?"

Suddenly, the stage lights came up and illuminated the blackened room. The brilliance blinded her, hurting her eyes. Savannah was so surprised that she whirled toward the stage without giving thought to the fact that her sudden movement could have resulted in a bullet in her back.

At first she couldn't make out the figure sitting center stage in a ladder-back chair, only that the shadow was of a rather slim person. She blinked but it didn't clear her blurry vision. She closed her eyes tightly, then opened them slowly and focused intently on the figure.

Her chest constricted; bile clamored up into her throat.

She saw clear enough to recognize her fourteen-year-old brother, Charles Parker, sitting in the middle of the stage restrained by ropes. A terrified expression curtained his face.

Swallowing was impossible, and her heart pounded in her ears. Shaking, she closed her eyes again, hoping the light had made the young man only look like her only sibling. It didn't help.

Then she spied a short, squatty man sporting a duster so long that no doubt he had to be careful not to trip over the hem, and a black hat pulled low over his face. He stepped closer to the prisoner, leveling a shotgun at her brother's head.

Anna whispered under her breath, "Stay calm, Anna. Stay calm."

Typically she tried to think things through several times, evaluate the situation and decide what the best course of action might be. But she didn't have that luxury. She needed to act fast to save her brother. These men wanted to make sure she cooperated and seemingly knew they held captive a person she would fearlessly protect at all costs.

Her heart pounded so hard that she figured the Cajun could hear its beat. A proper Southern lady would never use such a vulgar word as sweat *to describe perspiration, but Anna had to admit, at the moment, she was sweating bullets.*

She took a long look at the stage and softly asked, "Why my brother?"

"Security, mon cher, to make sure ya do exactly what ya're told, so nobody will get hurt."

She nodded an understanding. "Then you'll let him go?"

He shoved the gun deeper in her side. "Ye got my word."

A sense of calm came over her, although she knew better than to trust the crook. Anna lifted her head and said, "Just how do you foresee the robbery taking place, Mr. Graves?"

"Everyone has their job, and I'm here to guarantee that ye little brother Charlie there won't tell 'um anything."

As quickly as the stage came to full light, it went pitch dark, and in a flash of a firefly's flutter, the lights shone on Anna, blinding her.

"He'll say nothing because he now knows you are my hostage and he doesn't want anything to happen to you, mon cher."

From that moment on, Savannah had known that if she wanted her family safe she had to cooperate.

* * *

Anna now looked across the table at Ethan. Her throat felt parched and she was worn out, although she'd given Ethan only a glimpse of how she'd become involved with the gang.

Taking a sip of cold coffee, she continued to study Ethan.

"So, you see, I didn't do it because I wanted to be daring or do something exciting. I didn't even want to rebel. I did it to protect my family."

Anna wanted to scream at Ethan to say something—anything—just let her know what he was thinking. She continued, "They kept me under their control and forced me to take part in their bank robberies by reminding me how close they could get to my family."

She never took her gaze off Ethan.

If the expression on his face now was an indicator, he understood the position she had been put in and why she did what she did. But would he still be as sympathetic once he heard the rest of the story?

After an insufferable silence, Ethan asked the question she feared the most. "So, how does Dakota figure into the picture?"

Icy panic twisted around her heart. She forced herself to take a deep breath. "I met him in Amarillo when I went into town to pick up supplies." Swallowing hard, she lifted her chin, then boldly said, "He didn't have any place to live, so I brought him back to the dugout."

"And forgot to take him back?" Ethan asked.

"It wasn't like I kidnapped him. He needed a place to live. I had plenty of room for him here."

Anna wanted to run out of the house. Run in the rain. Yet she knew she couldn't run far enough away to escape the lies that would eventually catch up with her.

Chapter 7

Ethan felt like he'd taken a blow to the gut, realizing how difficult it had been for Anna to relive her nightmare. But something inside his heart warned him that she was trying to cover up fears that went much deeper than a gun stuck in her side or a rampage of bank heists or even taking in a homeless young man.

The lantern burned lower. Light flickered across her face, settling on the adobe walls of the dugout.

More questions were left unanswered than answered.

A big one stuck in his craw. Why hadn't she asked what had happened to Gator Graves and Shorty Duncan? It was as though she already knew, but did she? The outlaws were apprehended after she escaped, so most likely she had no idea they were not still dodging the law. And if she didn't know about them, was she aware of Arlis Buckley's death?

With the flooding and no horses, they wouldn't be getting out of the Palo Duro for several days, so there was no reason to hurry her up.

Ethan had spent enough years watching over his own shoulders and knew from experience what she'd been going through. Maybe it would help if she knew the rest of the gang was no longer a threat to her, or anyone else, for that matter. That should relieve the strain heaped upon her from worrying about what would happen if they caught up with her. He needed her to be focused and honest with him.

He truly wanted to lead into telling her about the rest of the gang in some sort of sensitive, gentle way. Ethan hadn't been nominated for any kind of do-gooder award and probably wouldn't now. He began the only way he knew how, most likely too brash, but straight to the point.

"Graves and Duncan are down in the Menardville jail and have pretty much spilled their guts, blaming one another. Even pooled together, they don't have enough brains to take a pistol apart and clean it properly. And Arlis Buckley is—"

"Dead," she said bluntly yet with deceptive calmness.

Anna's eagerness to fill in the blank made it clear she didn't just make a wild guess. Buckley's demise wouldn't be something that the law way up in the Panhandle would know or give a rusty rat's ass about either. She had to have been in their clutches when he was killed; otherwise, she wouldn't have known he was dead. But then, as far as he knew, little was known about how Buckley died.

Softly Ethan swore to himself for his unwelcome frankness. Enough for tonight. No more questions, he pledged, then simply confirmed, "He's six feet under."

"You're positive they're still locked up and you've seen proof that Arlis is dead?" She paled, then began chewing on her lower lip.

He nodded. "Your family is safe, Anna."

Anna let out a noticeable sigh of relief. Although a little color returned to her cheeks, she continued to bite on her lip. "Do you want some more coffee?" She spoke softly.

"No, thank you. I'm going to go outside and see if the water in the creek has receded much. Wanna go?" Ethan asked, not expecting her to accept. "A little fresh air will be good for you."

Thoughtfully, Anna rubbed her neck and jaw before answering, "It might." She grabbed up a knitted shawl.

Ethan helped her wrap it around her shoulders, and they proceeded out the door.

To their dismay the water neared the entrance to the dugout. They looked at one another in surprise. Down the hill a ways, the lean-to looked like a big hunk of wood floating in the middle of a playa lake.

"This is the third water crossing, so if this branch of the creek is this full, the other two are just as bad," she said.

Lightning sparked in the west. Another storm was gathering steam to pounce upon the rain-saturated earth.

"I guess you were right. The kid knew what he was doing when he took the horses to higher ground," Ethan said, hating to admit he was wrong about Dakota. "Are you sure he's okay?"

"He's tough, intuitive, and knows how to live off the land." She pulled the wrap around her tighter. "He's probably been enjoying roasted prairie chicken in the cave he likes to hide out in."

"You know where he goes, then?" Since Dakota was just a kid, Ethan didn't like the idea of leaving him to survive on his own in the wilderness and didn't mind letting Anna know how he felt either. "I'm still not sure about him being out there by himself."

"Don't worry. Dakota looks much younger than he is."

"How old is he, then?"

"Uh . . ." She hesitated before answering, "I'm not certain, probably eighteen, nineteen. I'm not sure he knows himself."

Ethan raised a questioning eyebrow. "Is Dakota his first or last name?"

"A nickname. I was told his mama gave birth to him up in the Dakotas and that's how he got it."

"Sure glad she didn't live in Virginia when he was born,"

Ethan remarked, trying to take her mind off the flooding. Very much more rain and the dugout could be under water.

Anna smiled meekly, hopefully a sign she appreciated his failed attempt at humor.

"Looks like there's nothing we can do, so let's go to bed," she said.

"Is that an invitation, Savannah?" He winked, trying to let her know he was kidding . . . or was he?

"When bulls fly, Dimples." She glared at him, then said, "But knowing you, you could probably convince a bull to try."

She flounced back into the house, and before Ethan cleared the threshold he was hit with a quilt and a pillow that made him think there was a chicken out there somewhere with more feathers than she deserved.

"Does this mean what I think it means?" Ethan laughed, knowing he was riling her up big-time.

"It means pull up a corner of the floor and make yourself at home or swim out to the lean-to, whichever you prefer." She yanked the curtain closed, separating him from where she stood next to the bed. "Good night, Mr. Kimble."

A few minutes later, Anna finished changing into a thread-bare gown, long ago missing four tiny pearl buttons that held it together. She combed her hair, without hearing so much as a peep from the man on the other side of the curtain.

Why in the world would he even tease about something as delicate as sharing a bed? He'd destroyed that possibility six years ago when he'd walked away from her without so much as a good-bye to become a Texas Ranger.

She cursed lightly to herself because she didn't think to bring the candleholder over to her side, so it remained on the table, illuminating Ethan.

From his silhouette, he appeared to be nonchalantly drinking coffee as he sat at the table. It was as if he were waiting for sunrise to announce the beginning of a new day.

Crawling into bed, Anna pulled the quilt up to her chin and wiggled her bottom around a couple of times until she got situated on the thin, worn-out mattress.

"Good night, Savannah," Ethan said in a rich, virile voice that could easily unlock her heart and soul.

"Sleep tight, Dimples." She smiled, remembering how his nickname had comforted her and given her quiet strength. Anna closed her eyes. With thoughts of the strapping lawman nearby to protect her, no doubt she'd rest better than she had in a very long time.

But sleep evaded her. She tried unsuccessfully to keep her eyes closed, but Ethan's every move enchanted her and she found herself watching him through the tissue-thin curtain.

He put his cup in the dishpan before spreading the quilt on the floor exactly in the place where Dakota typically played his game. That amused Anna a little bit.

Ethan leisurely began to remove his clothes, almost as if he knew she was watching. He tossed his shirt on the back of a kitchen chair and stretched, letting out a deep yawn, probably to aggravate her. "Sure is hot in here," he said.

She flipped over to face the wall without replying, closed her eyes again to remind her that she needed sleep whether Ethan did or not.

"About as hot as a branding iron on a bull's butt." He chuckled. "If the cowpokes weren't holdin' him down, he'd probably try to fly."

Ethan Kimble, you will not get to me, she reminded herself over and over.

Soft rain began to fall again, which typically would lull her into sweet dreams, but not tonight.

One at a time his boots hit the hard dirt floor with a firm thud.

Turning back on her side, Anna watched as Ethan unbuckled his gun belt and hung it over the chair, along with his pants. With the exception of a pair of sit-down-upons that fit him like a second skin, he was totally naked.

Refusing to watch any more of Ethan's shenanigans, which she had little doubt were for her benefit, she rolled to her back and focused on the wall where a single nail was precariously holding up one end of the rickety clothesline. The curtain seemed to bow lower by the minute.

Dern it, why hadn't she gone ahead and repaired the hole when she had noticed the moisture collecting earlier in the day?

The room did feel humid, exceptionally hot and somewhat stifling, but she wondered how much was due to the weather and how much was due to her own body heat rising from thinking about Ethan nearly naked in the same room as her.

Sagging even lower, the curtain caught Anna's eye again. Something had to be done or the clothesline would definitely fall down, exposing her to the lusty, two-fisted lawman.

As quiet as a whispering pine, she threw back her covers and eased a nearby ladder-back chair under the wobbly line. With the intention of pushing the nail back into the wall, she stretched as far as she possibly could and tried to reach the stubborn thing. She couldn't quite get to it, so why not use the chair for the purpose its name implied—a ladder?

The rickety chair groaned with rebellion about the time she stepped back down, realizing the rungs weren't sturdy enough to hold her weight.

Without warning, the cane bottom gave way, setting the whole dang thing in motion, tilting on one leg, then another until it could no longer stay balanced. She grabbed for the first thing she could find, pulling hard on a fistful of fabric. The curtain snarled around her legs causing her feet to slip out from under her.

In one fluid motion, the nail tore free, causing the line

to snap and sending material whipping across her face and obscuring her sight. Twisting one way and then the other, she fought being trapped in the fabric, eventually sending her head over teakettle toward the floor . . . right into Ethan's arms.

One moment Ethan had been thinking about hitting the hay, and the next thing he knew, his arms were full of a sassy redhead. He didn't even have time to realize what a pickle she'd gotten herself into before she landed right in his lap.

Every inch of her soft, sensuous body melted onto him like freshly churned butter on a hot day. She wiggled and heaved upward trying to get untangled.

As much as Ethan enjoyed her exquisite body against his, he tried to grab one edge of the curtain to pull it over her head and hopefully release her. In the process, he not only gathered the thread-bare fabric with one hand but managed to snag the hem of Anna's gown. He eased the edge upward toward her waist, not knowing what weighted it down.

Suddenly he touched silky smooth skin, as luscious as velvet. The scoundrel in him kept his hand on her shapely thigh before letting his fingers wander upward a bit. The second he realized he'd explored a little higher than he knew he should have, Ethan jerked the cloth over her hips and rolled over, straddling her.

Anna managed to free one hand and slapped at him, keeping Ethan moving until he got off her.

Although he enjoyed the feel of her smooth skin against him, her hot breath, and the signals her body sent to his as she tumbled and twirled, he resisted taking advantage of the situation, but barely.

Muffled, she continued to jerk and curl, tightening the fabric with each turn, entrapping herself like a mummy.

"Hold still, Savannah," he ground out between gritted teeth. "You're only making things worse by moving so much."

Loud mumbling came from beneath the swaddling. He couldn't make out the words and didn't waste time trying to either. Even though her tone was muffled he didn't miss the string of silken threats coming from her mouth. He heard at least one *hellfire and brimstone* and another couple of not so ladylike words he didn't think she even knew.

"Stay still!" he ordered.

She finally stopped fighting and settled down a tad. Slowly Ethan finished unwrapping her, almost enjoying it every time he touched her warm flesh, yet knowing when he got her loose she'd be coiled like a rattler and ready to strike at the first opportunity.

Once he pulled away almost all of the material, except for some across her hips and waist, the thought of kissing her hung heavy on his mind. Just the way she peered up at him, with dazzling white teeth and such kissable lips, made him feel what any man would feel under the circumstances. He just prayed she didn't feel it too.

Self-restraint won out. Ethan pushed up with both arms and stared deep in her eyes.

Trying not to drag her into his arms and kiss her deliciously tempting mouth ended up being a lot more difficult than he first thought. He had to scrounge up every ounce of willpower he had in him.

Ethan had an assignment—to keep Anna safe—and that didn't include being her lover.

Chapter 8

Anna and Ethan worked together, and it only took a short time, plus a sturdier nail, to reattach the divider separating her bed from the rest of the room.

Moments later, Anna once again settled in for the night. Fluffing her pillow for the umpteenth time, she reminded herself that she was safe and sound in her own bed, exactly where she wanted to remain until dawn.

From the edge of falling off to sleep, drifting dream clouds jerked her awake. Her thoughts were too riled up to rest. Everything from her being in the custody of one fine-looking, strapping lawman who could make her heart do summersaults with just a wink of an eye, to her concern over the flooding, rushed hither and yon in her mind.

While she tossed and turned, in the distance she heard Ethan moving every now and again.

Memories of his rock-hard body on top of hers resurfaced, sending a flame through her. Warmth she was unaccustomed to, but a sensation she could easily enjoy exploring.

For what seemed like an eternity, Anna's feelings flittered between passion and apprehension at having to leave the security of the Palo Duro to be prosecuted for her crimes.

But she could never lose sight of her promise to protect Dakota.

Emotions spiraled out of control entangling themselves with a mixture of desires and apprehension. She had wanted Ethan to kiss her but at the same time didn't want to give in to her passion.

When they had finally untwined themselves after she fell, she knew with his lips so close to hers, he was about to kiss her, yet he pulled away. Surely he wasn't all that chivalrous. Or was he?

Her mind continued to explore the what-ifs of his kiss. The thoughts probed and poked, keeping sleep even further at arm's length.

Enough is enough! Anna threw back the covers and sat up on the side of the bed. There was only one way to find out for sure if his kisses had matured along with the rest of his body.

In two steps she reached the edge of the curtain, where she hesitated before she lifted it back. Giving it more consideration, she eased it open to find Ethan lying on his back with his arms behind his head, eyes closed. Soft candlelight danced over his muscle-bound arms and chest.

There was no way a lawman of Ethan's caliber hadn't heard her slewfooting it in his direction, but if he did, he didn't let her know.

Kneeling down she kissed him full on the lips, at first lightly, but then as he returned her kiss, it became meaningful and heart-stopping. Tenderly, he slipped his arms around her waist but didn't pull her to him, just made sure she didn't escape until he had his fill of her sweet, luscious mouth on his.

Anna whispered, "Thank you, Dimples," and returned to her lonely bed.

The candle winked a final good night before it went out, as though the rain that continued to pelt down on the dugout had extinguished it. Another roll of thunder came from the west.

The nothingness of darkness, deep and quiet, encompassed her. Anna drifted off into slumber.

Coming in and out of sleep, she fought through her dreams, trying to distinguish between reality and nightmares. Darkness intermitted with brilliance, creating confusion. She felt herself falling into a shaft of muted sounds, down the slippery slope of life's occurrence she didn't want to revisit.

Ethan sat at her kitchen table, giving her a big, sensual smile, while braiding strands of narrow rawhide, which he then quickly knotted together to make cuffs.

Without warning his smile faded, replaced with the harsh, nasty face of Gator Graves. He was so close to Anna that she could nearly choke on the smell of yesterday's whiskey on his breath.

Belligerently, he bellowed, "See girl, ye cain't go no-where we cain't find ye." A thin trickle of spit dribbled from his mouth as he laughed.

His facial features slid away and were replaced with the face of Bradford Jackson III groping her, trying to kiss her. She fought back and screamed, "Ethan! Ethan! Ethan!" Jackson jerked away and with a wicked witch's laugh he re-leased her and began melting away, until he disappeared into the ground, leaving only a puddle of black nothingness.

Her frightfulness galloped along.

During daylight, the gang would ride the back trails from one heist to the next unsuspecting bank. Anna had tried to keep her mind off the pain of being hobbled like a horse who knew not to move if he got tangled in barbed wire. No matter how hard she tried, the nights weren't any better than her fears.

After throwing a camp in some out-of-the-way spot, she would be given rations of cold beans, which, after a while, began to taste good. At least she'd had something in her stomach besides bile.

If they'd had a good haul at the bank, Arlis Buckley, who was the only one of the outlaws she wasn't frightened of, would sneak her a piece of his hardtack or maybe a bite or two of dried beef. She had learned to eat slowly because she knew once she was finished her hands would be tied and she'd be hobbled with just enough rope for her to stretch out, but never without being uncomfortable. If it was cool, at least Arlis would give her his thread-bare blanket.

Anna felt herself tossing and turning trying to fight off her nightmares but couldn't. On gossamer wings she was transported to a campsite along a rushing river lined by stands of cottonwoods and wild berries.

Anna lay as quiet as a church mouse with a knot in her stomach, not certain if it was from not eating or the results of the whooping Gator had given her because he blamed her that their take at the last holdup wasn't as good as they had hoped for.

Blood coagulated on her hands from shielding herself from the whip he wielded.

Arlis suddenly appeared with a tin of salve used to tend the horses and offered it to her. "Don't cry. Don't cry. Don't cry," the dark-bearded outlaw whispered before disappearing back into the shadows.

After the lookout kid's pony fell due to exhaustion, she and Arlis rode double on a palomino he named Troubadour. For weeks afterward, she and the youthful outlaw forged a friendship three words at a time, but she was very cautious, realizing that if he got caught befriending her, he'd receive the same wrath handed her by Gator Graves.

Thunder or maybe gunshots, Anna couldn't tell for sure, bolted through her.

Flashes of bright light. The brilliance and blasts came together more frequently, louder and louder.

The images in Anna's mind became washed in red. Thunder became more intense and everything around her turned terra-cotta. The stream ran rapid with blood.

A man laid out by the undertaker came into view. Or was it an undertaker?

Another flash of light. She could see the deceased more clearly now, an expressionless face with innocent eyes full of wonderment. The face was almost hidden by a heavy beard. He wasn't a kid, but he wasn't a man either.

In a shaky voice, the undertaker whispered to the dearly departed, "Lie still, son." As if he wasn't experienced in what he was doing, he adjusted the kid's hat to obscure his facial features.

A black cloth appeared. Not over the lifeless body, but hovered over the undertaker, who hurried to a big, square black box. She could see more clearly now. He covered his head with the ebony material, trying to hide.

Boom . . . she heard the shot. And saw a flash of light. Lightning? But why had she heard the thunder first?

Could it be a flash from the camera?

Another boom ricocheted off the walls, followed by a louder one. Anna screamed, "No! No! No!"

Anna felt the big Cajun's whip lash at her as she ran down the dirt street with Gator Graves and Shorty Duncan closing in on her. Flogging and whipping her all the way. Something weighed her down to the point she couldn't move any farther. She looked over her shoulder and saw that the dead man gripped the hem of her skirt. Suddenly she realized she wasn't the one screaming the words, "No! No! No!" It was the deceased.

* * *

A burst of light illuminated the inside of the dugout, brighter than anything Anna had ever seen.

Startled, she pulled herself along a long path until she finally came fully awake.

Grabbing her chest, she tried to calm her racing heart. Closing her eyes, she took a deep breath.

The dreams again! She couldn't escape the memories that were permanently etched in her soul.

Her heart continued to pound out of control and sweat trickled between her breasts.

The same hideous nightmares again.

Night after night.

Week after week.

Month after month.

Tears rolled over her cheeks and meshed with the perspiration before settling on the thin fabric of her gown.

Another flash of lightning from the storm outside filled the air as she felt Ethan's weight on the side of the bed. He stretched out beside her and gently gathered her in his arms.

"It's okay, Savannah." Ethan cradled her and softly rocked her back and forth. "Nobody's gonna hurt you." He wiped the tears from her face and pulled her tight against him. "It was a dream, that's all." He kissed her temple and pulled her even tighter. "Trust me. I'll take care of you."

"I do." She was hardly able to raise her voice above a whisper. "I know it's late, but I need to tell you some things."

He brushed the hair from her temple and said, "Savannah, you don't have to tell me anything. I'm in no position to judge you. I know you're innocent, and my job is to protect you and get you back to Galveston safely."

"Thank you." She closed her eyes, and for the first time in months, she knew unequivocally she felt secure in the arms of the man she had loved for an eternity.

Chapter 9

Anna woke up to the sun peeking through the tiny window sending catawampus patterns of dim light across the walls of the dugout. She stretched and rolled on her side and caressed the mattress where Ethan had slept. She had vaguely heard him get up at daybreak. The smell of coffee still lingered in the air.

Closing her eyes again, she knew Ethan could never be kept indoors when the sun was up. He'd told her years ago that his pa figured that the sun coming up was God's signal to go to work.

With the storms, it wasn't likely that Dakota had brought the horses back down to the floor of the canyon because of the mud. Knowing Ethan, she was sure he was out scouting for Dakota.

She felt ashamed of herself for sleeping in, something she hadn't done in years. It was such a comfort to wake during the night and feel Ethan's protective arm flopped across her middle. Each time, she'd only partially come awake until his soft snoring lulled her back to sleep. She wasn't even sure it was snoring, but whatever it was gave her comfort that her Sir Lancelot was still there.

As much as she needed to stop lollygagging away her

day, she was enjoying, for the first time in a while, not having to be afraid of every sound, every movement, every moment of the day.

The significance of her nightmares haunted her. Everything in them portrayed a part of her life, but more vivid and grotesque than in reality. It was like a real world of make-believe.

Anna didn't want sympathy from Ethan, just acceptance, but still wasn't all that confident with how much of her abuse and heartache she felt comfortable sharing with him. Yet it was important to her that he know some of what she'd had to endure. With his understanding, eventually she'd tell him every detail.

If recent weather was any indicator, they still had a day or so before it'd be safe to travel. Time was on her side.

Although Ethan had questions that deserved answers, she had only one for him. One that had eaten at her for years. What had been so important that he rode out of Galveston and was never seen again until the day she robbed her father's bank? Something serious enough that made his own mother walk on the other side of the street to avoid Savannah and her family. But was it anything she needed to know right now? Wasn't it enough that they'd found one another again and had the opportunity to rebuild their relationship? That was, if he could help her avoid prison time.

If Ethan could be as caring and gentle as he had been under the present circumstances, maybe, just maybe, they might have a future together.

Her thoughts wandered back to the night before. One thing for certain: if Ethan still felt today about her like he felt last night when he straddled her, nothing could pull them apart again—nothing.

But, in the back of her mind, she still worried about what prison life would be like. Her father, the family man he was, wouldn't likely prosecute her once he knew the whole story about how she was trapped into participating in order to protect her family. If Gator and Shorty told the authorities even half the truth, which she doubted they were capable of doing, she could be totally exonerated for her part in the other robberies, but the reality of the severity of what she'd done lingered.

The concern that consumed her the most was her duty to shield Dakota from harm.

She wanted to enjoy the first day in a long time without rain and take pleasure in her newly found comfort level with Ethan, but regardless of what he said, they still had to have a heart-to-heart. Just like her mama and daddy used to do: have after-dinner drinks in the parlor and talk. Since there was no comfy settee in the dugout, two chairs at the kitchen table would have to do.

Jumping out of bed she threw a raggedy wrap over her gown, then hurriedly put on her mud-hardened boots before rushing outside to take in the new day.

Although there were still lots of white fluffy cumulous clouds with sagging black underbellies hanging around, the rain had been held at bay.

The birds forced to take cover by the storms had returned. The howling wind had settled to a hardy breeze, and she watched a blue jay pecking and searching for food. He flew into a mesquite bush when he detected her.

Water in the creek was now restrained between its banks but was still too dangerous to cross. The footbridge had managed to retain its integrity but obviously would require some extra support posts before it could safely hold a horse and rider.

But the biggest surprise to Anna was that the ground wasn't still waterlogged, and the dirt had begun to dry into walkable clay.

All with nature seemed to have been equalized overnight.

She noticed Ethan's boot prints heading off into a path she'd never explored. It was an area of open prairie with an abundance of cedar trees, mesquite, and wildflowers where feral animals and birds would find sanctuary.

Anna had never ventured far away from the dugout after the day she and Dakota came across a small black bear scurrying off to find shelter in a sandstone ledge. When she'd asked Dakota what he thought, he'd said, "Won't hurt, won't hurt," but didn't waste any time retreating back across the footbridge to safety.

As Anna now looked at the bridge, she knew they still couldn't ride out until it was repaired, but that didn't sadden her. She could get accustomed to spending time with the rugged lawman, at least until he had to hand her over to the authorities down South.

After tonight, she could relax and enjoy Ethan because he'd know all of her secrets . . . even the one about Dakota.

Quickly, Anna returned to the dugout and dressed in her pants and shirt. She combed her hair and grabbed her muddy dress and petticoat, then her pantaloons. The tub was filled with rainwater and she washed her clothes, along with a couple of tea towels, then hung them on the clothesline above the washtub. The wild, West Texas wind whipped them back and forth to dry.

Anna checked the area around the lean-to, which was still under siege by mud, but no horses were in sight. She became a little uneasy about Dakota's whereabouts. She thought for certain he'd have brought the horses back down by now.

Ethan trudged her way with a bundle slung over his shoulder. Even from a distance, she could see he was covered with red muck, not much unlike the evening before.

She waved at him. As he neared, she made out several ears of corn strung together, as well as a bird—a very big bird.

"Afternoon, sunshine." He dropped the corn and bird at

her feet and turned to the washtub. "You said if I'd kill it, you'd cook it, so here he is." He pulled up his sleeves to begin washing up.

"I never said that, Ethan." She looked from the dead turkey back to the lawman. "What do you want me to do with him?"

"Cook him." His mouth twitched with amusement, as he vigorously washed his forearms. "If you start now, he'll be tender in two or three days." He laughed in a deep jovial way.

Disconcertedly, Anna crossed her arms and pointedly looked away, repulsed at the thought of a dead animal deliberately dropped at her feet. Apparently, Ethan thought it more humorous than she did.

"Found him eatin' in a corn patch over yonder." Ethan nodded in the direction he'd come from.

"I didn't know there was any corn or I'd already have been out there gathering it." She took two steps back.

"It's an abandoned Comanche campground left over from when they lived down here huntin' shaggies before they were run out of the Palo Duro." He dried his hands on a towel hanging on the outdoor clothesline.

Anna's stomach felt slightly queasy, although the taste of fresh meat did tempt her taste buds. "How do I, uh, cook him?"

An easy whimsical smile played at the corner of Ethan's mouth, deepening his dimples. "Too big to pan fry, but I spied a pretty tough-lookin' piece of a green tree limb that should be strong enough to make a spit out of for him." He raised a playful eyebrow. "So, you'd better get a wiggle on if you plan on gettin' him dressed out and ready to cook before I have the fire ready."

Anna's mouth dropped open, and she could only imagine how ridiculous she looked. She wasn't a hundred percent certain whether he was kidding or not, but one thing she was sure about, she damn well wasn't about to go cleaning a turkey. Not only did she have absolutely no idea where to even begin, but the thought sent bile rushing up in her throat, making her want to throw up.

Ethan shot her another smile meant to win her over. "I'll make a deal with you. I'll take care of the bird and you can fix the corn. Presume you've shucked corn before."

"Of course I know how," she replied, praying he didn't notice the lack of finality in her voice. The handsome honyock knew full well she didn't know squat about cooking, although she'd seen the family cook prepare fresh corn. She took a deep breath. One thing for sure, it'd be less painful than beheading a turkey. "There's dry wood inside."

"So, we've got a deal. You fix the corn and I'll roast the buzzard." He smacked his lips and grinned like he knew something she didn't. "Some good grub tonight, *girl*."

Panic choked through Anna at his choice of words. She resisted yelling, "Don't ever call me a girl!" Instead she said way too harshly, "Ethan, call me a woman, a lady, or a floozy—I don't give a rip which one—but never a girl."

A muscle in Ethan's jaw quivered, and his brows narrowed, as if he was trying to figure out what had just happened.

Ethan didn't deserve her outburst. She immediately felt bad about it and tried to explain it away. "I'm sorry, it's been a long time since I was a girl."

"No offense meant."

She inhaled, hoping to shoo away the memories of Gator's voice that had ignited her flare-up, and offered, "I know."

Picking up the ears of corn still tied together, she added, "Do you want something to drink before you begin pluckin'?"

"Gotta do some choppin' first." A flash of humor crossed his face. "Had my fill of coffee earlier, but left some for you."

Ethan went inside and returned with a hatchet in one hand and a knife in the other. He handed off the knife to her, grabbed the bird, and headed back the way he'd originally come from, but not before he shot over his shoulder, "Nice drawers you've got hangin' up there." Then he stopped and turned back in her direction before adding, "Lady."

Anna rushed to the line and felt the clothes, which weren't thoroughly dry. Hellfire and brimstone, she had planned to have her unmentionables back where they belonged before he saw them. With Ethan's razzle-dazzle, she'd been distracted and didn't even notice they were still flapping in the breeze. Dang it, she couldn't win for losing with the man, but at least he showed her that he wasn't still angry with her.

Anna grabbed the first ear of corn and pulled back several layers of husks, exposing a green, well-nourished worm that squirmed around, probably angry that he was about to be plucked from his cushy abode inside the slimy brown cob. She thought she was going to throw up, but she put on her big-girl bloomers and with two chops she separated the desecrated cob from the edible portion, sending the worm on the ride of his life toward a bucket on the floor. After removing the silk, she wrapped the corn back up in the shucks and set it off to the side to be roasted.

One down, a baker's dozen to go, but so far so good!

Ethan returned to get a stew pot and quirked a grin as he headed back up the path.

Anna had just put up her dry laundry when he returned a second time to present her with the bird's innards, which he set on the potbelly stove. Now she really might puke.

"Ethan," she said, stopping him. "Has Dakota returned with the horses yet?"

"Not seen hide nor hair of the kid or the mutt," he said. "And I kept my eyes out for any tracks, but with the rain they were washed away."

"If anything was wrong, the horses would have come back by now," she said. "It's not uncommon for him to lose track of time." Anna tried to convince herself everything was okay, then added, "But I know where he likes to go, if you think we should begin looking for him."

"It's too muddy to try to climb up there tonight, so we'll have to wait until morning." Ethan looked up at the building thunderheads. "Remember, he can take care of himself, you told me."

"I know. I know. But accidents happen."

"Savannah, I'm concerned about him too."

Later that evening just before sunset Ethan and Anna dined on the first decent meal either of them could recall having in quite some time.

She washed the dishes and Ethan dried. Like an old married couple they cleaned up after supper before heading to the table to drink coffee.

"Anna, I know we need to get a few things straight, but I've had a really good time getting reacquainted with you, so unless there's something that can't wait until morning, let's enjoy what's left of our day. I don't want us to say goodbye before we say hello."

Relieved, she finally asked, "How about playing cards?"

"Only if I get the first deal." He finished off his coffee.

"Got cards?" Anna tossed out.

"Got more coffee?" Ethan fired back.

"I think I have something you'll appreciate more." She walked to the cupboard and on tiptoes stretched until an amber bottle was within reach. She turned and held it up for him.

"Whiskey?" Ethan fetched a deck of cards from his saddlebags.

"Half a bottle of some of Tennessee's finest." She picked up two cups and poured them each a swig. "Someone liked the good stuff apparently."

"Gin Rummy?" Ethan shuffled the deck.

Ethan teased that she won first only because he was off his game. She countered that she was more calculating as a card player. However, it wasn't long until their take-no-prisoner attitudes kicked in.

When they were tied four games each and the whiskey bottle was empty, the lantern flickered, reminding them it was either light another wick or get forty winks.

"Cheers." With about one good swig of whiskey left in it, Anna lifted her cup to Ethan, who goodnaturedly tipped it with his.

"Until the rubber match." He gave her a devilish, heart-warming smile.

In the distance, familiar thunder followed on the heels of lightning and announced another night of storms.

Concurrently, each spied the nail holding the clothesline up slowly slip out of the wall, allowing the willowy fabric to float to the ground.

The couple grimaced in good humor before breaking out into infectious laughter.

"I guess there'll be no modesty around here," she said.

"And I'm not gonna be hornswoggled out of gettin' the fluffy pillow tonight, either." He stood up, smiling with satis-faction.

Damn the sexual magnetism that made the lawman so self-confident and fueled her every fantasy.

Chapter 10

The sun blazed high overhead. Ethan mopped the sweat from his brow with the back of his hand, then picked up the ax. He split the piece of cedar in half. If all went well, he'd finish the repairs on the footbridge in no time. Then it'd be safe enough to carry the weight of a horse and rider. He'd gotten a lot of work done since sunup.

Thoughts of Anna crept to the front of his mind, as they'd been doing of late, and brought back recollections of the night before. Ethan smiled, thinking about the shocked look on her face when he'd teased her about their sleeping arrangements. Being a gentleman, in spite of how much it hurt, he had accepted the quilt and raggedy pillow and pretended he was sleeping in a warm bed with the lovely redhead by his side.

Apart from having to sleep alone, he was thankful that she hadn't fretted the night away with horrific dreams.

At daybreak, Ethan had dressed quietly and foregone coffee to get an early start on walking the bluff trail in search of any signs of Dakota or the horses. To his frustration, he hadn't found tracks of either, only those of wild animals and birds. He wasn't too surprised since last night's rains would have erased them.

Ethan reached in his shirt pocket and pulled out a playing card he'd found on the path near one of the banks of a wash running fast with rainwater. He studied it as if he'd never seen a jack of hearts before. Although it was pretty dog-eared, it wasn't weatherworn, so it hadn't been out in the elements long. The back was the same as that of the ones he carried, but there was no way it belonged to his deck. He returned it to his pocket.

When he finished fixing the bridge, he planned to begin preparation for their trip out of the canyon, so they'd be ready to travel the moment Dakota returned with the horses.

The sound of the screen door slamming shut distracted Ethan. Anna drew water from the well and filled a canteen before heading his way. She had dressed in pants and a shirt instead of her calico dress. A floppy hat topped her outfit. No doubt she was on a mission and it wasn't to keep Ethan from keeling over from lack of water.

The most difficult part of the day was coming his way.

Blast it! He could see the determination in her face and knew she was aiming to begin their search for Dakota. Maybe she'd relent once she found out Ethan had already been out earlier and hadn't come across any signs of the kid or the horses. To strike out again so soon would be down-right foolish since the day had already ripened into one hot son of a gun.

"Brought you some water," she said, handing off the canteen.

"Much obliged." He drank his fill, enjoying the gesture. "Nice and cool. Want some?" He handed the canteen back to her all the while knowing she hadn't come just to make sure he didn't parch in the heat.

Sure enough, it didn't take her long to begin. "No, thanks. I'm going to walk up toward the ledge where I'm pretty sure Dakota would have taken the horses."

"Savannah, it's way too hot and will only get hotter. With

the heat and humidity we're going to have bad storms again, and it'll be so sizzling in the floor of this canyon that lizards will be beggin' you to tote them water. It's too dangerous." He leaned against the post he'd just finished adding extra support to and waited for a backlash.

To his surprise, she said, "You're probably right, but will you go with me when it cools off some?"

"If it doesn't storm, but I know what we can do in the meantime. There's a rock formation about a quarter mile up that way that sits back off the path and is shaded. We can walk and talk a bit if you'd like."

Dang it! There he went again compromising. It wasn't in his nature, but she sure as hell had a way of doing strange things to his thinking.

"Let's go," she said, stringing the canteen over her shoulder. "Maybe we can find some tracks that way."

"Savannah, I've already been up there lookin' around this morning." He hesitated and tried to weigh his words carefully before he continued. "But I didn't find hide nor hair of them and it's still slippery, too. So let's not trouble trouble unless it troubles us, okay?"

Ethan briefly considered telling her about the playing card, but he didn't want to add to her concern over Dakota's welfare. Plus, he wanted to make sure that by chance the card hadn't come from his own deck.

"Deal." She flashed him a smile of thanks. "I haven't been too adventurous while we've been down here, so I'd really like to see the rocks you found." She continued to lock gazes with him, but Ethan saw the worry lingering in her eyes. "How long can we wait before you have to take me back to Galveston?"

"Until we find the horses," Ethan said. "I'll put up the ax and we'll take a walk."

"Just leave it in the lean-to. That's where it belongs anyway," she said.

They hiked along a path spotted with scarlet and orange Indian paintbrush and some yellow flowers that made Ethan think of scrambled eggs, something he hadn't eaten in a while.

It didn't take them long to reach the rock formation, and as Ethan anticipated, it was nice and shady.

They sat quietly and didn't speak, each absorbed in private thoughts. Feeling a need to protect Anna, he slipped his arm around her waist. They watched a bird graceful in flight dive-bomb a prairie dog, coming up empty-handed.

In the distance a dozen vultures circled overhead.

Tranquility of nature at its finest.

Anna was the first to break the silence. "Ethan, you told me that Gator and Shorty are in jail, but are you absolutely positive that my family is safe?" She lowered her head, as well as her voice. "I can't afford to go back if they are in any type of danger. I'd rather die first."

"Savannah, I promise you they are out of harm's way. Your father has hired a dozen men, even a Pinkerton agent, to protect your family. Bet your mama's having a hissy fit about now."

That caused her whole face to light up with a smile. "She's probably beat him around the stump a dozen times." She chuckled softly to herself. "But I'm truly worried about all of them." She looked up at Ethan with eyes filled with unspoken pain. "And especially Charlie."

"I know what it's like to have a need bigger than your own to protect a brother," he said.

Ethan hoped his words didn't reflect the ache he felt in his heart, but oh how he could relate to wanting to guard a sibling more than life itself. Walking to the end of the earth and back wasn't too far to go in order to guard a loved one. He felt sorry for her and really wanted to tell her something, anything, that would make her feel more at ease. Changing the subject, he said, "Your mama sure is enjoying the pocket watch you gave her for her birthday."

Anna stiffened and he could feel her quiver. She looked in his eyes and responded, "I never got the watch to give it to her, Ethan."

"She has one exactly like you described. When I complimented her on it, she said that it was a birthday present. Anna, I've thought all along that you'd given it to her before you were trapped into all of this mess."

"Gator never gave me the pocket watch. I never even saw it, so I surmised that he most likely didn't have one in the first place." Her voice died away for a second before she continued, "That was until I overheard him bragging to Shorty and Arlis about how he should have sold it to me and made some money off it instead of having to give it to someone he owed a favor to."

An alarm quaked Ethan's body. Whom did Gator owe a favor to? Who, besides Anna, even knew about the watch? And who had given her mother the birthday present?

Ethan gathered his wits. "But he never said a name or what type of favor?"

"No, but I've had plenty of time to think about it. And, Ethan, I believe there was someone besides the three of them who planned the robberies, but I never saw the person or heard a name." She swallowed hard and took a deep breath. "Gator and Shorty are just plain evil, but they aren't bright enough to stage such an elaborate scheme of bank heists."

"That's been a theory for a while, but I have to admit that a bastard like Graves is always in debt of someone, so there could be an endless list of possibilities."

Unless Gator had stolen the watch in the first place, which was a real possibility, he must've owed someone one hell of a big favor because a piece of jewelry with that many diamonds was worth a lot of money.

Somewhere along the line, the pocket watch got into the

hands of Anna's mother. But how? The lawman in Ethan made him want to know more about what had gone on while Anna was on the run. As much as he didn't want to have to make her dredge up bad memories, he'd given her enough opportunities to voluntarily tell him everything, and she hadn't. He wanted to help her out of the predicament she was in and avoid prosecution, but she had to be honest with him, whether the truth hurt or not.

"Savannah, in order to help you, I really need to know every detail about how you escaped. Maybe there's something I can do before you have to face the judge."

She wasn't sure how much to tell him, but when she went to trial, if she was prosecuted, all the embarrassing details would be exposed, but there was one thing she was absolutely sure about—she would not expose Dakota. "I'll try. What do you want to know first?"

"Did you get any of the money? Benefit from it in any way?"

"No. Nothing, but . . ." She stopped and held back the words *beans*, reminding herself whatever she did she didn't want Ethan to feel sympathy for her. Instead, she simply said, "One meal a day."

"From what you've already said, Graves took you against your wishes and it'd be pretty indisputable in any court of law that he kidnapped you. At least, that'd be my defense." The lines of concentration deepened along his brow and under his eyes. "That is, if I were your lawyer." He drew in his lips thoughtfully before he continued, "But I still have to take you back for that to be determined."

"I know you've got a job to do. I guess studying law was better than being forced to become a banker." She braced herself for his assault, reminding him of his failure.

"And ending up being a lawman instead?" He contradicted her with a quirky smile that punctuated his point. "Tell me how you escaped."

"Arlis helped me, but he paid for it in the end. He befriended me, but it took a while. Then when he got caught they beat him unmercifully." Her mind filled with sour thoughts . . . unpleasant memories. "Like they did me." She looked up with tears boiling in her eyes, realizing she'd just broken one of her own rules. She didn't want Ethan to feel sorry for her. "But they beat him much worse because he was a man."

"I'm sorry, Anna, I know it hurts to talk about it, but I've got to know every tiny thing that happened if I'm going to help you. You might think something is unimportant, but it could be exactly what can make the difference between clearing you and sending you to prison." The lines of Ethan's mouth tightened, and then he asked, "What happened to cause them to beat him up so badly?"

"It was because of me." She shuddered at the memories. "At night when we camped and he was on guard, Arlis would come to me and lie down beside me on the ground, but only when the others were either too drunk to know or sound asleep. At first it unnerved me, but I learned to accept it since he seemingly was harmless. After a while, I realized he really didn't mean any harm."

A cold shiver spread over her as she recounted the events. "Then one night he got closer to me than he'd ever done before and reached up my dress. For the first time, I was frightened of him. I wanted to cry out but knew whether it was my doing or not Gator would blame me, so I just lay still."

The right words began to elude Anna, but from deep within she found the strength to continue. "Arlis hushed me by putting his hands over my mouth, and I knew my luck had run out and he was going to take advantage of me, but he just continued to whisper, almost as though to calm me, that I should be quiet. It didn't come across as threatening, but all the while he delved deeper between my underskirt and my dress."

Ethan's jaw quivered and his face registered his disdain. Staring ahead, he finally said, "If he wasn't already dead, I'd kill the sonofabitch."

"But, Ethan, he never touched me in a sexual way, just seemed obsessed with my petticoat." In a show of understanding how Ethan might feel, Anna rested her hand on his knee. "So please don't pass judgment until you hear what it meant. He told me over and over to trust him, and he'd protect me. And he stayed true to his word. Night after night he'd come to me and do the same thing."

Ethan took her hand and raised it to his lips, lightly kissing it. She leaned into him, thankful for his support.

"Then one night he hushed me, as he'd been doing every night for a while, but this time it was different when he reached up my dress. He seemed interested in pleating the material, and then I realized that he'd stuck something in my petticoat. Ethan, he never intended to take advantage of me. He had cut slits between the layers of my underskirt and had threaded in a knife. It wasn't all that big, and certainly not that sharp, but it gave me what I needed to escape." Anna lifted her head from Ethan's shoulder and turned toward him. "He even had made a makeshift casing to keep the blade from cutting me."

"He played it slow and safe, staying in the background, making everyone think he wasn't all that sharp," Ethan said.

"He's smarter than the others, but they never gave him any credit for anything he did right, and they never missed an opportunity to kick him around for what he didn't do right."

Anna was tired and didn't want to go on with her story, but she knew Ethan would pressure her. There was no doubt in her mind that he intended to help her in any way possible. "I just felt sorry for him, that's all."

Three turkeys strutted between mesquite bushes about six or eight yards away, and Anna sighed, wishing she could be as free and as unconcerned about her future as they were about theirs.

She took a breath and gathered her thoughts, going on to tell Ethan that she didn't sleep the rest of that night thinking she was being set up by Arlis. She'd be shot by the Big Cajun or Shorty if she even tried to escape. She didn't know how to trust, but at that time Arlis Buckley was her only friend.

"So, Arlis ended up saving your life by helping you escape?"

"Yes." Sudden relief flowed over Anna. For the first time, she'd told her story out loud. "If it hadn't been for him, I'd be dead today. I knew from that second on that if I didn't return the favor and trust Arlis, Gator and Shorty would end up killing both of us."

"I'm trying to understand, but there're still parts missing." Ethan took off his hat, ran his fingers through his hair, and put the Stetson back on.

"When Gator pushed the horses so hard that the pony Arlis had died from exhaustion, Arlis and I began to ride double. So I was able to talk to him when we were far enough ahead of the others and the wind was with us. Gator hated the dust, but he hated letting us out of his sight more, so sometimes we'd get a pretty good lead on them."

Slipping his arm around Anna, Ethan tucked her to his side and rubbed her shoulder but said nothing, as though he realized if he stopped to ask questions she'd lose the need to tell him everything.

"I'd talk very quietly, reassuring him that we'd both be safe, but he always indicated he wasn't so sure."

"Not much of a talker, then?"

"Short on words, but long on smarts."

"So how'd you get away?"

"It doesn't matter now, Ethan. Arlis continued to come to me every night, and when we got on the other side of Menardville, he told me to take Troubadour and go to Abilene."

"And you eventually did?" Ethan asked.

"Yes."

"That pretty much explains what happened to Buckley—they probably killed him when they saw you were gone with his horse."

She closed her eyes, almost thankful that Ethan had come up with an excuse for Arlis's death. "If they did kill him, it was because they lost another horse, not because I was gone. By that time, I'd become a nuisance to them. The novelty of a gang led by a redheaded woman had worn off. I think they knew they were about at the end of the line with their bank heists. Each robbery was harder than the one before, and the haul became less and less."

"A bunch of outlaws could blend in no matter where they went, but not with a beautiful gal like you in tow. The law was on their butts, and they knew it."

Although the heat was stifling, the shade helped shield them. Ethan continued to hold her close, occasionally kissing her temple.

Now for the part of the story she'd been dreading since she'd laid eyes on the lawman. The truth about Arlis's demise.

Anna impatiently corralled her drifting thoughts, knowing what she had to do, while praying Ethan would understand.

Ethan pulled his big frame to his feet and reached down for her hand, tenderness and caring filling his gaze.

From the distance, a dog's bark broke the silence. A hound almost unrecognizable, because he was covered with red mud, bounced out of the brush and announced his arrival with a concerto of barks.

Bones danced at Ethan's feet circling around and around begging for the lawman's attention. "I never thought I'd see the day that I'd be happy to see such a mangy mutt."

A combination of apprehension and relief flooded Anna's thoughts. She knew the dog wouldn't have left Dakota's side if he was injured or lost, but where was the kid?

Bones wagged his tail and she swore he smiled at Ethan, a much different welcome than the first day they met. The pooch rolled over twice, scratched behind his ear, and yelped at Ethan.

Although he tried to ignore the dog, it seemed Bones wouldn't have anything to do with it. Ethan sat down, patted his knee, and the mud-clad dog jumped in his lap so Ethan could check his paws. "Anna, he's walked a long ways."

"You mean the *mangy mutt* walked a long ways."

"Might have to change his name." Ethan laughed and made a funny face at Bones, who tried to lick Ethan before he shooed him away.

Suddenly, Troubadour loped down the path in their direction on the heels of Ethan's palomino.

After Ethan gave both horses a preliminary once-over to make sure they had fared the storms, he took the reins and walked with Anna back to the small corral.

"Are they okay?" Anna asked.

"Troubador's front legs are pretty bunged up where someone who didn't know squat about hobbling tried to—"

"Then they weren't with Dakota, because he never would have hobbled them." An uneasy feeling squeezed at her heart. "If someone used that method to restrain them, it wasn't Dakota."

"What makes you think that?"

"Remember how he reacted when you mentioned that you'd hobbled Yellow Jacket the first day?"

Ethan nodded in agreement. "He certainly didn't take kindly to the way I handled my horse, and as I recollect, it really upset you the way he acted."

"It wasn't him. It was . . ."

Dark angry clouds overshadowed white fluffy ones, promising evening thunderstorms.

As they walked, Anna dug deep inside to tell Ethan about how Gator and Shorty would hobble her at night to keep her from escaping. The practice that, with the aid of the knife Arlis hid in her skirt, eventually helped her escape since they didn't watch her as carefully.

The closer they got to the dugout, the faster Bones ran.

"I don't think Bones would have left Dakota willingly either," Anna said as they neared the lean-to.

Ethan dug into his pocket. "This morning, I found this near a wash just a little north of where you said Dakota would take the horses." He handed her the jack of hearts. "Do you have any idea what it means, if anything?"

Anna examined the card carefully. "No. Unless the fact that Dakota doesn't like the jacks could make a difference. He always puts two of them aside when he plays cards and refers to them as his 'bad jacks.' Maybe he dropped it accidentally."

"Do me a favor. On the outside chance the card belongs to my deck, when you go in will you get my cards out of my saddlebags and make sure it isn't one of mine?"

"Sure, but unless you were hiding cards so you could win at gin and it fell out of your pocket, I can't see how one could get that far up the trail." She laughed at the thought of Ethan cheating at cards.

She thoughtfully rubbed the card. "Ethan, Dakota's cards are his best friends. He'd never misplace or lose one . . . unintentionally. That just isn't in his makeup. He has a purpose for everything he does."

The harder Anna tried to ignore the facts, the more they became real to her.

Like Arlis Buckley, Dakota did nothing without a reason.

Chapter 11

Anna chuckled all the way back to the dugout, thinking about how Bones wanted to follow her but kept running back to Ethan. Apparently the dog was undecided whether he should stay with his newfound friend or go with his master. A more fickle-minded dog she couldn't recall knowing.

Although clouds were building overhead, Anna felt only the sunshine. For the first time since the horrid day she saw her brother being held at gunpoint, she was shed of the cast-iron yoke that the robberies had put around her neck. Ethan not only understood what had happened, but wanted to help her get out of the mess. Although it had been heart wrenching to divulge every sordid detail, she had made it through the first step: making Ethan understand.

With Ethan's support, she could face anything, including her family and friends, whom she had betrayed. Once they knew the truth, she'd earn back their trust. She wished she had a crystal ball to see what the future held for her and Ethan.

Yes, she would still like to know what was so important that Ethan suddenly left town and became a Texas Ranger, but now that their relationship had matured, and might even have a future, it didn't matter.

Once inside the dugout Anna pulled out an iron skillet

and a bowl to make cornbread. While she worked, she imagined just how happy her father and mother would be to have her home safe and sound. Her father would be so indebted to Ethan that he'd offer him a job at the bank. The same bank where she'd always imagined he would work.

But what if he didn't want to be a banker? It didn't matter—she wanted him to follow his dreams and if being a lawman was what he wanted, she'd support him.

Maybe they could move away to begin a new life together. Only his happiness mattered to her, and since banks were in every town, if she wanted there'd always be work for her. But the job she wanted most was being a wife to Ethan and a mother to his children.

What in the Sam Hill! One very big problem existed: whether she'd seen it in his eyes or not, Ethan had never even whispered that he loved her or wanted to make a commitment to her for the rest of their lives. She'd pretty much gotten things bass-ackwards, thinking about white picket fences and baby prams. Had she gone loco?

Quickly she poured the cornbread mixture into the skillet, but kept her eyes peeled on the door, praying for Dakota's return. Something deep inside told her he was okay, but the fact that the horses and Bones had returned without him alarmed her. She was eager to tell him about their trip to Galveston, and if presented in a simple, direct manner where he came on board immediately with it, he'd probably even be excited and make it into an adventure.

For the first time since Ethan arrived, she knew in her heart that once she told him the truth about Dakota he'd do everything he could to help keep him safe, too.

If the flea-bitten mutt won the lawman over, no doubt Dakota could. As if on cue, Bones scratched at the door, and she let him in. She gave him a pat and returned to her chores, letting her thoughts wander around in her brain.

Ethan had made her realize that she truly wasn't a crook

but was an unwilling participant in the robberies. Of course, she knew that all along, but for some reason having someone acknowledge what she already knew seemed to exonerate her, at least in her own mind.

Ethan was the brightest kid in school, and that coupled with his good looks and charisma would have made him an excellent lawyer. If Anna had to select only one person to speak on her behalf, it'd be Ethan. But she knew her future would be placed in the hands of her father's personal lawyer, who always made her think of Sunday dinner—a roasted pig with a big apple in his mouth.

Anna washed the bowl she'd mixed the cornbread in and returned it to the cupboard.

Suddenly she realized she'd been so engrossed with fixing some supper and her dreams of what might be that she'd forgotten to look for the playing card.

Anna rushed to where Ethan left his saddlebags and dragged them over to the bed, where she heaved them onto the mattress. Digging deep into the first bag, she came up empty-handed. She turned it over and unbuckled the other side.

After moving around a number of items, Anna pulled out some and placed them on the bed, in order to locate the cards. She quickly checked the deck and accounted for all four jacks.

As she returned Ethan's personal things, she came across a tan box and recognized it as the one she had seen him with the first day he arrived in the canyon. Oh how she was tempted to open it. While she could blame curiosity for her desire to peek, she knew whatever was inside must be extremely personal for Ethan to keep it with him all of the time. Regardless of the temptation she would respect his privacy, as she would want him to do in return, and would forget about the box's existence.

Bones nudged her elbow. "Go away. Supper will be ready soon and you'll get your share, I promise," she said.

Anna shooed away the dog, although he only took it as a signal she wanted to play. The hound jumped at her, knocking the box out of her hand and onto the floor, spilling all of its contents.

"Now you've gone and done it, Bones," she said, as she bent over to retrieve the box. Faceup on the floor was a picture of a beautiful young woman with hair the color of wheat holding a baby boy of about six months. A pleasantly plump child.

Anna stared at the mother and baby. Carefully picking up the picture, she pored over it for a long time, examining every feature of the child. He was definitely a Kimble—she could tell by the shape of his forehead and the dimples.

Dimples . . . Her heart plunged.

A gamut of perplexing emotions trampled on Anna's soul.

She placed the picture in the box, along with a man's gold wedding band, before she noticed a card lying to the side. Written in an eloquent hand, it read:

I named him Ethan Robert Kimble. He looks just like you, even to his dimples. Never a day goes by that I don't miss you.

> *Love,*
> *Jenny*

"Ethan has a child," she whispered to herself. Tears welled in her eyes and a hurt deeper than anything she'd ever experienced stabbed at her heart. Worse than anything she had endured while on the run.

Anna took a deep breath to mask her inner turmoil, refusing to believe what was right before her eyes.

She picked up the ring once again and clenched it in her fist. Not only did Ethan have a son, but he had a wife. A beautiful family . . . the family she had just been visualizing as belonging to her.

Returning the ring to the box, she quietly put it back in Ethan's saddlebags, buckled the strap, and laboriously moved the bags to their original resting place.

Anna threw herself across the bed and let the tears flow.

Everything was clear to her now. Ethan had walked away from her six years before because he was in love with someone else.

The only word she never thought she'd ever use to describe Ethan—*coward*—speared itself through her heart.

Too cowardly to tell her that he'd fallen in love with someone else. Too cowardly to face her father and refuse his offer to work for him at the bank. Too cowardly to become a lawyer.

But what hurt the most was, Ethan hadn't lived up to his own commitments. Yet he had the gall to accuse her of running from her own.

Ethan took his time caring for the horses and preparing for their trip out of the canyon. When he finished, he'd make one more trek back up the Palo Duro in search of Dakota. It irked him to think that he might be right about the kid all along, that he was a horse thief. Otherwise, why was he nowhere to be found? He'd probably befriended Anna only for a safe place to hide out. Since she'd met him in Amarillo, he was likely already back there unconcerned about the good-hearted woman he'd trampled on.

Ethan could size up folks pretty good and didn't much like the idea of being hornswoggled, but Dakota had done a good job of it. No doubt he'd survive just fine by bamboozling other truly caring people like Anna.

Whether Ethan was willing to accept that he'd been fooled by Dakota or not, his real problem would be convincing Anna.

As he tended to Yellow Jacket's hoofs, his mind wandered back to the day of the bank robbery.

He'd left Galveston almost immediately after being hired by Anna's father to find her and wasn't armed with all the facts he would liked to have had. He was lucky that his captain was a comrade of Anna's father and was willing to give him time off to do the job for his friend. The sheriff, frankly, acted like he was glad he didn't have to assign a posse to chase down the Texas Flame Gang. It'd be just one less thing he'd have to take care of.

Maybe Ethan should have stuck around until they had pulled together all of the investigation, but to him it was pretty straight and to the point.

Finding Anna and getting her back to her family for protection was the job he'd been hired to do, not track down the outlaws and bring them to justice. But if they worked hand in hand that was okay too.

Ethan had set out on his own dime and time because he didn't want to be owing to anybody. He'd done it another way once with an outcome nobody wanted. Too many lives were destroyed and hearts broken. He'd never fall into that trap again.

But, at the same time, he had no reason to believe the Texas Flame Gang, whom nobody had ever heard of until Galveston, would go on a rampage up and down the Brazos River.

He shuddered at even the name . . . Texas Flame.

Going back over what was known about the bank heists, he sorted out fact from theory.

Most bank robberies were crimes of opportunity. Typically, it took at least four outlaws to carry it off. In a big operation such as the Galveston Merchant's Bank, it'd take that many or more.

Since Ethan couldn't afford to receive or send telegraphs along the way keeping him informed of the investigation, he had had to nose around from town to town to find out what he could. Although his captain allowed him to go off on his own as a favor to his friend, he'd made it clear that Ethan was not on official Texas Ranger business. As luck would have it, he was fairly well known around Texas, so without him presenting himself officially as a lawman, rumors flowed in his direction about as fast as the Red River after heavy rains.

Carefully, Ethan sorted out what he knew as truths.

In the Galveston robbery, Anna went to the bank at closing time flanked by shotgun-toting Gator Graves and Shorty Duncan. Without acknowledging anyone and acting like she wasn't afraid in the least, she strolled straight to the vault. She opened a big valise and cleaned out the safe, while the two outlaws held the lone teller and her father, Alexander Parker, at gunpoint.

Anna had confirmed what he'd been told that Arlis was the lookout who stayed outside to handle the horses, so they'd be ready for a quick escape. He was also assigned the job of alerting the inside men of any trouble brewing.

At this point, if Ethan's calculations were right, everyone was accounted for. Anna's mother was at the millinery shop, and Anna had already confirmed that her brother was being held at gunpoint at the Fillmore Opera House.

Ethan didn't recall being told who the teller was; however, he presumed him to be Bradford Jackson III, the same man who had witnessed Anna having dinner with Gator Graves. Ethan recoiled at the thought of even handling the same money touched by the slimy weasel bank teller, but apparently, Anna's father trusted him.

So, if everyone was accounted for, why didn't it feel

right? Ethan went back over the information again and again as he finished grooming Yellow Jacket and moved to Troubadour.

Graves and Duncan were in jail, and as many angry citizens seeking revenge as there were, a hemp committee might have already made them see the light.

Arlis Buckley was dead.

And Anna was with Ethan, but there was still something out of kilter with the whole picture.

Like a bolt of lightning the answer came to him.

Ethan hadn't been able to see the yucca for the prairie. If all of the gang was accounted for, who had stayed behind at the opera house to watch over their insurance—Anna's little brother, Charlie?

Anna had even mentioned that she thought there was another person involved, although in the past Ethan had discounted the theory.

Ethan released Troubadour into the corral and hurried to the dugout, eager to share his thoughts with Anna.

Maybe she could shed some light on who had stayed behind with her little brother—the fourth man.

Someone whom Gator owed a big favor . . . a favor worthy of a valuable diamond-encrusted pocket watch.

Just like the one Abigail Parker wore.

Chapter 12

Eager to learn Anna's thoughts on the identity of the fourth outlaw who kept her brother hostage during the robbery, Ethan reached the dugout just ahead of a late afternoon rain shower. Between the two of them, he was confident they could pare the list of possibilities down to a handful of suspects.

After washing up, he entered the dugout dodging Bones as he raced outside.

Anna stood in front of the dishpan staring at the pan in her hands. She didn't react when he closed the door with its customary bang.

"Smells good." He hung his Stetson by the door. "How long until supper?"

Only the distant rumble of thunder answered.

Taking a deep breath, she squared her shoulders, then set the pan on the cabinet top.

Her physical reaction, coupled with her ignoring a simple question, took Ethan aback. What could have happened in such a short period of time to distract her so?

No doubt Dakota's disappearance would cause her worry. It hurt Ethan to think how she would react when he'd tell her he didn't expect Dakota to return. How could he explain that there were no tracks whatsoever in any direction, and that the outlaw, who it was obvious to Ethan had snicker doodled everyone into thinking he was a young man with limited skills, had hobbled Ethan's palomino before riding up to the rim of the canyon on Troubadour? Not likely she would accept his theory that someone had provided Dakota with another horse nobody would recognize before he turned the Appaloosa loose to find his way back to the dugout. That was the best scenario Ethan could deduce from what he knew.

"What's wrong, Anna?"

She slung the dish towel aside indifferently and turned to face him. Although she was inches shorter than he, they came eye to eye. In a cold, cutting tone, she said, "You have a son!"

Ethan wasn't sure whether it was a question or a statement, but she hurled the accusation at him in such a manner that he knew she meant to rip out his heart. He'd gladly do it himself if it'd wipe away the anger in her voice and the tears in her eyes.

"What makes you think I have a child?" He took a step toward her, attempted to take her into his arms. "I'm not even married."

Rebuffing his advances, she moved away and returned to her sentry post at the window. "You don't have to be married to have a son," she snapped.

"Well, I do!" Ethan spat.

The sound of the door stopped the conversation.

Dakota entered wearing a scruffy, unkempt look. His disheveled dark hair was greasy and he exhibited the facial hair of a man, making him look much older than when he left days before. His black hat shadowed his forehead and eyes.

Without saying a word, Dakota walked over to the bed and dragged off the folded quilt. Settling in the corner, he pulled out the cards from the pouch hung around his neck.

As much as Ethan wanted to yell and ask him where he had been and didn't he understand how worried Anna had been about him, he couldn't bring himself to do it.

Something in Dakota's actions mesmerized Ethan. It was as if he didn't realize anyone else was in the room, not too unlike how Anna had been acting when Ethan showed up.

Removing one card from the deck, Dakota placed it to the side before saying, "Bad jack. Bad jack. Bad jack."

Dakota stared up at Ethan and Anna with a vacancy in his eyes that Ethan had never seen before, and he guessed from Anna's perplexed expression, she hadn't either.

Ethan took a step forward, and Anna caught him by the arm, stopping him. She shook her head and stepped around him.

Squatting down in front of Dakota, she asked, "Where have you been, Dakota?"

He returned the deck to the pouch and in measured strokes tore the remaining card into tiny pieces. He walked to the cold fireplace, threw in the pieces, and repeated three times, "No more bad jack."

Anna pulled to her feet, and before either of them spoke, Dakota cupped his hands over his ears and shuffled rapidly out the door, muttering the phrase over and over.

Ethan stepped forward, but again, Anna caught him by the arm. "Leave him be."

Without saying another word, Anna moved to the stove, stirred the beans, then began to set the table.

Standing near the fireplace, Ethan felt as though he'd just been dropped into the middle of someone else's dream. Shifting his gaze between Anna and the door, his thoughts darted around as he tried to figure out what in the hell had just happened. Confusion and frustration circled his head.

How could one Dakota leave and a different one return?

Thinking back to the maze of questions he had, suddenly the answer was as clear as the Texas sky on a calm day. He specifically recalled Anna's words as she'd asked the whereabouts of the other members of the gang: *you're positive they're still locked up and you've seen proof that Arlis is dead?* He recalled how pale she had become, almost acting as though she'd misspoken.

Savannah hadn't asked *if* he had proof, but if he'd *seen* the proof. But why did she even use the word *proof?* Evidence of the death of a fugitive to collect a reward had just recently become accepted. So how did she know to ask?

Grabbing his saddlebags, Ethan found the reward poster for Arlis Buckley. He stared at the picture for a long time before he slipped it in his shirt pocket.

Ethan hadn't gotten that good of a look at Arlis Buckley during the bank robbery, but the resemblance between Arlis and Dakota was uncanny. Why would someone want to send a photograph of Dakota to collect Arlis Buckley's reward money?

There was only one logical explanation: to make sure the law stopped searching for Buckley.

And the one person who knew the difference between the two men? Someone in the Texas Flame Gang.

Ethan wanted to slam his fist into the adobe wall. How stupid could he be?

The shadowed face.

The age discrepancy.

The stubble.

Ethan was too angry and confused to confront Anna about his accusations, but her words that Dakota did nothing without a reason ate at him. If that was the case, then why the obsession with his playing cards? The significance of the jack of hearts he had found?

Silently he gathered the discarded card pieces from the fireplace, sat down at the table, and like a jigsaw puzzle put them back together.

He studied the jagged pieces intently. "Anna, didn't you tell me that Dakota doesn't like the jacks for some reason?"

"Yes. Why?" she said curtly.

"It's the jack of spades," he said out loud.

Anna looked up at him, then down at the card. "He generally puts two back in the deck. You've already found the heart, so what does it mean?"

He took out the jack of hearts he'd found earlier and placed it alongside the jack of spades. "So, what's the difference in these jacks over the others?"

They locked gazes, and their voices blended into one as they said, "One-eyed jacks."

"He hasn't been saying bad jack, Ethan, but *Brad Jack.*" They looked at one another, knowing they had the answer to the identity of the fourth gang member: a man who wore a black patch over one eye.

Softly she said, "Bradford Jackson," then stopped, apparently to organize her thoughts. "He wasn't at the bank the day of the robbery." She slid down in the kitchen chair opposite him. "Father fired Bradford the week before and had just hired a new teller to replace him."

"The sorry sonofabitch," Ethan lashed out. "He's the one Graves gave the watch to for your mother. Bradford was the brains behind the heists. If Dakota knew who the fourth man was, why has it just now started to bother him?"

Thunder rumbled in the distance.

"Something bad happened while he was gone, Ethan." Anna's voice was stifled and unnatural. She bombarded him with questions. "Do you think Bradford has found us? Threatened him? Or was holding Dakota against his will?"

"That'd answer why the horses were gone so long." Ethan grabbed his shotgun. "And if that's the case, there's only one witness and Bradford is out there ready to ambush him." He checked to make sure the gun was loaded. "You stay here, Savannah, and after I find him, we've got a lot to talk about."

"I don't know how I can ever explain it to you where

you'll understand. But, Ethan, please don't blame Dakota for my mistakes. Be angry with me, not him."

"You can rest assured, Savannah, that I'm damn well beyond angry with you right now." He crammed his Stetson on. "And when I get back I'm expecting a lot of answers from you."

Ethan pulled the paper from his pocket and tossed it in the middle of the table, then said, "Beginning with this."

Anna's heart plunged as she unfolded the reward poster for Arlis Buckley.

Chapter 13

After ripping off her apron, Anna grabbed the Winchester from above the fireplace and followed Ethan out the door, stopping long enough to fetch the canteen still sitting on top of Dakota's saddlebags. "Wait, Ethan."

Kneeling down to examine tracks near the bridge, he looked up when he heard her. "What in the hell are you going to do with that?" He stared at the shotgun.

"I'm going to help you find Bradford Jackson," she said, settling the gun in the crook of her arm, like she'd seen her father do when he hunted.

"If you don't intend to use the damn thing, leave it behind, because all it'll do is get you killed, Savannah." His tone left no room for argument.

"I can use it when I need to, and *will* on Bradford Jackson, if I get the chance."

"There are tracks leading both across the footbridge and back up the trail, and it's hard to say which ones are the fresher." His profile was somber, and he nodded dubiously before standing. "With the rain and our comin's and goin's, I can't tell which prints are Dakota's, except that Bones stayed with whoever went past the lean-to up to higher ground."

"Then I know where he's headed." She tried to depict a confidence she didn't necessarily feel. "Let's go."

Ethan caught her eye. "Savannah, this is going to be a rough climb up those rocks in this weather."

"I'm going, Ethan." She meant business and wanted to make certain he understood. "So don't try to stop me."

"For the record, I don't like it, but—"

"For the record, I don't give a damn what you like." She boldly met his disapproving look without flinching.

"Just walk behind me, so I can stay focused on tracking. This is not a game, Anna." And with conviction he added, "Bradford means business."

"And I do too." She squared her shoulders and reminded herself that she owed Dakota a lot. Without him, she'd be dead or worse, still imprisoned by the power-crazed Cajun.

Anna hadn't had to pick up the reward poster from the table to know that Arlis Buckley's face was on it. Knowing that Ethan had no reason to trust her because she'd betrayed him by not divulging Dakota's true identity caused her heart to sink down into her stomach. But to save Dakota, she'd do it all over again if necessary.

Hopefully, this time it'd be with Ethan's blessings.

"Tracks can be pretty confusing," she said.

"I'll do the tracking, and keep that damn gun pointed far away from me," he replied sharply. "And give me the canteen. I'm not sure you're big enough to carry that and a weapon."

Courage and determination coursed through every vein in her body. She'd show him! He might be a strong lawman, but she was a strong-willed woman . . . and never the twain shall meet.

Anna had no idea how long they'd been climbing, but judging by the spasms across her shoulders and trembling limbs, she figured it'd been longer than even she realized.

From where she stood, the worse was yet to come, as the incline was becoming steeper the higher they went.

Soon the rocky, dirt-packed trail widened and forked, giving way to overgrown grasses and brush.

They stopped to rest.

Droplets of perspiration mixed with rain danced across Anna's forehead. Stray tendrils of hair plastered against her face and neck. Anna pushed the hair away from her face. "See where the rock overhang is shaded by trees? That's where I'm fairly certain you'll find Dakota's favorite hideout." She took a deep breath.

"This is the only place up this high where it'd be safe enough for the horses to roam freely." Ethan opened the canteen and handed it off to her.

"Thanks."

"I'm going over to check it out, so stay put." He headed in that direction.

The rain had lightened up somewhat, but Anna couldn't tell whether she was wet from humidity or perspiration. Hell, today it was nothing but purdee ol' unladylike sweat.

An unexpected roar of thunder startled her.

Ethan returned shortly. "He's been there, but isn't now. There are signs of a campfire a few days old and hoofprints that aren't very fresh, so he hasn't been there today."

Anna stood up and handed the canteen back to him. "Were you able to follow the tracks?"

He took a big gulp of water. "Yep, they disappeared a ways north of the cave. Dense scrub brush kept the rain from washing them away completely."

"So let's go. We've come this far, and I don't plan on going back now."

"Just be warned that if you think the first part of the climb was treacherous, it'll only get worse. The trail skirts the ridge line and doesn't look like it flattens out for a while. So this is a good time to turn around and go back."

"No. Considering everything Dakota did for me, I'm not giving up on him now," she said.

The rain fell in earnest as they snaked through monstrous switchbacks dotted with mesquite and cedars.

She stayed behind Ethan as instructed and refused his help when a small boulder got in their way. With his long legs, Ethan stepped over it as though it were little more than a puddle, while she had to make two attempts to clear it. She landed on two feet but stumbled over a rock slide.

Ethan grabbed her arm to steady her. "Savannah, this is your last chance to go back to the dugout. Are you sure you want to go on?"

"Please don't ask me that again."

"Okay, then don't look down, and keep as close to the inside of the ledge as possible. Just watch for more rock slides. It's only a few feet across, and I'll be right in front of you."

Eyes focused ahead, she tried to forget that the trail skirted the eastern edge of the ledge and overlooked a creek bed brimming with rainwater.

Her throat constricted and her feet rebelled. Panic rose from the pit of her stomach. She closed her eyes and took a deep breath. If she set her mind to it she could scurry across the ledge before she had an opportunity to think about the distance between her and the water below.

Another breath and she prepared to make her move. She looked ahead. Ethan had already passed through the narrow path and disappeared around the bend.

Beads of sweat rushed down her spine. She rubbed her moist palms on her pants, while her heart pounded out of control.

"Ethan, wait a minute." She inched forward.

A clap of thunder drowned out her words. Yet another cloud-to-cloud strike of lightning zigzagged across the backdrop of the ancient layers of earth.

"Slow and easy. Don't look down," she said under her breath. "One step in front of the other."

As she snailed her way along the winding ledge, mesquite bushes, sagebrush, and cactus jutted out of the rock formations like a prickly porcupine.

Gushing rain, mixed with dust and sand, cascaded over the rock beneath her feet. Cautiously she slid one foot from side to side and felt the uncertainty under her.

A howling gust of wind sucked her against the jagged wall.

"Ethan!" His name echoed out of the bowels of the canyon.

"Savannah!" Ethan stood within two arms' length of her. "Are you okay?"

She could barely make out his words over the wailing winds and piercing claps of thunder.

"Just a little scared." Damn, she hated to admit to herself that coming along to prove a point was probably a little on the stupid side.

"Don't move. I'll come to you." Ethan tested the ground before stepping forward.

A vicious burst of wind sucked her legs from beneath her, and she tumbled forward, falling on her right shoulder.

In slow motion, Savannah grabbed at the slippery mud and felt her body drift farther and farther away from the security of Ethan's extended hand.

The Winchester slipped from her grip and slid over the edge of the trail, landing somewhere below.

A stabbing pain shot through her body, and she forced herself to take a deep breath to absorb some of the discomfort.

Cold air and rain slammed against her face. Anna closed her eyes and blundered into the warm protective arms of unawareness.

She remembered Ethan sweeping her into the cradle of his arms. A salty taste penetrated her lips. Blood mixed with rain soaked her shirt.

Anna slowly peered through heavy eyelids. "Dimples . . ." She gasped with pain, and her eyelids dropped shut.

Visions of losing her footing and sliding in the mud within only inches of the trail's edge clung in her mind for what seemed like hours.

The light crunch of breaking stones echoed in the vivid darkness. Cold air settled around her, yet she felt warm and safe.

Anna forced her eyes open to see gray skies somewhere beyond the mouth of a cave.

Chapter 14

For about the first time in his life, Ethan was happy to see rainwater. To stop any infection from setting in, he had to get Anna's wounds cleaned pronto. He hadn't hesitated to pull up her dress and tear the hem off her petticoat to make bandages.

Ethan had no idea how long they'd have to be holed up in the cavern. Even if the weather permitted, Anna needed rest before they could set out, plus darkness would overtake them soon, but that was the least of his concerns at the moment.

Anna moaned and tried to sit up. Ethan grabbed the canteen and kneeled beside her. "Try not to move, Savannah."

"Did I die or did you find Dakota's cave?" she murmured.

"You didn't die, but you've got a nasty gash in your back just below your shoulder blade." He checked her forehead for fever.

She flinched. "My head is splitting open."

"You've got a few fair-to-middlin' scratches and scrapes, but nothing worse than a goose egg on your noggin. I think you probably passed out from pain."

Anna reached back and touched the wet rag covering her shoulder. "How'd you make a bandage?"

"I ripped up part of your petticoat."

"Thanks." She squirmed and made a feeble swipe at her lips with her parched tongue. "Did you wash my mouth out with a cactus?"

"No, but over the last week, there've been times I thought about washing your mouth out with soap." He smiled, hoping to draw attention away from her pain.

Ethan lifted her head and placed the canteen to her lips. "Take a sip, and when you're through, I'll help you to sit up, so I can get a better look at your back."

She took a drink. "You don't need to check it. It's fine. I'll dress it when we get back to the dugout."

"Savannah, I know what you are trying to hide from me, but I've already found the scars left over from some pretty bad beatings you took, so let me help you."

As Ethan thought of the welts and jagged scars on her perfect skin, furor rushed dangerously through his body like nothing he'd experienced in a long time. Only once before had he been that sickened and angry, but that was a long time ago and he kept those memories at bay as much as possible.

Anna gave in and stopped fighting him. She clenched her eyes closed and bit at her lower lip but allowed him to assist her to sit up.

"Bear with me. I'll see what I can do to make you more comfortable."

Anna didn't resist his touch when he unbuttoned her shirt and pulled back the fabric to expose an ivory camisole protecting full, deliciously tempting breasts. Rolling her halfway onto her left side, he removed the blood-soaked rag. She gasped in agony.

Slowly Ethan washed away the surface blood and inspected the wound. Lingering much too long, he savored the feel of her warm flesh and wished he could erase her suffering.

Although riddled in pain, Anna dropped her chin to her chest, almost as though she enjoyed his touch.

He folded a strip of the cotton fabric into a bandage and tied a longer piece of cloth around her shoulder. Closing her eyes from time to time, she grimaced, then took a deep breath.

"Hurts pretty bad?" Ethan asked.

"No. I might be scared of the dark, but after everything I've gone through, this is little more than a scratch from a mesquite bush." She attempted a faint smile. "I made up my mind not long after the first beating that it's my spirit, not my body, that dictates what I can tolerate."

"It got you through some really bad times, huh?"

She nodded.

"Finished until we can get you out of here. Even without the rain, we won't be able to go back down until morning," he said.

"And Dakota?"

"Nothing. But someone was here not too long ago. There's dried wood, saddlebags with everything needed to survive for a day or two. So if he left them here, he plans on coming back."

"They aren't his. Dakota's bags were at the dugout when we left." She buttoned up her blouse.

Ethan helped her move to her back, then slid down beside her. He took her into his arms and pulled her close to him. "Rest while we wait for the sun to set."

She snuggled against him.

Swirls of purple and orange washed the western rim of the canyon wall as the sun slowly sunk behind it. Shadows of night enveloped the hideout.

Anna shivered, and he tucked her closer to him.

"You're cold, but I can't light a fire because we sure as

hell don't want to let whoever staked their claim here know they have squatters, especially—"

"If it's Bradford Jackson," she completed his sentence.

"It's gonna get dark soon, but with the rain washing away our tracks, whether it's Bradford or not, they won't expect anyone to be inside."

"I'm not as scared of the dark as I am of spiders." She rested her hand on his thigh.

He tried to put a trace of laughter in his voice. "I plan to stay up all night, so I'll take the first spider watch."

"And coyote?"

"And coyote too. I brought you as far back into the cave as possible, so if anyone gets past me, they probably can't see you. We have the advantage of the dark. If anybody comes from outside, they'll have to wait until their eyes adjust before they'll be able to spot us."

"But we'll be able to see them." She rested her head on his shoulder. "Thank you. Ethan, I'm sorry I didn't tell you about Dakota sooner—"

"Sooner?" He found himself frowning. "How about not getting around to mentioning it at all? You know my mama always told me that not being honest and justifying it by omission is just nothing but a bald-faced lie in sheep's clothing."

"I tried to so many times but could never find the right words, or the timing was bad."

"And you couldn't just say . . . sit down, we need to talk?"

"I tried, but something always seemed to come up that caused me to lose my courage. Dakota saved my life and I felt like I owed it to him to keep him safe, knowing he couldn't stand up for himself. Gator and Shorty took full advantage of him because he was good with the horses and did what he was told to do without asking questions. So I figured if they thought he was dead, they'd not track us down. I was more scared of them than any lawman."

"I'm trying to understand, but why didn't you just take him back East or somewhere nobody knew either of you? A church or something?"

"My heart wouldn't let me. He'd been discarded enough in his life, so I couldn't just send him away. Find someone to take him in like a lost puppy." She took a deep breath before she continued, "I just couldn't do it. So when I finally found him in Abilene and the situation presented itself where a photographer with a traveling medicine show was there and was showing off the pictures he'd taken of outlaws, the idea came to me. It seemed such a simple plan to get a picture taken and send it to the sheriff so everyone would stop looking for Arlis Buckley. The photographer didn't care as long as he had a picture for his collection."

She shifted around so she could see him. "I didn't even send a name along to collect the reward because I was afraid someone would try to track us down."

"I know your intentions were good, but . . ." He wanted to be the hard-assed lawman who saw everything in black and white or right and wrong, but he realized she'd done what she knew was right, not necessarily legal—and with total disregard for her own well-being. That shone a different light on the subject. He continued, "But we've got more problems than Dakota being charged with anything. We've got to find him before your friend Bradford Jackson does."

"My friend?" She sounded perplexed. "He's never been my friend, Ethan. I could hardly stand the sight of him, but because his daddy was Father's attorney and Brad worked for him, I had little choice."

"Don't give me that, Savannah. I saw you kissing him the night I had planned—"

"*Me* kissing *him!*" Her voice was weak but irate. "You didn't see me kissing him, but him trying to take advantage of me," she said with a renewed vigor in her voice. She stiffened in his arms before managing to sit upright. Facing him she added, "I can't believe you'd ever think I'd jeopardize what I *thought* we had over someone like Bradford Jackson." Her voice was even more unwavering with anger.

A rush of dejection flooded over Ethan. For six years, he'd made choices based on something he thought he saw, not on the facts. He'd always prided himself on never going off half cocked, yet doing just that had caused him to recklessly veer off the path to his dreams.

One night had changed his life forever . . . and Anna's too.

Breaking into the loneliness of his thoughts, she hurled at him, "Plus, you have no room to hold grudges, since you forgot to tell me about Jenny."

"Jenny!" Just the fact that Anna had brought up her name flat-ass infuriated Ethan. "What does she have to do with any of this?"

"How could she not?" Anna's emerald eyes danced with annoyance.

"How do you know about Jenny?" Ethan asked.

"And don't forget your little boy." Her voice was heavy with cynicism.

"Here we go again. Why don't you just drop the subject? I've already told you that I don't have any children."

"Ethan, please don't play me for a fool. Now that I know you saw me with Bradford, I realize that's why you left town without saying good-bye, but why into the arms of another woman?"

"Let's get a few things straight." He attempted to check his furor, because he knew she spoke out of pain, and he was afraid he wasn't equipped all that well to help her get through it.

He took a deep breath, corralled his anger, and continued, "I didn't leave for another woman, Savannah. I had just received notice that I'd passed my test to be a lawyer, and I had already gone to your father and turned down his offer to work for him so I could take a position in a law office in San Angelo. I wanted you to go with me—as my wife—and that's why I was looking for you that evening."

She gasped. "You came looking for me?"

"Yes, to tell you that I loved you and wanted a life with you."

"But you found me and Bradford instead. So you decided not to work under his father . . . the lawyer who trained you?"

"No. I could never work for a man who had the personality of hog slop." He almost shuddered at the thought of having to spend his whole career under the helm of such a shyster pettifogger as Bradford Jackson Jr.

"And that's why you turned down Father's offer to work at the bank?"

"Yes. I'd envisioned a life in a big city like Austin with you someday, but thought San Angelo would be a good beginning. But even that turned disastrous . . ."

"So that's the reason your mother never spoke to our family after that?" she asked curtly. "Because I hurt her little boy?"

"No." He tried to disguise his annoyance at her comment. "It had nothing to do with it. She was madder than a hornet at him long before that, because your father tried to buy our land when Pa died. When Mama refused, he insulted her by telling her that a woman shouldn't be trying to run a few head of cattle on land that was more valuable to the cotton merchants." The memories of his mother's disappointment rushed through his mind. "She never forgave him for it, because she said he meant to say a woman couldn't run it like a man could. Mama was just that way."

"And, unfortunately, my father is just that way too." Her voice rang with perplexing emotions. "Oh God, Ethan."

He watched the sadness come over her face in the near darkness.

"Your mother is dead," she whispered.

"Yes. I came back to Galveston a couple of days before the robbery to see her for the final time. She passed the next morning. That's the reason I was even around to listen to your father's plea to find you."

"So you're here at my father's request—not to arrest me?"

"Yes, but I've never forgotten that I'm a lawman first. And if I had to arrest you, Savannah, you can bet your sweet cheeks that I would have done so without giving it a second thought."

"So you're a lawyer and a lawman? You left Galveston years ago as a lawyer, and ended up joining the Texas Rangers because you were mad at the world?"

"More or less, but it wasn't right away." On safer ground now, he took time to gather and weigh his thoughts. He hated to divulge the remainder of the story, but he had come too far to turn back now. He expected the truth from her, and she should get nothing less from him. "I went on to San Angelo—"

"Where your brother, Robert, lived."

"And his wife . . ."

It took all of the courage Ethan could muster to tell her how not long after he got settled into the law office at San Angelo his brother was charged with horse thievery when a gelding was found in his corral. Robert was set up, and Ethan was well on the trail of proving it. Being a young legal eagle, Ethan didn't take the advice given to him by more experienced lawyers to not go to trial. Instead, he was hell-bent for leather to clear his brother's name . . . with an outcome nobody wanted.

Ethan found himself keeping a steady eye on the entrance

to the cave as he relayed the vile events for which he felt responsible. "And since the horse belonged to one of the town's favorite sons, while I was occupied with reading case law and trying to show off what I'd learned in my training to be a lawyer, some of his friends thought I was abusing the judicial system with delays, so they took things into their own hands. A vigilante committee broke into the jail and lynched my brother right before my own eyes."

Taking a deep breath as he experienced the agony all over again, he remembered the hurt and how weak he had felt being unable to stop them. Helpless and angry. No matter how hard he tried he couldn't prevent what he felt he'd set in motion.

"After Jenny and I buried—"

"Jenny." Terrifying realization washed over Anna. "And Jenny was pregnant with your—"

"My nephew, and his name is—"

"Ethan Robert Kimble," she said in a broken whisper.

"How did you know?"

God how she didn't want to tell him because she felt so small, but she had no choice. She'd told him too many half-truths already. "I saw their picture when I got the deck of cards out of your saddlebags."

Ethan clenched his jaw and his intense blue eyes narrowed. His stare drilled into her.

"Ethan, I wasn't snooping. Bones jumped up and knocked the box out of my hand."

"So that's where you got the idea that I had a child?"

"Yes. And I'm so sorry." Her heart broke for all the things she hadn't been totally honest about with him, thinking he'd jump to conclusions, when in fact she was the one who was equally to blame for doing the same.

"He has dimples just like you," she whispered.

"Jenny calls him Bobby, after his father."

Tears flowed down her face.

Ethan looked deep into her eyes and brushed away a tear. In one forward motion, he took her into his arms. His mouth moved over hers, devouring its softness. His hands slipped up her arms, bringing her even closer.

Anna relaxed, sinking into his cushioning embrace.

They momentarily parted a few inches, and then his lips seared a path down her neck, her shoulders before they recaptured hers, more demanding this time.

The touch of his lips was a delicious sensation, and she gave herself to him, having a burning desire, an aching need, for his kiss. He caressed her mouth with his, his lips more persuasive than she cared to admit, and she found herself swallowed up in his slow, drugging caresses.

They shared a dreamy intimacy.

Like a lariat around his neck, rationale jerked Ethan out of the moment and back to reality. In his arms he held the one woman he'd loved since the first day he'd laid eyes on her.

"Ethan, did you mean it when you said you loved me?"

He nudged the hollow of her neck with his nose, ran his lips down its length, but not kissing, only nuzzling. He lifted his head. "With all my heart and soul."

"And I love you too." She let her eyes droop shut, then opened them again.

As hard as it was on Ethan, he forced himself to say, "Sleep while you can. We've got a lot of years left." He kissed her on the temple and held her even closer. "Inside a cave with you being injured feels too much like taking advantage, so when it's the right time, we'll both know it."

A shadow slowly backed away from the mouth of the cavern.

Chapter 15

Uneasiness mocked Ethan as he continued to watch the entrance to the cave. He couldn't shake the feeling that someone lurked outside, which only heightened his awareness. He roamed the cave like a caged animal . . . watching, listening, and wondering.

Except for the occasional howl of a lonely coyote, Ethan heard nothing but Anna's soft breathing and his own footsteps.

The rain moved out, leaving a ceiling of sky flooded with a million stars and a moon that watched precariously over the countryside.

Even with the tranquility of the night, every now and again Ethan spied shadows crossing the entrance to the cave. More than once he raised his shotgun and aimed it into the darkness.

At first dawn, Ethan walked outside and scanned the outskirts of the ledge. In the east, a new sun iced the edge of the canyon's rim in red and blue. After taking care of nature's call, he walked back into the cavern. Low, soft light filtered beneath the rock overhang into the darkened cavern.

Anna stirred and he was instantly by her side. "Are you okay?"

"It's nothing." She twisted a little bit, holding her shoulder with her free hand. "I've been hurt more having to carry my wanted poster over my head for so long." She managed a feeble chuckle.

"Do you think you can make it back down to the horses, Savannah?" Ethan asked.

"I'm no quitter." She took a deep breath. "I made it up and I'll make it down."

He kept his gaze on the opening as they talked, still a little gun-shy from watching for movement for hours on end. It wasn't the first time he'd stood watch all night long, but it was the first time he'd watched over someone he truly cared about. Hell's bells . . . *loved.*

"When you feel like it, we can start back." He reached down to help her up but halted when he heard a noise.

He recognized footsteps a split second before the cave darkened dramatically, and not from a wayward cloud dancing in front of the sun.

Someone stood at the entrance of the cave.

Defensively, Ethan dropped to his knees and gathered Anna to him. Taking her with him, he rolled to the far side of the cavern, within reach of his shotgun. He put his hand over her mouth and whispered, "Don't move," as he drew his Colt.

Anna nodded her head, and he could see by the fear in her eyes that she recognized the danger. He rolled off of her and came to his feet in lightning speed, aiming at the figure at the entrance, whom he could now make out to be a man with a gun aimed back at him.

"Hold it where you are right now or I'll shoot," Ethan warned, prepared to fire.

"Do you think I can't see you as good as you can see me?" Bradford Jackson's helpless, almost pitiful words echoed off the walls of the cave. "I've waited a long time to even up the score. So when Savannah's father fired me because he thought you'd come back to Galveston to take the job he'd offered you years before, I had the perfect opportunity."

"And to even up the score with her father by masterminding a bank heist," Ethan egged him on.

"So, you just had to come to Savannah's rescue and be Alexander Parker's lackey."

Uncontrolled rage coursed through every bone in Ethan's body, but before he could respond, a second figure appeared out of the shadows with a gun drawn and pointed somewhere between Bradford's back and Ethan's chest.

"Bad Jack. Bad Jack," Dakota said. "Bad Jack."

Ethan's heart missed a beat, and his emotions wobbled between dread that he was about to commence his last gunfight and confidence that he had backup . . . but he wasn't sure which gut feeling to trust.

"Okay, Bradford, you've got me. But if you get off a shot, Dakota will have you down before the bullet hits me," Ethan warned.

"Huh," Bradford guffawed. "You think Buckley is going to kill me after everything I did for him?" He shot over his shoulder, "Right, Dakota?"

His only response, the loud, throaty *check-check-check* of a blue jay, as he glided overhead.

The silence didn't deter Bradford. "I've been sitting out here all night long listening to you cooing over one another. Talk about how much in love you all are, but I don't think Savannah was feeling that much love for you when she cornered me and kissed me, just to get even with you for not taking the job at her father's bank." His thin lips spread into a satanic smile, and he let out a deep sordid chuckle.

The sun had pulled itself full into the sky, making it

easier for Ethan to see the man with the black patch over one eye and Arlis Buckley one step behind him.

"I never did that and you know it," Anna stormed.

Before Ethan knew what happened, she stepped to his side, so close that he could feel her breathing. "Bradford Jackson, you're a nasty, despicable person who took more than the money from my father."

Ethan wanted to look at her but didn't have to. He heard the defiance in her voice. He kept his eyes leveled at the two guns facing him. Suddenly he felt her hand on the small of his back when she nudged him a little as she slipped the knife she always carried in her underskirt into his gun belt.

Anna continued, "You took his pride. His dignity——"

"And his daughter, don't forget," Bradford snorted.

"Bad Jack," Dakota repeated twice again, never changing the blank expression from his face, but Ethan saw something in his eyes, a recognition, as he added, "Uncle Ethan."

"Dakota, put my shotgun down." Anna came around Ethan in such a hurry that he couldn't catch her. "Bradford, you'll have to shoot me if you want to get Ethan, but if you don't let me handle Dakota he'll kill you." She stood tall and proud. A true Texas woman plannin' on defending those she loved. "It's your choice."

With Anna a good seven inches shorter, Ethan still had a clear shot at Bradford, but he wouldn't take a chance on return fire. "I'll make it easier on you, Jackson. Let her talk to Dakota, and I'll holster my gun."

Ethan could tell by the look in Bradford's eyes as he cut them from the lawman back to Anna that he wasn't sure which the better choice was, but finally he said, "Slide your gun this way."

Laying his Colt on the ground, Ethan put his hands behind him, fingering what he thought was a knife . . . but instead he distinctly felt a pistol. He wanted to laugh and would have if things hadn't been so serious. He thought all along that Anna still carried a knife in her underskirt, but apparently she'd traded it in for a small-caliber Derringer. And a pearl-handled one to boot. Pretty much a woman's gun, but with his skills and the short distance between them it'd be deadly in his hand. This was one time he was glad she hadn't been totally honest with him. He felt a whole bunch better drawing a pistol on Bradford than a knife.

Anna knelt down, so she'd be eye to eye with Dakota, and as Ethan had seen her do before, she reached out to him. Then she said, "Dakota, go to your safe place until it is suppertime."

Dakota turned around and said, "No more bad Jack," then repeated, "Ruts," three times before heading back down the path.

"No more bad Jack," Anna repeated softly and prayed he'd remember to follow the path to the ruts in the trail that would lead him to Amarillo just in case she and Ethan weren't able to get out of this mess she'd gotten them into.

Frustration and anger took control and pulled Anna to her feet. She took a step back, lifted her skirt, and with a kick that would have made a bucking horse proud waylaid Bradford with the toe of her boot somewhere between his brains and his most prized possession, causing him to drop his gun and yelp like the injured weasel he was. He fell to his knees, bellowing words that even Ethan couldn't understand.

Ethan had the Derringer at Bradford's head so fast that any of the gunfighters at the O.K. Corral would have been impressed.

"The next time you decide to tell a lie, you'd better make sure who you're dealing with." Just for good measure, Anna gave him a second kick in the cojones, sending him into another fit of anguish. "That's for hobbling Troubadour."

"Savannah, get those ropes out of the saddlebags," Ethan ordered.

Within seconds, Ethan had Bradford Jackson III hobbled and tied to a tree. "Sit tight you sonofabitch. The law ought to find you in a day or two." Then he stood and enjoyed saying, "If the coyotes don't get you first."

Ethan picked up his Colt and returned it to his gun belt, then took Anna by the hand. Putting the Derringer in her palm, he said, "I don't know what in the hell this is, but the next time you want me to shoot someone give me something more threatening than a knitting needle." His gentle laugh rippled the breeze.

Watching the lawman, she joined him in laughter. For the first time in as long as she could remember, a release valve opened and she could laugh with life. Anna picked up her Winchester shotgun from where Dakota had dropped it. "I'm glad he found this."

Bones shot up the path from nowhere and bared his teeth at Bradford, who was still babbling in agony. A slow growl came from the mutt's throat as he nipped at the captive's pants leg before lifting his leg and taking care of nature's call on the tree trunk Bradford was tied to.

Taking another look at the man, apparently Bones thought his time would be wasted on him, so he chased ahead of Ethan and Anna as they descended into the bowels of Palo Duro Canyon.

"And you accused me of going to bed mad and waking up madder." Ethan laughed in a deep, jovial way, enjoying the camaraderie with Anna.

Ethan whistled, then called, "Hey, mutt."

Bones stopped in his tracks and looked back as though he recognized his new name.

It wasn't long until they caught up with Dakota on the path, and they walked another few miles in silence.

As the threesome neared the dugout, Dakota turned to Ethan and said, "No more bad jack, Uncle Ethan."

Ethan dropped to his knees, where Dakota could see him eye to eye, and with tenderness the lawman hadn't felt in many years, he said, "No more bad jack, son."

The sun smiled down on the newly forged family.

Epilogue

News Reports
All Around Texas

Amarillo Champion, January 23, 1887

Quinten Corbitt, publisher of the *Amarillo Champion*, says he'll start a weekly newspaper in Kasota Springs, Texas, and operate it as the *Kasota Springs Bugler*. Mr. Corbitt also predicts that this winter will be the worst in the history of Kasota Springs.

Dodge City Times, July 28, 1889

The Panhandle has been suffering for the want of rain, as several weeks have elapsed since rain has fallen; and if we don't soon get rain we will have a long dry spell.

Amarillo Champion, August 11, 1889

The Panhandle has been blessed with a soaking rain, which was much needed.

Amarillo Champion, August 14, 1889

A man with a patch on one eye was found hobbled and tied to a cedar tree in Palo Duro Canyon on Saturday. He doesn't know who he is or where he came from or how he got tied to the tree. Suffering from severe intestinal problems, he requested to borrow money to take a train to Fort Worth. Wishes granted.

The Galveston Daily News, October 31, 1889

The case of *State vs. Savannah Kathleen Parker Kimble,* daughter of prominent Galveston citizen Alexander Parker, who didn't much want to see his only girl charged for the bank robbery, continued the entire day in the justice court. Mrs. Kimble, who was represented by her duly married husband, Ethan Robert Kimble, Esquire, was discharged, but the other bank robbers were bound over till the next term of the district court. Their bond was fixed at $500 each prisoner and paid by their lawyer, Bradford Jackson Jr., and they were taken to the Kaufman jail this afternoon.

The Galveston Daily News, November 9, 1889

Five miles north of Galveston, Gaylord Graves, a big Cajun with a bad temper, and Shorty Duncan, a short man prone to wearing long black dusters, became engaged in a difficulty, both being under the influence of whiskey. Graves struck Duncan just above the temple with a blacksmith's hammer, smashing his skull. There was a strong suspicion of foul play.

Graves made his escape, with an officer in pursuit, going in the direction of Louisiana, his former home. Graves, who was taken back to jail on Thursday night last on suspicion of murder was denied bond before the district judge of that county and will be in jail for a while.

The Galveston Daily News, November 20, 1889

Lawyer Bradford Jackson Jr. died very suddenly last night. He had been feeling poorly and complaining a lot for several days but was feeling better yesterday. He ate a hearty supper last night of pork and apple cobbler, retired to his room, and was found dead this morning. This brought about a closing of his law office.

The Galveston Daily News, January 11, 1890

Mrs. Abigail Parker donated a Patek Phillipe pocket watch, valued at a lot of money, to the children's home. The watch was a birthday present given to her by a no-good-scoundrel-of-an-employee of her husband, prominent banker Alexander Parker, owner of Galveston Merchant's Bank, the same bank that was robbed some time back.

Attending the presentation was her son, Charles Parker, along with her only daughter, Savannah Kimble née Parker. In attendance was Savannah's husband, Ethan Kimble, who had procured a license to marry shortly before Miss Parker was bound over for trial for the robbery of her father's bank. Looking on was their adopted son, Dakota Robert Kimble, a handsome, clean-shaven youth a bit older than her brother.

The whole town is happy for the new family.

MOST WANTED

DEWANNA PACE

Like John Wayne once said,
"Courage is being scared to death—
but saddling up anyway."

To Dionne and James:
Life will throw you for loops sometimes.
But if you always remember who you love
and what you want most out of it,
you'll always find the courage to
saddle back up and find the best road.

Mama loves you both.

Chapter 1

Longhorn City, Texas
West of Fort Worth, 1888

Shadow Rivers leaned back against the cell wall and stretched his long legs out over the wooden cot, wishing he had a smoke to ease him into a better rest for the night. Spending what little money he had for tobacco was a luxury he hadn't chanced, and asking the sheriff for a second favor in one night wasn't his way.

Sheriff Pickens, the seasoned lawman who ruled this neck of the Texas prairie with a fair hand and a mean pair of Colts, stood and grabbed his holster, strapping on his guns. His square jaw looked set in granite and his eyes were narrowed by years of watching for trouble coming. The law dog appeared rougher than he did ten years ago when Shadow first met him. His nose had been broken more than once and half an eyebrow was missing. Many a man had tested Rafe Pickens's balding gray hair and expanding flesh to see if the lawman was past his prime, and all of them had come up short on judgment.

"I thought I'd heard of just about everything till now,"

Rafe told him, his eyes studying Shadow's long lank. "Ain't nobody ever *asked* me to put him in jail before."

"Makes good sense to me." Shadow reached up and rubbed the dark whiskers along his jaw. He had gotten pretty scruffy during the long ride from Fort Worth and was itching for a bath and a shave. Maybe everybody would leave him the hell alone long enough to get a haircut, too. "This is the last place anybody would come looking for me."

The ancient wooden jail was little more than flatboards slung together with a few nails and some wishful thinking by the city council and their tax budget. A lit match or a high Texas wind would take it down faster than a bucket line could be formed to save the hoosegow. Still, a night spent out of the unpredictable Texas summer weather and not having to keep one eye open for trouble made this place feel like a grand palace to Shadow.

"If you were anyone else, Shad, I'd think you were running scared, but I know better."

Anyone who had ever rode with or tangled with Shadow Rivers knew he wasn't a coward. He was afraid of no man, just himself and this strange force within him that compelled him not to care about anything or anyone. If anyone knew him at all, it was Rafe Pickens.

Pickens grabbed his hat and a handful of wanted posters. "Hard bed you chose to lie down in, but I guess you had your reasons."

Shadow knew it wasn't the cot his old friend was speaking of. Though Rafe probably knew more about him than any man alive, Shadow had never shared the real reason he had chosen to live the life of a gun for hire. Maybe he never would. "Every shootist has reason," he told Pickens.

"Just as sure as he's got those who come gunning for him," the sheriff reminded, "even when he's ready to put up his guns." Pickens paused a moment at his desk before pulling open a drawer. "How long has it been since you quit hiring your gun out to the highest bidder?"

"Not long enough, apparently," Shadow admitted, being as honest as he could. He remembered those loco days of playing both sides of the law.

Not long enough gone to fade a reputation nor to expect redemption. Even after he'd paid three damned hard years of debt to society and a justice-minded lawman had decided to set the record straight to help him get paroled.

It damned sure hadn't been long enough to put away the hurt and anger that burned in him when he learned that his pardon had come too late. A hundred years of working the right side of the law would never ease the stupidity of his youth.

"Once a fast gun, always a fast gun," Shadow said, uncustomarily staring into his future. Yet it was the past he saw all too clearly. "Everybody wants to play the game I've played. No one believes a man like me can ever put away the boy he once was. Maybe there *is* no right time to put it away. Like I said, Rafe, I appreciate the good night's sleep."

Pickens took out a whiskey bottle and opened the door to the jail cell. "Guess I owe you the night and this. You did the same for me once. Now we're even, but I expect you'll be gone by morning so my town can stay peaceable."

"Expect I will." Shadow took a long drink and remembered how he'd saved Rafe's life during the holdup that later sent Shadow to prison. He wished the fiery liquid could quench the dark restlessness burning inside him now just as he'd wished he could have found a cure for the dark excitement he'd felt at fifteen wanting to be part of a gang. Best way he could pay back Rafe for his kindness then and now would be to move on and take his trouble with him. Do what he always did—just pass through.

"Appears somebody knew you were headed this way or else spotted you already." The sheriff's brow creased. "Word is spreading fast. Come morning every fast draw in the territory will know Shadow Rivers is in the vicinity and every whore will want to notch her bedpost with your favors. You cast a long—"

"Don't say it," Shadow said. It wasn't the first time his name and reputation intermixed and preceded him. Someday the joke that his life counted could be put to rest even if it meant burying it all away in a six-foot grave.

"I'm gonna make my rounds and hang up these posters out on the community board," Rafe informed, taking a moment to lift the cell keys and hook them around a loop in his belt. "See if I can't quiet down this Saturday night a might so you and the law-abiding folks around here can catch some shut-eye. You sure you don't want me to bring you something to eat . . . order you a tub of bathwater . . . maybe a cigar?"

Everything within Shadow said yes, but he shook his head. "No, just leave the cell unlocked in case I change my mind and hightail it out of here before morning."

"Headed somewhere specific?"

"West."

"Got plans, do you?" Surprise lifted the damaged eyebrow.

Shadow sighed, releasing the frustration of the long road ahead of him with little money, a near-lame horse, and no way to improve either. "Nothing's changed. I don't make plans. Just looking for work."

"Do us both a favor, son."

"What's that?" Shadow asked.

"Make sure it's legal."

If he had any luck remaining at all, Shadow hoped he hadn't said what he was thinking out loud before the door shut. *Gonna try my damndest, partner.*

* * *

"Psst. Mister? Catch this."

Shadow's eyes jarred open, the sense of possible threat bolting him upright on the cot. His hand automatically went for the gun that usually rested strapped against his right thigh, but it wasn't there. He scrambled to his feet, his thoughts racing to remember why he wasn't wearing his holster and where he had put it. *Under the cot. Within arm's reach. Thought you were safe for the night.* His hand snaked out and found the peacemaker, readied it for action, its deadly force now aimed toward the cell window that rose slightly over his head.

Whoever you are, don't make me use it. He listened intently, waiting for the sound of a hammer being pulled back or a burst of gunfire. Instead, all that came was a voice. A feminine one at that.

"Can you see it?" the woman asked from beyond the brace of iron bars that held off freedom from the prisoner. "Grab the end of the rope and wrap it around the other bars, then throw the end back out to me, please."

Soft, sweet voice. Polite. His instinct for taking in details of those he met sharpened his skills so he could hear anything else going on outside. Nothing discernible. Just the sound of Saturday night hell-raising somewhere down the street. Well, if the lady was aiming to gun him, she'd have fired already. If she meant to hang him, she was making a mistake letting Shadow get his hands on any part of the rope. He could easily outmaneuver her.

A quick look toward Rafe's office revealed that something had kept the sheriff out on his rounds. Probably the rowdy cowboys over at the saloon having such a good time. She had to know Pickens was away. Did she have any idea whose cell she was roping?

I must have fallen dead asleep, Shadow decided, not seeing well enough into the night beyond the window to know just how long he had snoozed. "Before I take it, ma'am, you mind telling me what you're aiming to do?"

The sound of exasperation echoed from the other side of the bars. "Well, gosh almighty! What does it look like? I'm trying to pull these off the wall so I can break you out of jail. That is, if you've a mind to help me a little, sir. I'm having to stand on a crate so I can reach it."

Short, southern, and full of sass. Intrigued, Shadow decided to play his hand and call her on her game. After all, she was going to a lot of trouble for a stranger. He sure didn't know any woman who cared enough about him to follow him to Longhorn City and take such a risk . . . not even the widow he had visited once in this part of Texas when he was looking for an evening of quick courting.

"Well, pardon the heck out of me, ma'am. I wasn't sure it was *me* you were attempting to rescue." He tossed his gun on the cot and looped the rope as she'd asked, then handed the other end back to her. A small gloved hand reached up and grabbed it, making a quick knot on the other side. "You sure you got the right prisoner?"

How did she mean to pull those bars down by herself? It sure sounded like she was alone.

"Is there anybody else but you in there?"

And if there were? He almost felt insulted. He was accustomed to being the preferred choice. She was full of brass, this one. All the more reason to see what she was up to. "Pretty slim pickings around here, little lady."

"You're handy with a gun, aren't you?" Uncertainty filled her tone for the first time. "A gunman?"

"Don't much use one these days." Maybe he could discourage her to give up her efforts. "What would you be wanting with such a man?"

Shadow took a step up on the cot to look out into the night and see more about her and how she planned to pull this off. The thin mattress sunk to its bed, the wooden housing squeaking beneath his weight.

No sign of any horse or a wagon, but then he didn't have all that much of a view. Maybe they were tied off farther in the alley so no one would see them. All he could determine was that she wore a floppy hat and a light-colored duster. If the crate was any height at all, she was no bigger than a small man or a boy big enough to have his first shave. Only the sweet lilt to her speech hinted at her true gender.

The alley between the sheriff's office and the mercantile was so dark he couldn't even tell the color of her hair. Guess the moon hadn't risen high enough to shine overhead, so it couldn't be midnight yet.

"Heard you needed work," she announced.

Obviously, she'd been listening to his and Rafe's conversation. How long had she been out there and what had she heard? "And I suppose you've got some sort of job to offer me?"

"Yes, if I can get you out of there without too much ruckus. We're wasting time and we need to take advantage of all that noise over at the saloon to get done before the sheriff gets back."

"No need for any ruckus whatsoever or for that rope." Shadow realized she'd thought this through and wouldn't be easily persuaded to give it up. She was about to make a major mistake counting on somebody she didn't know hell or high water about.

Maybe he needed to show her just how dangerous that could be.

Maybe she should find out just how hard it is to correct a mistake.

Maybe if someone had done the same to him a long time ago, he wouldn't have gotten himself into trouble.

"My cell's unlocked," he informed. "Just come on in and speak your piece. That way I can see who I might be taking the road with."

"Unlocked?" She hesitated before adding, "Strange way to keep killers off the street."

"You in need of a killer, Miss . . . ?"

"Kilmore," she sighed heavily. "And don't say anything about my name. I know it's a twist of bad luck for an outlaw to carry such a handle, but it was supposed to have been my father's."

She was revealing a lot about herself just by that admission. She didn't know who her pa was. All kinds of hard-luck circumstances came to Shadow's mind, making him do his own bit of hesitating about scaring her off from her planned rescue. But just as rapidly as the hesitation sprang up, it quickly fell away when one of his longtime codes flashed through his mind. *Sorry don't stop a bullet.* That would trip a man up quicker than a dance hall girl with loose garters. "Then you're an outlaw, I take it? Is that why you waited until the sheriff went on his rounds before you made your play?"

"Yeah," she said, unknotting the rope and loosening it. "I would have just walked on in and used his keys, but I noticed he had them with him. I heard him jangling all the way uptown. That's why I thought of trying the rope. I figured with you pushing and me pulling, those old boards would probably loosen up enough to break free. I'm sure glad it wasn't necessary. I was afraid the sound of it coming down would give me away."

"Not afraid of a little effort, are you?"

"I knew I'd get it done one way or another."

He was beginning to like this lady. She was feisty and Shadow admired feisty in anyone.

"Now, would you mind coming on out and meet me back here?" she insisted. "I'd rather not show my face out front, which I'm sure you can understand. And while you're at it, Mr. . . . uh . . ."

"Rivers. Shadow Rivers."

Silence ensued long enough that he thought she might have changed her mind. She obviously knew his name.

"*The* Shadow Rivers?"

"Does it matter?" He heard the astonishment in her voice. Maybe what else she knew of him would end all of this now. She hadn't heard as much of the earlier conversation between him and Rafe if she hadn't already been aware of his name. That meant she truly had been willing to take on any man who'd been locked away. The thought that she'd been that desperate made him wonder what kind of trouble the lady could be in.

Something long forgotten stirred within Shadow and it felt more than a little rusty. Here was a chance to help someone instead of hurting her. It wasn't exactly feeling sorry for her. It would be giving her a chance not to get herself into more trouble. And hadn't that been what Rafe had done for him ten years ago? Paroled a boy of eighteen from a life of crime?

Was he up to the challenge? It had been a long time since he'd promised Rafe he would pay him back someday by helping somebody else who needed it. A long time since he'd concerned himself with anyone else. "Your offer of work still stand?"

"You bet it does!" she said excitedly, sounding relieved. "I just might have done something right for once if I've got you willing to come along."

Shadow stepped down off the cot and grabbed his holster, strapped it back around him. Settling the peacemaker into place, he snatched his hat from the peg where he'd hung it and headed for Pickens's desk. There he set the barely tasted bottle of whiskey and tossed his last coin next to it. Rafe would know it was his way of saying thanks for the few hours of pure sleep he'd gotten in months. That was the least he owed the man.

"Hey, Mr. Rivers, on your way out do something for me, will you? I hate to ask, but it's important."

She was the politest boss who'd ever sought him out, that was for certain. There seemed to be an edge of worry in her tone, and he couldn't help but wonder what was so important. He didn't have to wait long to get his answer.

"Check the office wall and then the pegboard outside. If you see a wanted poster with the name Odessa Kilmore on it, would you tear it off, please?"

So she'd been telling the truth. She really was an outlaw. Maybe he had better proceed a little more cautiously and not take her so lightly. She just might bring a lot more trouble than earning a little redemption was worth.

Shadow decided not to light the lamp on the desk just in case someone might see the office lit and wonder why the sheriff was in one place and someone else was roaming his office. Though it was hard to read with little more light than that shining past the tied-back curtains at the window and door, Shadow was accustomed to reading trail at night and peering through the darkness for signs of threat. How hard could it be spotting a woman's likeness amid a roster full of men's? It wasn't all that common for a woman to be posted.

As he studied the documents lining the wall, his gaze finally focused on one in particular. He took it down and stepped toward the door, needing more light to read the writing.

Odessa Kilmore. Fugitive from justice. Reward of one thousand dollars for her capture. If you have any information on her whereabouts, please contact Sheriff Cassius James at Jerkwater, Texas.

One thousand dollars was a lot of money. What had she done? Didn't say robbery or murder. Just fugitive from justice. Maybe because she was a woman and the offense wasn't one a man usually made, they'd spared the details. He didn't know her well enough yet to care one way or the other what she'd done short of murder, but something inside said the lady didn't have any true meanness in her. If she was willing to pay him for work, he might as well try to earn a little grub money to see him through to the next real employment. If his instinct was wrong about her, then he'd just cut to the chase and earn a thousand dollars the easy way.

He took one last look at the wall just to make sure part of his own former deeds hadn't found their way among the posters. Nothing there. Maybe he was wrong earlier and it had finally been long enough to quit roaming, to find a place to breathe clear again. Maybe if his instincts were right after all and he helped this Kilmore woman from destroying her future, the road to redemption might just be stretching straight ahead of him.

Chapter 2

Odessa Kilmore watched from amid the shadows as the stranger strode around the corner and entered the alley. He was tall, better than six feet, she'd bet, and he moved with a sense of purpose. He was a man unafraid of the dark and what it might bring—that was clear. Just the kind of man she needed.

He wore a battered hat and his dark hair long enough to touch his shoulders. She couldn't see the color of his eyes, but a deeper shadow under his nose and along his jaw hinted that he needed a shave. His trail coat moved with him like wings of a dark angel and his boots were once of quality. She wasn't sure what she'd expected a man of his reputation to wear, probably something more like what she'd read in the dime novels about him. Not that it mattered as long as he didn't prove himself to be some saddle bum with a lot of hokey made up about him and no sand.

Her attention immediately went to the sidearm strapped to his right thigh, and that made her aware of the hand that swung in and out of the shadows as he strode. His right hand was bare. She glanced at the left. Gloved and gripping papers. Probably the wanted posters.

A tiny shiver of trepidation sent gooseflesh beading

down her spine, and she knew it was from more than the posters that must hold her likeness. His ungloved hand was a shootist's choice, she realized, to make him faster with his gun hand. Something she might need to count on. But what was it he'd said earlier before she knew his identity and she'd asked him if he was handy with a gun? *Don't much use one these days.* Did that mean he could still pull leather if he had to?

He halted and peered into the dark. He didn't speak, just waited, staring. The intensity of his gaze made her heart feel as if it rose in her throat and fluttered. Her pulse seemed to quicken in her fingertips that gripped the rope. She didn't know whether to show her position and make herself more vulnerable to him or run as fast as she could away from him. What the devil was she getting herself into?

All of a sudden, someone hurled himself from atop the roof of the sheriff's office.

"Watch out, Mr. Rivers!" she yelled.

Both men went down and a fight ensued. Fists connected with flesh and the crunching of bone echoed through the alley. Blow after blow landed hard and deadly, filling the night with grunts and the sound of feet scuffling.

Dust stirred up from all the scuffling. Odessa's nose suddenly itched and she had to wiggle it to ward off the coming sneeze that would give away her hidden location. Her eyes blinked and she felt them tear up. She had to get out of there, away from the stirred-up dust. But she couldn't just leave Rivers.

Without a moment's hesitation, her hands formed a loop on the rope and she threw, praying it would be long enough to reach the jumper. Before she could see where it landed, a shot rang out. Then another. Odessa braced herself for the impact, her eyes shutting away the image of her coming death. Something whizzed past her.

"Missed, damn it!" someone shouted. "Now the sheriff will be on us."

Racing feet warned that she couldn't wait to see if they were headed toward her or away. Her eyes sprang open, blurring as she yanked as hard as she could. The two combatants jerked apart. One went down, groaning. The other fought like a wildcat to remove the rope.

A third man raced from the dark, a flash of metal warning that he was one of the shooters. Just as he reached the struggling men, the roped fighter's legs flew up and landed a gut-bending blow to the new threat. Metal flashed, then thudded hard against the jail wall and fell to the dirt. The kicker sprawled backward from the momentum, and Odessa grimaced at the sound of him cursing as he hit the hard-packed ground.

"Damn it, lady," Shadow complained, "you roped me, not him! Stop pulling or you'll choke me. Now, run! Get out of here!" He scrambled to his feet, wrestling to remove the rope that was still tangled halfway up his shoulders and in the flap of his trail coat. "Before they decide to call in their brothers."

Of all times to hit her mark. How many times had she missed when she'd practiced with a rope? Now she had lassoed the wrong man. Stranger or no stranger, Shadow Rivers had gotten into trouble trying to make a deal with her. She refused to leave him. "You don't know where to meet me," she argued. "I can't go."

"A *lame* excuse. Now run, lady. Better find a horse and get to riding it. If this is going to work between us, you need to listen and listen *good*."

Shadow hoped Odessa Kilmore was as smart as she was desperate. Otherwise, he'd gone to a lot of trouble to give up a comfortable bed for the night and would endure more than a few bruises on her account. Maybe she'd been wise enough to hear the double meaning in his command and understand that he meant her to go where she would find a lame horse. It was nearly three in the morning and the livery was no place to be milling about if she wasn't there. The mountain of a smithy that ran the blacksmith shop and livery was no man to tangle with.

Creeping silently past some hens that were roosting and a couple of stabled horses that whickered softly, Shadow managed to find his own mount located in the third stall. The bay immediately sensed his presence. The animal raised his head and moved over to the edge of the gate. Shadow reached up to stroke him and whispered, "Sorry, Dollar, it doesn't look like we're going to get to stay long enough to give you that rest I promised. Maybe next time."

At least the blacksmith had repaired the horse's shoe, given him a good brushing, and saw that he was fed properly. More than Shadow could say he'd gotten for himself. His stomach grumbled, reminding him that he should have kept that last coin for some grub in case this thing with Kilmore didn't work out. Good thing he'd paid Dollar out in advance and had saved a little beef jerky in his saddlebags.

"Ahh-choo!"

Shadow's eyes jerked upward to focus on the hayloft that rose above the stables. "Is that you, Miss Kilmore?"

A slow rain of straw filtered down from above as the hay shifted once, then twice. Suddenly a face peered over the edge. A heart-shaped face, high cheekbones, and plush, bowed lips promised pretty features, but he couldn't take his focus from the puffy eyes that looked swollen almost shut.

"It's m-me, all right," the pretty lips answered. "And I hope you know that I'm highly sensitive to all this . . . this . . . achoo! All this hay. Couldn't you have thought of somewhere cleaner?"

The hens cackled at the sound, stirring the other animals.

One of the horses whinnied, making the chickens squawk even louder.

"You want to wake up the smithy?" Shadow warned. "We'd be hard pressed explaining what we're doing out here before dawn. Besides, I didn't tell you to get up there."

It had taken him a while to deal with the shooters who had given chase in the alley. Then he'd turned over the other two he had fought with to Pickens. Rafe hadn't been real happy with him until he found out the pair were two of the men in the lineup of posters wanted in Kasota Springs up in the Panhandle. Close to where she was in trouble. "He'll be mad getting woke up so early this morning. And from the size of the man, I'm not looking forward to messing with him."

"It's morning? *Sunday*?" She immediately bolted upright and turned around, climbed down the ladder as if the hay had caught fire.

"Whoa there, surefoot. You'll kill yourself in the dark." Shadow grabbed some matches from his coat pocket and struck one on the side of the stall. The lucifer flared red, then blue, sending a sulfuric odor wafting through the livery and offering the light he had meant to lend her safety. The sight of a nicely rounded bottom backing its way down the ladder in a stretch of nankeen trousers was a pleasant surprise. Only then did he realize she was missing something that had afforded him the view. "What did you do with your duster?"

"It's thrown over that stall there, near the horse with the new shoe. I figured he was yours, what with the instructions you gave me. The other two aren't lame so I figured it had to be him. Lucky for you the shoe was all he must have needed."

Yeah, she's plenty smart. Shadow swung the match to see where she pointed, but he had forgotten the flame and it burned his fingers. "Ye-ouch!"

A chuckle a few feet away said she had crossed the

distance that separated them and knew she'd caught him staring at her backside a moment too long. "Serves you right for having me hole up in a place that'll make me look like a strawberry patch for days. Everybody's going to think you've beaten me to a pulp, and that'll hurt my plan. I've got to get my hands on some water, quick. If I don't get this off me, I'll start breaking out in lumps."

"Was that the only place in here you could hide?" Shadow could spot a handful of dark havens. "Was the smithy still around when you got here?"

Her hair was golden, that much he could tell. Moonlight shone through the slats of the boarded livery wall and her hair could have matched its shine. He'd have to wait till daylight to see its true color and the color of her eyes. That is, if they weren't swollen shut. He'd bet they were full of piss and vinegar, no matter what the color or condition.

"I waited till his wife called him into their house and then I snuck in. I bet I wasn't here ten minutes when a couple of men came in. I thought they were going to search the place, but the smithy suspected them up to no good since none of the horses must have belonged to them. He ran them off. While he was out there warning what he'd do to them if he caught them back around his place without business for him, I thought it best to hide up there under that haystack just in case he decided to look around the stalls and see what they were searching for."

"Do you think they were after you?"

"Who else?" She sounded confident in the matter. "It was probably some of those men after me in the alley."

It wasn't the men from the alley. He would let her know what had happened to them and who they were once he got her somewhere she felt safe. The fact that the two he'd fought with were near neighbors of hers suggested that they might also have been after her instead of him. But he couldn't be sure until he asked what she knew of them.

"They were smart to go on." Shadow tried to calm her. Her breathing was a little rapid and he could tell that she still felt threatened. "Any man who could lift an anvil like it was an empty carpetbag is nobody to rile. So unless we want to deal with the smithy ourselves, I suggest we find a better place to hole up until we can figure out if I'm going to take your offer."

"You mean you might not?"

"Didn't say that." He could sense her stiffening, just by the way her shoulders went back and her chin lifted. She had to be about four inches shorter than him, not nearly as little as she'd looked in the confines of the dark alley. "I've got to know what the work is before I agree to it."

"So you're a man with a code."

Was she taunting him? Not a wise thing for her to do since she didn't know his temperament yet. She couldn't have been a desperado for very long or she wouldn't be so quick to challenge a man.

"I mean, I didn't know hired guns were so choosy."

"Like I said, I don't use my gun much anymore. I'd rather settle matters other ways if I can."

"Oh . . ." She sounded almost disappointed. "Then I don't know if I can hire you after all."

"You need someone shot, do you?" He'd never shot a man who hadn't drawn on him first. Not even during the holdup that had put him in prison at fifteen. He wouldn't do it now.

"Not exactly. At least I hope not, but maybe."

"Do you know what you really want, Miss Kilmore?" Shadow's patience was wearing about as thin as his last meal. He wanted nothing more than to get on with his payback to Rafe and put her on a safe road back to a decent life.

"I'd like you to start with taking me over to the church."

Of all the places he'd expected her to want to go, church was not it. "Well, ma'am, I'm not exactly familiar with the house of worship here in Longhorn City, and I expect that you could have done a sight better than breaking me out of jail to take you." Maybe he was the one who needed to walk a little cautiously here. The woman was beginning to sound a few stitches loose from a full seam.

"Look, Mr. Rivers, I know I'm not making any sense, but if you'll just give me time to get rid of this itch, I'll explain. Then if you decide to walk away, I'll buy that lame horse from you so you can get yourself a better one."

"You saying money is no object?"

"I'm not made of it if that's what you mean, but I've got some put away for better times. I figure this is about as good a time to use it as any."

"You got it with you?"

"Do I look like a fool? How do I know you wouldn't rob me blind?"

"Well, lady," Shadow chuckled, "with all that swelling, I couldn't honestly say what you look like and, near as I can tell, you're about half blind now. And just to set the record straight, you're the one on the wanted poster. Not me." Despite her grit, she was getting more interesting by the minute to him, loco or not. "And just so you make no mistake, Dollar isn't for sale. We've rode too many trails together."

"Good. You're a better man than I hoped." Her tone had softened. "Go ahead and bring him along. I'll figure out some other way to thank you for taking on those men in the alley."

"You so sure *you* were their target?" Shadow moved to the stall and handed Odessa her duster.

"Like you said, I'm the one currently wanted. Why? Do you think they were after you?" She accepted the duster but didn't put it around her. "I didn't want to get this all full of hay or I'd have been sneezing from here to Jerkwater."

"They *could* have been chasing me," Shadow admitted as he began saddling the bay. "Are you planning on heading back to where you're in trouble? Most known criminals run the other way."

"That's just it, Mr. Rivers." She lent him a hand so they could be quick about leaving. "That's why I need you. The harder I try to go back home, the more men come after me and the faster I'm chased away. Somebody plain and simply doesn't want me to return to Jerkwater bad enough that they've hired men to stop me. I want to hire you to figure out why."

"Why me? Why not a lawman?" He expected her to say she'd picked him because of his reputation, but then she hadn't known whom she was actually rescuing from that cell.

"They tend to help only the innocent."

"Are you guilty?" He stopped what he was doing and looked straight at her. Her head shot up and, to her credit, she met him swollen eye to eye.

"No . . ."

She did the one thing that he hoped she wouldn't do.

She blinked. ". . . but sort of."

Great, now he would have to "sort of" figure out whether or not he was willing to work for a liar.

Chapter 3

"Rein right."

Shadow guided Dollar down the street away from the white building with a steeple. Snuff-clop! Snuff-clop! The sound of the bay's hooves against the dirt kept time with the slight squeak in the saddle. "You decided not to head for the church after all?"

"I mean rein *left*. And you ought to whisper in case anyone hears us."

"Sorry, Dollar." Shadow tugged the reins the other direction. "Seems the lady can't make up her mind where to go. And sorry, lady, but this *is* me whispering."

"I am half blind at the moment if you remember . . ." The feminine curves that had felt pleasantly distracting bouncing up and down against his back moved away, cooling the snug cocoon Kilmore's body had plastered against him. "And I can't see with a wall of muscle and coat in front of me."

"Muscle, huh?" His chuckle exited husky enough to reveal that he found her description flattering and the nearness of her body against his more than a little distracting. "Left or right looks pretty much the same whichever direction you're headed. Don't want to confuse the poor beast, do we? Better hang on tight in case he decides to bolt."

"Don't let him wake up anybody. I want some time at the church."

Just as Shadow hoped, her arms shot around him like two iron bands and she pressed her body against his once more. He was peeved earlier when he had learned she didn't have a horse of her own. How in the blazes did she think they were supposed to make good use of daylight with one horse? But the press of her body against his had instantly taken away the irritation. It had been one hell of a forever since someone had been this close without expecting payment of some kind. Since anyone had been near enough to touch him. He felt like a man dying from thirst without knowing what it was he needed to drink. He didn't want to reach that church anytime soon.

At least now he understood why she'd been alone in the alley. This particular outlaw didn't know how to sit a horse. It might be a long ride to Jerkwater later on, but it was becoming more appealing by the bounce.

A few minutes later, he reined to a halt behind the sanctuary. "Better I tie him up back here in case someone spots him." Shadow looked up at the position of the moon. Dawn would break in a couple of hours. "Someone might recognize my horse."

Her arms unbound themselves from his waist and he grabbed her hand to help her down.

"Thanks," she said, looking up at him, her smile suddenly turning downward as she caught sight of his grin.

He couldn't help it. He'd gotten a pretty good feel of her ample breasts as her body slid down his leg. He was still rogue enough to admit his wayward thoughts.

"You have a dirty mind, sir." Her brows knit into an angry vee.

If you only knew. Yes, ma'am, there's a real sweet possi-

bility of you being pretty damned good-looking once your eyes get better, he thought. "I'm not the saint needing church this morning, miss. You are."

She bustled off around the corner and disappeared from sight. He jumped down and wrapped Dollar's reins around one of the hitching posts that had been provided to help the overflow of congregational needs out front. "Don't know how long I'll be, fella. Maybe she'll just send me on my way."

Shadow wasn't surprised to find the church unlocked. Most left their doors open night and day to offer sanctuary to souls in need. In his years of riding the hard trail, he had spent many a winter or rainy night stretched out on a pew to keep warm. Without fail, each collection plate had soon contained some of his coins to express his appreciation. Better to sleep there than have to keep watch for the inevitable man wanting to challenge his gun in a boardinghouse or hotel.

Church was the farthest place to look for a man who made his living in questionable ways and tended to deter all but the most hardened of those wanting to test Shadow's fast draw. Maybe Kilmore had the same experience and she intended for them to get some sleep before the preacher showed up.

He stepped inside and saw her about to light one of the candles near the altar. When she turned, he noticed that two now burned. Had she lit one for him? The thought touched Shadow and he was surprised that such sentiment still dwelled inside him. He couldn't remember the last time anybody had included him in a prayer.

She walked toward him and said nothing, then took a seat at the back pew. Bowing her head she began to pray.

Why hadn't she sat up front? Shadow didn't know whether to sit beside her or choose another pew. A person's talk with the Almighty was something personal, something he did by himself. His awkwardness was short-lived when she suddenly began talking loud enough to wake the saints.

"And Lord, thank You for not letting me accidentally hang Brother Rivers when I accidentally roped him. I promise I'll practice more when I get a chance, but You and I both know I meant to lasso that other man."

Shadow chose to sit beside her. He needed to be close in case someone heard her and came in. If they had to run, better he could get to her quickly.

"Lay it on his heart, Lord, to help me. You know I didn't mean to take that . . ." One swollen eye suddenly opened slightly wider and peered at Shadow. Then her head quickly turned and bowed again. "Well, You know I said that I would explain better when and if I ever get there. I pray that You forgive me for not going to church that day. I promise never to miss another Sunday ever again. I learned my lesson.

"Oh, and one last thing"—her fingers traced the trail of a cross from her forehead to her tummy—"make us better."

"Amen." Shadow's agreement echoed in unison with the end of her prayer. He stood and waited for her to do the same. "You ready to get on the trail?"

She stood face-to-face for the first time in any kind of light. "I thought Shadow Rivers would be bigger."

"I am bigger sometimes." Shadow noticed that her hair was more wheat colored than blond, hung almost to her waist, and had been tied back with a string of violet ribbon. Her voice might sound young, but her figure was not boyish by any man's calculations. She curved in all the right places. Dangerously.

He wanted to see her eyes. "You said something about getting water to wash your face. I saw a pump out back near Dollar. Maybe the preacher won't mind me using the offering plate or that container over there to fetch you some."

She gasped. "That's holy water. Use the plate."

"It's the water that's been blessed, not the container. I'll go to hell for a lot worse than that." One of her eyes seemed to narrow at his statement, and Shadow thought maybe it would be best to fetch the plate, save time and an argument. He had just one question to ask before he left. "Are we finished or are we gonna stay a while? If we're staying, I'm going to round us up something to eat out of my saddlebags. If not, then we'll make camp somewhere down the road."

"I thought we would have our talk and, if you agree, then we'll rest until the six-ten from Fort Worth pulls in. The whistle will wake us."

Good idea. Shadow nodded. "Then I'll get the beef jerky and some water and be right back."

Odessa was grateful for the few moments alone. It would give her time to decide how much or how little to tell him. She couldn't leave several facts out, but maybe she could find a way to stretch the truth so it wouldn't make him change his mind about helping her.

Then it dawned on her where she was. Deciding how much of a lie she should tell while standing in church was a sure indication that this might not go as well as she wanted. *Let's see, Lord. Which kind of lie would this be? A black lie? No, it isn't a total falsehood. A yellow lie? Partly, since I've been coward enough to run away in the first place. A white lie? That's it. A lie for someone's good.* She glanced toward the altar. There was no need to destroy what she'd spent her whole life trying to disprove.

Odessa looked around for a piece of cloth to wash with and spotted only the altar adornments. She would just have to tear off her shirttail, dust it real well, then rinse it out good. Unfortunately, the sanctuary was small enough that it didn't have a curtained-off area to hang choir robes. So, she would have nowhere for privacy. She'd just have to make

Shadow turn his back while she freshened up more. She didn't need him finding out where she hid her loot, and she sure didn't want him looking at her like he had when he'd helped her dismount or she'd never . . .

"You sure are thinking hard about something."

Odessa gasped, her heart leaping in her chest. She hadn't heard him return. But she wouldn't let him know he'd frightened her out of a day of her life. She definitely didn't want him to see any hint of what she'd been thinking. The thought of sliding down his leg had sent heat rushing to her cheeks. She could only hope the candlelight wasn't enough to reveal her blush. "Back already, Mr. Rivers?"

"Look, if we're going to work together, we don't have time to be so polite. Call me Shad and I'll take the same shortcut with you. Now where do you want me to put these?" He juggled the water-filled offering plate in one hand and something rolled up in the other.

"Set it on the back pew for now," she instructed, assuming it was the beef jerky. "And if you don't mind, I'll ask you to take a seat up front."

"You don't like company while you eat?" He set the roll of jerky on the pew and propped the plate on one edge of the roll. At her look of curiosity, he offered an explanation. "The seat leans. Don't want to spill the water."

She heard something different in his tone. Almost as if he was disappointed. He'd been kind enough to get the things they needed. The least she could do was share a meal with him. She would have to get used to doing so in the next few days. "I'd rather your back was turned for a while. Just sit there for a few minutes until I'm finished."

"That reminds me. I brought you this." Shadow reached into his trail coat and pulled out a fresh bandanna from an inside pocket. "I thought you might prefer something clean to use as a washcloth."

She accepted his gift and appreciated his thoughtfulness. "Would you like to be first?"

"Bustles before boots." He winked and headed up the aisle.

He was a gentleman of sorts and that eased some of the questions in Odessa's mind about whether choosing him was a wise decision. She turned, dunked the bandanna into the water, and let it soak generously before ringing it out. With anticipation she lifted it to her eyes and squeezed the material just enough to let a few drops of water wash through her lashes. "Ohhh, that feels good."

She wiped the dust from the corner of her eyes, her cheeks and forehead, along her neck and the valley of her breasts. "This is pure heaven, Shad."

"I could do without the moans. Just get yourself washed."

Odessa heard the slight strangle in his words, as if he were setting his jaw. "Oh, sorry. It just felt so good." A long sigh escaped her.

"You're making it hard on a man, Odessa . . ." He cursed to himself. "Will you just be done with it!"

Maybe it was the sound of her name in that low, husky baritone. Maybe it was the sudden crispness of his demand to end the washing. Or maybe it was the simple fact that he looked like he was braced for a shoot-out with somebody that made her realize why he was so disturbed. He thought she sounded like one of the doves in her mother's brothel during the throes of passion.

The bandanna flew across her skin as she wiped like a madwoman to clean the hay dust away. Then she immediately readjusted the lacy chemise she wore beneath her shirt and refastened her buttons. "There, I'm finished," she said loudly, making sure she kept any more expressions of relief to herself. She rinsed the bandanna and held it out to him. "You're next."

It took a minute for him to turn around and she didn't want to think about why. So she busied herself with finding a way not to spill the water while trying to unroll the cloth that stored the beef jerky. His boots clicked across the slatted floor.

"Thanks, hold the bandanna a minute and I'll pour out that water." Shadow grabbed the offering plate, stepped to the door, and slung out the water. He returned and placed the plate on the opposite pew from where she sat, then asked for the cloth. "I'll clean my face and hands for now. Somewhere down the trail we'll get a bath."

She sensed him looking at her, intensely. *We'll?* She wasn't going to let him think that she had read any meaning into his words or his stare, nor was she threatened by either. She had fought off many a man's advance in all the years growing up in a brothel. He wouldn't be the first one who tried to take what wasn't being offered. She hadn't reached adulthood untarnished by being stupid or easily swayed. "Of course we will. We'll have to clean up before we get to Jerkwater if what I have planned will work."

"What's your plan?" He took a seat beside her as he washed his face, then his gun hand. "But before you tell me, I want to know why you're sitting here instead of up there. Seems to me you deliberately chose the back pew."

Well, this was it. The perfect opening to explain what had happened to her. At least some of it. "I'm the daughter of a local madam in Jerkwater, and I'm told an outlaw named Moon Kilmore is my father. I wouldn't know—I've never met the man. Anyway, the back pew is the only pew I've ever been allowed to sit on. The good folks don't like their soiled doves sitting in front of them."

"You're not one."

Odessa's heart filled with something so warm that she felt the icy wall of defense she had built around it thaw slightly. "How do you know?" she asked softly.

"You have innocent ways, Des. A man doesn't need daylight to notice something like that."

The warmth of his words flooded her eyes, urging her to look up at him. She realized his were a curious shade of blue-gray, like bluebonnets or a far horizon breaking into a stretch of Texas sky. "I seem to be saying thank you a lot."

"No need to say anything. Fact is fact." He reached out and gently wiped away the tear that trickled down her cheek. "Are you running from the brothel?"

His touch was equally warm, his fingers igniting something in her bloodstream, something promising in her soul. She shook her head and immediately regretted it when he misunderstood and let his hand fall back to his side. "Someone thought I tried to rob them and I didn't mean to. It's a long story. I'll tell you down the road, I promise. Right now all you need to know is that I really did try to give the loot back. But I saw something I shouldn't have when I attempted to return it. I got scared and fled town, afraid they'd call the sheriff and have me jailed. Then I thought it all out and decided I would go to Sheriff James myself."

The urgency to make him understand erupted in her tone. "You see, I've made a couple of friends I don't want to lose. People in Jerkwater who are willing to look past my bad blood."

"There's no such thing as bad blood, only bad choices. Everybody makes those, and you shouldn't be held responsible for the ones anyone else made."

There was something hidden in his quiet insistence. Something he had experienced personally. If she weren't sitting in church, she would swear anger now set his jaw.

Odessa waited but he said no more. She had heard of quiet fury before, but this was the first time she'd ever witnessed it. She could only guess at the past mistake that had forced his strong reaction.

She flung her hands wide, shrugging her shoulders. "Bad

blood or not, every time I try to go back to talk to the sheriff, someone keeps stopping me. I thought if I traveled with a man as a married couple, maybe with a gunman, then that would at least get me back there. Once we hit town, you could go with me to the sheriff's office and I can tell him what really happened. Then you could leave after I paid you." Odessa crossed her heart. "I promise, I do have money of my own, Shad. I have some with me, but we'll need that for traveling expenses. I'll have to pay the rest of whatever you ask once we get there."

"Something's not adding up right." His eyes seemed to stare through her. "Why is there a thousand-dollar reward on your head?"

"A thousand dollars?" She bolted to her feet. "Someone will kill me for that amount."

"Not while I'm around they won't." Shad gently took her hand and guided her back down. "Here, eat that." He handed her a piece of the forgotten jerky. "No telling when we'll get another chance."

"You'll help me then . . . for sure?"

"Definitely."

"How much?" she asked cautiously, not exactly certain what a man like him would charge for his services. What had that dime novel said? Forty dollars a week and keep. She took a bite of the jerky.

"What am I worth to you?"

"My future's in your hands. You name it."

"Got a hundred dollars?"

She had a lot more on her but she couldn't let him know how much. "Yeah."

"Then I'll take the hundred and a promise."

She stopped chewing. "What kind of promise?"

"That when I say come close, you do. Every time. Without question." His eyes locked with hers. "And exactly how I tell you to."

Odessa looked into that blue horizon and sensed that he would accept nothing else for the bargain. Still, she had to know his reason. "Why?"

"So your plan has a chance to work. You want to make people believe we're married, don't you?"

Though she suspected his demand for the closeness stemmed from something far more than logic, she finally whispered, "Done."

Chapter 4

Odessa lay across the back pew restless, staring up into the rafters of the steeple lit by the beginning rays of dawn. Prisms of color filtering from stained-glass windows danced along the church walls warning that morning had come and there would be no more chance to sleep.

The pew in front of hers creaked beneath Shadow's weight as he shifted and stirred, mumbling something. She couldn't tell what he said, but he was clearly talking. Maybe he was dreaming.

She didn't want to wake him until the whistle announced the arrival of the 6:10. Best to let him get as much rest as possible. She wanted him alert if any trouble presented itself that morning.

Suddenly, Shadow sat up and turned toward her, his eyes wide, unseeing. "Don't do this, Laurie. Don't walk away. Give us time." The words exited in a ragged rush of desperation. "Forgive me . . . just this once."

Emotion that she didn't know him well enough to recognize etched his face. Maybe heartache. Maybe loss. Maybe the end of his world. She wasn't sure she wanted to know. Whoever Laurie was to him, she counted deeply in his life.

But she had apparently left him. What had he done to need her forgiveness?

Compassion consumed Odessa and she gently reached out to touch his arm, hoping the touch would wake him from his dream talk. Instead, Shadow looked at her with such need that she almost wished she was this Laurie person and could somehow soothe his troubled heart.

"That's it," he whispered softly, his ungloved hand reaching out to take hers and lace their fingers together. "Never stop wanting me. Come near me one last time. Just lean against my heart. I'll die if you don't."

It was clear he thought she was Laurie. Odessa couldn't have moved away if she'd wanted to. The plea in his voice was so compelling in its need that she was amazed it had come from such a rough-edged man.

"Nothing's changed for me. I'll make things up to you." His thumb caressed her thumb, the race of his pulse pressing warmly against her palm. "You won't ever be sorry for loving me."

He lifted their hands to his lips and kissed her knuckles one at a time, his breath brushing each as if it were a tropical wind wafting over them. Gooseflesh pebbled up Odessa's wrist and arm, igniting heat in the wake of his sensuous touch. Attraction shivered its way to the tips of her toes.

Her own breath quickened and she realized she had to stop him before he went any further. She was not Laurie. She would be no woman's replacement. She saw that too often in the brothel. If she was ever the woman in some man's dream, she wanted it to be *her* face he was seeing. *Her* touch he needed so desperately.

She attempted to pull away without startling him. "Wake up, Shad. It's me, Odessa Kilmore. You're asleep."

She watched contrasting feelings war through him. Confusion about her abrupt withdrawal. Realization that he'd been dream talking. Discomfort about what he might have said or done.

His brow furrowed for a moment as his wayward hand unlocked itself from hers and ran through his hair. Unease filled his eyes as he looked at her and apologized. "I hope I didn't do anything to . . ." He couldn't quite meet her gaze. "Hurt you."

Odessa shook her head and motioned toward his hat lying on the pew. "You didn't. You were only mumbling in your sleep." Had he hurt Laurie? A man with his kind of background could be . . . no, she wasn't going to do what others did to her. She refused to judge him. "Maybe we'd better be on our way."

The unease didn't leave him. A guardedness that had not been there before now layered the space that divided them as he rose to gather his wits. She didn't want to set out on the road together with uncertainty standing between them. "Whoever Laurie was is your business," she said quietly. "I don't care if you mumble her name all night as long as your terms of our agreement have nothing to do with her."

His eyes met hers and it felt as if they were burning the very edges of her soul. "Not a damned thing," he assured her.

As Odessa straightened the wrinkles from her clothing as best she could, she silently added another type to the list of falsehoods that had been told in church that morning. A bold-faced lie.

She felt the untruth clear down to her bones, which were being rattled as a whistle blared over the countryside. The slatted boards that made up the church's flooring shuddered, revealing the 6:10 was coming in right on time. "Good, 'cause we have a train to catch."

"We're taking the train?" He moved toward the sanctuary doors. "What about Dollar?"

"I've got enough to see we all ride in style for the trip."

Hearing her plan seemed to be just what the man needed to put his unease away. "Remind me later that I want to ask how you make your money. I think I could use some advice, boss."

By the time Shadow got Dollar loaded, Odessa had awakened the mercantile owner and managed to buy an armload of clothes. Two shopping stops later and she had finally convinced Shad not to call her boss.

"Pretty fancy . . ." He was admiring the lace gracing the eight single-sash windows along the touring car's west wall when he suddenly realized he could see her from the oval dressing mirror that stood on hinged legs in the corner of the Pullman car. He had turned his back to allow them both privacy in dressing, but the full image of her stepping into the serge travel skirt and bringing it up to a perfect flare of hips made him stumble over his words. "A-arrangements you made."

She sported her own share of lace that looked delicate against her shoulders, and he watched in disappointment as a blouse the color of newly churned butter quickly hid the lace away.

He instantly got busy looking the other way and finished dressing in the fancy trappings she had bought for him. Brocade frock coat, tailored vest, clean white shirt, and string tie. Pants that fit him as if they were a second skin. She'd guessed his size well.

"Personally, this is all too girly for me. The car and these clothes. My, don't you look good," he remarked.

Glad that she had finished, Shadow turned around just in time to see her unpin the ostrich-feathered hat from her hair and let it sail onto a chair.

"I've seen worse, believe me," she informed.

He supposed she had, being brought up in a brothel. He

admired her ease at talking about her past with him. It showed how strong her confidence was. She must have more than her share of grit to face what society doled out to people of so-called bad blood. He too had suffered that particular branding, from those far closer than "society."

Odessa motioned to some of the furnishings. "I figured a married couple would travel this way, and the Pullman would be an easy way to avoid passengers in case any of them were on the lookout for me."

"The tickets cost you a pretty penny." *And they call me a thief,* Shadow grumbled inwardly as he remembered how much of Odessa's money the ticket master had demanded for their travel arrangements. Lucky for them, the train had to take on water, allowing time to make all the necessary arrangements.

Shadow eyed the rosewood chest, high-backed chair, and washstand lining the same wall as the mirror. The tickets were worth it, he guessed. A stove offered a way to heat water if they decided to enjoy a bath in the provided water closet. His new duds were a pleasure, but getting a good bath was something he looked forward to. The image of joining Odessa in hers seemed a tempting option but a closeness no promise he'd demanded would ever ask of her . . . unless she offered the invitation first. From what he knew of her so far, that wasn't likely to happen.

He ran a hand across the top of one of the chairs. Upholstered in the best grade of plush, it offered a place to sit and shone with a polished pattern that someone of better society than himself probably could have named. Even the four-poster bed housed against the car's back wall promised an interesting way for a real married couple to appreciate a long train ride. To him, it just all looked rich and offered more luxury than he'd seen in a while. Pullman knew what it took to make people comfortable.

The car suddenly jerked forward, then back, causing

Odessa to stumble. He grabbed her and helped her regain her footing. Once she was steady, he escorted her to the chair, then parted one of the curtains to look out.

"I didn't hear the conductor call, did you?" she asked, facing Shadow. "And the whistle didn't sound, did it?"

As if on cue, the whistle blared and the Pullman began to move. "I guess I didn't hear him yell all aboard because we were talking."

"Stay put," Shadow ordered, not sure he wanted to tell her what he'd seen going over the eave of the touring car. Trouble had already tracked them down. "I want to check on something. I'll be right back."

When she had informed him about wanting to reach Jerkwater by train, he'd thought it was unwise, but she'd insisted that it would be the fastest way to get there. He couldn't argue that point, but he didn't like being boxed in anywhere. He learned a long time ago that that limited his getaway possibilities.

The train was well under way now, chugging at its maximum of thirty-seven miles per hour.

Shadow grabbed the other chair and headed for the door that led out to the platform. "Here, prop this against the knob and don't remove it unless I come to get you. Don't open that door for anyone, not even the conductor. If I see him, I'll tell him you're bathing and he should come back for the tickets later."

Though his tone demanded no argument, her back slammed against the door, blocking the exit. "You saw something you didn't like out there."

Hazel. Her eyes were hazel, a combination of green and brown with streaks of gold in their midst. Eyes darkened with worry for whose safety? Hers or his?

She would be stubborn enough not to listen to reason, so he told her the truth about the boots he saw slipping up and out of view over the farthermost window. "Someone saw through your disguise or spotted me. Either way, the train ride's impossible now."

"I'm going with you," she stated flatly, refusing to move away.

Maybe they did stand a better chance if she stayed with him instead of him trying to come back for her once he took care of the threat. Maybe if they could reach Dollar's boxcar before anyone found them missing from their car, they'd have a way to get off this rolling cell and make a run for it. But it would challenge them both to reach him. He wished the hell the Pullman offered a two-ended exit. Now they'd have to go up and over.

"All right, but stay close," Shadow invoked his first demand of the promise she made, then added, "and behind me."

He opened the door and pointed to the roof's scalloped edges, waiting for sight of the attacker before attempting the next move. Sunlight glinted off the window of the car in front of them, making him blink to ward off the glare.

A man squatting over the coupling between cars stood abruptly and swung at Shadow.

"He's trying to pull the linchpin to disconnect us!" Odessa shouted from behind him.

A shot rang out, the noise deafening. Another quickly followed. Odessa screamed. Someone was firing from the direction of the tool car. The man swinging at Shadow took the bullet, crumbling below the fittings, disappearing between the crush of iron wheels. A third bullet hit the car wall above Shadow's head.

He grabbed Odessa's hand and rolled, landing on his feet only to have the momentum send him and his employer into the passenger door in front of them. The door flung open, apparently striking whoever was opening it from the other side. Shadow felt himself falling into the opener's torso.

"He's going for his gun!" Odessa warned. Women screamed

at the fracas. Children began to cry. Passengers looked on in surprise, but no one got up to help.

Shadow wrestled with the culprit, trying to grab the man's gun before he did. He couldn't keep Odessa's hands out of the fray. She was being too helpful. "Back away, Des," he ordered. "You're getting in the way."

The gun left leather and the fight for control of the weapon intensified. Both of Shadow's hands deadlocked around the fighter's wrist. As he tried to twist away from Shadow's grip, the sound of a pain-filled curse and bone cracking rent the air. In an act of desperation, the man's other fist slammed into Shadow's chin, meeting its mark.

Shadow reeled backward but held on, wrangling the weapon from the broken wrist as the impetus took him backward into Odessa. Her hand shot past him, grabbed the gun from Shadow, and reared back. Suddenly, the fighter's head took a hard blow from the butt end of his gun. The man went limp.

"Remind me never to make you mad," Shadow half teased Odessa and her handiwork, but the moment he got a good look at the unconscious man and recognized him, his tone took on a deadly seriousness. "Cole Lambert."

"You know him?" Odessa took a long look at her victim.

"Yeah, this one was after me." If Cole was there, that meant his older brother, Sal, was on board somewhere. That explained a lot of the suspicions Shadow had felt lately. He knew someone had been following him since Fort Worth. If Odessa weren't with him, he would just wait until Cole revived and demand to know the whereabouts of his brother. He would call Sal out and finally have the reckoning they both knew was coming.

From the other end of the car, passengers finally started moving toward them. Shadow didn't wait to see if they had finally found a sense of duty to help or if any of them were part of the Lambert gang. He couldn't take a chance.

"Back to our car. Stay close enough we can move like we're seamed together," Shadow commanded, grabbing a parasol from one of the ladies sitting nearby. "Sorry, ma'am, I'm just borrowing it." *That is, if someone doesn't try to bust the door down and break it.*

Once outside, Shadow hooked the curved end of the parasol's handle over the doorknob and stretched its stem under the metal that formed a handrail to climb the boarding steps. It wouldn't hold long, but maybe just long enough to offer them time. He pointed to the roof and, with tremendous effort, swung himself atop the Pullman, praying that the man whose boots he'd seen go up earlier was the same one who had tried to pull the linchpin. A quick look offered relief that he'd been right about the linch puller. He leaned over and extended Odessa a hand up.

"Is this any time to tell you that I haven't walked a roof before?"

He suspected the teasing in her tone meant to cloak her fear, but safety lay in reaching Dollar. The freight cars that housed the animals and hay for their travel lay behind the touring cars for passengers. "Once is all it takes to give you experience. You trust me, don't you?"

She accepted his help and gripped. "With my life."

He boosted her up and, once there, she nearly flung herself into his arms. He gave her a moment to gain her balance, but he couldn't linger in their nearness, no matter how much he would have liked to do so had circumstances been different. They would be visible to anyone brave enough to follow them.

"Crouch low as you walk," he instructed, showing her how to turn slowly.

"Why?" she asked, the wind whipping at the serge to make her petticoats billow out behind her. "We're a target no matter how short we are."

He grabbed her hand and urged her forward. "The wind.

Grab your skirt and tuck it up into your waist." He reached to help her, but she quickly pushed him away and followed his instruction. "Yeah, just like that. Keep your arms in close and curl your body like a half bowl. You'll be more compact and that will steady you better."

They managed to make it to the end of the car, down and over the top of the next one. When they walked midway of the second touring car, Odessa suddenly held a finger to her lips and cupped her ear, signaling him to listen. Voices carried on the wind and it was difficult to discern which direction they came from.

Stealthily, Shadow made his way to the edge of the car and listened. Men arguing below. He took in their conversation, then signaled Odessa closer, raising his boot heels to indicate she should tiptoe. She looked at him as if he'd lost his mind. They weren't exactly taking a stroll. To her credit, she kept her body curled and moved forward, looking very much like a condemned man heading to the gallows.

When she reached him, he pointed downward. "Danger."

She nodded understanding and waited for further instructions.

"Cole should have been back by now," a man bellowed. "See what the hell is keeping him. No, wait a minute. Let me think."

Shadow went into full alert. Whoever followed those orders would have to climb over Odessa's Pullman in order to get to the passenger car Cole Lambert had been in. He and Odessa had to get off of the top of the car in case the man turned around and saw them.

"That linchpin should've already been pulled by now and this train stopped. One of the hell of you had better see if you can't give Sanderson a hand, and the other of you go after Cole."

The rush of wind died off enough that Shadow could plainly hear the man giving orders this time. A distinct voice Shadow had known since childhood. It hadn't changed much over the years. Just as demanding and full of threat if it wasn't obeyed. *Sal Lambert's.* He'd been right about the brothers being together.

"Who do you think the woman is?" another man asked. "The conductor said a married couple had taken the Pullman for the ride. You think she's his wife?"

"No, dipweed. She must be some kind of cover. He swore he'd never marry if Laurie hitched Banker Patterson."

Shadow stiffened, wishing he'd gone ahead and had them jump to the next car before Odessa heard Laurie's name. Her mind needed to concentrate on what they were about to do, not on connecting his dream to what she'd just heard.

"Your Laurie?" she whispered.

Shadow shook his head and grabbed her hand. "She was never really my Laurie," he whispered back, glad he wasn't really lying to Odessa. If Laurie had ever been in love with him, she never could have told him to get out of her life. To keep away. "You ready to take a big leap of faith?"

She looked over at the next car, her eyes widening as he squeezed her hand in reassurance. She understood that they couldn't take the chance of climbing down to make the transfer. This car had two exits. "I think I already have," her voice quivered as she squeezed his hand, "in *you*. I've just got one question before I do it, though."

"Ask it."

"I wonder which of us is the most wanted?"

Chapter 5

Being on the outlaw trail with Shadow Rivers was more than Odessa had bargained for. Already she'd been shot at, walked the roof of several cars on a moving train, and nearly fallen off into the mesquite trying to swing herself into the open side door of the boxcar. The man thought she was one of those monkeys the organ grinders used to draw in customers.

"Where did you learn to do all that?" she asked, still lying sprawled on her backside atop the hay that littered the floor of the animal housing. It had taken her several minutes just to get her heart to quit galloping from sheer fright.

"I never swung into a side door before." He sat alongside her, dusting off his legs. When a gust of hay dust rushed up to billow around them, apology wrinkled his brow. Shadow started dusting off her legs and working his way up. "Sorry, I forgot about your itchiness."

She pushed his hands away, her nose wrinkling in response as she busied her own hands to the task. "I can do that." Her gaze shot up to glare at him. "You mean to tell me you had me go *first* through the door because you were afraid?"

He chuckled and reached up to wipe away a piece of

straw from her cheek. "You were doing so well, jumping that last car before I did. I figured why not give you some rein. You knew as much about it as I did."

"If I had a gun right now, I'd shoot you myself."

He stood and offered his hand. "If you were wearing a gun, you'd probably have shot Lambert back in the passenger car. Instead you just plunked him with his own. If we plan on getting you back to Jerkwater to prove your innocence, then it might be best you don't go murdering anyone before we get there."

She accepted his offer and stood, her feet still a little wobbly from what they'd just done. The smell of animal excrement indicated they'd found the right car, and she was extremely grateful that she'd landed only in hay, no matter how much it itched. "Where's Dollar?"

"Give me a second." Shadow moved away. "I'd whistle for him, but someone might hear him trying to bite through his hitching or kick the stall down trying to get to me."

Not long after, Shadow came back leading the bay by the reins. The horse had already been saddled and his bags looked full.

"You ready?"

Odessa looked at Dollar. "You mean we're going to ride him?"

A dark brow arched higher over one blue eye. "Well, why do you think we went to all this trouble to reach him?"

She looked out into the passing scenery, then back at the horse. "We're going to jump?"

"Would you rather stay here and let them find us? They're sure to shoot me, and I wouldn't want to guess at what they might plan for you. Lambert isn't fond of women and even less of witnesses."

"We're really going to jump." She'd hired the man to save her, not kill her trying to get there. "All three of us?"

Shadow saw her start to raise her foot into the stirrup and

stopped her. "Not on top of him. That would kill us all. We'll give him a shoo, then you and me will follow. Got to get past some of this mesquite and wait for some buffalo grass. It'll cushion the fall."

He quickly secured the reins around the saddle horn so they wouldn't get tangled in the bay's legs or a bush and break the poor beast's neck. Then he grabbed hold of the side of the door and scanned the passing countryside. "Looks like there's a place coming up. You ready? You hesitate and we're both dead."

She nodded, taking a deep breath as her heart thudded in her chest and her pulse felt like it would drum her ears off her head.

Shadow moved to Dollar's flank and counted, "One. Two." He swatted the bay's rump. "Hii-yah!"

The horse bolted through the door, taking a flying leap that made him look suspended in air for a flash, and then he was gone. The train rushed on.

"Ready?" Shadow grabbed her hand and swung her toward the door edge. "When I say three, jump, then tuck and roll. Got me?"

"Do *you* got *me*?" she asked through gritted teeth.

"One. Two. Threeeee . . ."

"Ho-o-ly . . ." Her curse was lost on the wind as she remembered midair that she was supposed to tuck and roll on the way down.

"Oof!" Breath left her lungs as she landed on something hard yet soft and rolled, rolled, rolled, finally ending on her back. A second later, Shadow crashed into her with such impact that she was certain she plowed a foot deeper into the buffalo grass. She tried to push him off, but her legs and arms were still quivering from the bone-jarring jump. "Get off me, Shad. Let me breathe."

"Can't move. Gotta lay here a minute," he mumbled

against her neck, his body completely stretching down her length. "I p-promise. Not trying to grope you."

"Move your hand, please."

His hand slowly removed itself from her breast.

She could tell by the sound of his own breath that it was taking everything he had to regain his calm. So she just lay there and willed strength back into her bones. Five or so minutes passed. Her own breath had steadied despite the extra weight on top of her. Dollar had found them and grazed a few feet away, but Shadow didn't stir. She raised one hand and pushed at his shoulder. "Shad? Are you conscious?"

No response.

"Shad?" Worry instantly gripped her. Was he hurt? Had he taken his last jump to save them? Spoken his last words to assure her he wasn't taking advantage of her? Had she been so worried that he would feel the money stuffed in the chemise she wore beneath her shirt that she hadn't considered he might be hurt? She managed to wiggle her other arm loose to try to use both to flip him over.

The man had the audacity to chuckle.

And she'd felt sorry for him. "You'd better get off me or, I swear, when I get up from here I'm going to hook your boot in Dollar's stirrup and hii-yah him myself."

Shadow rolled to his feet and stood, offering her a hand up. When she refused to take it, he laughed. "Can't blame a man for trying, can you? I've been good. I haven't asked you to come near me once that it wasn't to save your hide. It's not my fault you happened to land right where I was landing."

"You haven't had reason to demand it," she sputtered. "And, if you'll take a good look around, there's nobody here but Dollar to prove anything to. I'm the one who comes to you, remember? I decide just how close I want close enough to be. Got me?"

She rose and went to the bay, untied the reins, and motioned for Shadow to take them. "You ride him. I think I'll walk for a while."

"Don't worry yourself. You don't have to sit near me." Shadow grabbed her around the waist and thrust her up on the saddle. "You ride him. If anyone's walking, I am."

Three hours later Odessa stared at the sweat stain that darkened the back of Shadow's once white shirt as he walked in front of her and Dollar. He had discarded the frock coat in the first hour of walking. Thirty minutes later, the string tie had decorated a patch of Indian paintbrush. In the past hour, he had rolled up his sleeves. Thank goodness he'd insisted that he keep his old pair of boots back in Longhorn City. He would have worn blisters into his feet breaking in a new pair in this manner. She wished they hadn't been forced to leave the train in such a hurry and left their hats back in the Pullman. Too long in the Texas sun would blister the hide off anybody.

She reined Dollar to a halt. Shadow kept on walking. "Where are you going in such a hurry, partner?"

He kept walking. "Got to find shade somewhere."

Looking around, she urged Dollar to move again. "There isn't a tree in sight."

"That man who planted apple trees must have never traveled this part of Texas. He'd earn his keep down here."

"Don't you think we'd find that shade a little quicker if you rode with me?" she insisted.

He finally stopped and turned, shielding the sun from his eyes to look up at her. "Well, actually, I do. But whether I do that or not depends on whether you feel comfortable if I'm up there with you."

When she reached where he stood, she reined up short again. "I'll be comfortable. Besides, I think we need to talk."

His hand went down and he headed west again. "I think I'll keep walking. I'm not fond of gabby women, and I don't like being a captured audience."

She laughed. "I won't talk your head off, although you deserve it after that last stunt. I want *you* to talk to *me*. Tell me some things I need to know about that Lambert fellow who's following us. The one we didn't knock out."

"Sal," Shadow said over his shoulder. "You won't have to worry about him till we get to Jerkwater."

Surprise filled her. "How do you figure that?"

"He knows by now where we're headed. You heard what he said. He had already learned our destination from the conductor, and by now he's found out anything anyone else might have known about the married couple in the Pullman." Shadow stopped and waited till Dollar reached him.

Odessa extended him a hand up and Shadow took it, nestled into the saddle behind her, and gently took command of the reins.

"Will he send his men after us?" She settled against the warmth of his chest and was a little irritated for liking the way it felt to have him there. His heart beat strong against her back. His breath brushed warmly over the crown of her hair, and the scent of sun-dappled skin and something pungently male lent an intimacy to their closeness.

"Why send anyone to follow when they know where we intend to go?" His left arm became a band of iron around her waist while the right held the reins.

"I don't understand." Puzzlement swept through her. "Then why didn't we just ride the rest of the way with Dollar in the boxcar?"

Shadow bent slightly and whispered against her ear, "And have you show up looking like a strawberry patch?"

Surely he hadn't made them take that death-defying leap to save her vanity and a little suffering from itching.

His chuckle ended abruptly, offering a more serious tone to his question. "You don't remember, do you?"

"What am I forgetting?"

"The two shots when we walked out of the Pullman. They were from in front of us, not the back, where Lambert and his men were riding. And I hadn't fought with Cole in the passenger car yet. So he hadn't attempted to go for his gun. He was probably just stationed ahead of us in case the linchpin didn't get pulled and we tried to escape into the forward car."

"The shots were meant for me, weren't they?" She knew the truth before he confirmed it.

"Not for sure, but it makes sense. If anyone's after us on foot, it's probably whoever's trying to stop you."

"You haven't looked back once since we jumped," she realized aloud. "Don't you believe anyone is following?"

"No, if they're smart, they rode the train ten or fifteen miles ahead and got off. They'll make their play somewhere between here and Jerkwater. That's why I'm hoping we can find some shade, give Dollar a little rest, and hit the trail in the dark. We'll be harder targets to find and they'll be expecting us to camp for the night."

The land stretched long into the western horizon with no sign of trees and the only shade offered by an occasional cloud drifting by. "I'd pray for rain," Odessa said, "but that would just make it worse for us tonight."

"If we don't spot something quick, we'll find an arroyo and make a lean-to out of my trail coat with whatever reeds we can find. Maybe the wind will give us a break and won't get worked up."

Odessa let wait the questions that she wanted to ask Shadow about Sal Lambert. At the moment, she owed both Shadow and herself total focus. Her eyes already stung and staring into the Texas sun was blinding. Seeing would be even more difficult the longer the sun rode the western sky.

An hour later, Shadow suddenly urged Dollar into a trot. "Spotted something," he said.

She would have known it even if he hadn't spoken up or hastened the bay. Shadow's body changed behind her. His heart sped up. An exhale of relief cooled the top of her head. He patted her tummy as if telling her everything was okay now.

She noticed the land sloping slightly downward, not so much that she thought they were on the downside of a hill of any sort, just that the prairie had taken on a gradual roll.

"Look there, a wild boar." Shadow pointed to the southwest. "He's spotted us. Going to run for it."

"You're heading toward him? Isn't he dangerous?" She'd heard of the wild boars in this part of the Panhandle. They'd killed men before.

"They tend to graze near a waterhole." Shadow spurred Dollar into a gallop. "We could use the water, and he'll be supper."

"*If* we catch him," Odessa complained, grabbing the saddle horn to anchor herself for the hard ride.

Shadow's right hand disappeared for a flash, then came up holding the peacemaker. "I'll catch him." His face dipped closer to her ear. "Think you can shoot him?"

"At full gallop?" She didn't want to let go of her hold on the saddle horn, and she sure didn't want Shadow to let go of her long enough to shoot. "I've only shot bottles off a fence rail before, and they didn't move even after I shot them."

Shadow dared to press a kiss against her ear. "That's for luck then, little sureshot. I don't know about you, but my stomach feels like it's pressing against my backbone. I could eat that critter clear to his hooves. I'll do the shooting if you think you can take the reins."

"Hand me that blasted gun." Her teeth gritted against the power of the bone-jarring ride. "If I didn't know anything

about outlawing before I met you, I'm sure learning it now."
She let go of the saddle horn with her right hand long
enough for him to thrust the gun into it. Odessa pulled back
the hammer and curled her finger around the trigger.

The boar's hindquarters disappeared for a moment and
she was certain they'd lost him, but Shadow kept pursuing.
Another slight roll of the prairie brought the beast into
view again. Her hand bounced with each pound of hoof
against prairie loam and she could only pray she held on to
the peacemaker long enough not to end up shooting Dollar's
ear off by mistake. She couldn't take another chance of
losing sight of the boar either.

"Here goes," Odessa warned, closing her eyes and squeez-
ing the trigger. "Duck, Dollar!"

Chapter 6

Odessa watched Shadow stake two ends of his trail coat to the ground. The lavender ribbon that had once tied back her hair was now laced in two pieces through the first and the last buttonhole on the coat, helping to attach it to the bay's saddle horn and cantle. After they'd watered him, Dollar had been hobbled in the plushest clumps of buffalo grass so he wouldn't wander off and move the makeshift lean-to.

"You've done that before," she complimented Shadow, appreciating his cleverness. The lean-to made a nice triangle of shade. "He's perfectly content with what you're doing. You must have taught him a lot in your time together."

"He's smarter than me sometimes." Shadow turned around only to stop still as he stared at her. "Leave it unbraided. It looks pretty down."

Odessa quit braiding her hair, not because he'd told her to, but because of the frank appreciation in his voice. She'd heard many a man's excitement for a woman echoed in her mother's place of business. It had been difficult to miss no matter how many doors away she'd slept. But there was something purely innocent in the way Shadow offered his compliment about her hair. Something fine and clean and good. One of the best experiences he had given her since she'd met him and certainly one she would treasure long after he left Jerkwater.

Realizing she was staring back at him in a daze, she rose from her crouched position in the buffalo grass and dusted her bottom. "Want me to get the beef jerky?"

He shook his head and motioned to the trail coat. "I will. Go ahead and get some shade." He reached up as if he was going to touch her cheek, then didn't. "You're blistering."

The rest of the clothing he'd worn in the cell lay beneath the trail coat, forming a cushion over the grass beneath it. Shadow's thoughtfulness pleased her and she thanked him. "I'm just sorry I missed that shot."

"You tried your best." Shadow searched through the saddlebag, then sat down beside her. The lean-to rose behind them shielding off much of the sun, but the great scorcher still glared from the other side of Dollar. Despite her reasoning that they would have more shade angling the tent from the east, Shadow had insisted the open end face the western horizon so he could look between Dollar's legs and still see anything coming by.

He unrolled the jerky, took a piece himself, then handed her the rest. "At least you scared him off. Lucky for us we noticed him or we wouldn't have found this waterhole."

"He won't try to claim his territory, will he?" Boars were mean and nasty, from everything she'd heard about them. She didn't want to find out personally.

"I'll take first watch." His right hand gave her a couple of reassuring pats.

"And I'll wake you up if he comes back while I'm on lookout." She patted right back, too quickly to make it the jest she'd planned.

"How about we eat, then get washed up." He laughed as she strained around him to look at the arroyo and the welcoming oasis of water springing between two rolls of the prairie. "I can't promise how long we'll have it to ourselves. It may be the only water for miles."

"I can't wait to get out of these clothes," she admitted, then realized how that had sounded. "I mean *change* my clothes. The serge is hot."

Shadow's attention slowly swept from her face, down the slim column of her neck, over her breasts, and ended at the top of her knees, where she wrapped her hands. She was grateful for the cloth of jerky she held for it gave her something to hide her trembling fingers with.

"Greasy jerky," she muttered, hoping he couldn't discern the utterly black lie she used to ward off the attraction those glorious blue-gray eyes of his now stirred within her.

"So you've decided not to go into Jerkwater dressed as a married woman?"

"We're kind of worse for wear, don't you think?" She eyed him closely now. His shirt might be stained, his dark hair could use a good cut and combing, and his scruff of whiskers needed the sharp edge of a razor strop. But the man was better looking than any she'd seen duded up for money spent at Maddy Kilmore's Gilded Garter. "Maybe that wasn't the best plan after all. It only got us in trouble."

"Could have worked. It just didn't."

"You don't worry much about anything, do you?" She took another bite of the jerky and handed him back the cloth, waiting for him to answer.

"Try not to. It just makes a man old." He accepted the cloth and remained silent.

She wanted him to talk. "Tell me more about yourself, Shad."

He stood, looming over her. "Talking's for later. Time's wasting and we need to wash off and get to sleep. We'll have to be on our way at sunset."

He was right, of course, but she couldn't help feeling disappointed. They seemed settled for a moment there, and she thought he was willing to reveal some things about himself. Things she was sure the dime novel had wrong. "Okay, but before I go to sleep I want us to have that talk. I'm the boss, remember?"

He helped her up, his fingers lingering a moment too long just to be offering aid.

"You're not going to leave it alone, are you?"

She shook her head and withdrew her hand. "Not if we're going to spend time out here sleeping. In case you decide to do something in your sleep, I need to know a little more about this Laurie person and a whole lot more about Lambert."

"You might lose sleep if you do."

"Let me worry about that."

Though no one he knew would consider him a gentleman, Shadow found himself being one despite the great desire to watch Odessa bathe. He'd thought it best that they bathe at the same time, just keep their backs to each other. That way, they could get done quicker, have their talk, then get some badly needed sleep. But he knew from his time in the Pullman with her that a turned back didn't mean he could stop thinking about what she might look like in all her naked glory.

The past two days had tested him to the limit in several ways, most of all maintaining his willpower not to demand the last term of their agreement every time he got the urge. Odessa needed rest if she was going to survive what miles separated them from here and the next sign of civilization. That needed to remain foremost in his thoughts. He hadn't told her, but he'd just pretended to eat. The jerky was just about gone, and he'd put the rest away to save it for her.

Not wanting to be too long without the peacemaker, he'd rushed through his bath and hair washing and cleaned the shirt she'd bought him. It now hung over Dollar's saddle, drying. He'd also made sure the canteen was filled. It had taken everything within him not to join Odessa to wash the dirt from her hair. Everything in him to keep his back turned to her bathing.

But if he had joined her, he would have been the kind of no-good Laurie had called him. The kind of man who hadn't been good enough for her after his prison stay. The kind of man whose nearness no genteel woman would ever want. The words Laurie had yelled when she left him lashed like a jerk of a bullwhip.

Odessa might not be able to hit the wide side of a barn with a bullet. She might not handle a rope well, but she wasn't ignorant by any means. The minute she started learning anything about Laurie, she was going to figure out that he'd demanded Odessa's closeness for more reason than just to convince people they were married. She would know it was some kind of test he'd made of her. Some kind of soothing to his ego. The truth tasted sour and he thought maybe Laurie was at least partly right. No gentleman would have lied to someone like Odessa.

"That was worth the wait." Odessa startled him from his thoughts.

He glanced up and watched her approach, dressed in trousers, shirt, and the lacy something she wore beneath her slightly unfastened shirt. But she looked like no man he'd ever seen. Her hair shone like wheat ripening in the sun, curling past generous bosoms and brushing against the top of her hips. When it completely dried, it would look like a shawl of gold about her.

Her face and slender neck glowed pink from the cleaning, and her eyes had taken on a deeper shade of green, enhanced by the color of her shirt. "Beautiful," he whispered, not caring that she heard it. The truth demanded to be heard this time.

"Thank you." She smiled, stowing away the roll of serge. Her gaze met his, then swept appreciatively down his bare chest. "You clean up pretty good yourself."

Her smile warmed him to the tip of his boots. He liked her feeling comfortable enough to speak her mind. "My shirt ought to dry in a little while. I'll check it when we finish our talk."

"Okay."

She started to take a seat beside him, but he half turned and patted the spot at the back of the lean-to. "Go ahead and lie down. We'll fit better under here if at least one of us is lying flat. You can put your head on my leg for a pillow, if you want."

She hesitated. "My hair's still wet."

"I'll dry. It's the least I can offer you. I promise I won't make any demands I shouldn't."

She eyed him for a moment as if gauging his sincerity, then accepted the offering. She lay the back of her head against his thigh. Good, she was beginning to trust him. A closer look at her face revealed a slight splattering of freckles across her nose.

"You sure I'm not too heavy on you?" Her gaze met his.

"See what I mean about worrying? Makes a woman fret."

"You said it makes a man old," her lips scolded gently. "And by the way, how old are you?"

"Is that your first question for the talk, boss?"

"I told you not to call me boss." Her chin lifted and he liked how it set stubbornly. "Yes, and if you want me to hurry and get to sleep, then I'd appreciate quick and honest answers."

"Depends on what you ask me." At least that one was easy to answer. "I'm twenty-eight. How old are you?"

"Twenty."

"I wouldn't have guessed."

"Why, do I look older?"

"There you go again, worrying."

Her arms linked beneath her breasts and he rather liked the way they emphasized their generous size. When she caught him staring, she immediately unlinked them and started to lift her head.

"I'm sorry," he said sincerely, gently touching her shoulder to silently ask her to stay. "I'll be a good boy, I promise. You'll be more comfortable there."

She lowered her head slowly. "Okay, but if I catch you doing anything like that again, I'm off of here."

He let her settle down. "Question two?"

"Who was Laurie to you? She must have once been very important in your life."

The truth, Rivers, he told himself. *Get it over with.* "My former fiancée."

"Why did she leave you?"

Her hazel eyes held such sympathy Shadow wanted to look away but couldn't. Honesty kept him riveted to her face; he needed to see her reaction. "Because I went to prison at fifteen and when I got out three years later, I wasn't good enough for her anymore."

"Did she *say* that?"

"She told me she wanted nothing more to do with me. That a good woman would never want me. She refused to let me near her, even walk down the same sidewalk she did. She liked me well enough as long as I bought her pretty things and didn't have a bad name."

The memory raged hard within him. "Then I learned the real truth. While I was imprisoned, she'd become engaged to the town banker. A better man, she told me. I didn't stay around to find out if it was true." Shadow's jaw set firmly. "I felt raw for a while, went down a bad hole. Maybe tried to prove I was what she said I was. That's the *boy* they wrote about in that dime novel." He glanced into the distance for a moment. "I didn't know she actually married Patterson until Lambert said so this morning."

Odessa's hand reached out to touch his. "I'm sorry, Shad. Some people can be so cruel."

He returned his attention to her, staring at her fingertips on his. Odessa's touch was genuine, the most sincerely offered that he'd ever known. He would take the memory of it with him and treasure the closeness for the long nights that stretched on the lonely road ahead of him. "They say men like me are cruel," Shadow whispered, "making a living off settling the west whichever way the dollar lures us. But so-called society can be cruel too. Not giving a stupid boy a chance to prove himself a man. The real cruelty comes from making us feel once we get out of prison that we've got a chance to make good. That's why I don't make plans," he confessed. "That's why I don't worry. I take each day and whatever it offers. Good or bad."

"That's the saddest thing I've ever heard."

He wanted no pity. "Just a hard truth a man has to live by because of his own mistakes."

"What mistake *did* you make? You were only fifteen at the time, you said."

At least she hadn't moved away. It was more interest than some folks had given him to learn his past criminal record. "I was stupid enough to think riding with a gang was something to brag about. We were kids trying to be stagecoach robbers. Wanted a little spending money to spoil our sweethearts or help our mother. So, we held up a Wells Fargo shipment." He cursed at the memory. "That was the day I grew up fast. The day I lost my best friend."

Odessa sat up and faced him. "He was one of the gang?"

Shadow nodded. "Him, Sal Lambert, and his brother, Cole."

"What happened to your friend?"

"After we stopped the stage, he and I realized we were in

over our heads and decided we were playing a man's game too soon. My friend got scared when the shotgun rider who rode on the seat next to the driver pulled his weapon and aimed it directly at him. Right at that moment, Cole and Sal jumped from an overhanging ledge just as we'd planned to surprise the drivers. The next thing I knew the shotgun went off, the four of them went down, and my best friend hit the ground. Sal and Cole made off with the gold shipment while I tried to revive the two drivers to help me get my friend to the doctor."

Grief poured through Shadow at the telling but the words came out hard and bitter. "They wouldn't let me out of jail long enough to attend his funeral, even though both drivers said I helped them and hadn't done any of the wrestling or hitting. I had a gun on me and the sheriff checked it. It hadn't been fired. But the gold was gone and a kid had been killed. The townspeople wanted somebody to go down for the robbery and the drivers never saw the other two who attacked them."

"So Sal Lambert and his brother got away with the money. Did you tell anyone?"

Shadow shook his head. "I'm not sure you'll understand this, Des, but at the time I figured staying quiet was the right thing to do. Sal said if I didn't squeal on them, he'd make sure my part of the take went to my friend's mother. She's a widow woman with three kids. I figured five years wouldn't be much to pay for my part in his death."

"Five years? You said you served three."

"Sheriff Pickens back in Longhorn City got me paroled. After I couldn't find work anywhere, he took me in and let me do odd jobs for him. I asked him once why he did it, and he just said that I got a raw deal. I think he suspected the Lamberts and they probably threw enough money around to add to the suspicion. All I know is, after three years, the judge issued a pardon and released me into Rafe Pickens's care. Because of him I found a way to earn a living and send my friend's family money now and then."

"So you weren't in jail for doing anything wrong when I found you, and that's why the cell was unlocked."

Shadow explained why he'd been there.

"Why do you think Sal Lambert is after you? You kept your word. You never told, even though I'm not sure I agree with honor among thieves." She looked apologetically at him. "Oh, I didn't mean you were a thief, I—"

"I almost was. I just got attacked by a moment of good conscience that ended up saving my life for whatever it is. If I'd used my gun that day, I'd have hung."

"You're a good man, Shadow. I'll bank my life on it. In fact I have. You've had plenty of opportunity to rob me and you haven't. You've done right by your friend's mother."

He reached up and touched one of the golden tendrils that cascaded from her shoulder. She didn't push his hand away. "Only you would think so, Des. And I still haven't gotten you to Jerkwater."

"At least I'll know not to trust anyone named Lambert I meet, although I wouldn't know him on sight."

"Did you get a good look at Cole?"

"How could I miss? I knocked the man silly in the head."

"Saloon Lambert is just an older version, maybe a few inches taller. Has a bully of a voice."

"His brother was lying flat when I looked at him," she reminded. "Saloon? That's Sal's real name?"

"He's a bit testy about the handle his parents gave him. Something you and I both can understand."

"That we can. You still haven't really answered me about why you think he's after you."

"I heard tell he wants to be somebody important up north and thought well of in the community."

"What does that have to do with you?" Curiosity filled her face.

"I'm the only living link to the robbery. Cole will never tell or he'd implicate himself. That leaves me a loose cannon. Sal's afraid that with me walking the right side of the law these days, I might just talk and ruin any chances he has to become an upstanding citizen. I don't know who he's trying to fool, but it can't be good for them."

"Would you tell?" she asked softly.

"A man always hopes for redemption. Like I told you before, I don't make plans. But neither will I run from the reckoning that has been building between us ever since I went to jail. Guess he's decided it's time to bury the past." He stared at her, waiting for any sign of disapproval.

"Then I'd better get to sleep so you can too. I don't want you tired when he finds us."

Chapter 7

"Campfire ahead." Shadow caught wind of an aroma that made his stomach growl its discontent. Someone was cooking on an open fire. The distinct smell of coffee blended with the other appetite-stirring scents urged Shadow's tongue to flick out and lick his dry lower lip. Just as Dollar carried him and Odessa over a rise in the prairie, a thin wisp of gray smoke and a flicker of firelight captured Shadow's attention. He drew closer.

The camper was a lone man with a covered wagon. A tripod with a surveyor's glass stood a few feet away from the wagon. Shadow let Dollar continue in the same direction. They'd been picking their way in the dark all night. Though she had not complained once, he could tell by the way Odessa kept shifting from one hip to the other in front of him that she was getting saddle sore.

"You think it's safe?" Worry echoed in her question. "You don't think it's someone after us?"

"He wouldn't have taken the time to make a fire, much less coffee."

"Not even to draw us in?"

"I'll go around him if you want and leave you with

Dollar. Then I'll circle back and check him out. I'll come get you when it's safe."

"No, stay with me." Her order came in a rush of breath. "I'd rather stay with you and take our chances." She took a deep breath and set her shoulders as if gathering her courage. "Coffee sounds good."

She was about as much outlaw as he was saint. Couldn't shoot, couldn't rope, was afraid of being left alone in the dark. Shadow smiled, enjoying the sense of protection her presence demanded of him. Made him feel good about himself and about what he was doing for her. She was going to be a handful for whichever good man asked her to be his wife.

"Well, let's see if he's hospitable. Keep real close. You take the reins so my gun hand's ready if necessary," Shadow whispered in her ear. His other arm remained locked around her waist, his right hand pressing against his leg as if they were sauntering in from a joyride. "Ho the camp!"

"Come in, pilgrims. Have a cup. Just got it brewed."

Shadow went in slow, his eyes searching the immediate surroundings, taking in every detail. "You a surveyor?"

The man rose from a bent-knee position near the campfire and his hat immediately swept off his slightly balding head and into one hand. "Sorry, ma'am, didn't see you clearly. I thought you were two fellows riding double. Did your other horse come up lame?"

After reining Dollar to a halt, Shadow dismounted, then quickly helped Odessa do the same. His hand lingered at her waist for a moment too long, but she didn't move away. In fact, she turned and pressed her cheek against his chest and said, "Thanks, sweetheart."

Shadow returned her hug, taking pleasure in her role playing. "You're more than welcome, honey."

The camper grinned. "Newly married?"

Shadow reluctantly let go of her to accept the handshake

being extended to him by the fellow. "Name's Rivers," Shadow introduced himself. "And this is—"

"His bride," Odessa interjected, not letting Shadow finish.

Maybe it was best to keep her real name secret in case the man was a decoy. Shadow followed her evasive lead. "We ran into a little trouble a ways back but looks like a better string of luck finding you here. Coffee smells good."

Odessa shook the man's hand too.

"Glad to meet you, ma'am. I'm Timothy Hobart. I work for the New York and Texas Land Company." He motioned toward the cast-iron skillet warming food next to the speckled coffeepot. "Would you folks like to share a meal with me? I haven't had company for more than a week now. And I have plenty of oats for your horse."

"We'd be obliged." Shadow grabbed Dollar's reins and led him toward where Hobart had tied off his team. "Darling, you go ahead and fix you a plate. I'll get Dollar settled."

"I'll fix you one too, honey." Odessa pressed a hand against her throat and whispered something to the man that Shadow couldn't quite hear.

"A gentleman, he is," Hobart said. "A man who saves the last bite for you thinks more of you than he does himself."

So she knew about the jerky. He thought he had been pretty slick pretending to eat, but she proved herself even slicker keeping quiet about her knowledge. Letting him think he was being some kind of hero.

Shadow kept his attention riveted on Odessa while he settled in Dollar with some water and oats. Like she'd done with him in Longhorn City, she had no trouble striking up a conversation with a stranger, and she was being smart in steering it toward Hobart's reason for being out on the prairie alone instead of theirs.

"I'm surveying about a million acres of open range up

here in the Panhandle," the broad-shouldered man informed. "But it's sad to say they won't be worth more than fifty cents an acre to homesteaders because water's so hard to find. Frankly, what water is here has already been claimed mostly." He started to scoop a tin of food for her, but Odessa told him she could do it herself. Instead, he poured two mugs of coffee.

While she scooped, he continued with his explanation. "My company has managed to fence off some of it at about four cents an acre for cattlemen to graze their herds on, but it's going to take some mighty stubborn people to really settle this part of Texas."

"Fifty cents?" Shadow's interest was caught. "A man could build himself a life out here if he knew how to divine water."

"Or if he had a good idea of where water was that hadn't been found yet," Odessa said softly as he joined them at the fire.

Could she be thinking the same thing he was? That they had found the ideal spot for settling.

"If you wanted to buy a certain piece of land"—she scooped beans and cornbread into a second tin, then handed it to Shadow—"how would you go about doing that, Mr. Hobart?"

Her interest sounded sincere or else she was one hell of an actress. But what if she wasn't just role playing? For the first time in ten years, he allowed a spark of hope to ignite deep inside him. *If a man was willing to make plans, maybe something other than a long ride might always lie ahead of him.*

Shadow accepted the tin and began to eat, his eyes watching her while he listened to Hobart's answer.

"Well, the nearest land office is in Jerkwater, a little town just a few miles west of here. You could probably get there by tomorrow evening if you didn't stop for anything.

The next morning you could go in and circle on a map which acres you have in mind. If they haven't already been claimed, then you pay the money to the county and they're yours. Or you can get a loan from the bank as long as you have some money to put down up front. Why? You folks got somewhere particular you're interested in? Is that what you're doing out here?"

Odessa stretched the truth a little. "We weren't speculating on it at first, but now we think we've spotted just the place."

"I'm headed to Jerkwater myself soon as I break camp. It will be daylight soon and I have to get on my way. I'd be pleased if you would keep me company. You could give your horse a rest and we could tie him off to the back of the wagon. You could either ride up there beside me and your husband, ma'am, or if you're tired, we could make you a soft bed in the back of the wagon."

"Thank you very much, Mr. Hobart." Odessa looked up over the rim of her coffee mug. "But I wouldn't want to be any—"

"No trouble at all, Mrs. Rivers," Hobart insisted. "Frankly, I hope to be married soon, and I'd like to ask you a few questions about how a man goes about helping his lady arrange a proper wedding."

Shadow thought the man's offer was a stroke of luck. Now they'd still be able to travel as a couple. Best of all, if someone was out there looking for them or awaiting Odessa's approach they wouldn't question two men in a wagon. Probably wouldn't even try to stop them. Having her ride in the back and get some rest was exactly what they needed. No one would be able to see her.

"My bride could use some sleep. It's been a long night." Shadow noticed the yawn she tried to hide. "When she wakes, she'll be more than happy to tell you all about how she worked up our wedding."

Odessa started to protest even as she attempted to stifle

the yawn. "And while I sleep, I know my husband would just love to tell you how we met amid a hail of bullets and ended up in church together."

"My, my." Surprise filled Hobart's face. "Sounds like I'm going to have quite a story to tell my Minnie."

"If you'll excuse us, Mr. Hobart"—Shadow took Odessa's tin, noticing she was finished eating—"I'll make a bed for her and then I'll help you break camp."

He gently leaned toward Odessa, then decided not to whisper for her to come closer. Instead, he said loud enough for Hobart to hear, "Now come with me, sleepyhead, before you make our host think that I don't take care of you properly."

"Yes, do, Mrs. Rivers." Hobart tipped his hat at Odessa. "But I wish you folks would just call me Tim or Timothy."

"Thank you for everything, Timothy." She linked her arm through Shadow's. "We'll never forget your kindness."

Shadow escorted Odessa to the back of the wagon and suddenly swept her up into his arms. He set her on the wagon bed and kissed the top of her head. "You little minx, now what am I supposed to tell him?"

She didn't protest the kiss. It felt more than a little endearing. "He's a nice man. Why not tell him the truth?" she suggested. "As he said, he'd have quite a story to tell his Minnie."

"You just might be right."

She warmed to the approval in Shadow's tone, aware of how much she'd done in the past twenty-four hours to seek his compliments. Several times she'd caught herself trying to please him, watching his eyes just to see if she could break his concentration. And she had, sending a thrill through her that made her feel more woman than anything else in her life ever had. She'd allowed herself to enjoy the way his hand caressed her even when he didn't know he was doing so, stopping short only when he noticed her looking. It wasn't one of those grabby touches men at the Gilded Garter tried, but one that Shadow made almost unconsciously as if she were a favorite pet he was stroking.

Odessa especially liked the way his lips curved and withdrew momentarily from their thin line when he was pleased with something she said or did. She knew she was letting her heart pull her from the goal she'd set for herself never to trust or care for any outlaw or gunslinger, but Shadow Rivers was different. He made her *want* to feel different. Whatever type of man he truly was, he had somehow defined himself as his own kind.

"Stop looking at me like that or I'm going to ask you to honor your second part of our deal even though Hobart can't see." Shadow's words exited soft and husky.

"You mean, move in close like this?" She scooted forward, rubbing her thumb gently over his lower lip.

His tongue darted out to taste her touch, his eyes sweeping over her hungrily. Only then did she realize she'd ridden into Hobart's camp with her top shirt button still unfastened to relieve the heat. Her fingers rushed to refasten the breech, but the warmth of Shadow's gaze prickled the back of her hand as if it were heated tingles from the sun. Odessa glanced up at him again, staring as he did at her.

A strangely exotic silence ensued. She *had* to find a way to somehow be closer now, the urge so compelling that she couldn't satisfy the need unless she felt the span of muscles that had encompassed her since they'd began the ride. Her fingers splayed across his chest, traced the ridge of each shoulder, then delved into the ebony hair at his collar, silently asking him to draw nearer.

"You want Hobart to come back here finding out what's taking so long?" Shadow half groaned, half teased as he glanced around the edge of the wagon.

She giggled. The idea of Shadow being nervous about anything was too blamed funny to hold back her laughter.

"He's going to hear you." Shadow sounded like he could have been applying for membership to become a monk and it made him seem all the more endearing. Now who was worrying?

"So keep me quiet," she challenged, her heart taking voice. She realized what her words suggested and refused to find fault with her feelings.

It was as if she'd given him license to live. Shadow pulled her into the hard planes of his chest, staring deeply into her eyes as if he was measuring her in some way. "I've never met anyone like you, Des. I think my luck turned for the better when you broke me out of jail. I know my life has. I've just been waiting for you to say that what's stirring up between us is a good thing."

As if one had asked and the other had agreed, she slipped her arms around his neck and their mouths met softly. His warm, wet tongue teased until she could do nothing but answer its quest and appease her need to taste him and discover why he had come to mean so much to her. Odessa surrendered to the feelings that had been building since she met him—the beckoning from somewhere deep in her soul, a tender acceptance of her heart's revelation, a treasured taste of heaven that made her tremble in its wake.

She felt herself unfolding, blossoming like the bluebonnets his eyes reminded her of. Years of wanting to be cherished, to feel like she counted as something good and fine and honest to someone, melted away with each pass of his hands along her back, with each caress that traced the curve of her hips.

He finally pushed away, his breath ragged, his eyes smoky blue and hooded.

"I think that ought to do it for now, don't you?" she lied breathlessly, motioning behind her. She needed some way to stop the world from spinning. Teasing him by reminding him that they did have company seemed to be the necessary call of order. "Timothy might think we weren't affectionate if you left your new bride too soon to help him. That should convince him we're married, don't you think?"

A look of hurt swept across Shadow's face as he backed away, misunderstanding her need to regain control of her senses. "You made a believer out of me, darling. Just be glad I'm still gentleman enough to remember that we really aren't."

"I'm sorry," she whispered as he walked away, "for making light of something that shifted my world."

Chapter 8

"That's quite a story," Timothy admitted, continuing to drive the team over the rutted trail that led to Jerkwater.

Shadow admired the man for not pulling up rein and demanding that he and Odessa leave his company. She had been sleeping all morning and had not risen even once to ask them to stop for personal reasons.

"You say she's innocent?" Timothy glanced back at his female passenger. "She sure seemed plenty nice to me this morning. Hard to think a woman like her could be much of an outlaw."

Though their situation wasn't one bit humorous, Shadow chuckled, maybe just to release some of the tension from leaving her last night. "She's not much of one." In a more serious tone he added, "I've got to get her home before she's forced to really become one, Tim. She's fit for more in this life than that."

"I've got to admit when you introduced yourself by your last name, I thought I'd heard it before and she looked kind of familiar but I couldn't quite place her. Then when you told me your first name this morning, I almost stained the inside of my trousers."

"You didn't pull that hog leg under your seat there."

Shadow added honesty to one of Tim's traits. "But you could have."

"Maybe." Hobart's gaze left the roadway momentarily to sweep to the bench where they sat and the curled blanket that rested just below it at the back of his legs. "But if you're as fast with the gun as they say you are, Shadow, I fear I'd been dead before my rifle ever left the blanket."

"When I was younger and if you had pulled it first, probably," Shadow admitted to the possibility. "But I've put that life behind me now. I wanted you to know it all because I think you're a fair man. Odessa does too because she was the one who said we should tell you the truth. Now the question is, what will you do with that information?"

"You say this Lambert chap plans to meet you in Jerkwater and she's being kept from town, right?"

Shadow nodded. "That just about sums it up."

"Then there's only one thing I can do." Timothy shrugged and faced Shadow for a second. "I've got to take you both straight to Cassius James."

"The sheriff?" Recalling the name on Odessa's wanted poster didn't reassure any qualms Shadow might have concerning his new friend. In fact, Shadow didn't like the sound of this at all.

"She'll be safer with him than anywhere else, guilty or not, at least until he gets it all looked into." Hobart focused on the team again. "And if there're any warrants for Lambert's arrest, they'll be posted. That might prove helpful to you. Come to think of it, that's where I know Odessa from. I've seen her wanted poster."

"Tell me about the sheriff." He didn't want Tim dwelling on whether or not she was innocent. Poster or no poster, Odessa had been wrongly accused. Shadow was sure of it. "What kind of man is he?"

"I'm surprised you haven't heard of him. He rode with George Jordan of the Ninth Cavalry during their successful defense of New Mexico territory against the Apache. Near Tularosa, I think."

"The Ninth, you say? That's a unit of Buffalo Soldiers."

"Right you are. Cassius is one of only two black men to serve as sheriff in Texas. That's how well he's respected."

Hobart's list of respectable traits was building in Shadow's estimation. The surveyor suffered no prejudice except for a way a man conducted himself.

"He's a crack shot and has won more than a dozen shoot-outs with men who all drew on him first, and he's never suffered a wound. It's said that only one man has ever gotten away from him."

"You sound like you know James well." Shadow hoped Timothy did if he was going to trust the sheriff with Odessa's future.

"I do. Being a land surveyor, you sometimes have to rely on the local authority to keep you from getting shot. There's an occasional dispute about who owns which water rights. Anyway, Cassius is a skilled detective, a master of disguises, and an expert tracker when he has to be. I expect that's why those Apache feared him so much."

Odessa finally sat up behind them, stretching and yawning. "Sheriff James is someone we can trust, Shadow. He was out of town the morning it all happened. I couldn't go to him and I was afraid to involve my mother. I knew I'd be tracked there. The only thing to do was leave. I just couldn't get back to return the stuff."

"Do you mind telling me what you're trying to return?" Curiosity filled Hobart's tone.

"This."

Shadow turned around in the seat and saw the wad of cash she was pulling from the lace that made a delicate triangle at the top of her slightly unbuttoned shirt.

She dug a little deeper. "And this. Ouch, that itches like sin."

She rubbed the place where the ring she held up must have been pressing between her breasts. She saw Shadow gaping at her. "Close your mouth, darling. I'm sorry they're not as big as you hoped."

"What's this?" Hobart asked, unable to turn around well enough to see what was in her hands.

Odessa fanned the wad of money. "About five thousand dollars and a man's ring."

She had kept saying Shadow could have robbed her but he didn't. He had thought she meant the extra money she might be carrying with her. He didn't know it was a blasted fortune. "And tell me exactly how you *didn't* steal that," Shadow said.

"Mind if I put it away and crawl up there with y'all?"

Shadow waited until she'd hidden the stash away again, making her breasts look much larger than they actually were. He shook his head wondering what other little secrets she had that she'd not told him. He scooted over on the bench and held a hand out to help her over. It took a moment or two, but she finally managed to squeeze herself between him and their host.

"We're waiting," Shadow reminded.

"I know," she said. "I'm trying to find the right words."

"Just the truth, Des. That's word enough." Shadow didn't know how long she'd been awake. "I've told Tim the truth and what I know of your story. You can trust him with the rest."

She took a deep breath and splayed her hands on her knees. "Well, you know how I told you about me being from bad blood?"

Shadow linked one arm through hers to make sure she rode safely on the seat, to silently tell her he'd put away the anger that had stirred from her teasing last night, but mostly to anchor her from whatever it was that seemed so difficult to say.

"You aren't your family's keeper," Timothy said softly. "You answer only for your own deeds."

"Did I tell you I'm happy to have met you, Mr. Hobart?" Odessa's eyes looked upon their host in sincere askance.

"*Timothy*," the surveyor reminded. "And yes, you did."

Shadow owed the man for many kindnesses since they'd come upon him, but the biggest kindness of all was his willingness to hear Odessa out.

"Well, I allowed enough people to convince me that I had such bad blood I thought why not just be what I was accused of being." She turned and looked at Shadow, tracing the place where their arms linked. "I got drunk one Saturday night and decided I would shoot a man. Oh, I had good reason. He tried putting his hands on me one time too many. He thought I was one of my mother's working girls. I work for her, all right, but not in that kind of way and I told him so, plenty of times."

Shadow wanted the man's name and where he could find him. But that would come later after Odessa had cleared herself.

"Trouble was, sober I couldn't have shot him if he'd been standing two feet in front of me. Shadow can attest to that. I sure couldn't have shot him drunk to the gills. So instead I got mad at God and started shooting the hell out of Him."

Unable to help himself, Shadow started laughing.

"Stop it. It's not funny. It wasn't then and it isn't now."

She tried to unlink her arm but he wouldn't let her. "I'll behave," he promised, catching his breath. "It's just that the image of you drunk and shooting at anything ought to have sent everyone in the vicinity running for cover."

She sighed heavily. "Actually it did. I happened to be in an alley between two places I thought the vagabond would be, and when I started shooting, I couldn't stop myself. All those years of being called bad and not deserving it. All that dodging from grabby men. I wanted to shoot out every star in the sky because none of them seemed to be shining for me."

Tears welled in her eyes. "That's when I heard a scream. In my drunken stupor I figured I had lost my aim and shot somewhere other than up. Before I knew it, a woman and a man who'd been passing by on the sidewalk were stripping off their coats and threw them at me. The man almost clobbered me with his ring. They thought I was trying to rob them. They took off running like . . . well . . . like Shadow Rivers himself was gunning for them."

Her gaze locked with Shadow's. "They didn't wait around long enough to listen. All they heard was me shouting, not what I was saying, apparently. You believe me, don't you, Shad?"

He patted her hand, then reached up to wipe a tear from her cheek. "I believe you, Des, and I'll make the sheriff believe you if I have to."

"I don't understand." Hobart slowed the team a little so their harnesses wouldn't jingle so loud. "Why didn't you just take everything to the sheriff?"

Odessa exhaled a deep breath, then continued with her tale. "That would have been the easiest thing, but you remember that I said I was drunk."

"And that Sheriff James was out of town," Shadow recalled.

"So smart me decided I would wait till morning—which, by the way, was the only Sunday I've ever missed church— and I would go to the lady's house while she was at service. I meant to return their coats and the ring."

"So you know who they belong to?" Shadow saw hope in that fact. It would go a long way in aiding the lawman to help Odessa.

"Yes. At least the lady's, I do. Like I said, it was dark, I was drunk, and they were not exactly around long enough for me to see their faces well. But Cathleen Cullen wore that coat any night there was a cool breeze stirring. She liked to show it off. Got it from Paris, France, so she said. I'd admired it for a long time."

"So how did the money come into play? I understand about the man's ring, but is it common for people in Jerk-water to walk around with that kind of money?"

"That's just it, Shad, it's not. And I only found that by mistake."

"You mean there's more to the story?" The surveyor's eyes widened in response. "Minnie's going to want to meet you, I can already tell."

Odessa looked uncomfortable for a moment and Shad realized it had nothing to do with her seat on the wagon. "Go ahead and tell us. It can't be that bad."

"I tried that coat on just for the sport of it. I figured she'd never know. It was only when I thrust my hands into the pockets and twirled around that my hand came out with a wad of cash in it. By the time I quit counting, I discovered I had about five thousand dollars. I knew I was in big trouble then and had to get it back to Cathleen as quickly as possible."

Shadow put two and two together. "So that's why you missed church the next morning."

"Cathleen always goes every Sunday and sits on the front pew. She's one of the town's society matrons. Come to think of it"—something lit in Odessa's eyes—"her husband was away on business down in Austin. That couldn't have been him with her that night." She squeezed Shadow's arm. "That explains a lot about the next morning."

"Go on," he encouraged.

"When I got to her house, I checked around to see if her buggy was gone and it was. Then I snuck into her parlor and was just taking off the coat when I saw a man's boots at the top of her stairway."

"It wasn't Mr. Cullen, was it?" Hobart asked, though none of them had any doubt that it wasn't.

Odessa shook her head. "No, Mr. Cullen wears fancy tooled boots. The man at the stairs wore boots of a lot less quality. I got a good look at him as I stripped off the coat and threw the other one on the settee. I assumed he really might be robbing Cathleen so I couldn't take the chance of leaving the ring or the money."

Frustration filled her tone. "I had to take them with me. I barely got out of there without him shooting me dead. He didn't have a gun on him at the top of the stairs but he sure did just before I managed to reach my horse. Lucky for me he wasn't a good shot. Since I didn't know him, I couldn't count on that being a bad day of shooting for him. I knew the only thing left for me to do was get out of town before he found me and where I lived. I didn't want to bring any-thing down on my mother's head."

"Are you sure Cathleen Cullen isn't the one keeping you from returning?" Shadow asked. Too many things weren't adding up right.

"What makes you feel that?" Hazel eyes met blue.

"Let's say the man in her house was the owner of the ring. With her husband away in Austin, I'd say Mrs. Cullen has plenty of reason not to let you return to Jerkwater."

"You mean he was . . . they were . . . ?"

"Hold it right there and put your hands up!" a man yelled from behind the wagon. The sound of horses moving toward them warned that he wasn't alone. "That means you too, Odessa."

"Hog leg," Shadow whispered, slowly unlinking his arm from hers and bringing his hands up.

"What?"

At the moment, he couldn't ease her confusion about his words to Timothy. All he could do was lean over and kiss the side of her head, adding one more hurried whisper, "Re-member what I told you to do when you left the boxcar?"

"Jump, tuck . . ." She didn't turn but started bringing her hands up slowly.

"And roll!" Shadow ordered.

Odessa jumped toward the team.

Shadow's right hand flashed to his peacemaker. The hog leg slipped from its blanket. Two chambers emptied just as a resounding boom echoed from Timothy's direction. A volley of gunfire answered them back.

Chapter 9

Gun smoke reeked all around Odessa as she dared to peer over one of the team's flanks to see who was moaning. *Please, God, don't let it be Shadow.* When she rose, pain echoed up her back. "Ouch!" she complained aloud, then remembered to duck again in case she had just made herself the perfect target. *Scratch that. If he's moaning, he's alive. Let him be the moaner.*

"Are you shot?" Shadow jumped down from the wagon to check her injuries.

His beloved face was all she needed to breathe again. "No, I got a splinter in my butt, of all places. Somebody shot the wagon up pretty good." She allowed him to check her over and even to pull out the splinter. "Is Timothy all right?"

"He's holding that hog leg on them at the moment." Shadow kissed her, quickly and full of relief. "If you're sure you're okay, I need to tie them up."

"They're not dead?"

"I told you, Des, I'm done with people thinking I'm a killer. Tim did most of the scaring. Their horses didn't take too kindly to the sound of that boom. One of the men was thrown and the other one won't be using his trigger finger anytime soon."

"What are we going to do with them?" She managed to work her way out from between the team and follow Shadow to the back of the wagon, where Tim stood. Cob and Harlin Barriger!

"We didn't do nothing," Harlin said sullenly, looking in disgust at the horse who had thrown him. "We were just having a little fun. That hog leg spooked my horse and that's why my gun went off."

"Made it go off several times, did it?" Timothy glared at the chubby man.

"Get me to a doctor," his slender brother demanded, gripping his hand in pain. "I'm going to bleed to death."

"What you did was try to kidnap my wife and shoot up our wagon." Shadow grabbed the pistols that littered the dirt near both men, handed them to Odessa. "I'd say that's on the wrong side of funning and reason enough to take you in to have a little talk with Sheriff James."

"Your wife? That's Odessa Kilmore," Cob complained even louder. "She ain't nothing but a dirty—"

"Finish that sentence and you'll lose the whole hand." Shadow's tone echoed with deadly intent, the peacemaker already pulled and aimed.

Cob shut his mouth and wouldn't look at Odessa anymore.

"You know these two?" Shadow asked her.

She nodded. "They work for the Cullens. Cob's the bleeder. Harlin is Mr. Innocent."

"You got some rope, Tim?"

Timothy's head motioned toward the wagon. "Sure, Shadow. In the back under a sack of horse feed. Or we could use some of that barbed wire I've got rolled up in the corner."

"Decent folks don't use such things." Harlin backed up a few inches. "Shadow? Shadow *Rivers*?"

"One and the same. And as the story goes, I ride the short side of decency. Considering what you intended for her, I'd say you'd best shut your mouth before I change my mind and show you how hateful I can be." Shadow waited until Odessa found the rope. "Good thing for you she's making me a better man."

"Tim, give her the hog leg and tie that one up." Shadow waited till Odessa took the surveyor's rifle. "No offense, darling."

"None taken." She smiled, knowing he was thinking about her lack of ability with a rope. "It will be tighter if he does it."

When they finished, Shadow had already untied Dollar, mounted him, and was handing Tim a bandanna. "Give this to the bleeder for his hand, then tie him to his partner."

Once Shadow was certain Timothy had everything well in hand, he looked softly at Odessa. "Go on and ride up top with Tim. These two bushwhackers and I are going to take the lead."

"You're gonna make us walk back to town?" Cob looked up at Shadow.

"There's a perfectly good wagon," Harlin added his two cents.

"With too much in it to help loosen those ropes. No, boys, I want you right where I can keep my eye on you." Shadow motioned for them to hit the trail. "Now get to walking."

Chapter 10

A magnificent sunset streaked wide across the western horizon as they finally reached the edge of Jerkwater. The lake that had given the town its name shimmered with a million sparkles as the fading sun glinted off its surface. When the railroad had first come through this part of Texas, it had been forced to stop and take on water there, the engineer not knowing how much farther a water tower and a bigger town lay to the west. The crew had carried buckets from train to wallow and back again, jerking water for the steam. The town that built up since that time had simply taken on the name the men had given the whistle-stop.

A sense of homecoming engulfed Odessa as she caught sight of the business district and the people lining the thoroughfare. Peddlers hawking their wares, prospectors readying their wagons for places unknown, and men visiting the whiskey mills were moving about, showing that the place was thriving and unchanged since she had left it.

"Which way is the sheriff's office?" Shadow asked from ahead of them.

"Keep heading straight," she informed. "Then when you

get to Main Street rein right. It's at the end of the street near the land office."

Timothy breathed a heavy sigh beside her. "It's good to be here. I could use a nice meal and I plan to soak in a hot tub of water for the rest of the evening."

"My mother's got room for . . ." Odessa spoke without thinking, then realized a man like Timothy Hobart probably didn't visit such places. She glanced at the two-story gallery standing at the north end of town with all its lights shining brightly downstairs and dimmer ones upstairs. The Gilded Garter was probably just getting wound up for the evening ahead. Odessa couldn't help wondering what her mother was doing at the moment and whether or not she'd even missed Odessa.

As Timothy commanded the team to make the turn toward the sheriff's office, people started looking up and noticing the two bound Barriger brothers and Shadow riding behind them. Their eyes immediately focused on the surveyor's wagon that followed and the woman sitting next to the driver.

"Ain't that the Kilmore gal sitting up there on that wagon?" someone announced.

"Somebody get the sheriff."

"No need," Timothy told the gathering crowd. "That's where we're headed."

"What did the Barrigers do?" a peddler asked.

"Who's he?" another pointed at Shadow.

Odessa recognized many of them, visitors at her mother's house of business. Some acknowledged her directly. Others turned away as she rode past, not wanting to make eye contact. Those were the more upstanding of Jerkwater's citizenry. Men who didn't want to admit they recognized her well enough to know her name.

"Stop." Shadow informed the Barrigers that their journey had come to an end. "Des, you got that hog leg?"

"Aimed straight at them," she said, not caring that others were looking at her like she was truly the outlaw plastered on the poster.

"Keep it there until I get dismounted." Shadow reined Dollar just past the men and dismounted near the hitching post in front of the sheriff's office.

Tim stopped his team in the middle of the street. "I'll take the rifle from here, Odessa. You hop on down and I'll keep a bead on them. While you're talking to the sheriff I'll go to the livery, then I'll join y'all there."

"Thanks for everything, Timothy. We couldn't have done it without you." Shadow's peacemaker motioned for the Barrigers to head on into the office.

"No need, Shadow. I've got quite the story to tell now. You bet I do."

"Shadow? Shadow Rivers?" His name echoed through the crowd.

Odessa could almost feel the collective one step backward by all of them. His legend was known far and wide.

"You okay to get down by yourself?" Shadow eyed her quickly.

"I'm right behind you." She hopped down to follow him through the now-open door to the sheriff's office. Someone had gone in ahead of them to inform the lawman of their presence.

"What's all this about?" The tall, muscular black man stood behind his desk, his hands resting on his hips near two pearl-handled Colts. When he caught sight of Odessa, his teeth flashed white against the ebony granite of his skin, revealing two gold fillings spaced just enough apart to make his teeth look like wolf fangs. "I should have known this had something to do with you."

"Why do you say that, Sheriff?" Shadow scowled, sending furrows across his brow.

Sheriff James waved toward the two cells that had gone

unnoticed until that point. "Seems to be family reunion night for the Kilmores."

A gray-haired man with his head bowed looked up from where he sat on the cell cot. His elbows, one of them bandaged, were resting on his knees. Odessa recognized him almost immediately. It was the same man she'd seen in Cathleen Cullen's house. "He's the man who shot at me!"

"You sorry wad of tobacco spit!" cursed a lady's voice Odessa recognized all too well from the cell next to his. She wore a gown of emerald satin and black lace that showed more cleavage than Odessa ever hoped to inherit.

"Mama! What the heck are you doing here?"

Maddy Kilmore grabbed her matching black parasol and poked its rib through the bars that separated the two cells. "I shot your father, that's what the heck. Sorry cur was trying to hitch his holster on that Cullen woman's bedpost when he had a perfectly good one waiting for him over at the Garter." She glared daggers at her husband as she spat out the words, "And if I ever get out of here again, I'm gonna shoot you twice for shooting at your own daughter."

"My daughter?" Moon Kilmore dodged the poking parasol and jumped up to race over to the front of the cell so he could take a better look at Odessa. He squinted, his hazel eyes sweeping her from head to toe. "She don't look much like me."

I shoot like you. Odessa realized where she'd gotten her lack of skill.

"Took after my ma," Maddy bellowed, "and be glad she did. That kid hasn't got one bad bone of yours in her body, thanks to justice. And she's got more sense than I ever had."

"She robbed the hell out of me," Moon sounded almost proud. "Lucky all I had on me was my wedding ring."

"You were the man in the alley, too?" Odessa hadn't been sure of the man's identity; she just knew it hadn't been Mr. Cullen. She'd had far too much to drink that night and been running scared since. The man's dark image evaded her no matter how much she'd tried to think it through.

"Your wedding ring!" Maddy's face turned livid. "I told you if you ever took that off I'd haunt you till your dying day." Suddenly, it dawned on her what he'd said and she looked at Odessa in puzzlement. "What does he mean you robbed him?"

"A fine way to meet one's father, don't you think?" Odessa whispered, wishing she were anywhere but there right now.

"She'll explain everything just as soon as you lock up these two fellows, Sheriff." Shadow nudged the Barrigers forward.

"Care to tell me what they did?" Sheriff James took the keys from the peg near his desk and started to open Maddy's cell, then instead moved to Moon's. "On second thought I'd best put the brothers in here with Moon. I can't put the Kilmores together. They'll kill each other for sure."

Shadow began to explain how the Barrigers had tried to ambush them and take Odessa. The brothers joined Moon reluctantly, not sure whether his cell was a safer place than the other. Her father didn't lay a hand on them even after he heard that they'd shot at her. But then he was guilty of the same crime. He'd have to choke himself too.

"You sorry excuse for blood donation." Maddy shook her fist at Moon. "If you were any kind of a pa, you'd beat those two to a pulp with your bare hands."

Moon shrugged. "What do you want me to do about it, Mad? You done shot me up. I'm one armed. You got to give me a little healing time, then I'll take care of them."

About that time Timothy walked in, escorting Cathleen Cullen with him. "This lady asked if I'd heard anything about the capture of the woman who robbed her. I believe that she said her name was Odessa Kilmore."

Odessa realized he was pretending not to know her so as not to give anything away to Cathleen.

"Now what?" Sheriff James looked at Odessa sternly. "Just how many people were you supposed to have robbed?"

"I didn't rob anybody," she insisted, finally telling the lawman how everything had happened and why she'd run from town. "Somebody just kept trying to stop me from coming back home. We found out from the Barrigers that it was Cathleen who had men gunning for me."

"You fools!" The town matron glared at the Barrigers as she began backing away. "I told you to say nothing."

"We didn't say anything, we swear," the slender of the two argued.

Odessa grabbed Cathleen. "I thought maybe it was because you thought I meant to rob you or maybe that I saw him"—she nodded at her father—"in your house. But now I know it's all about the five thousand dollars. You just told on yourself."

"What five thousand dollars?"

"The money you probably took from your husband's account while he was gone to Austin. I bet you and my father were planning to do something with it. Maybe leave town with it, weren't you? I think maybe we should ask Mr. Cullen to join us and find out if he knows he has that kind of money missing from the bank."

"Your father? Maddy Kilmore's husband?" Her chin lifted haughtily. "I thought that was all a rumor the whore spread."

Odessa reared back and threw a punch at Cathleen, sending her sprawling. "Don't you bad-mouth my mother ever again. Got me?"

"Like I said earlier"—Shadow winked at Odessa—"innocent ways."

Odessa giggled and faced the sheriff, stretching her hands out in front of her, crossing them. "Might as well lock me up, Cassius. It looks like you're going to have to jail the whole family."

"I don't think Mrs. Cullen will press charges, do you Sheriff?" Timothy helped the lady up. "And frankly, Odessa, there are too many witnesses that can testify that you were provoked and the results were justifiable."

"I've got only one thing to say to all of this." Cassius James looked from Maddy to Moon to Odessa then Cathleen. "Where the hell am I going to put her?"

"Not here, that's for darn sure. I'll pull every red hair out of that saintly sister's head for messing with my husband and daughter."

"Now, Mama," Odessa tried to calm her. "Don't do anything else. I've got to think of a way to make bail for you."

"Or break her out," Shadow whispered for her ears alone.

Odessa giggled again, relieved that at least it all seemed settled now, if being a part of this rowdy family could ever be called settled.

"I can make my own bail," Maddy informed. "I put up that thousand-dollar reward money for you myself. Now that you're found, I guess I can take it back."

"You put it up?" Odessa had thought Cathleen had been the one. "I assumed Mrs. Cullen had."

"You're the best thing that me and your pa ever did together. I figured somebody would dang sure track you down and bring you home for that kind of money."

"Or shoot her." Moon stated what he most likely would have done.

"Thanks, Mama. I know you did it for the right reason."

"Just like I'm going to do this." Maddy's parasol pointed toward the wall of posters beside the sheriff's desk. "Cassius, you see that there poster at the far end about halfway down? Yeah, that one right there. It says there's five hundred dollars reward for Moon. I reckon that's mine since I shot him and brought him in for justice."

"Well, technically, Maddy, justice wasn't exactly what

you had on your mind but, yes, you brought him in. The money's yours."

She nodded at Odessa. "I want you to see that she gets it. She deserves it for no other reason than her pa shot at her and, after leaving her high and dry for nearly twenty years, that's the least he owes her."

"Looks to me like he did you both a favor by leaving you to yourselves," Shadow said.

"Who the devil are you, handsome?" Maddy caught a good look at him.

"He's mine, Mama. Keep your garters on." Odessa moved back and linked her arm through his.

"Well, I always said you had good taste, honey." Maddy's hand spread over her ample breast, an act Odessa knew she deliberately did when she wanted a man's attention.

"You in town for long, Rivers?" Sheriff James's eyes scanned the wall of posters. "Don't have reason to hold you, I guess."

"Just long enough to settle some private business."

"An old score or something more pleasant?"

"Maybe both." He glanced at Odessa. "Depends on how close the second convinces me to stay and finish what got started."

"I don't want any killing. I run a clean town."

Shadow nodded. "If there was any killing to do, I'd have done it when those two took a bead on Odessa. As you can see, I brought them in a little worse for wear, but they're alive."

Odessa tugged on his arm. "Please don't go looking for Sal Lambert. He's not worth the trouble. Finish what *we* started."

"Sal Lambert? Got a brother named Cole?" Sheriff James's body went on full alert.

"Yeah." Shadow met the lawman's gaze. "Why, do you know him?"

The sheriff pulled one of the Colts, checked its chambers, then did the same to the other one. "Let's just say he's the one who got away. Is he nearby?"

Shadow relayed the story about the train ride and how he felt that Lambert and his men had probably reached town yesterday. "I can't say exactly where he is, but I know what will draw him out. Just pass it around that I've reached town. The snake will crawl out of whatever hole he's curled up in. Meanwhile I'd like to get over to the land office if Tim there isn't too tired to take care of it tonight."

"I'm not too tired and I have a storage room where we could put Mrs. Cullen, if you like, Sheriff." The surveyor waved toward the door.

"No." Sheriff James unlocked one cell. "I think I'll let Maddy go home in her daughter's custody."

"About dang time." Maddy gathered her parasol and patted her hair to wait while he swung open the cell door.

"Keep your hands to yourself." Cathleen glowered at the madam, but Maddy behaved long enough for Cassius to settle the matron in the cell.

Maddy laughed. "I got worse plans for the likes of you, husband stealer. Wait till the good folks of Jerkwater find out you've been cavorting with my husband. Ought to make prime pew gossip come Sunday. Hope you've made bail by then so you can hear it firsthand."

She linked her arm with Odessa's. "Now tell me all about your new beau, sugar pudding. I want to hear all about him. Has he kissed you yet? Has he . . . well, of course he hasn't. Not my Dessie." She eyed Shadow up and down. "But he will, dumpling. And from the looks of him, he'll do you proud."

"Mother!"

Chapter 11

"Hold it right there, Rivers!"

Shadow pushed Odessa back behind him as he stepped out into the street. Sal Lambert stood about thirty paces away, looking like he was gunning for blood. "Get back, Des. He means to have his reckoning."

"No!" she shouted, trying to move in front of him, but he held her at bay. "Stay close to me, Shad. Stay close."

"Timothy?" Shadow spoke a volume of words in that one single question.

"I've got her."

Her hands suddenly disappeared from view. The surveyor now held her back from doing what Shadow knew would only irritate Lambert more. "He's pushing to see if he's faster than me," Shadow explained. "He won't leave me any room till he finds out one way or the other. He'll shoot anything that stands in his way, including a woman."

"Damn right, jailbird. They'll finally see which one they should have been writing about all this time."

"I love you, Shad. I didn't tell you that I love you."

Shadow heard Odessa's whimper and the sound just about killed him. She had sucked up all kinds of trouble like a twister swallowing countryside and never showed one hint of fear for herself. But now for him she sounded truly frightened. The thought of Sal Lambert causing her to cry set Shadow's stance in stone. "You've made your last mistake, Sal," he warned.

Envy took its toll on a man. Lambert looked older than his years. He was dressed in black, silver decorating his hat brim, his belt, and the spurs at his boots. Like some fools under the sad impression that dressing like a fictional legend made them one, Lambert had chosen funeral black. Apparently, from the absence of his brother, he'd come calling alone, a decision of pure ego and no sense.

Despite his need for retribution concerning Odessa's tears, Shadow offered the man one more chance. "Look, there's still time to make something of yourself. Just walk into the sheriff's office and turn yourself in. You may have to do time and pay back the Fargo money, but that's better than lying dead in the street."

"You so sure you're faster than me?"

"I wish I weren't, Sal. We were friends once."

Sal laughed. "You sat in prison for that weakness, Rivers. Thought that people could have second chances. There ain't any for men like you and me."

"I thought so . . . until I found out different."

Sal's arms fanned out near his pistols and held, his eyes locking with Shadow's. "Go for it, anytime."

"I'll not draw on you first."

"Your mistake, partner." His eyes blinked. His hands went for the gun. Two shots echoed over the street.

Smoke cleared from Sheriff James's Colt as Sal fell backward. Lambert's bullet had hit the sign that swung under the eave jutting out from the mercantile. Shadow's peacemaker settled back into place, unused.

The sheriff ran forward just as Sal revived and groaned, groping for the gun still housed in the other side of his holster. The lawman grabbed it and hollered for a couple of the townsmen to take Lambert into custody.

As Sheriff James passed Shadow with his prisoner in tow, Shadow thanked him. "Looks like I put up my gun just in time. Seems there *is* someone faster than me."

"No matter how fast you are, friend, there's always somebody faster."

Epilogue

Not only did Shadow receive his hundred-dollar payment from Odessa, but Sheriff James had wanted to give him the price on Sal Lambert's head too. He'd fussed about not really earning that money since it was the sheriff who had stopped him in the street, but the lawman said he wouldn't have been able to if it hadn't been for Shadow's help in locating the man. Shadow had ultimately quit arguing about it and split the money with him, feeling that his best friend's mother might as well reap the rest of the reward for Lambert being put away for his crimes.

"Got any plans for your hundred dollars?" Odessa asked.

"As a matter of fact I do," he admitted as they left the telegraph office, where he'd wired the widow about the coming money. He could tell Des wanted to ask something more important: would he be moving on? "I'm going to buy me a new hat."

Odessa reached up and rustled his dark locks. "You could use one."

"You too, freckle face." He tapped the tip of her nose. She was wearing her hair down, just like he liked it. "Then I'm thinking about using the rest to buy some acres of prime Texas land a few miles east of here. Got a good-sized waterhole on it. Maybe build Dollar a big corral to spend his old age in. One for me too, if I can find enough trees around this prairie to build them."

"Sounds like you're going to need a lot more money." She smiled up at him. "Are you going to try raising anything in particular?"

"Maybe some cattle, wild boar. A couple of kids—the human kind." He took her into his embrace, not caring that they were standing in the middle of the street in front of the Gilded Garter within view of the townsfolk and anyone else who thought it might be improper.

"You asked me once, Des, which one of us was the most wanted." Shadow had no doubt about the answer to that particular question anymore. "It's you. I want you more than anything or anyone else I've ever wanted in my life. Will you love me and help me learn how to be a better man? Will you marry me?"

"Only if you make one promise."

He chuckled, knowing her well enough now that he had no doubt they both would enjoy whatever she demanded. "And what would that be?"

"Come close anytime I ask you," she whispered, her eyes full of the love he couldn't believe was shining there for him. "Never stay away so far from me that I can't spend every night in your arms. That I can't press my ear to your heart and hear it beating with love just for me."

"Sounds good. Sounds real good." At last, Shadow exhaled the catch that had been deep in his throat for ten long years. He could finally breathe right again.

He had found true love and the only woman who could ever make him the kind of man he wanted to be.